The nightmares have lost some of their power by now. I can haul myself out of one almost at will, knowing that the sweat-soaked sheet under me is not wet jungle floor, that the pressure against my back is not the barrel of an enemy rifle or a terribly wounded Vietnamese but my sleeping cat.

Still, most of the time, I retain the feeling that it's the nightmares that are real and my life here and now that is a dream, the same dream I dreamed in the hospital, in the jungle, in the Vietcong tunnels. I'm always afraid that someday I'll be dragged out of this dream, back to Nam, to a war that goes on and on for real in the same way it replays itself in my memory.

"That is what stops your power, Mao," Nguyen Bhu tells me. "You cannot provide a clear path for the amulet's power until your own mind is clear." Nguyen Bhu knows what I have to say, and insists that it is not too much to ask people to believe and forgive. Charlie knows part of it, but he has his own nightmares to chase. Of the others who know, I keep hoping that at least one or two survived, and that someday I might see and recognize them among the refugees. One hope I have in writing this is that maybe they will read it or hear of it and find me.

And we can heal together.

# The Healer's War

# PRAISE FOR **THE HEALER'S WAR:**

"What moves the novel is a sense of catharsis. The story with all its horrors *must* be told, not for sensationalism, but in the hope that someone will listen and understand."

—*Locus*

"The heroes in *The Healer's War* are those who strive to save lives, who see life as sacred, in whatever color skin it is wrapped. I read this book straight through and so, I predict, will you."

—Tom Paxton

"*The Healer's War* is a tale of truth full of living people, emotions, and events that cannot be denied, ignored, or forgotten. At every turn in the story, Scarborough reminded me of the war I left behind but can never leave behind. I did not want to go back to Vietnam, yet I am glad I went with her. I did not want to return to those hospital wards, but returning with her I gained a new perspective—and a new respect for Elizabeth Ann Scarborough and those we served with. There is magic in every war—especially for those of us who have been on the battlefields and in the hospitals, closest to the magic of life and death. *The Healer's War* captures that magic in a way that makes the unbelievable real—just like war itself."

—Warren Norwood,
author of *True Jaguar*

# The Healer's War

## ELIZABETH ANN SCARBOROUGH

**BANTAM BOOKS**
NEW YORK · TORONTO · LONDON · SYDNEY · AUCKLAND

All of the characters in this book are fictitious,
and any resemblance to actual persons, living
or dead, is purely coincidental.

This edition contains the complete text
of the original hardcover edition.
NOT ONE WORD HAS BEEN OMITTED.

THE HEALER'S WAR
A Bantam Spectra Book / published by arrangement with
Doubleday

PRINTING HISTORY
Doubleday edition published November 1988
Bantam edition / October 1989

ISBN 0-553-28252-2

Published simultaneously in the United States and Canada

PRINTED IN THE UNITED STATES OF AMERICA

O       0 9 8 7 6 5 4 3 2

This book is specifically for Lou Aronica, who asked the right questions.

It is also for my fellow Vietnam veterans, living and dead, male and female, military, civilian, and pacifist, American, South Vietnamese, North Vietnamese, Australian, Dutch, Laotian, Cambodian, Montagnard, Korean, and Chinese. And for our children, in hopes of arming them with hard questions to ask leaders selling cheap glory.

# Acknowledgments

The perspective, extrapolations, fantasy elements, and selection of story material in this novel are entirely my own. This story is a work of speculative fiction, not an autobiography, although some of the more mundane aspects and background are based upon my own experience as a nurse in Vietnam. This work does not, however, claim to be representative of the viewpoint of any group or of any other person but me. However, I have obtained nonjudgmental help, support, information, and reference materials from the invaluable sources listed below.

I would most especially like to thank John Swan for generously sharing his experience as a field medic, combat soldier, Vietnam Veterans Outreach Center counselor, and human being, for helping me cope with the initial stages of this book, and for introducing me to the Fairbanks Combat Veterans Rap Group. Another debt is owed to a Vietnamese lady whose perspective was of real help but who prefers to remain anonymous. Thanks also to Mack Partain; Megan Lindholm; Dr. Sharan Newman; Dr. Peter Cornwall; Janna Silverstein; Karen and Charlie Parr, my parents; Don and Betty Scarborough, my agent; Merrilee Heifetz, her assistant; Kathilyn Solomon and others at Writers' House; and Walt Williams of the Seattle Vietnam Veterans Outreach Center. In addition, I owe a great debt to all of the veterans who have been courageous enough to tell their stories, whether they thought what they had to say would be acceptable or not. Without their example I would not have been able to write my story. Particular thanks to Lynda Van Devanter, author (with Christopher Morgan) of *Home Before Morning*; to Cheryl Nicol, a portion of whose story is in *A Piece of My Heart*; to Patricia L. Walsh, author of the novel *So Sad the Hearts*, based on her experiences as an American civilian nurse who treated Vietnamese patients in Da Nang; and to Huynh Quang

Nhuong, author of *The Land I Lost*, a portrait of the author's boyhood in rural Vietnam before the war. Also thanks to those who collected the stories of other veterans: Keith Walker for the excellent *A Piece of My Heart*; Kathryn Marshall for *In the Combat Zone*; Stanley Goff and Robert Sanders for *Brothers: Black Soldiers in Nam*; Wallace Terry for *Bloods*; and Mark Baker for *Nam*, among many others. I owe special gratitude to Robert Stone for suggesting *Dispatches* by Michael Herr, to Shelby L. Stanton for advice on technical aspects of the story (all mistakes are purely mine, however), to Frances FitzGerald's *Fire in the Lake*, and to Jeanne Van Buren Dann and Jack Dann, editors of *In the Field of Fire*, for suggesting that writers of fantasy could have anything to say about Vietnam.

# Glossary

Spellings are phonetic and meanings are approximate, not literal, translations. Many terms are not actually Vietnamese but pidgin. My apologies to any Vietnamese speakers for inaccuracies. I wish I had had your assistance when compiling this.

*Ba*:   Vietnamese term for a married woman.

*Bac si*:   Vietnamese term for a doctor.

*Beaucoup*:   French for "much" or "many," used in pidgin Vietnamese-English.

*Bic*:   Vietnamese term for "understand." (*Bicced* is author's Americanizing of past tense.)

*Cam ong*:   Vietnamese term for "thank you."

*Cat ca dao*:   Vietnamese term meaning "cut off head."

*Chung wi*:   Vietnamese term for a lieutenant.

*Co*:   Vietnamese term for an unmarried woman or girl.

*Com bic?*:   Vietnamese term for "Come again?" or "I don't understand."

*Dao*:   Vietnamese term for "head."

*Dau*:   Vietnamese term for "pain."

*Dau quadi*:   Vietnamese term for "much pain." (*Dau quadied* is author's Americanizing of past tense.)

*DEROS date* (military jargon):   The day a person can leave an assignment; in Vietnam, when one leaves country.

*Didi* or *didi mau*:   Vietnamese or pidgin used often by

GIs and Vietnamese; approximate meaning "Go" or "Go quickly."

*Dinky dao*:   Vietnamese or pidgin for "crazy."

*Dung lai*:   Vietnamese term for "Stop."

*Em di*:   Vietnamese term for "Shut up."

*La dai*:   Vietnamese term for "Come here." (*La daied* is author's Americanizing of past tense.)

*Mao*:   Vietnamese term for a cat.

*Mao bey*:   Vietnamese term for a tiger.

MOS:   Military Occupational Specialty.

*Sin loi*:   Vietnamese term for apology.

*Tete* or *titi*:   Pidgin for French word *petit*.

TPR:   Temperature, pulse, and respiration.

Triage:   As used in medical emergency situations, this term refers to the process of sorting victims of a mass casualty situation or disaster into categories, i.e., those who can be treated and released, those who can be saved by quick intervention, and those who will need more extensive help if they are to recover. The last category are those so seriously injured they will probably die without immediate, extensive care and may die anyway. In triage situations, patients are treated in the order listed, the worst injuries requiring the most care left until last so the greatest number of people can be treated.

# Prologue

The nightmares have lost some of their power by now. I can haul myself out of one almost at will, knowing that the sweat-soaked sheet under me is not wet jungle floor, that the pressure against my back is not the barrel of an enemy rifle or a terribly wounded Vietnamese but my sleeping cat. When someone in a suit or a uniform frowns at me, it doesn't always make me feel as if the skin over my spinal column were being chewed away by pointed teeth. Sometimes I can just shrug, and recognize the authority in question as an uptight asshole with no legitimate power over me—none that counts, that is, nothing life-threatening.

Still, most of the time, I retain the feeling that it's the nightmares that are real and my life here and now that is a dream, the same dream I dreamed in the hospital, in the jungle, in the Vietcong tunnels. I'm always afraid that someday I'll be dragged out of this dream, back to Nam, to a war that goes on and on for real in the same way it replays itself in my memory.

"That is what stops your power, Mao," Nguyen Bhu tells me. "You cannot provide a clear path for the amulet's power until your own mind is clear. When you turn your face from your fear, that fear bloats with the power you give it. Look it in the eye, and it will diminish into something that is part of your life, part of your memory, something that belongs to you rather than controls you."

Nguyen Bhu sweeps the floor at his cousin's grocery store. Charlie says he's a former Cao Dai priest, a mystic like old Xe, and the wisest man to escape from Vietnam. He is sixty and looks ninety, has lost three fingers from his right hand, has more sense and is far less expensive than a psychiatrist whose lifelong concern has been to avoid obesity rather than starvation.

And most important, Nguyen Bhu knows what I have

to say, and insists that it is not too much to ask people to believe and forgive. Charlie knows part of it, but he has his own nightmares to chase. Of the others who know, I keep hoping that at least one or two survived, and that someday I might see and recognize them among the refugees. One hope I have in writing this is that maybe they will read it or hear of it and find me, and we can heal together.

# PART ONE

# The
# Hospital

# 1

I didn't know old Xe was a magician the night I began to be aware of his powers. If anybody had told me there was anything magical going on that night, I'd have told them they were full of crap, and assumed they either had a sicko sense of humor or had been smoking too much Hanoi Gold.

I was in the worst trouble of my life, to date, and had brought someone with me. An eleven-year-old kid lay comatose, barely breathing, on the bed by my chair.

Every fifteen minutes I repeated the same routine.

Right arm, right leg, left leg, left arm, I pulled up a spare lump of flesh from each of the little girl's limbs and pinched hard, silently daring her to kick me or slug me. Then I ground my knuckles into her chest, counted to ten, and prayed for a sign of pain.

A kick or a slap, a whimper or a wiggle, even a grimace would have gladdened my heart. But the kid just lay there, her disproportionately long limbs limp as wet rags, her breathing so shallow that it barely stirred her skinny ribs a quarter of an inch up or down.

I peeled back her eyelids one at a time and dazzled them with the beam of my flashlight, checking to see if the pupils contracted at the same rate, to the same size, or if they expanded at all. If they stayed fixed, or if one was the size of a dime while the other stayed the size of a pencil lead, both of us were in truly deep shit. I had to try them five or six times before I could be sure they were not contracting more slowly than they had fifteen minutes before. I'd been performing this same cruel routine continuously since she had been wheeled back from O.R., already deeply unconscious. Thank God, they had not yet anesthetized her for surgery.

"Come on, baby, come on," I prodded her encouragingly, as if she were my kid up to bat at a Little League game, and pumped up the blood-pressure cuff that circled her skinny upper arm. I had to pump it and release it three times before the faintest throb of pulse came through the membrane of my stethoscope. Partly that was because her pulse pressure was so weak. Partly it was because the papasan in bed five had started up again.

"Dau quadi," he whined ("much pain"), twisting in the padded cuffs binding him to the side rails. He sounded like a night in a haunted house, with the rails rattling like hail on windows, his sheets thrashing like those of a particularly agitated ghost, his bedsprings squeaking like unoiled ancient portals.

"Dau quadi!" he shrieked this time, his voice shrill with the hostility head injuries inevitably display when and if they start to heal.

All eleven of the patients then on ward six, the neurosurgery ward, were Vietnamese with some kind of trauma to the head. Most of them were civilians, war refugees. Before, we'd had two poor GIs on Stryker frames. One was a gork—a vegetable, who didn't know that he wouldn't ever move by himself again. The other guy wasn't so lucky. Both of them had been medevaced to Japan that morning, so tonight there were just Vietnamese on this side, them and George, the corpsman, and me. Ginger Phillips, who was officially in charge of the graveyard shift that night for ward six, was staying on the other half of the ward, across the hall. The EENT patients were over there, injuries and ailments of the eyes, ears, nose, and throat, a couple of GIs with sinus infections and a couple more with superficial facial wounds, as well as elderly Vietnamese suffering from cataracts and facial cancer. Men and women were mixed together on both open wards, which was true throughout the hospital. On most wards the division was between GIs and Vietnamese instead.

Papasan dau quadied again and the old man in the next bed stirred restlessly. I pulled my stethoscope out of my ears.

"Can you shut papasan up, George?" I asked. "I can't hear a damned thing for the racket."

George nodded, rose from his semislumped comic-book-reading position, and lumbered sleepily down the aisle between the beds. I waited while he threatened in a gentle, soothing voice to do hideous things to the old man, pulled the gnarled and squirmy body up in bed, and smoothed the sheets. Then I tried again. I could hear the systolic—140—but the diastolic eluded me until the second reading—it was 60. Up 6 points from the previous reading. A widening pulse pressure—the difference between the first throb I heard and the last—was a sign of increased intracranial pressure. But last time the spread had been 144/52, so it had decreased slightly. I hoped I could take that as a good sign.

The girl's respirations were still so slow and shallow I had to measure the movement of her ribs against the sheet to be sure she was breathing. Her right radial pulse, before slowed to 50, was now 56, but that was not necessarily a good sign. As the pressure on her brain increased, her pulse might start racing as her squashed brain sent wild signals to her heart, panicking it into an essentially useless flurry of activity. I took pulses in both wrists, at both ankles, and at her carotid pulse, at the base of her jaw. They were within two points of one another.

Her Foley catheter was still draining urine from her bladder, her I.V.s were still dripping on course. I wrote everything down on the chart at the end of the bed, sat on the metal folding chair, and used a towel to wipe the sweat off my face and neck.

The sweat wasn't just from the heat. It was from fear: fear that this child was going to die and I was going to have to live with it, and with myself. The fear soured in my throat and I leaned forward again and took her hand. It was clammy with sweat. How could I measure intake and output when she was sweating gallons like that, poor baby?

Her bald head was bandaged with a strip of white gauze, like an Indian headband, and her face didn't look like a child's. It looked like death, the high cheekbones jutting through the shiny flesh like carnival apples bleeding through caramel.

Her original problem was a depressed skull fracture. She'd tumbled off a water buffalo, something Vietnamese kids always seemed to be doing. I only wished the water buffalo had sole responsibility for her current condition.

But unfortunately for us both, the poor kid had fallen right off that water buffalo into the hands of a numskull nurse, namely, me. Now I was waiting to see if my carelessness had turned her simple, easily treatable injury into something that was going to kill her or make a zombie out of her.

I forced myself not to brood about how unfair it was, not to worry about what they would do to me if she died, or about what I could have done to prevent it.

Instead I held on to her hand and, in my mind, held on to her spirit, apologizing over and over and begging her to stay. "Tran, come on now, baby, keep it together. You know Kitty didn't mean to hurt you, and she's sorry, honey, she's really sorry. Just come on back. That shit of a doctor will fix your head and your hair will grow back and you can go back to mamasan and papasan and eat that bad old water buffalo, okay? Aw, hell, sweetheart, I'm so sorry. . . ."

The old man in the next bed, another depressed-skull-fracture case, with bilateral above-the-knee amputations, shifted slightly in bed so that his head lolled toward us. His name was Cao Van Xe, according to the strip of adhesive that had been taped to his wrist. His arrival had caused something of a stir. Some idiot with Special Forces had called a chopper out to a really hot landing zone just to load this one old man, who was probably going to die pretty soon anyway. The pilot had given the redheaded GI who loaded the old man a piece of his mind, but the man had grinned and waved and walked back into the bush. The object of all this dissension slackened his lower jaw so that it seemed to drop into a grin.

"What's with you, papasan? You think I'm as dinky dao as you, huh?"

Maybe it did sound crazy to be carrying on a monologue with first one comatose patient, then another, but in nursing school they taught us that hearing is the last sense to go, the first to kick back in. So I always chattered at my unconscious patients, telling them what I was doing, commenting on what was happening, and musing on life in general, as if talking to myself.

Papasan's breath emerged in a sort of groan, and I turned in the chair and leaned toward his bed, touching his bony hand. "You okay, papasan?" His other hand fluttered like a bird to his neck and touched what I figured was a holy medal. To my surprise, the hand under mine twisted and caught my fingers for a moment before sliding back to lie flaccid on the sheet.

Well, good. At least somebody was responding. I patted his hand again and turned back, a little more hopefully, to Tran.

No dice. She hadn't stirred. Her breath was inaudible. I held on to her hand with both of mine and concentrated. I had done this before, while trying to hang on to someone who was dying, collecting my strength, and any other strength I could suck from the atmosphere, God, or whatever, building it into a wave and flooding it through my hands into that person, almost as if I could wash her back to me, back to herself. She lay there quietly, and when I pulled my hands away, her small pale ones had red marks from the pressure of my fingers.

George clomped up, large and olive-drab, his walrus mustache drooping damply at the ends. "How's it going?" he asked.

"Not good," I told him. "BP's a little better, I think. It's about time for an encore."

"I'll do it, Lieutenant. You get a cup of coffee, why don't you? I just made some."

"Thanks, but I'll do it."

He shrugged and clomped back to the nurses' station.

As soon as his back was turned I leaned over Tran again, but when I looked into that vacant little face I just lost it. My calm, I'm-in-charge professional mask, the one no nurse should be without when on duty, dissolved. I had to pretend I was wiping sweat away again.

Then I repeated my routine: vital signs, neuro checks, and as many prayers as I could fit in between.

The prayers were for Tran, because I didn't know anything else to do, not because I'm this holy, religious person. Like all my family, I've always been a lukewarm, nonchurchgoing, nonspecific Protestant. People like us pray only on ritualized occasions, like funerals, and when there's a really big crisis. It isn't nice to pray for something you want for yourself, according to my upbringing, and God expects you to help yourself most of the time. But this was for Tran, not for me—not mostly. Well, not only me, anyway.

Maybe that was the trouble. Maybe God wasn't listening because my heart was not pure. Every time I squeezed my eyes shut and started mumbling humble apologies for my sin and error I ended up snarling that it wasn't *all* my fault. Even though I knew damned good and well I was going to have to take the whole rap. Despite the fact that pre-op orders were supposed to be written, pre-op medications and all narcotic medications double-checked and double-signed. But our high-and-mighty new neurosurgeon had handed down his commands to our high-and-mighty new college-educated head nurse, the twit, who had demanded that I do it, damn it, didn't I know enough to give a simple pre-op?

I should have. I'd done it often enough. But not pediatric doses, and not on head injuries, not that often. I hadn't been giving meds long on this ward. And I was so mad at their sheer goddamned pompous arrogance that I kept jumbling it up in my head. I was mad a lot in Vietnam. My best mood, in the heat, with the bugs, and the lack of sleep, and these gorked-out patients, was cranky. But that day I had gotten so mad that .25 cc of Phenergan turned itself into 2.5 cc of Phenergan. And I gave it to Tran.

As soon they came to take Tran to surgery, I got to thinking that that had looked like an awful *lot* of Phenergan. By then the doctor was on his way off the ward and the head nurse was in a more human frame of mind and I asked her. . . .

Had Tran been anesthetized already, she would have certainly died. The overdose I had already given her, combined with her head injury, was potentially lethal as it was. She was quiet as death when she returned to the ward, and I had been at her bedside ever since, watching for some sign of reprieve for both of us.

I couldn't just blame the doctor and Cindy Lou for the orders. I had to blame myself, too, admit that maybe I was getting rattled, after three long months in what was vulgarly known among staff members as "the vegetable patch." Maybe it was the Army's fault for sending a sweet young thing like me to Nam. But one thing for sure: it wasn't Tran's fault, and she was the one who was going to die. I tried to explain all of that to God to account for the impure static in my prayers. Unfortunately, there were a lot of distractions that kept me from formulating a really good defense.

"Beaucoup dau!" This time it was bed seven, a fourteen-year-old boy whose Honda motorbike had collided with a tractor-trailer unit. The boy had a broken arm as well as a busted head. Once more George's jungle boots slapped wearily down the concrete floor.

Somewhere in the distance, mortars crumped. Outgoing. I knew the difference now: what was incoming, what was outgoing. After 124 days in country, I was fairly blasé about anything that wasn't aimed specifically at me, despite the fact that another nurse had been killed by a piece of a projectile just before I arrived in Nam. Mortars bothered me no more than receding thunder, ordinarily.

But, God, it was hot! This had to be the only country in the world that didn't cool off at night. I finished Tran's neuro checks and vital signs again and tried to touch my toes with my fingertips. My uniform was sticking to my skin and my hair stuck out at all angles, I had run my hands through it so much.

Pain boomed through my skull louder than the mortars and probed at the backs of my eyeballs. The odors of the ward were making me faintly nauseous. The smell of disinfectant and an Army bug spray so strong that when I accidentally used it on the telephone it melted the plastic was bad enough.

But the reek of pot drifting in from the Vietnamese visitors' tent, a shelter set up between the neuro side of ward six and the general-surgery side of ward five for the families of our critical patients, was potent enough to give an elephant a contact high from half a mile away.

At least the disinfectant and the pot smoke covered up the aroma of the scenic beach, which stretched beyond the hospital perimeter, between the barbed wire and the South China Sea. It was off limits to us because it was used as a latrine by the residents of the villages on either side of the compound.

The smells were something everyone complained about a lot. When George had gone on his R&R to Australia, he said he'd felt light-headed getting off the plane and figured out it was because he wasn't used to clean air anymore. He said he had to poke his nose into a urinal for a while until he could adjust to the change in air quality.

My own headache made me wonder about how Tran's head felt, with all that pressure in her brain. By now the bone fragment pressing into her head could have been gently lifted, she could have been recovering.

Since they'd brought her back, I'd replayed the scene in my head hundreds, thousands of times, hearing bits of their snippy put-downs. Next time they could write down their goddamned orders as they were supposed to, so a person could read them, or give the medicine themselves, and the hell with Army wrist-slapping and nasty pieces of paper with snotty words like "insubordination." Better to go head to head with them than this. At the same time, in the back of my mind an accusing voice wondered if I hadn't overdosed Tran while entertaining some adolescent subconscious desire to "show them"—Chalmers and Cindy Lou—what happened when they didn't listen to me. The idea scared the hell out of me, and I shoved it away. I was a nurse, a helping person, a healer. The whole thing was a mistake. I hadn't realized the difference in dosages. I'd never harm a patient out of spite. Gutlessness, maybe, being too chicken to challenge orders until I was sure of what I was doing, but that was different, even if the results were the same. Sure it was.

She had to live. She had to. What in the hell could I do to get some response out of that floppy childish body? The hard thing about somebody you've met only after they've nearly been brained is that you don't have any idea what you can promise them to induce them to do what you want. What did this kid like? What was her favorite color, her favorite toy? Did she even have any toys? Was a water buffalo a Vietnamese kid's teddy-bear substitute? How would she look in a pretty dress? Would she get a kick out of wearing a funny hat while her hair grew back? Would her hair have a chance to grow back?

And why in the hell would she listen to me anyway? I tried to concentrate on my prayers, visualizing not some holy heavenly father in a long white beard but other patients I had been close to, people I had comforted as they died. Nice people. I saw their faces as if they were watching over Tran with me. Mr. Lassiter, a kind man with a daughter a year ahead of me in nurses' training. When the doctor told him he had lung cancer, I'd held him in my arms while he cried and tried to get used to the idea. Later, when the cancer bit into his brain and he began doing weird, sometimes obscene things, I led him back to his room and talked to him and soothed him while he talked nonsense, and I remembered who he really was while he acted in ways that would have mortified him if he'd known. Mr. Franklin, an incontinent old man who was in a coma with a high fever all the time I cared for him, but who made me wonder, until he died, where *he* really was, and was he feeling the pain of the hideous bedsores that ate up skin and fat and muscle. And the baby born with its insides so scrambled we couldn't tell if it was a boy or a girl, but whom I rocked and eventually persuaded its mother to rock before it died. Those people were who I was really asking to help Tran—them and the handful of my own friends and relatives who had died before I came to Nam. I thought about all of those people, visualizing them as a cross between ghosts and angels, relieved to be free of suffering and looking down at us with a sort of benign interest. They wouldn't be overly anxious to have anyone, especially a child, join them prematurely. "Do me a favor, folks," I urged them. "Nudge her back this way."

Old Xe stirred, and I realized I'd been babbling aloud. I stood and stretched, my bones creaking louder than the mortars, and leaned over him. He didn't seem comatose now so much as dreaming. The fingers of his right hand still gripped the medal thing to his hairless chest. He mumbled a word and groped toward me with his left hand. I thought again of Mr. Lassiter, who mistook me for his daughter in vaguer moments, and gave papasan my hand to hold. He grasped it with a power that was surprising in someone whose bones looked like a bird's.

Whatever he was dreaming, it must have been intense, because he held on to me as tightly as if it were a matter of life and death that we remain connected. I stayed there as long as I could. It made me feel a little stronger, a little more confident, to provide even such a small measure of comfort. I thought that was what I was doing, at the time.

When I tried to pull away, his hand clenched over mine so tightly his ragged nails bit into my wrist. Well, the beds were on wheels. I tugged them a little closer together and counted Tran's respirations, then checked her pulses and pain reflexes with one hand. The old man refused to relinquish either my hand or his holy medal. The wrinkles of his forehead and between his eyes deepened, as if he was concentrating. As I knuckled Tran, I thought I felt her stir slightly.

I was reaching for the blood-pressure cuff when the other patients started up again.

"Troi oi! Troi oi! Troi oi!" (Omigod, omigod, omigod!) The old lady from bed fourteen padded toward the desk, holding her head. "Beaucoup dau," she complained to George, who headed her off halfway down the aisle.

"Mamasan, you just have numbah one pill. No more now."

"Beaucoup dau," she insisted, showing her betel-blackened teeth. She was not used to taking no for an answer. The interpreter said she was the scourge of the marketplace in downtown Da Nang. She'd been clobbered with a rifle by an ARVN guard who wanted some trinket from her shop. She was lucky he'd hit her in the head, where she was well armored by a thick skull. If he'd hit her in the abdomen, he might have killed her.

Leaving George to handle her, I pulled away from the old man to take Tran's blood pressure. When I pried my hand loose, old Xe's hand, as if worn out from the exertion of holding on to mine, flopped between the rails and brushed my back.

I dreaded starting the neuro checks again, and my hands fumbled as I lifted Tran's lids to check her unseeing pupils. If she died, nothing would ever be all right for me again. I wished I could trade places with her. My own skin crawled when I pinched hers, my own lids twitched when I lifted hers, and I felt a knot in my chest when I knuckled her.

I apparently felt more than she did. "For Christ's sakes, Tran, that must hurt like hell. Snap out of it. Come on, kiddo, wake up." The breath eked out from between her lips with little sighs. I wanted to smack her awake, anything, just so she'd move. *That* would be compassionate and helpful, now, wouldn't it, nurse? Shit. I just wasn't cut out for this. I was okay with the gallbladders, cancer cases, and geriatric patients I'd cared for while I trained in Kansas City, but we just hadn't had a lot of skull fractures, traumatic amputations, or people with parts of them shot and melted away. I could take each case individually, but the collective weight was driving me down until I was simply too tired and depressed to try anymore. I was merely going through the motions, reacting automatically, leaving myself and my patients wide open to something like this.

The old man's hand brushed my hip and I swiveled around and looked at him suspiciously. He seemed the same as before, one hand still clutched at his sternum, the other now curled against my waist. Another mortar crumped and the bedlam in the ward broke loose again.

"Dau quadi!"

"Beaucoup dau, co!"

"Troi oi! Troi oi! Troi oi!"

I tucked the old fellow's hand against his side and stroked Tran's arm as if she needed soothing, not I. Through one of the three windows set high in the curve of the corrugated wall of the Quonset hut ward the sky was streaked with lemon, turquoise, and deep purple. Dawn was dawning and everybody on the ward seemed to have something loud to say about it.

"Jesus Christ, George," I said, stilling Xe's questing hand by holding it again, "can't you at least get them to do it in harmony?"

George grunted and rolled his eyes above his *Archie* comic.

Maybe the noise wasn't really loud enough to wake the dead, but then again, perhaps all that restless energy was contagious. Because this time, when I knuckled Tran, her mouth twisted and from it came a thin cry, like the kind that comes from a baby doll when you squeeze it.

I mention that incident for several reasons. I guess the first is to get it out of the way and tell it myself before anyone else does. There are those who may use that particular medication error to hint that I was an unstable nurse, which, of course, I was, and that my judgment was faulty, which it also was. However, I think it's important to note that my initial assessment of how the situation should be handled was rejected, which was also the case later, with Dang Thi Thai. That's what made me realize how power-less I was to do what I knew was right, and what made me take Ahn's case into my own hands. Maybe in a war situation there's no way to avoid tragedy, but I was trying, at least, to do what I thought was right. But most important of all, Tran's case was the first unknowing link between Xe, the amulet, and me, and what led to my transfer. And that, of course, led to everything else.

Tran's vital signs had stabilized by the time the day shift came on, and she was reacting to painful stimuli again. She was rescheduled for surgery that afternoon. I was scheduled for a meeting with Lieutenant Colonel Letitia Blaylock, the Chief Nurse of the hospital, that same morning.

I wasn't afraid of Lieutenant Colonel Blaylock by that time. As long as Tran didn't die from my carelessness, there wasn't really very much the Army could do to me that would be as hard to take. And after twenty-four hours of bedside-hovering, I was too drained to take much of anything except sleep seriously, least of all the good colonel.

A couple of weeks after Lieutenant Colonel Blaylock arrived at the 83rd there'd been a mass casualty situation —one of the biggies with chopper after chopper of mutilated people, both Vietnamese and Americans. One corpsman covered all but the most hard-pressed wards while every other available person spent the night in the E.R., cutting bloody clothing off patients, applying pressure bandages, starting I.V.s, giving meds, and going over surgical checklists. By the time I finally returned to neuro, it was almost time for the day shift to come on and I was drinking coffee, catching my breath, and waiting. The new patients were all taken care of, all I.V.s, catheters, and chest tubes were patent, and I felt we'd all done a good night's work. Lieutenant Colonel Blaylock arrived early for an inspection of the ward, her carefully smoothed, former-model-perfect features contracted in the barest hint of a frown; I was sure I couldn't be the cause, as hard as I'd been working that night. She toured the ward slowly and stopped several times to look at patients. In the middle of the ward she lifted her arm to summon me to the bedside of an elderly rice farmer who had been hit in the head by a bomb fragment.

"Lieutenant McCulley, I would like to know why this man's toenails are so filthy," she said sternly.

"Because he's worked in the rice paddies all his life, I

guess, ma'am," I said. "He's been bathed, like everyone else."

"That is not enough," she said, her voice soaring above my fifteen new I.V.s. "I want these Vietnamese patients properly cleaned. It is our original mission to take care of these unfortunate war casualties, as you no doubt know, since you have been in country longer than I."

What do you say to a colonel who insists on a damn-fool thing like that when you come to the end of an awful night? "Yes, ma'am," I said, but neither I, nor other personnel to whom she had amply demonstrated her deficient grasp of priorities, had much respect for her.

Nevertheless, she was the Chief Nurse. And this time she had something legitimate to yell at me about.

Yelling, however, was too coarse for the colonel. Instead, when she had released me from my stance at attention and bade me be seated in the metal folding chair allotted visitors to her office, she smiled a smile of sweet patient understanding. That made me far more nervous than if she'd yelled. I had learned to beware of smiling colonels at Fitzsimons, where I inadvertently got caught in a political battle between two of them.

I sat. The metal folding chairs used throughout the hospital compound in deference to our unit's "semimobile" status always reminded me of funeral parlors. When I was little, every time you went to an ice cream social at church or a school assembly, the folding chairs brought in to seat the multitudes were stamped with the name of the Peaceful Passages Funeral Parlor, from which they had been borrowed. They seemed an amenity particularly suited to Nam, where Uncle Sam and Uncle Ho were running such an enormous wholesale client-procurement racket for the funeral business. Although, in country, disposal of the dead was not expedited by agencies like Peaceful Passages with hushed tones speaking of loved ones. Here the departed were shoved into body bags, if there was enough left to bother with.

I suppose sleeplessness and release from tension caused me to drift into such thoughts instead of the trouble at hand. Because when I had composed myself, I saw that the colonel's smile was wearing pretty thin. She blinked, the dried glue of one of her false eyelashes giving way and detaching itself a teensy bit at the edge. The colonel had been a runway mannequin in New York before going into nursing, as she was fond of saying at parties, little realizing she gave us much fodder for cruel puns back in the barracks. Her modeling experience had to have been fifteen or twenty years ago, though, sometime before her makeup had petrified into varnish. Still, her years of charm school had imbued her with a poise that wasn't even challenged by dealing with delinquent second lieutenants.

I would have found a firing squad led by General Patton infinitely more reassuring than that *Vogue*ish smile.

"You do realize, do you not, lieutenant, that you are a dangerous nurse?"

"Well, yes, ma'am, but I did ask for a written order—" I began.

"The doctor gave you an order, Lieutenant McCulley. You were supposed to follow it. Instead, you administered ten times the prescribed medication. Didn't they teach you dosages and solutions in nursing school?"

"Yes, ma'am, but—" But that had nothing to do with it. I was not told to figure the proper dosage from the child's weight. I had been given a specific order that was incorrectly transmitted or received, I still wasn't entirely sure which. Had it been written, there would have been no question, and no error. But I was not going to get a chance to make even that meager point.

The colonel overrode my objections. She knew what was needed to mend the situation. Busy work. "Apparently you need a refresher course. You will report to my office during your lunch period until I am satisfied that you know how to properly compute them."

"Yes, ma'am," I said.

"Meanwhile, I'm afraid I must agree with Dr. Chalmers that despite your training in advanced medical-surgical nursing, we can't continue to risk entrusting you with such seriously ill patients."

"Yes, ma'am." Well, of course that was right. I was definitely feeling too shaky to work on the neuro ward anymore, particularly with Chalmers and Cindy Lou. But it was stupid of Blaylock to ignore Chalmers's share of the responsibility for bullying me out of verifying his order. If he could do it to me, he could do it to others, with results just as disastrous. I was not the only insecure, half-baked nurse who would ever work at the 83rd.

On the other hand, she wasn't in charge of him, she was in charge of me. And he *was* the doctor. Anything I said would only make it look as if I was being defensive, not taking criticism cheerfully, as they say on evaluation forms. I had only to look at Lieutenant Colonel Blaylock's face and listen to her voice to know that the arguments clenched behind my teeth would be construed as sniveling and caviling.

Why was it that when I was called on the carpet I felt as if John Wayne and every grain of sand on Iwo Jima would descend upon my head if I tried to explain myself? When I tried the colonel's roughshod tactics on some of my alleged subordinates, like the guys in the lab, they told me to stick it in my ear, it didn't mean nothin', and they weren't *e*-ven going to listen to no butter-bars lieutenant. Maybe I ought to take lessons from them instead of the colonel, I thought. I was no good at totalitarianism. My voice betrayed my age and inexperience. In my taped messages to my folks, my lisp made me sound like a third grader.

Obviously, I wasn't the kind of officer men or anybody else followed to hell and back. If Blaylock had been chewing out John Wayne or Jimmy Stewart, they'd not only convince her to exonerate them and court-martial Chalmers, but would come up with some new strategy that would win the war. Those kinds of guys never have to question how much of the blame is theirs. They're never wrong.

But right then it was rapidly dawning on me that I was wrong about more than Tran's Phenergan dosage.

Why, oh why, had I ever gone into nursing and joined the Army?

When I was a kid, I'd dreamed of being either a world-famous mystery novelist or a Hollywood costume designer. I wrote stories and doodled elongated models in glamorous getups during idle time in school. But what I wanted to be when I grew up was eclipsed by wondering if I'd get the chance.

Almost every week we'd have civil defense drills at school. The fire bell would ring and our teachers would herd us into the corridors, assumed to be the safest during bombings, or direct us to huddle under our desks. We listened to the mock alerts on the radio and memorized the conelrad call letters. At home, my mom and dad wondered if the cellar, which made a good tornado shelter, would also be effective against atomic bombs. On TV, Russia threatened us, then we threatened Russia, Khrushchev pounded his shoe on the table, and nobody seemed to be able to get along. War with the Reds was inevitable. I'd be walking home from school, enjoying brilliant autumn leaves or a fresh snow, and all of a sudden hear a thunderous explosion that rattled nearby windows. I'd check the sky, see the telltale jet stream, and relax. Just a jet breaking the sound barrier again. But I was afraid that one day I'd hear a sound like that and there'd be no more leaves, no more houses, no more cellar, no more school, no more Mom and Dad, and no more me or anything else. No matter what paltry precautions the adults tried to take, from what we kids had seen of the films of Hiroshima and read about the new, improved destruction perfected by atomic tests, nothing was going to do any good. If they dropped the Big One, the only thing to do was bend down, put your head between your knees, and kiss your ass good-bye.

Later, I read *On the Beach* and began thinking about what I would do if I wasn't vaporized. I'd have to be useful, that was for sure. Know how to do something the other survivors couldn't get along without. If I was designing costumes or writing stories, I'd be one more mouth to feed. But if I went into nursing, like my mother, and knew how to take care of people, I'd be valuable.

Vietnam had been a pimple of conflict when I entered training, but by the time I was a senior, it was obviously another of those undeclared wars like Korea. The military actively recruited student nurses. I was short on money to finish my senior year, and tired of being broke. I was restless, too, and wanted out of Kansas City. I didn't approve of war, God no. But Vietnam seemed to be a comparatively piddly conventional war with men and guns and tanks and stuff, like most of World War II, instead of nuclear warheads. I was so grateful that the world was restraining itself that I felt a rush of patriotism unmatched since the last time I'd watched the old movie about George M. Cohan. Surely, if I joined up and took care of casualties, I wouldn't be helping the war, I'd be repairing the damage as it occurred and doing my bit to keep the war contained until we could win it, without recourse to monster bombs. I never thought I'd actually end up in Vietnam. I'd have to volunteer for that, I was told. But on my first assignment, I ran afoul of one of those colonels I mentioned before, and discovered that I had been volunteered whether I liked it or not.

My mom had a fit, but after six months at Fitzsimons taking care of casualties and hearing my patients' war stories, I was curious to find out what really *was* going on in Vietnam. And it wasn't as if I'd actually be risking my life, really, not the way the men were. Female nurses were stationed only in the more secured areas, well protected by several thousand of our finest fighting men. I'd be able to test my ability under emergency conditions, be in the thick of things.

My skill had gotten tested, okay, and I'd flunked. Instead of getting sharper, I seemed to be losing what efficiency I'd had when I graduated second in my nursing school class. I had not, even at first, conned myself into thinking I was going to be another Nightingale, but neither had I anticipated becoming the Beetle Bailey of the Army Nurse Corps.

Apparently the distress from that notion showed in my face sufficiently to satisfy Blaylock, for she was now ready to deliver her coup de grace.

"After giving it some thought," she said, "I've decided to transfer you to another ward." She said "transfer," but her face said "banish." "Major Canon needs help on ward four. You'll start tomorrow, on days."

Ward four? Glory hallelujah, I must have overprayed. God not only helped Tran but delivered me from mine enemies as well. I felt like falling to my knees and begging Blaylock to please, please, Brer Colonel, please don't throw me in that brier-patch, just so she would be sure not to change her mind and spare me. Ward four was orthopedics. All the patients there were conscious. You could actually talk to them. You could actually watch some of them get better. You didn't run the risk of nearly killing them every time you gave them a cotton-pickin' pill.

"Yes, ma'am," I said, trying to hide my smile and refrain from clicking my heels together until I was safely away from her office.

"Dismissed," she said.

I felt so giddy with relief that I was ashamed of myself,

so I chastised myself by sneaking back onto neuro for another look at Tran. Chalmers and Cindy Lou were at the far end of the ward.

Tran was making up for her lack of activity for the preceding twenty-four hours. She'd wriggled halfway to the foot of the bed, her feet pushing the sheet overboard to drag the floor. I slid my arms under her hot little back and boosted her up again. She was so light she felt hollow. She let out an irritating but relatively healthy wail. I smoothed her covers and wiped the sweat from her knotted forehead. "Give me hell, sweetie, but thanks for not croaking," I whispered to her.

In the next bed, old Xe lay quietly with his hands over his chest. The deep frown lines I had noticed earlier were smooth now, his wrinkles gentle as the furrows made by wind through a wheat field. The dreams that had disturbed him earlier seemed to have quieted, and his sleep was peaceful.

Chalmers and Cindy Lou trotted up the ward with bundles of charts tucked officiously under their arms, the two of them looking for all the world like Dr. Dan and Nancy Nurse. They exchanged a look that pointedly did not acknowledge my unclean presence.

# 2

I tramped up the wooden stairs of the barracks and down the landing to my own hooch too tired to spare a glance for Monkey Mountain or the South China Sea, and unsure whether I wanted to continue to beat my breast, lick my wounds, or gloat. What I really wanted to do was sleep, but as soon as I opened the door to my hooch I knew that was going to present a problem.

The sun glinted blindingly off the tin roof of the building, giving my room the climate of a kiln. I had nailed a Vietnamese bedspread, an institution-green brocade of a phoenix, over my window in an attempt to provide myself with shade and privacy. Otherwise the hooch's decor was a scant improvement on the miners' shacks outlaws use for hideouts in old Western movies.

I flopped down on my cot and groaned for a while. The cot was covered with another Vietnamese spread, which was, like everything else at the 83rd, habitually sandy. I had no sooner lain down than I knew I was going to have to sit up again and pry off my boots. My socks were wringing wet, my feet swollen and sore. I twisted on the bed and opened my door and dumped the sand from the boots. Mine were standard issue leather because I have big wide feet and the quartermaster couldn't find the lighter, canvas-and-steel-reinforced jungle boots in my size. The plywood floor of the room did not cool my burning soles, so I lay back down on the bed and let the room spin around for a while.

The whole hooch was about the size of my clothes closet at home in Kansas City, and it didn't have a closet. It did have, courtesy of my mother's care packages, contact-paper flowers stuck around on the bare plywood walls and

21

a mobile of paper cats, a pop bottle with Mexican crepe-paper flowers stuck in it, also gifts from home. My hot plate, assorted food, a midget refrigerator, and a reel-to-reel tape deck, along with my folded clothing, even my underwear, freshly rice-starched and ironed by my hooch maid, were arranged on a wonderful wall of shelves constructed by the orthopedic surgeon I would soon be working with. Joe Giangelo, a doctor who had somehow managed to escape ascending to deity when he gained his M.D., was better known as Geppetto by the nurses, because of the kindness with which he deployed his carpentry skills. With Geppetto for our local architect and interior designer, the hooches of several of the nurses were pretty plush by Vietnam standards.

Correction. This whole assignment was *very* plush by Vietnam standards. So what the hell was wrong with me? I wasn't being asked to build the Bridge on the River Kwai, just to do my job, for very good pay, under much better circumstances than most of the people in Vietnam. I wasn't in any foxholes, or in danger of being shot at, and even the concertina wire and sandbag bunkers were more for joshing the folks at home than taken seriously, at least by me. Of course, the work hours here were a little longer, the heat and bugs were atrocious, and I was unable to get enough sleep because of all of the above, but compared to what the average grunt went through I was living in fat city. So why was I screwing up so badly I almost killed people?

Well, actually, I wasn't almost killing just anybody, but specifically a little Vietnamese girl with a head injury. There was a double dehumanizing factor there. She wasn't one of "us," of course. Didn't speak English. Was automatically suspect of being a grenade-tossing junior terrorist just because she had the gall to be Vietnamese in Vietnam. And the head injury made it worse, because even though I knew theoretically that some of the neuro patients would get well, I could remember only a handful of encounters with patients alert enough to display whole personalities. I really wanted to blame someone else so that I didn't have to admit that I had gotten not only careless but callous.

Looking closely at why I was so mad at the doctor and the head nurse and the others who were justifiably alarmed over what had happened with Tran, I think I took the whole thing personally because I felt they didn't really care about her as much as I did. They were just tsk-tsking me to get me. Because only a couple of months earlier, it had been standard operating procedure to give the Vietnamese patients life-threateningly dangerous care on a routine basis, when we transfused them with O-positive blood.

Before I came to Nam I had only read about transfusion reactions in textbooks, because a routine laboratory procedure, typing and cross-matching a patient to ensure compatibility with the donated blood, eliminated most of the danger.

I began to realize the difference between wartime and peacetime nursing the night one of my Vietnamese patients went into a transfusion reaction and nobody but me was even upset about it.

The patient was a middle-aged woman who had been too near when a bomb went off, drilling a hole in her skull as well as peppering her body with frag wounds, from which she lost a lot of blood. The first unit of blood had been hung as I came on duty. My assignment was to monitor the patient for a transfusion reaction. Although transfusion reactions are rare in the States, it's routine to keep track of the patient's vital signs and general well-being for the first hour or so, just to make sure everything is okay. Only this time everything wasn't okay. The woman spiked a temp even higher than the one she was already running from dehydration, and began chilling at the same time. It's eerie seeing goose bumps rise on somebody when their fever is 104–105 and the room temperature is the same or higher. It happened so fast that she was starting to convulse before I quite realized what was happening. As soon as I did, I yanked the unit of blood, tubing and all, and replaced it with a bottle of Ringer's lactate. I put in a call for the doctor, who was, I think, in downtown Da Nang that night (though that was supposed to be off limits), and called the lab to ask them to repeat the cross match.

"Why?" asked the stoned young thing on the other end.

"Because the unit you brought me was wrong—it almost killed my patient."

"Then so would anything else I bring you. O poz is all we got for gooks, lady."

"What do you mean by that remark, soldier?" I asked in my best John Wayne growl. "The woman almost bled to death already. We surely aren't going to bring her in and just finish her off with bad blood."

I meant to be sarcastic, but the fellow was full of herbally induced patience.

"It ain't bad blood, Lieutenant. It's good ol' American universal-donor blood. The gooks are lucky to get it. American donors donate for 'Mericans, get it? There'd be hell to pay if they knew their blood was going to keep some gook alive. But bein' the Good Samarit—the kind-hearted suckers we are—we let 'em have a little of the cheap-and-easy brew."

"If O positive is the universal donor, why is she reacting to it?"

"Oh, it ain't all *that* universal. Lots of AB types don't handle it real well, and uh—AB is a lot more common among the gooks than it is with us. Oops, gotta date with a hot centrifuge. Have a nice night, Lieutenant."

The doctor was even more offhand than the lab tech, who was indeed repeating hospital policy. Nobody said in so many words that they didn't care if the Vietnamese patients lived or died. But the lifers, the career Army sergeants and senior officers, were fond of reminding us new recruits that anyone who had served in the Pacific in WW II or Korea could tell you gooks didn't value human life the way Americans and Europeans did.

It wasn't until the neurosurgeon left and a fill-in, a doctor who had been serving in the field, was reassigned to us on temporary duty that something was done about the problem. Dr. Riley was a very logical man. He decided that if gooks bled, gooks could give blood. He grabbed a handful of tourniquets, needles, and syringes and he and Major Crawley, our head nurse at the time, raided the visitors' tent and availed themselves of its walking Vietnamese blood bank. Most of the visitors didn't mind donating. Nobody had ever thought to ask them before.

I had thought myself above the kind of bigotry that had willfully overlooked what was so obvious to Dr. Riley; the human body works pretty much the same no matter what kind of upholstery you put on it. Now I had to seriously question whether I hadn't at least inwardly begun to buy into all of that "anti-gook" stuff. Had I harmed Tran because I secretly didn't give as much of a damn about her as I did about my "professional image"?

Was I really more concerned with stupid appearances than I was with hurting somebody who was so totally helpless and dependent on me?

Oh well, so I'd screwed up. Nobody had been making it exactly easy for me. *Let* them transfer me to an easier assignment. What did I care? Except—except that I still hated like hell that I had failed, that I hadn't measured up. Because I wanted to do more, not less. I really wanted to be in a field hospital, as a surgical nurse, doing the rough stuff. But of course, after my screwing up like this, there was no chance of that. So I'd have to accept what they told me and watch myself and make sure that it never, ever . . .

I wanted to cry, but I couldn't. I was furious with myself now, not just with everybody else, and it was a cold kind of furious that made the center of my chest ache as if I had pleurisy. My throat was as gritty and parched as the beach. I trolled with my fingers until I found the refrigerator door, and popped it open long enough to extract the dregs of a flat Coke. I popped two Benadryls and chased them with the Coke.

It tasted metallic, and there were little solid pieces at the bottom, like worms. Probably from having been shipped and stored so long. But there were all those stories floating around about the Vietcong taking the tops off pop bottles and putting ground glass in the Coke, then recapping and resealing it. I couldn't help wondering if their evil little minds hadn't dreamed up a similar way of getting into cans. I generally tried to drink 7-Up or Shasta, but with the PX, you took what you could get.

Despite the Benadryl, I couldn't get comfortable. My elbows and knees were in the wrong places, and vast patches of my skin stuck to the cot.

Someone climbed the steps to the upper porch and walked toward my room, the footfalls sending tiny vibrations across the floor and up the cot legs. A face and a pair of hands squashed against my screen door.

"Kitty? You there?"

I grunted, and Carole Swenson opened the door and plopped herself on the edge of my cot. Her ditty bag and another of the Vietnamese bedspreads slid to the floor beside her boot. "Hi. How was your night?" she asked as if it wasn't already all over the compound how my night had been.

"Oh, you know. Long," I said.

Carole was maybe my best friend at the hospital, but I couldn't talk to her about this. She waited a moment for me to continue, then started pawing through her ditty bag, the little olive-drab cloth sack we all used as a purse. Triumphantly she extracted a stack of three-by-five cards. "I had a brainstorm. Lookit here."

"What are those for?" I asked.

"My schedule. I got tired of reciting it to guys who keep forgetting it and call me up while I'm on duty, so I decided to start copying it out on three-by-five cards. It'll save time."

"Uh huh," I said, mild amusement lapping at the edges of my bone-tiredness. Carole did tend to carry her talent for organization a little far sometimes. But that talent was part of what made her such a good nurse. She handled the ICU, which was a nightmare, as if it were routine ward work, and conducted emergency triage situations as coolly as if she were planning seating arrangements at a party. Her I.V.s always seemed to hit the veins on the first punch, she always found the bleeder, she always managed to hold someone where it didn't hurt, and she seemed to know before the patients did what would make them more comfortable, feel a little better. She was the kind of nurse who would be there with a glass of water half a second before a patient realized he was thirsty.

"If you have your schedule, you could do the same thing . . ." she suggested, which was supposed to give me an opening to tell her about my transfer. The hospital compound was a small place. Rumors had probably spread far and wide about how I had nearly killed Tran and what Blaylock had done about it. Carole, who would never have made the same kind of an error, nevertheless had probably already put herself mentally in my place and was trying to help.

I grunted noncommittally, because I still didn't want to talk but I didn't want her to go away mad either. I needed all the friends I could get.

"Be that way," she said, and tucked her cards back inside the bag, and abruptly changed the subject. "Judy's ward master is going to the PX and said he'd drop us at the beach on the way. Wanna come?"

She'd done it again. Suddenly I knew that I needed to get off the compound and away from the hospital more than anything. I nodded, plucked my beach bag from the corner, and followed her out the door.

Carole, Judy Heifetz, and I crowded into the Jeep driven by Sergeant Slattery, the ward master on Judy's ward. Getting a ride all the way to the beach was a rare treat. Usually we had to walk to the gate and hitch a ride with a passing deuce-and-a-half or whatever other vehicle was willing to pick us up. Women weren't allowed to drive vehicles off post. Too dangerous.

The Jeep bumped its way through the gate and down the dirt road through Dogpatch, the Vietnamese village that separated the southern side of the compound from American-built Highway 1. The highway ran down the coast of Vietnam, and led past Tien Sha, the naval base north of us, past Freedom Hill and the China Beach R&R Center, to the south. Somewhere along the way was a turnoff for the bridge across the river to Da Nang and another road that led to Marble Mountain Air Force Base.

Vietnamese children stopped and watched our Jeep sputter past. A little boy, who was probably eight but looked five, ran toward us. "Hey, GI, you want buy boom-boom?"

"Get lost," Slattery yelled.

"Hey, man, numbah one boom-boom, no shit." The child continued with the hard sell. After all, family pride was no doubt involved, since he was probably pimping for his mother or sisters.

We laughed, and Judy leaned out and waved him away. "Hey, man," she said. "We mamasans. No need boom-boom."

The kid, undaunted, trotted along beside our dust cloud, calling, "Hey, mamasans, you want numbah one job?"

Later, out on the highway, Slattery had to stop the Jeep for an overturned Honda while the three occupants reloaded two baskets of chickens, their laundry, two water jugs, and a pig onto the little vehicle. While stopped, we all assumed the sort of hunchbacked position required to cover your watch with your right hand while keeping your elbows tight over your pockets and, in our cases, our ditty bags tucked firmly into our armpits. Vietnamese street kids watched for just such incidents to dart out and strip the valuables off the passengers of stopped vehicles before the suckers knew what happened. It occurred to me more than once that it was a damned good thing Jeeps didn't have hubcaps.

Carole and Judy had worn bathing suits under their fatigues, but I had to stop at the ladies' room of the officers' club to change. My mom had picked my suit, a gold velour modified bikini, out of the Sears catalog. Needless to say, it was not particularly revealing, but it wouldn't have made any difference if it had been cut like a pair of long johns. Stepping from the ladies' locker room onto the glaringly sunlit beach, surrounded by a couple three hundred males, I squinted down the long stretch of beach between me and the blankets Carole and Judy had stretched by the edge of the water. I felt I was running the gauntlet, like the guy in that old movie *Flight of the Arrow,* although the scenario was more like Annette Funicello in *Beach Blanket Bingo.* Or maybe it was Sally Field in *Gidget Goes to War.*

Heat pulsed from the sand, and I smelled the rubber of my flip-flop soles, hot as a teenager's tires. I was glad I had my new tortoiseshell-rimmed aviator-style dark glasses to hide my eyes as the usual chorus of wolf whistles and catcalls followed me down the beach.

"Hey—hey, Joe?" someone on the enlisted side of the beach called.

"Yeah?"

"Get a load of that funny-shaped guy in the two-piece suit."

I turned around and saw two tanned-to-the-waist, white-legged specimens of American manhood staring after me with a cross between bewilderment and awe. One of them looked mildly mortified that I was staring back. The other one gave me a cocky grin. I waved hello and kept walking. A month ago I would probably have struck up an acquaintance, gone swimming with them, or played beach ball for a little while. But during the last month, our fellow officers had decided that female nurses were not safe consorting with all those horny enlisted men, most of them marines on in-country R&R from combat duty. Our fellow officers thought we were much safer consorting exclusively with horny officers. Carole, Judy, and I, as well as a lot of the other girls, were pissed off about it. The guys on the enlisted side of the beach were the ones who were taking all the risks. They were the ones who needed the morale maintenance that officers on the make were so quick to remind us round-eyes women was part of our patriotic duty. Probably some of those guys were dangerous—I mean, they were supposed to be dangerous to the Vietcong and the NVA, weren't they? But the treatment I'd received from them hadn't frightened me. Though there'd been some tentative passes, so respectfully tendered as to almost be comical, most of the guys had just seemed happy to be reminded that there were other kinds of people around besides Vietnamese and men.

Carole was busily filling out her three-by-five cards when I arrived, while Judy tried to get to sleep. I waded into the sea. It was warm as urine and about as refreshing, but I wet myself down anyway, then waded back out again to lie face down to bake on my blanket.

I dug little holes in the sand with my toes and tried to snuggle the sand into conformation with my body. The skin of my back twitched when I lay still, my muscles relaxing only slowly as they grew accustomed to the warmth of the sun.

An aircraft carrier rode the waves on the horizon, a guardian beast for the beach. I felt, as much as heard, the distant rumble of artillery, the sand vibrating beneath my breasts and stomach.

The tepid gray-green sea lapped the beach, its rhythm soothing. I lay still until the droplets of water evaporated from my hide and were replaced by droplets of sweat. Then, feeling like a dolphin needing to keep her skin wet at all times, I waded back into the sea.

Before I could settle back down on my blanket, a shadow interposed itself between the sun and my body.

"Hi there, young lady. You look like you could use a drink. What'll it be?"

I peered up at this aspiring cocktail waiter. He had thinning grayish hair, an eager expression, and a white band around his left ring finger where his tan stopped.

"Nothing, thanks," I said. "I'm trying to get some sleep right now. I'll get something to drink later."

He plopped down beside me. "Don't be crazy, hon. You'll get all dried out in this sun. Hey, you're starting to blister already. Better let me rub some suntan lotion on you."

"It'll just wash off again," I said, but he was already squeezing my lotion onto his big pink ringless hands. I thought about making a lunge for it and asking Carole or Judy to do the honors instead, but they had found new friends and wandered off down the beach.

"My name's Mitch," the man said as he smeared goo onto my back. "What's yours?"

"Kitty," I said. I didn't care how good it felt. Name, rank, and serial number were all he was entitled to.

He chuckled as if he'd already made a dirty joke out of my name. I glared at him and he put a lid on it. I was surprised. It was the single indication he had given of sensitivity. Or perhaps he just felt vulnerable in swimming trunks.

"What do you do, Kitty?"

"I'm a nurse. I just got off a twenty-four-hour shift and I'm *trying to get some sleep,*" I repeated. A little reinforcement is never amiss when dealing with slow learners.

"A nurse? Army?" he asked, and I nodded into the blanket. "Say, we sure do appreciate you girls. Me, I'm over at I Corps HQ."

I grunted. If good ol' Mitch was from I Corps headquarters and had time to hang out at the officers' beach, he had to be some kind of brass, which accounted for the amount of it in his approach. He took my grunt for an invitation instead of what it was: the most eloquent communication I felt I could spare, and that only because I was brought up to be polite. I was so tired I would have gone to sleep with him there if I'd dared.

He lay down on my blanket beside me and got even chummier. "Yeah, we supply this whole area, you know. Do you like those fancy dishes in the Pacex catalog? We got a whole load of those the other day by mistake. I'll bet I could get you some really cheap."

"Um," I mumbled.

"What?" he asked, a little starch creeping into his voice when I did not instantly offer him my undying gratitude. You usually got that sort of unrealistic expectation only from lieutenant colonels and above.

"I said to let me know, after Mrs. Mitch makes her choice of pattern, and I'll talk to my fiancé and see what he thinks."

He sat back up and dusted sand onto my freshly oiled back. "Well, I sure am getting thirsty, Kitty. Sure you won't take me up on that drink? Nope? Nice talking to you."

Judy had returned to her blanket, alone, this time, and had been eavesdropping. "Hey, Kitty, what pattern is Colonel Martin going to get for *you* just out of the goodness of his little old heart?"

"He asked you too?"

"He's asked every nurse in Da Nang, I think. Somebody ought to let the poor schmuck know he's real confused about our particular military occupational speci*al*ity, and even if we were what he seems to think we are, who ever heard of a hooker who does it for china?"

"Hanoi Hannah might—do it for China, I mean, get it?"

"You are on the *very* seriously ill list, McCulley, and that's a fact. Get some sleep, woman."

I slept, and in my sleep kept doing vital signs and neuro checks, vital signs and neuro checks. Tran's eyes stared up at me, just the whites, and I knew I was going to fall asleep on duty and she'd die because I wasn't awake. . . . I jerked myself awake and saw the sand and smelled the oil. My back felt slightly tight, a little too hot.

I wet down again and tried to bake the other side, but even through my sunglasses, the light pried my lids open. I now felt the artillery rumble in my spine. Oddly enough, it drowned out other, less predictable noises and lulled me back to sleep. I don't remember dreaming that time.

It must have been at least two hours later that Carole shook me. "We have to get back now and shower for work. Coming?"

"I think I'll stay here and have something to eat. I'm not all that anxious to get back."

Carole gave me a stern look of the "once you fall off a pony, pardner, you just have to climb back on" variety, but I had better things to feel guilty about than staying at the beach all day.

# 3

The China Beach Officers' Club was a rambling French colonial building on a hill above the beach. It commanded a splendid view of the South China Sea and the adjacent mountains and jungle. It was a romantic-looking place if you overlooked the concertina wire and sandbags and disregarded the attire of the clientele. With its lazily rotating ceiling fans, latticework of white painted wood, wide veranda, and potted palms, the place always made me feel as if I should be wearing a white linen safari suit and a pith helmet and walk in on the arm of Jungle Jim. I kept expecting somebody to come riding up on an elephant and call me "memsahib."

Right then, however, the *Gunga Din* illusions of the place were of less allure than its distance from the hospital.

I usually dressed up to go to the club and went in a group, or with an escort. This time I just pulled on my rumpled fatigues over my swimsuit, which was by then bone-dry, tried to brush the sand off, and stuck my hair up under my baseball cap. I looked like a grunt, which was fine with me. I didn't feel very glamorous.

The club was half-empty at five, which was a little early for dinner. I really wanted to be alone to mope, but that was a sure way to attract even more attention than usual. I looked around for someone I knew. Just anybody harmless and familiar.

Even as messy as I looked then, I no sooner stepped inside than the clatter of stainless and restaurant pottery died to an occasional clink and the muted conversations stopped altogether. I felt like the Fastest Gun in the West entering a saloon just before High Noon, but I pretended not to notice. Since coming to Nam, I had gotten used to stopping traffic. Literally. I had always considered myself attractive in a sort of wholesome, moon-faced way. I had nice hazel eyes and brown hair carefully kept reddish, and a figure that ten pounds less made "stacked" and ten pounds more made "fat." But none of it mattered, because the attention was nothing personal. It was not my sheer breathtaking gorgeousness or incredible charisma that was causing apnea among the male diners. The standard female reproductory equipment and round eyes were all that was required to be the Liz Taylor of China Beach.

I just stood there kind of dazed from the sun and sleepy and tried to decide what to do. The very idea of all those men just made me tired right now.

One reason I hadn't minded coming to Nam so much at first was that I had already talked to a lot of bewildered boys my age who didn't want to go but saw no other choice. It seemed unfair that they had to serve, just because they were men of the right age. Like discrimination. I thought, if this war was for the benefit of the U.S., why were men the only ones who had to go? The North Vietnamese, or at least the VC, had women troops, and so did the Israelis. Of course, two days after I was in country it was pretty clear that no American, male or female, should have had to be there. If I had to enlist again, nothing short of the invasion of Kansas City would have gotten me into uniform. Furthermore, I knew that many of the men who had been gung ho before they got to Nam agreed with me. Even the South Vietnamese stayed out of the military if they could, and it was their damned war.

Nevertheless, there I was, and my idealistic notions of brother-and-sisterhood failed to prevent me from being an exotic novelty item in the war zone, no matter how much I wanted, or was able, to contribute. Most of the guys most of the time were okay, even downright gallant. But there were those like Mitch who decided that we nurses were just working twelve-hour shifts, continually suffering from lack of sleep and incipient heatstroke, as a sort of hobby. What we were really in Nam for, of course, was to get laid. By them.

Nurses, Red Cross workers, entertainers—we were all nymphos if not actually whores, according to the predominant mode of wistful thinking. Even fairly nice men swore to us nurses that all doughnut dollies were making big money as prostitutes, and apparently the same men told the same story about us when they were talking to the Red Cross workers. I remember having a conversation with one of the Red Cross girls at Marble Mountain. "Funny, you don't seem as—ah—you know . . ." she said at one point, when we had been talking about what we were doing in Nam. "I know," I said. "You don't look like a hooker to me either."

The whole thing made me want to smack somebody, but unfortunately, most of the people I could smack here would outrank me.

But basically, as long as the guys kept their cruder notions to themselves, I could handle it, and even enjoy the attention. What really got to me was the ones who made Mitch look like Mr. Suave. On Carole's birthday, one of her boyfriends had brought four of us girls to the club to celebrate. Drunken marine officers had converged upon us to woo us with obscenities and innuendos delivered with typical Corps couth, which vies with that of convicted multiple rapist-murderers for gentility. "No, thank you," "I'm not interested," "Please go away or I'll tell my boyfriend, King Kong," "I'm engaged," and "I'm married" did not deter them. Neither, at first, did "Get your goddamn hands off me," and "Fuck off and die," until voiced with sufficient volume to attract the interest of other officers, who wandered over to reinforce Carole's boyfriend. Our rescuers then stayed around for drinks and any possible demonstrations of eternal gratitude. Most of them were somewhat better behaved than the marines. One of them suggested that we had had no call to get so mad, since if we didn't want marines lusting after us, we wouldn't be there.

That was so unfair. I for one had been expecting a different Marine Corps altogether—the one with the lofty Latin motto, the one my dad had joined in WW II. He had had such a good time with those other marines, and often told long, funny stories about the adventures of his group of lads on Ishi Shima. They never, in Dad's stories, killed anybody, they just camped out in the rain a lot and scrounged and gave candy to children and nylons to women and converted POWs through sheer kindness and wrote home to Mother. And they certainly didn't say "fuck" every other word. Of course, by now I did. Dad would be very shocked at all of us, I supposed.

Maybe from this you can gather that our lives were a bit on the schizophrenic side. While we were on duty, we were responsible for the lives and deaths of our patients, for calming their fears and administering treatments that could cure or kill them. Off duty, we were treated as a sort of cross between a high-ranking general who deserved to be scrounged for, taken around, and generally given special treatment, and a whore. It was a little like that old saying of water, water, everywhere, and not a drop to drink. All those men and you could still be so lonely.

On a date, after you talked about where you were both from, your escort would brag about his aircraft or his unit or, God forbid, his body count. If he was feeling disgruntled, you were supposed to keep up his morale. But you were expected to do the same attentive little cupcake act the football players had expected in high school. Nobody wanted to hear about your day at work. Some of the girls dated doctors, who at least had some idea of what the rest of their life was like. I was awfully glad I didn't. All I'd have needed just then was to have to spend my off-duty time, too, explaining what I'd done to Tran. Dating doctors, to me, was a good way to screw up both your social life and your work life. Besides, doctors were married.

A nurse captain I'd met at Fitzsimons who had been to Nam twice and Okinawa once told me her prescription for handling one's love life on overseas duty.

"Keep it light, honey. Keep it light. What happens is you have these real killer romances and then the love of your life leaves country, promising to write, and all that shit, then he goes back to his ever-lovin' wife or his *real* girlfriend, and forgets all about you. It's just not real, see, whatever it feels like. The partying is great, but you can't take it seriously. What you do is you find a nice guy who has about three months left in country, just long enough to have a little fun. You don't tend to get so involved when you know how soon the end is coming. You date him and meet his friends, and when he goes, you take up with the nicest of the friends who have only about three months left in country, and so on. It's the only way to keep from being burned."

I agreed and tried to maintain a properly cynical attitude, but naturally, I hoped she was wrong in my case, and that I would find true and requited love just for being so goddamn noble. Oh well, at least I was drawing combat pay.

A rugged-looking fellow sporting a blond crew cut and a lightweight flight suit marched up to me and smiled, showing enough teeth to look friendly and not enough to look as if he were about to bite. "Excuse me, ma'am, but if you're not with anyone, my buddies and I would appreciate it if you'd be our dinner guest."

"Well, I was sort of . . ." I glanced around the room again, but it was full of strangers. "Okay."

"I'm Jake."

"I'm Kitty. Where you from, Jake?" I asked, the usual opening conversational gambit in Nam. Everybody wanted to talk about where they were from. Damn few wanted to talk about where they were at.

"Florida originally, but my family lives in Tennessee now. Where you from?"

"Kansas City," I replied and decided as he led me to his table that he was probably okay. Mentioning his family in the first sentence and not hiding his wedding ring were good signs. Whatever else he was, he was not that bane of the single military nurse, the geographical bachelor.

The table was on the veranda, and at it were two more men in flight suits, one sitting and one standing, his feet spread as if he were about to straddle his chair, his hands on the back of it, his face shrouded in mirrored aviator glasses. Those lenses hide a lot, but I felt them locked on me as surely as if they were the sights of a sniperscope. He wore his hair longer than the other two and it was dark, with a rather rakish forelock brushing the tops of the glasses. He was tanned and rangy and his grin was lopsided and only slightly tobacco-stained.

"Pay no attention to this fellow, ma'am," Jake said. "He's just one of your run-of-the-mill dust-off pilots. We let him eat with us, hopin' he might learn how to conduct himself in proper company. Tony, you don't propose to eat standin' up, I suppose?"

"Nah. Not that I don't appreciate educational opportunities, sir, but I ate already, as I would have explained if you hadn't gone trotting off after the prettiest girl in the room like a—well, anyhow, I got to get back to Red Beach. I'm on alert. But I wouldn't pass up an introduction."

"I didn't think you would, somehow," Jake snorted. "Kitty, this is Warrant Officer Antonio Gutierrez Devlin."

Warrant Officer Devlin gave me the full impact of that slightly snaggle-toothed grin and swept my paw to his lips. "*Very* pleased to meet you. What was the name? Kitty what?"

"McCulley," I said.

"From over at Single Parent?"

"What?"

"Single Parent, the 83rd. You're Army, aren't you? Your code name over there is Single Parent."

"No shit?"

"I kid you not. Also referred to more casually as Unwed Mother. Where do you work?"

"Uh—ward four, ortho, as of tomorrow."

"Hmm—"

"Didn't you say you were just leaving, Tony? Urgent mission?"

"Yeah, well, I'm sorry, Kitty. I have to go rescue stranded casualties, unlike these heavy-machinery haulers. Since we all work so *closely* together, I'm sure I'll be seeing you real soon." He tilted his sunglasses down to the tip of his nose and gave me a meaningful look out of hazel-green eyes with curly dark lashes that should have been outlawed on a man, then did a smart about-face, swiveled around again, and said to Jake, "Make sure *she* comes to the party, Cap'n, sir," then sauntered through the door. Have I mentioned that not all of the masculine attention we girls got was unwelcome?

I was catching my breath when Jake gently lowered me into a chair and continued introductions.

"This fine gentleman here is Tommy Dean Kincaid. Say hello to the pretty lady, Tommy Dean."

"Hello, pretty lady. Ain't it awful what you meet on your way to Grandma's house in the middle of this war?"

These two were definitely going to be all right. They sounded like Bing Crosby and Bob Hope on *The Road to Da Nang*, with me as Dorothy Lamour. Of course, what I was really wondering about was the Errol Flynn type who had just left, but the comic relief was comforting. I was still feeling a little too fragile to withstand the kind of internal fireworks Tony generated.

But these two good old boys really were good. Like

Jake, Tommy Dean mentioned his wife within the first fifteen minutes, and asked my advice about what kind of a present to send her for her birthday. We told each other where we were from, and later Jake and Tommy Dean, between mouthfuls of steak and baked potato, talked about aircraft while I ate in what I hoped passed for awe-stricken silence. I'm a fast eater, though, being used to institutional half-hour lunch breaks during which fifteen minutes was spent in a cafeteria line, and I finished before either of the men.

"What did Tony mean about you guys hauling heavy equipment? You *are* pilots, I gather?"

"Yes, *ma'am,*" Tommy Dean said.

"Fixed-wing?"

"Goodness no."

"What do you fly, then? Cobras? Hueys? I rode in a Chinook when I first got here. The guys up at Phu Bai had us up for a party. Boy, are those things noisy."

"Honey, you ain't seen nothin' yet," Jake said proudly.

"You seen anything flyin' around in the air looks a little like a big grasshopper?" Tommy Dean asked.

"Well . . . I can't say as—"

"You'd know if you'd seen it. It's a flying crane. Looks a little like this." He pulled a pen from one of his zippered pockets and drew a picture that did indeed appear to be the product of a marriage between a helicopter and a grasshopper.

I examined the picture, wondering if this might be another one of those strange in-country jokes to impress newcomers and girls. Finally I handed it back and asked, "Why in the world would anybody build a chopper that looks like that?"

"It's a flying *crane,* Kitty," Jake said, and then, of course, I understood. I had been associating the word "crane" with the bird, or with the long, spindly legs of the Disney version of the Ichabod Crane who saw the headless horseman in Sleepy Hollow. Jake eagerly pointed out the features of his aircraft to me. "This space under here is for a cable to haul cargo. Watch the air sometime. You may see one carrying a tank or another chopper." His face lapsed into an expression of almost paternal fondness as he spoke.

"Aw, seein' it from the ground is nothin' compared to watchin' something swinging from its belly."

"I can imagine," I said honestly, because I was by now as intrigued as it is possible for me to be by a piece of machinery.

"If you'll come over for that party Tony was talking about, maybe we can take you for a ride," Jake said.

"I'm changing wards right now," I told them and found my voice was a little unsteady at the reminder. "I don't know my schedule."

"That's okay, honey," Jake said, patting my hand. He obviously mistook the hint of distress in my tone for disappointment that I wouldn't be able to make an immediate date to acquaint myself with the ungainly object that was the current love of his life. "The cranes will be there when you can make it over. And there'll be other parties. Don't worry. . . ."

The talk turned to their families again, then, abruptly, Tommy Dean ducked out to see if the sergeant they'd ridden over with was done with his carousing at the NCO club. "Is he okay?" I asked.

"Oh sure, honey. Just a little homesick. You know, I don't think you realize how much it means to him—to both of us—to have you come over and talk to us for a while." He stopped looking at me for the first time that evening and studied his fingernails, and the ceiling fan, and took great interest in the comings and goings of the waitresses. "Now, I'm not sayin' we wouldn't either one of us take somethin' if we could get it, if you know what I mean, but mostly we are happily married men. I miss my wife like hell. It feels so good to be able to talk to a woman without, you know, havin' to use sign language all of the goddamn time."

It was my turn to study my fingernails. I couldn't find the right expression to let him know how good it was to talk to men who didn't treat me like a servant (the doctors), a policewoman (most of the enlisted men), or a piece of ass.

"If you guys have a Jeep, would you mind dropping me off at the PX gate so I can hitch back to the hospital?" I asked.

They insisted on taking me all the way back to the 83rd, of course, and kept me laughing all the way. I was hoping one or the other of them would mention something else about Tony, but they didn't, though Jake reminded me of the party.

I felt pretty good until the Jeep drove out of sight and I turned to walk past the sign that said "Welcome to Hell's Half Acre."

Beyond the gate, floodlights from the guard towers illuminated the compound, sandbags, concertina wire, plywood barracks, and administrative shacks. The hospital's white humps shone from within, the three long windows at the top of each ward glowing faintly with the light over the nurses' station. The hospital building was actually two sets of Quonset huts connected by a long, enclosed corridor. It resembled eight enormous oil drums that someone had split open and spread apart so that half of each drum lay directly across from the other. Each entire oil drum was a whole ward, with space enough for maybe another Quonset hut on each side of the ones already in place. You could almost see the cloud of pot smoke swirling above the visitors' tent, defining the atmosphere between wards five and six.

Smelling it, I forgot about Tony and Jake and Tommy Dean and could see the inside of ward six again as clearly as if I'd never left Tran's bedside. Shame and grief not only for the harm I might have caused Tran but for the nurse I was not and was never going to be welled up in me again, returning in a massive sodden lump. The closer I got to the hospital, the bigger the lump swelled, until it filled my chest and throat and brought the taste of sirloin and stomach acid to my tongue. I should stop and check on Tran, just so everyone would know that I really did give a damn about her. But what if something had gone wrong? I took a shortcut through the hospital, my boots loud on the concrete hallway. No one else was out there, just the mingled smells of antiseptic, pot, and Nam, and the collective sound of deep breathing, restless sleep, shifting feet, and the occasional clank of metal trays or bedpans. The light glowed softly over the desk on ward six. Ginger was pouring meds. George was behind his comic. Tran's bed was still occupied. I crept just a little closer, not wanting to greet anyone. The body in the bed was Tran's, and she was breathing.

I passed through the hospital, out onto the boardwalk, and up the stairs to my quarters, gratefully closing the door behind me. My side of the building had been out of the sun for several hours, so the temperature in the tiny room was more or less bearable. I turned on the fan and let it blow through my hair, evaporate the last moisture from my skin as I pulled off my fatigues.

My laundry was lying freshly pressed on my shelves—well, most of it was my laundry. Looked as if mamasan had left me somebody else's rice-starched and ironed lace panties.

I grabbed a clean set of underwear, slipped on a shift, and headed for the shower. It was cold, as always, but washed off the sand and the stink. No one seemed to be home in the barracks that night, but the light at the 83rd officers' club across the road still twinkled and "Proud Mary" warred with the sounds of Aretha Franklin coming from the barracks in back of ours.

Returning to my cot, I slouched back against the wall with my stationery box on my knees and tried to write a long, philosophical letter to Duncan. Duncan was—well, it's hard to explain about Duncan now. He was—is—a former professor of mine, a great storyteller, and in my own heart then my own true love. Only he didn't seem to know it, or value it, and tended to treat me like a kid brother. Of all the men I could have had, he was the one I wanted, though I wasn't damn fool enough not to have my spirits lifted by the proximity of men like Tony Devlin. Still, it was always to Duncan, rather than my mother, that I wrote the letters that really explained, more or less, how I felt about Nam. I'd been composing in my head, in my sleep, in between snatches of conversation, what I would tell him about the situation with Tran, but halfway through I tore it up. If he found out what a fuck-up I was, he'd never love me. Instead, I wrote a short, funny letter about the beach and meeting Tommy Dean and Jake. I'd save writing about Tony for when and if there was something to write about that would make Duncan realize what an incredibly desirable woman I was.

I stuck the letter in an envelope, and took two more Benadryl. I thought I might finally be able to sleep.

# 4

Nobody shuddered in horror when I reported for duty on orthopedics. Nobody said, "Oh no, not her." Nobody gave me knowing glances that said, "Lieutenant Colonel Blaylock told us about your kind." Major Marge Canon looked up from counting narcotics only long enough to give me a quick, slightly distracted smile. Sarah Marcus, who occupied the hooch next door to mine, wiped the sweaty hair off her forehead with her arm, pouched out her bottom lip to blow upward to cool her face, and looked straight through me in a spacey way not unusual for night nurses just coming off a twelve-hour shift. Then her eyes focused, and she sighed and nodded her head in my direction before resuming the count.

Sarah's morning report was rushed and perfunctory. "All five of the casualties from yesterday are going out today. I haven't had time to get their tags done yet. I was supervisor last night and there was a push of Vietnamese from some village that got shelled. I think we may get two or three of them. Joe was triage officer last night and didn't get scrubbed for our first case till about five-thirty, so you probably have an hour or two before recovery room calls. Right now you've got three I.V.s on the GI side, one on the Vietnamese. I'll do those tags now."

"Don't worry about it, Sarah," Major Canon told her. "We're finally getting some extra help around here. Blaylock sent us Kitty instead of making us wait around for Joanie's replacement from the States, so there's no need for you to stick around."

"Yeah, well, g'night," Sarah said. "I have to go give supervisor's report to the colonel. By the way, Kitty," she added casually, *"every*body on your old ward had a pretty good night."

"Thanks, Sarah. Sleep well."

She waved good-bye, tucked the supervisor's clipboard under her arm, and disappeared down the hall.

Before the day crew disbanded from report, Marge made introductions. "Troops, this is Lieutenant McCulley. She's been transferred to us to replace Lieutenant Mitchell. Kitty, this is our ward master, Sergeant Baker, our interpreter and nursing assistant, Miss Mai, and Specialists Voorhees and Meyers."

I nodded and said "Pleased to meet you" all around. Sergeant Baker was a broad black NCO with a habitual expression of long-suffering tolerance. Miss Mai looked like an oriental elf who'd been out in the rain too long. All the time I was there, it was Mai's unvarying custom either to come to work early to wash her hair or to wash it during her break, so maybe she was more of a water sprite than an elf. Voorhees was a compactly built, sandy-haired corpsman of about nineteen. Meyers, the other corpsman, was a tall, chubby-cheeked black guy who looked as if he belonged in high school.

"Come on, Kitty, we'll try to give you a little orientation before it gets busy," Marge said. First she showed me how to fill out medevac tags for the wounded GIs, all of whom were bound for Japan for further care, and then to the States. So few of my seriously injured GIs on neuro had lived long enough to stabilize sufficiently for medevac that I didn't have much practice in filling out the forms.

I was so glad nobody seemed to be mad at me about my screwup on neuro that I wanted to prove myself, show the major how gung ho I could be. As we started rounds, I saw that one of the patients wore a badly saturated dressing over what was left of his right leg, so I pointed it out to Marge. According to the nursing care plan on the guy's chart, he had been backed into by a tank driven by a friend who had taken too much herbal remedy for the Vietnam blahs.

"Yeah, that needs reinforcing okay. Let's wrap it with another couple layers of gauze. We're just going to reinforce most of the dressings on these guys. We don't usually change them when they come straight from the field and are medevaced the next day. Too much danger of infection. Open up a wound here and it sucks germs out of the air. Pseudomonas, staph, you name it, Vietnam's got it."

"I didn't see much of that on neuro, but then, a lot of times we didn't get open wounds," I told her. "And I suppose the Vietnamese have a certain tolerance built up."

"Probably, or anyway those that don't are dead before they get here. But we get a lot of infection on the Vietnamese side of the ward, too. You'll see that later."

Another soldier, this one with frag wounds of his upper torso and compound fractures of the right clavicle and humerus, couldn't wait for us to reach him. He had been using his good arm to scratch frantically at his cast and dressings. "Ma'am, ma'am, you can change my dressings, can't you? I mean, since I'm asking. You've just got to. They itch like hell."

Marge said something soothing and regretful and examined his bandages, then pointed to a fly that had lighted on the dirty part of the dressing. "Probably maggots."

The soldier, who looked about fourteen, turned a green only a shade or two lighter than my fatigues. "Yuck. Get them the fuck off me," he said, trying harder than ever to scratch.

Marge gently restrained his left hand. "Leave them alone, soldier. They're saving you from gangrene. Maggots only ea—maggots clean up dead tissue, sort of nature's way of debriding wounds. They won't hurt you. They just itch a little. They keep wounds like yours from putrefying."

The boy, red-faced and almost in tears, lay back with a whimper. Not knowing what else to do, I handed him an emesis basin. He appeared neither convinced by the major's explanation nor willing to revise his no doubt longstanding prejudice against maggots. He was in for a long trip to Japan. I could only hope he'd get accustomed to the idea of bodily dinner guests.

There was also a marine with a self-inflicted gunshot wound to his right foot, and two other patients with less serious multiple frag wounds, overflows from the general surgery ward.

Voorhees and Meyers were already at work with razors and basins of water. Sergeant Baker brought the dressing cart, and Marge and I put fresh layers of bandage around the filthy, seeping dressings. It felt like sweeping dirt under the rug.

The boy with the maggots groaned when we raised him to reinforce his dressings and cursed us as we manhandled him, but when we were done, lay back and said, "Thank you, ma'am," as sweetly as if he were talking to his Sunday school teacher.

We were headed for the Vietnamese side when recovery room called to tell us that the first of our new admissions was being transferred to us.

After that, three more arrived in fairly rapid succession. The corpsmen were still busy escorting the GIs to the helicopter, so Marge, Mai, and I did routine vitals. I wondered where the charts were, but every time I asked about pain or nausea medication or whether to touch a bandage, Marge referred me to a little recipe box containing standing orders. These orders authorized nursing staff to administer medication for pain, nausea, or fever, to reinforce dressings, and to perform other routine care without doctors' orders written specifically for each patient. I was finishing the vital signs on the second patient when the third was wheeled onto the ward.

Joe Giangelo, red-eyed and barely able to lift the soles of his paper scrub shoes, pushed the last gurney in front of him and stopped at the desk to hand the major a stack of charts.

His scrub suit was dotted with a fine spray of red droplets up one side, blood that had soaked through his scrub gown while he worked. His hair was matted from being tucked under a scrub cap all night. He opened the refrigerator door and gulped down a canned Coke as if he'd been dying of thirst. He looked a lot different from the twinkly-eyed benefactor who whistled while he built cabinet shelves. I thought he was about to drop. But when I reached for some of the charts, he said, "Why don't you grab a clipboard instead, Kitty, and make rounds with me. I'll tell you what I know about some of these folks and what we're going to try to do with them."

The Vietnamese side of the ward was more vigorously noisy than neuro had been. A bedlam of troi ois, dau quadis, and less articulate moans and whimpers greeted us, along with a cheerful wave from the end of the ward from a girl who squealed, "Bac si Joe! Bac si Joe!"

Bac si Joe drew himself up to his full five feet four inches and summoned Voorhees, who was counting vitals on one of the new patients. "Specialist Voorhees."

"Sir?" Voorhees asked, his head snapping up as if he expected to be called to attention.

"What's the matter with you, Voorhees? Why haven't you informed these patients that they, as Orientals, are stoic and inscrutable? Look at them! Listen to them! Scrutable as hell!"

Voorhees gave him a "Give me a break" sigh and started counting the pulse again.

Joe's face turned serious as he bent over the middle-aged woman in the first bed, however. She was curled on her side, biting her knuckles, her face and pillow wet with tears, and she cried a little harder for a moment when he stooped down to say something soothing to her. Her patient gown was rucked up over a saturated pressure dressing covering her from waist to knee.

"This is one of our new admissions from last night, Kitty, Dang Thi Thai. Mrs. Dang's husband was murdered in the assault that brought us most of these people. He was the village chief. After they killed her husband, the VC shot her too."

"At least they didn't kill her," I said.

"No, but this way she makes a good example to anybody who wants to cooperate with us. And it will take time and money to take care of her. You'll see what I mean when we get to another patient, a couple of beds down. Now then, Mrs. Dang, let me show the nurse where you're hurt. That's right." Dang Thi Thai gasped a little as he pulled the dressing off her wound and showed me a smallish entry hole. She cried out once as he gently turned her to show the gaping crater of medicated bloody gauze where her left hip had been. "You see here the tumbling effect of the bullet. Little hole here"—he pointed to the front—"totally blasts away or pulverizes the entire structure back here. We did a preliminary debridement in O.R. to clean out the worst of the necrosed tissue and dirt and tie off the bleeders, but of course we'll have to delay closure until infection is no longer a problem, and we can maybe get some skin to graft onto the area. It's going to be a long haul for her, but there's nothing else to do except maybe sew a volleyball in there."

"Dau quadi, co," the woman said and stretched her tear-slicked hand toward me, then dropped it again, as if the effort of holding it up was too much for her.

"She's been medicated within the hour," Joe said. "I don't think we could give her much else right now." He adjusted the flow of one of her two I.V.s and moved to the next bed, where an ARVN soldier with bilateral below-the-knee amputations lay.

The man ignored Joe's greeting and held out his hand for a cigarette. Joe shrugged. "No can do. They're in my other pants. You bic? Other pants?" The man just looked disgusted and turned away, ignoring us while Joe told me about his unsuccessful attempts to save at least one of the legs. "He's been here about three weeks. You know how to do the figure-eight wrap to mold a stump for prosthesis?" I said I did.

I had to say it loudly because about half the noise on the ward was coming from the next bed, a small boy with a big mouth.

The stump of one of his legs was tightly bandaged, but draining. His right arm was in a plastic splint.

"*This* little devil is Nguyen Tran Ahn, a ten-year-old orphan, parents killed by the VC before this last raid. He keeps saying he wants to go home, but nobody's claimed him. He was apparently up in a tree when a shell took his right leg. He fractured his right radius and ulna when he fell out of the tree. I—Jesus—" He looked down into the screwed-up little face, which reminded me of a monkey face carved out of a coconut, only smoother, of course.

The volume of the kid's howling and sobbing increased as Joe started to unwrap his stump dressing. I tried to shush him, but that made him howl even more loudly. Joe cut his examination short and sprinted two beds down. "I would have debrided him this morning, but the little devil got ahold of a candy bar somewhere and I couldn't operate."

Sergeant Baker, a towel draped over one shoulder, paused to catch what the doctor was saying. "Yeah, well, bac si, you can do somethin' for me when you take him in to surgery. Sew his mouth shut, will you? Whoo, that child sure can holler." He tugged his ear, shook his head, and ambled toward the back door.

The next patient sat stone-still in bed, disregarding

the slings around her shoulders and arms, staring at the far side of the ward.

"What's the matter with her?" I asked, dropping my voice.

"Bilateral fractured clavicles and shock. Remember what I told you about the VC?"

I nodded.

The question was rhetorical. He used the pause to swallow. He'd been doing a fairly good job of putting on the Jolly Joe Giangelo Show for my benefit and that of the patients, but the jolliness vanished suddenly and it was easy to see that the man had been working all night.

"They, uh—the VC—shot—she was walking down the street, see, coming back from taking dinner to her husband, who's one of the CIDG civilian guards. She had her one-and-a-half-year-old on one hip and her three-month-old on the other. The sniper shot both babies out of her arms. They were small. The impact fractured her clavicles." He continued talking in a flat, chart-dictating voice about what he was going to do for her. He had two daughters, a toddler and an infant, back home.

The next two beds were empty, but in the last a pretty young Vietnamese girl ostentatiously pouted until we turned toward her, then bounced up and down like a puppy while she waited for us to reach her bedside. Bouncing up and down when your leg is in traction is not all that easy to do, so we hurried, while she beckoned urgently with her hand and called, "Bac si Joe, Bac si Joe, I no see you long *time*."

"This is Tran Thi Xinh," Joe told me. "Xinh, this is—"

"This your girlfrien', huh?" she asked.

"Nah. You know you're my best girl. This is Kitty. Lieutenant McCulley. She's going to be working with us now, so I want to show her your leg, okay?"

"Okay, Joe. Kitty, how old you? You marry? Have children?"

We straightened the sheets under her while she pulled herself up in bed with the help of the metal trapeze suspended from her overhead bed frame. I told her I was twenty-one, not married, no children, and she said, "Ah, same-same me," though she looked no more than seventeen.

"Xinh here is going to put me in the textbooks, Kitty.

She has an unusual spiral fracture of the distal femur. We don't really have the equipment here to work with. I'd send her back to the States except that her family doesn't want her to go. So I ordered the equipment through channels. Needless to say, Xinh is going to be one of our long-term patients."

Xinh flashed a cover-girl smile, followed by a torrent of Vietnamese. Mai, also speaking rapidly in Vietnamese, rushed over, half hugging Xinh every time she winced as Joe examined her. The two of them were almost as noisy as the little boy, Ahn, who was still alternately caterwauling and whining.

Both were drowned out by the sudden boom of Sergeant Baker's bass voice. "Wait just a goddamn minute, soldier. What you think you're doin'?"

"Bringin' you a new patient, Sarge. Ain't that nice of me?" The response was from an equally forceful voice with a thick overlay of Southern drawl—which didn't necessarily mean the guy came from the South, not in Vietnam. For some reason, even guys from Boston started talking like Georgia crackers by the time they'd been in country a week.

"Not without no authorization you ain't," Baker replied, pulling his towel off his shoulder as if he would flip the tall redhead with it if he made a false move.

Joe flipped the sheet back over Xinh and headed toward the two men fighting over the gurney.

"Hi, Joe. You want to tell the sergeant here that you authorized this transfer?" the redhead said. His uniform was funny-looking: a regular camouflage shirt mixed with green tiger-stripe trousers, his only insignia a Woody Woodpecker pin he'd probably picked up at the PX. From his manner, I thought he might be one of the doctors in from the boonies. They all spurned Army dress codes.

Joe temporized, "Now, Doc, I didn't . . ."

Marge popped her head through the door. "Something the matter, Sergeant Baker?" she asked cheerfully.

"This man bringin' us this patient got no authorization, ma'am. Unless, that is, Captain Giangelo, you authorize it, sir?"

"If Chalmers is all finished with his head, I—"

"Nothing wrong with his head," the redhead said.

"There was a depressed skull fracture," Joe said, not arguing, just informing.

"That was a mistake, Captain. If you X-ray him now you'll see there's nothing wrong with his head. He needs to get somethin' done about replacin' his legs so he can go back to the villages, though. They need him out there."

"Wait a minute, wait just a minute here," Baker said. "You a doctor? You don't look like no doctor."

"Yeah? Say the same thing to me when you've got your ass shot off or are burnin' up with fever and I'm the only dude in sight with a first-aid kit and some kind of training."

"I'm real impressed. Been a field medic myself in two wars. That don't mean I haul patients around makin' unauthorized transfers or sassin' the real doctors. What's your name and your outfit, soldier?"

"Spec-6 Charles W. Heron, Special Forces medical supervisor assigned to C-1 operations detachment attached from B-53 Special Missions Advisory Force."

"Uh huh," Baker said. "And who might this man be? Your C.O.?"

"Sergeant Baker, Specialist—uh—" Major Canon said. "Whoever this patient is, don't you think we'd better make up our minds where he's going and get him back to bed?"

"I'm tellin' you, Joe, there's no head injury," the redhead said.

"I'll have to clear that with Major Chalmers, Doc."

"Chalmers! That asshole has his head so far up his—"

The man seemed to be a good judge of character anyway.

I remembered belatedly to try to reassure the patient, the object of all of the argument. It took me a moment to recognize old Xe. His color was much improved, his head unbandaged, and his face less sunken. His eyes were open and alert, seemingly staring at the ceiling, though as I watched I saw that he shifted them from the redhead to Joe to Baker like someone watching a three-way Ping-Pong match. I probably wouldn't have recognized him at all in a couple of days—legless, bald elderly Vietnamese men weren't uncommon at the 83rd. But his hands were crossed at his chest, over the medal, in the gesture I remembered well from the night before last.

"Way to go, papasan," I said, patting his shoulder. "You sure healed in a hurry."

"You should watch how you touch him," Heron told me. "It's disrespectful to touch a holy man casually."

"You're the one who's disrespectful—" Baker began, but Heron wasn't paying any attention. The old man was speaking to him in a soft, hoarse voice.

When Heron looked back up, his face wore an odd expression, as if he was trying to assess me, and at the same time resented me.

Marge, who had been on the phone, reappeared. "Neuro got swamped last night with ICU overflow, apparently. When I told Captain Simpson that we had one of her patients over here, she spoke to Major Chalmers. He said he didn't know why we didn't take the old man in the first place, and if you need help with the mild concussion the admitting physician misdiagnosed as a depressed skull fracture, Chalmers will be happy to consult with you, Joe."

Mai helped Heron put Xe to bed. I transcribed the orders, trying to hurry so I could talk to Heron before he left. It occurred to me that he was the mystery man who had called in the air evac on old Xe's behalf. But when I looked up from my chart, the old man was sleeping fitfully in the bed between the woman who had lost her children and the whiny little boy. I thought it might have been the light, but he looked sicker and wearier than he had a few moments before.

Joe Giangelo, when he returned to the ward, evidently agreed with me, because he ordered a new antibiotic, an extra I.V., and two units of blood for the old guy and scheduled him for surgery as soon as he was judged strong enough to withstand anesthesia.

We were moderately busy those first few days I worked ortho. One morning the husband of the woman with the fractured clavicles simply appeared and packed her off. Marge called Joe, and Joe, with help from Mai, tried to talk the man out of it, but the husband just gave a tight bow and a tight thanks. Mai said the woman would feel better with her own people and would want to be present at the funeral of her children. Personally, I thought the woman looked as if she would die of grief very soon and the man looked as if he blamed us for the tragedy and himself for ever becoming involved with "our" side. Which irritated me. "Our" side was supposed to be the side of most of the South Vietnamese, wasn't it? We were helping them, not the other way around. And he wouldn't even let us try to repair some of the damage.

Nor was he the only one who didn't want our help. The day Ahn was scheduled for surgery, the O.R. tech wheeled him away and then, a short time later, came back scratching his head, wondering if we'd seen the boy.

Voorhees and Sergeant Baker divided up the hospital and started searching, but a few minutes later a sergeant I vaguely recognized carried a wailing Ahn back onto the ward. "I understand this might belong to you ladies," the sergeant said. I showed him where to deposit the boy while Marge tried to call Joe in O.R.

I took Ahn's vital signs, thinking Joe would want to know, but I couldn't hear much. The kid shrank from my hands and bellowed at me, all the time watching me with a mixture of fear and loathing. I couldn't understand it. I hadn't done anything to *him*.

The ARVN in the next bed blew a smoke ring and smirked at us as we passed.

The sergeant said, "Say, you're the lady we brought home from the club."

I rounded the nurses' desk and he poured himself a cup of coffee and leaned over the chart rack.

Marge looked up and said, "The O.R. supervisor says Ahn will have to be rescheduled. When they couldn't find him, they gave the room to Dr. Stein for a gut wound. Some vertebral damage, so Joe's scrubbed in with him. He said he's glad we found the little darling, though. Guess we can call for a tray."

The sergeant, who looked vaguely like an Irish prizefighter, was giving Marge an appreciative once-over. "This major looks like a nice lady to me, Lieutenant. Have you asked her yet about the weekend?"

"Not yet—"

"What about the weekend?" Marge asked.

"Well, ma'am, we're having a sort of a special do over there, and my executive officer has asked me to extend an invitation to you for Saturday night but was hoping we could have the loan of this young lady over at the company so's she could do a little flight training in a crane—kind of a goodwill mission. He's already checked about the guest room with the commanding officer. It's our anniversary weekend. Hell, we even got a Filipino band."

"What time's the party?" Marge asked.

"We'll send birds to pick the ladies up at 1900 hours. Skip evening mess and we'll barbecue you some numbah one steaks."

"You want to go, lieutenant?" she asked me.

"Sure," I said. "I just thought, since I hadn't been here very long, I might not be up for a weekend yet—"

"Shoot, girl, you make it sound like you just got in country. I hadn't planned on getting you, so I didn't count on you for the weekend. Go ahead and have it off, but if we have a big push the minute you get back we'll know who to blame."

Things were definitely looking up. Nobody looked over my shoulder or breathed down my neck and somehow I managed very well without the supervision. Even the noontime sessions with Blaylock weren't all that painful, though she looked mildly insulted when I did know the answers to the math questions she drilled me on. Voorhees just happened to mistakenly order an extra lunch tray every day I missed my turn at the mess hall.

Friday evening during my shift, Tommy Dean came to the ward and spent the last hour drinking coffee while I finished report. I collected my swim tote, into which I'd packed a couple of dresses and toiletries, including the Shalimar perfume I got for under ten dollars at the PX. The chopper was waiting for us on pad by the back doors of the emergency room. The dust flew higher than our heads as we ducked under the thundering blades. Tommy Dean flew in the copilot position and I took the backseat, accepting earphones from the crew chief with mimed thanks.

The routine was familiar to me. Some outfit or the other was always inviting a group of nurses to their party and sending a chopper as cab service. Most of the time the chopper came because someone owed someone else a favor. Scrounging and barter were as big a part of the economic system for the military in Nam as the black market was for the Vietnamese. So I knew how to put on my earphones and listen through the bone-shaking throb of the chopper and the crackle of static to the wisecracks and

CB-type lingo exchanged on the radio. The crew chief was often also the crew, especially on the smaller birds, and he was the one who took care of anything that happened in the back end of the chopper, manned the door gun, and sometimes took care of patients in medevac situations.

I've never been afraid of heights and I enjoyed looking out at the ground as we flew past China Beach and over Highway 1 to several miles of cleared ground devoted to hangars, barracks, other ugly buildings, barbed wire, sandbags, and row after row after row of every imaginable kind of helicopter.

I didn't really know what to expect of that weekend. At Fitzsimons, I had gotten into deep trouble with an unreasonable colonel for having a man in my apartment after midnight. We weren't doing anything, but my roommate, a professional virgin who was irked to come home and find Willie there, and the colonel refused to believe me. I was called a slut in front of several other senior officers, and the colonel promised me she would personally drum me out of the corps if I ever again disgraced the sacred name of the Army nurses with such depraved behavior. Shortly after that, I got orders for Nam. I hoped her spies were watching, writing back, "Oh sure, she *says* she's just going to learn about flying cranes, making 'friends' with the men, while staying chastely in the guest quarters." I'll admit it seemed a little unlikely, but that's exactly what happened. Well, mostly, anyway.

Friday night, after Jake had met us and escorted me to my room so I could change into a dress for the sake of troop —and my—morale, we barbecued steaks on a quadrangle the men had constructed. The C.O. liked funky country and western songs, such as "Cigareetes, Whusky and Wild, Wild Women," and I knew quite a few myself, so we took turns playing C-F-G on his beat-up guitar while the troops sang along with varying degrees of tunefulness and ethanol-enhanced enthusiasm. It reminded me of the Texas bars I had loved while I was in basic at Fort Sam, and we sang and played until 0100 hours, when Jake told me I was going to have to get up early if I wanted to fly a mission in a crane.

I trundled off to the guest room singing my favorite new horrible song, a parody of the "Green Berets" song by

Barry Sadler. It ended with " 'cause that is where berets belong, down in the jungle, writing songs." I intended to send a copy of it to Duncan if I could remember all the words, and glamorize the weekend for him the way Jake and the others were glamorizing their unit for me.

The next morning Tommy Dean sat me down in the eye of the great airborne grasshopper, a glass bubble that gave me an unimpeded view of the countryside and the mission. We flew over fishnet-strung seas, lush green mountains fading to purple in the distance, golden rice paddies, and aquamarine waters. Gauzy mists puffed up beneath us, veiling the valleys. It was still extraordinarily beautiful. But even from the air, the beauty was marred by the bomb craters pitting its surface, like Never-Never Land with smallpox scars. I was used to thinking of Vietnam as ugly, hot, smelly, dirty. It had never dawned on me that the Rice Bowl of the East, as they called it in social studies, would have to be lush, that a country that was once a resort area for the French would of course be lovely. What a crying shame to hold a war here.

The crane hovered over a chopper stranded on a small island. A cable was dropped, and a man below attached the great heavy hook to the stranded Huey. A short time later, the crane lifted again, bearing the swinging Huey under its belly as if the smaller aircraft were a fly intended for the larger one's dinner. There were a couple of nervous moments when they had to pause and wait for the momentum of the Huey's swing to decrease, so that it wouldn't send the crane off balance. Watching the Huey appear at the bottom of the bubble first from one side, then from the other, I thought of the string-and-ring test done to tell if a baby was going to be a boy or a girl: back and forth for a boy, round and round for a girl.

By the end of the day I had lots of pictures and an exciting adventure to write home about. My grin almost split my face when Jake met me at the airstrip.

"God, that was great!" I told him, latching chummily onto his arm. "I think I could write a song about that myself."

He grinned like a father being told his newborn was adorable. "Well, good. Hope it put you in a partying mood. Meet you in about forty-five minutes and we'll all walk down to the club together, okay?"

I agreed happily and changed into my bright pink embroidered Mexican sundress and sandals. Then, feeling a little like a mascot, I walked down the road with thirty or forty of the men from the flying crane unit.

I sailed in between Tommy Dean and the C.O., captured a steak, and watched a thoroughly oriental woman who didn't look as if she spoke a word of English, and who wore a strapless sequined evening gown and high-heeled shoes on bare feet, belt a Patsy Cline song just like Patsy, twang, warble, and all. Then the dancing started and I, who had never been asked to dance at any Stateside party I had ever attended without a date, in high school or out, was in hog heaven. Marge was there, along with several other girls from the 83rd. I sat down to talk to her when the band took a break, but we couldn't hear ourselves for the noise.

As the band started again, someone tapped my elbow and I looked back and up to see my own fun-house reflection in Tony Devlin's mirrored sunglasses.

He turned his hand palm up, inviting me to grab it, and nodded toward the dance floor. I suppose in a movie the band would have been playing a Viennese waltz right then, but actually they were playing something more compelling: "Proud Mary." I never could sit still to that. Tony danced well, his knees, elbows, and wrists more than his feet keeping time, a style which is a boon on a small floor. He frowned slightly to himself as he swayed and bounced and snapped his fingers, like a Russian about ready to go into one of those numbers where they get down on the floor and kick. The frown was sexy. I'd seen it on hippie men friends who seemed to use it to say, "Sure I may be doing something frivolous like dancing, but I'm supporting civil rights" or "saving the world from the bomb." In Tony's case it said, "You better believe I'm dancing while I've got the chance." I loved watching him dance, but I enjoyed playful stuff, too—pretending to be Mouseketeers with Tommy Dean, or line dances and circle dances with everybody. When I danced with Tony, I double-timed like an Indian ready for the warpath. Maybe that should have told me something.

But I was feeling good. New friends, a new adventure, and maybe a new romance. I lasted much longer than the girls from the 83rd, and when Marge waved good night, neither of us had stopped dancing long enough to talk much. It must have been quite a while later—I was dancing with one of the crane pilots, I don't remember who—when I noticed that Tony had slipped away from the bar, and that Tommy Dean and Jake were gone, too. I saw the top of Jake's head come through the door and his finger make a circle in the air. The girl singer tapped the lead guitarist on the arm and jerked her head in Jake's direction, and they cut the song a chorus short and began packing up the instruments.

He stopped and said a few words to one or two guys and the club began emptying.

He started toward me and I met him halfway. "What's up?" I asked.

"I don't think anybody else is going to be able to leave tonight. Would you mind if the girls in the band shared your room? I don't want any of the guys who've had too much to drink giving them a hard time."

"Sure," I said, bewildered. "But why?"

"There's a sniper at the gate. I got Sarge to get some cots for the entertainers, but I wanted to let you know what was going on before we set them up."

"I'll help," I said. We walked back up to the quad in a tight little group, me, Jake, and the crane jockeys with the Filipina girls from the band and the Patsy Cline–clone singer mincing behind us in their too-high heels and too-tight outfits.

The sergeant had a stack of cots and linens set out. I started unfolding cots and sheets. I could have let the girls do it themselves, but after working in hospitals as candy striper, student nurse, and graduate for the best part of five years, I automatically tended to make any unmade bed that crossed my path. Besides, it made me feel useful in a potentially dangerous situation over which I had no control. I was used to rockets and mortars, but a sniper? Somehow that seemed a lot more personal.

I was cussing a stubborn hinge on the last cot when Tony poked his head in the door, "Jake said to tell you relax. Looks like the girls may get to go home after all. We called in an air strike from Phu Bai."

"Oh," I said, looking at my row of neatly made up cots.

"Forget that. Come on with me. I've got something to show you. I think you're going to find this real interesting."

"Where are we going?" I asked.

"Just to the water tower. Come on. Hurry."

He practically pulled me past the quad, where a few of the crane company were entertaining the Filipinas and vice versa, through the dark part of the compound to a squatty water tower. We climbed a rickety wooden ladder and lay face down on the top of the tower. He lay beside me with one arm flung across my back. His fatigue shirt was damp with clean-smelling sweat mingled with the odor of rice starch, whiskey, and cigarette smoke. He hugged me closer so that his forearm braced us against the top of the tower. With his free arm he pointed ahead of us.

"Watch," he told me.

"Is that where the gate is?"

"Uh huh. But watch the sky."

All I could see was buildings, trees, and stars. The occasional pop of gunfire sounded like distant fireworks, an effect heightened by the red streaks of tracers streaming into the air and bursting.

"Hear that?" he asked, and pretty soon I did: a chopper, from the rhythmic beat of the blades, but a very quiet one, as if the rotor had been muffled with oil and velvet.

"Where is it?" I whispered, the excitement of the darkness, the danger, and being half-squeezed to death by Tony making it hard to keep my voice low and serious. The whole scene reminded me of when I was about eight years old and my cousins and I played combat in Army surplus helmets and belts underneath my Aunt Sadie's bridge. Except my cousins didn't smell or feel like Tony.

Tony swung his hand in an arc. Following it, I saw the outline of the slim nose of the little chopper, hovering overhead like an airborne cat watching a mousehole.

"What kind is that?" I whispered.

"Cobra," Tony said, his breath tickling my ear.

Suddenly the Cobra pounced, spitting fire, covering the area in front of the gate with burst after burst. "Jesus Christ," I said, "all that for one little guy with a gun?" It seemed like using a tank for a flyswatter.

But the Filipinas were able to go home after all, which was great, since by the time we left the water tower I had other company in the guest room.

# 5

Xe was scheduled for surgery my first day back. The antibiotics had helped prevent the spread of infection in his stumps, but they still had to be debrided; that is, the dead tissue had to be removed so that the new could form a clean scar.

Of course, I had no idea who the old man was or how great his power had been until it was nearly gone, even though he had already shared it with me once. I'm glad I didn't know. If I had, I would have missed the point: that even a great master like Xe was only a part of the process. I think if I had known about him I would have been quick to discount my own role in that process. That would have been a fatal mistake, in more ways than one. As it was, the mistake we all made of treating Xe like an ordinary, slightly crazy old man is only embarrassing. And though I'm sure some of his anxiety was real, I wonder now if the old man wasn't having a secret laugh at our expense.

The fracas started when Voorhees began prepping Xe for surgery. Xe had permitted Voorhees to shave and bathe him and clean his nails without a problem. Xe had never been combative before, but I'd noticed when I did his dressings his eyes were always angry and troubled. Once I caught him watching me while I did Dang Thi Thai's wound irrigation, and his expression was unfathomably miserable. Mostly, though, he had been withdrawn and almost sullen. I thought perhaps he was still suffering the hostile stage of brain healing I mentioned earlier. On the other hand, it was normal enough for anyone to be angry and confused on awakening from a head injury to find his legs missing.

He sometimes spoke briefly to Mai, their exchanges no

more than a few careful words, as if they were trading eggs. When he was sleeping, he mumbled and clasped his hands to his chest. When he was awake, he stared at the wall or followed us with his eyes, though if we said something to him, he looked away.

"I bet he's a VC," Meyers said once. "He looks sneaky."

"Oh no," Mai objected. "He very holy man."

"So were those monks that barbecued theirselves, and look what they got us into," Sergeant Baker snorted.

Mai carefully refrained from looking offended, but lowered her eyes. "I hear about him from my friend," she said and turned away. I could have kicked Baker for discouraging her from saying more. According to Marge, Mai's "friends" told her a lot of things—like when there were likely to be heavy rocket attacks or when it would be unsafe to go to downtown Da Nang.

But while Voorhees didn't treat Xe with any particular reverence, he had shaved and bathed the old man with his usual stolid gentleness and patience, as if he were grooming some prize piece of livestock for a 4-H show. The trouble began when he tried to remove the pendant the old man wore.

Xe clutched his fists to his chest and glared defiantly at Voorhees, who turned to me, looking hot and perplexed.

"I don't think he's real impressed with the surgical checklist, Lieutenant. We better get Mai to explain it to him."

I was hot and perplexed myself and sick to death of hearing little Ahn's incessant crying. "They borrowed her in ICU," I said. Lucky her. She was as frustrated with babysan's nonstop wailing as the rest of us. The kid hadn't stopped crying, or thwarting efforts to get him to surgery, since he arrived. Mai had told me that morning that some of the Vietnamese patients were threatening to smother him if he didn't shut up, so they could get some sleep.

"Well, we got to find some way to tell the old guy he can't wear jewelry to O.R.," Voorhees said. "I'm sorry, but I'm not going to fight him for it. I didn't sign up for hand-to-hand combat. Any ideas?"

I rose from charting my meds and walked to Xe's bedside. The old man's bony jaw thrust pugnaciously forward over his doubled fists and his narrow black eyes snapped from me to Voorhees and back again as if we were threatening him with torture and further dismemberment.

"God, papasan, don't look at me like that," I said, in English, of course, but hoping he'd find my tone reassuring. "I'm not going to hurt you. Nobody's going to hurt you. Not here. But you gotta give me that." I pointed to the thing he clasped to his larynx. "I keep safe for you."

He looked suspiciously at my outstretched hand. How in the hell was I going to explain to him that he couldn't wear his necklace because it would get in the anesthetist's way? For all I knew, his idea of anesthetic was biting a rock.

Fortunately, Xinh had forsaken Vietnamese TV for the live entertainment we were providing. She had too much energy not to get antsy lying in bed day after day, and now she clearly itched to get involved. Her English wasn't as good as Mai's, but she seemed to understand more than she spoke. "Xinh, you know when you go O.R.," I began in the simplified English that, mixed with a few words of Vietnamese and a few words of bastardized French, made for a sort of pidgin common language between Americans and Vietnamese.

"O.R.?"

"Surgery? Doctor fix your leg?"

"Nooo . . ."

Well, actually, she hadn't been to surgery yet. "Uh, well, anyway. Papasan Xe go surgery. His legs numbah ten. Doctor fix. Make better."

Xinh nodded energetically, her gleaming black pigtails waggling. I thought I was getting through to her. "But before go surgery, must take off *all* jewelry." I demonstrated, removing my own rings and putting them in my pocket. But although Xinh's eyes followed everything I did, she looked puzzled. So I reached for her watch, and though she looked doubtful, she unbuckled it and handed it to me.

"Jewelry," I told her, and jingled the watch and rings together in my hand. Xinh looked scornful. She knew that. I continued. "Now then, you papasan." I pointed to her, and Xinh shook her head that no, she wasn't papasan.

"Play like. Play like you papasan."

Xinh drew in her breath and nodded. She bicced—understood—"play like."

"I take your jewelry and lock it up," I said, and walked to the narcotics cabinet, looking back to see if Xinh was still watching. Xinh's head bobbed like a buoy on a windy day.

"Then you go surgery, get legs fixed." I pantomimed Xinh's bed rolling down the hall and made vague fixing-up gestures at her knees. "Then you come back"—I continued the charades with more laborious gestures, then scuttled back to the medicine cabinet and with a flourish worthy of a magician produced the watch again and handed it back to Xinh—"and you get your jewelry back. Bic?"

Xinh looked puzzled for a moment, then broke into another flurry of earnest nods.

"You explain to papasan for me?"

I expected maybe three or four more explanations and charades would be necessary, but Xinh drew herself up with the self-importance of a teacher's pet chosen to be hall monitor, leaned over the edge of her bed, and shouted to Xe in strident Vietnamese loud enough to be heard over Ahn's whimpering. Xe, who had steadfastly refused to watch my shenanigans but had withdrawn into staring through the corrugations of the tin wall opposite him, looked startled. He shifted onto one hip to face Xinh, then loftily turned away and said something argumentative, gesturing at me and the ward with more animation than I'd seen in him so far.

Xinh assumed the airs of both a princess and a mother as she replied, lecturing him. The old man set his jaw even more firmly and she repeated what she had said, this time in a more coaxing tone, intermittently pointing to me.

Xe watched me impassively for a while, his fingers idly stroking the thing at his neck. After a couple of minutes his jaw relaxed and he beckoned me to his bedside with a lift of his head.

This time Xinh shouted her encouragement to me, no doubt urging me not to drop the ball after she, Xinh, had gotten things rolling. I leaned over the old man and he pulled the thong from his neck and tenderly handed me the object on the end. I started to carry it to the medicine cabinet, but Xinh, like a referee calling a foul, began bouncing up and down, crying, "No, co! No, Kitty!" and indicated that I was supposed to put Xe's necklace around my own neck.

I hesitated, doubting the professionalism of wearing a patient's jewelry—particularly since it didn't look like very hygienic jewelry. But Xe was making small nodding movements. He was urging me to wear it, not lock it up. Once I slipped it on, he seemed satisfied and with lordly dignity allowed Voorhees to finish prepping him.

I remember thinking that the necklace could have had value to no one but Xe, and even at that the value had to be purely sentimental. The pendant on the grungy thong looked as if it had been carved, or melted maybe, then molded, out of the bottom of a soda pop bottle. It was still roughly round and had a deep wave running through the middle, with something like ears on the side. It sure wasn't the Hope diamond, but then it wasn't mine to worry about either. Just so the thong didn't contain living creatures. I detected nothing more noxious than the old man's sweat, so I tucked his treasure inside my fatigue shirt, the pendant lodging under the top button above my cleavage. I'd promised to guard it with my person, if not in so many words, and I would, though why anybody would want to steal such a thing I couldn't imagine. But even as Voorhees rolled Xe off to surgery, the old man cast a backward glance my way to make sure I was living up to my end of the bargain.

That incident exhausted all of the good humor I had for the day, and when I sat down to do the chart, I felt like a boiling lobster. Sweat saturated my hair and dripped into my eyes. My fatigues stuck to my back and armpits, the backs of my legs, and my crotch. My bra was soaked and clammy. I hate heat and always have. It shuts down my thinking ability by at least 75 percent. I get slow and clumsy, and my skin feels like a freshly tarred road gumming onto everything that touches it. I get faint and headachy and my temper is about as stable as nitroglycerin. I gulped two salt tablets and sat down with my head between my knees for a moment, my hands, where they pressed against my eyes, feeling sticky as those of a two-year-old who's just finished eating candy. Ahn's shrill whine sawed through the heat, irritating as the buzzing of a thousand mosquitoes. Damn! And I still had to do the little bastard's dressings. I peeled myself off the chair and jerked the dressing cart away from the wall so hard it clattered. Jesus, it was so hot even my skin seemed to be sending off red light, as if it were boiling. I paused for a moment, closing my eyes just so some part of me could be cool in the shade my eyelids provided. I couldn't touch the kid feeling like this. I took three deep breaths and opened my eyes again. Well, better. My skin was only giving off a hot rosy glow now. I wheeled the cart over. Now it looked as if the kid was glowing red—red and kind of a murky eggplant color that intensified and darkened when he glared up at me and started shrieking.

"Oh, shut up, I haven't touched you yet," I snapped. He looked right at me and howled louder.

"Okay, kid, that's it. I've had it with you and so has everybody else. You're not the only one around here who's been hurt, you know." But he just kept howling. I couldn't, I simply could not, keep listening to that racket while I worked on him. I pushed him over on his side and swatted his rear. "Now, em di, dammit. We're all tired of you. Just shut up." I gave him about four swats, the pink of my hand blurring to red as it hit the red around his rear.

He didn't yell any louder. In fact, his shrieking died off to a whimper, then a snuffle, by the time I got control of myself and stopped abusing my patient. He sniffed and looked at me for the first time without the hatred and terror I was used to seeing in his face. I couldn't figure it out. I was feeling like the Marquise de Sade and the kid was definitely in the best mood he'd been in since he arrived. The light around him looked cooler somehow, too, and less murky. My own had faded to dusty pink. I laid my hand on his forehead, thinking that maybe the color had something to do with fever.

His skin was sweaty but cool, and he watched me, not fearfully, but with a funny kind of anticipation. And it came to me that he didn't know nurses weren't supposed to paddle their patients. He knew he'd been thoroughly annoying everybody, but he felt lost and abandoned. The spanking and my scolding voice, even speaking English, had made it seem as if his mother were still with him, in control of the world, telling him what to do. I knew that as certainly as if he'd told me, though I didn't know then how I knew it. But whatever passed between us he didn't ask to understand but simply accepted with relief. His face smoothed out of its monkeylike scowl and his lids dropped like rocks as he passed into long-overdue sleep.

"Ooh!" Xinh cried and shook her hand. I left the dressing cart by Ahn's bed and walked to hers. A blur of blue-green light surrounded her. I blinked hard, but the light remained.

"What's wrong, Xinh?"

She held up her hand so I could see the fingernail broken into the quick, a thin line of burgundy light pulsing from it. "Nothing. Tete dau," she said, her frown vanishing.

She took my hand in her sore one and swung it back and forth, companionably. This made me a little uncomfortable, but I knew from watching Vietnamese people that same-sex friends often held hands in public. I was grateful for the gesture, since I was still feeling a little like an ogress for spanking Ahn, despite the surprising way he had reacted. Xinh was impossible to dislike. Her emotions swept across her face like weather on a seascape, sunny one minute, stormy the next, but open and changeable. She painted her nails and tried different hairdos and watched the performers on Vietnamese TV. I was sure that if I could understand what she and Mai gossiped about, it would have been what my friends in nursing school talked about, boys, clothes, normal things that had nothing to do with the war. The only thing funny about her was that blue-green stain. I must have a bad case of heatstroke, I thought, and reclaimed my hand. "I have to get back to work, Xinh," I said.

She pulled her own hand away and started to suck on the broken nail, then stopped with it halfway to her mouth. "Heyy! Numbah one!" she said, her eyes shining. She held up her nail, perfectly intact, with about a quarter inch of unpainted growth showing above her ruined polish job. She looked at me as if I had pulled a coin from behind her ear. "How you do that?"

"Huh?" I said stupidly. Maybe Xinh wasn't feeling so good either—she *was* that funny color around the edges. Maybe we were both sick. I looked at both of Xinh's hands —all of the nails were intact. I shrugged. She shrugged and happily accepted the mending of her manicure as a miracle of American medicine. I felt distinctly dizzy as I started back for the nurses' station.

Mai returned to the ward, her hair newly washed, and

glowing iridescent pink. I rubbed my eyes and looked away from her.

The lunch cart arrived, and Meyers and Voorhees started passing lunch trays. I joined them at the cart and pulled a tray out, then started giggling helplessly. Not only did a baby-pink glow wrap both corpsmen, but the food was also color-coded: a pale green wisp over the cottage cheese, a faint orange to the fish.

"You okay, Lieutenant?" Voorhees asked.

"Uh—yeah. But I think I'd better sit down. Everything looks funny to me." I turned back toward my chair and tripped over my own feet.

Meyers caught my arm. "Whoa there, ma'am, what you been *on?*"

I stared hard at the dark brown center of his face and ignored the fluff of pink tipping his modified afro. "I dunno. One of you guys put a drop of acid on my fizzie or something? You're all weird—" I started to say "colored" and was afraid Meyers would take it wrong, so instead I asked for a drink of Kool-Aid and sat down again with my head between my knees. Maybe I was having some kind of drug reaction, but I found that hard to believe. More likely it was the heat. I had fainted during my first scrub, when I stood in a closed operating theater in muggy ninety-degree heat and watched a particularly bloody mastectomy while unwiped sweat ran down my face and pooled under my surgical mask. I'd also fainted during my first O.B. case, also in the summer, when the heat made the blood smell like hot metal. But I hadn't ever seen colors like this before —a roar in my ears and a sudden blurring of vision, but never distinct shades surrounding perfectly well-defined individuals. And I'd been sick those other times. Today I didn't actually physically feel any worse than I'd felt every day since I'd been in country.

Maybe I should have my eyes checked? But that wouldn't explain why Xinh had a blue-green halo while everybody else's was pink. Did only staff get pink halos? I'd have to ask Chaplain O'Rourke about that one. Maybe there was more to that angel-of-mercy stuff than met the eye. Trying to figure it out did make me start to feel a little nauseous, so I avoided the whole issue by refusing to look at anyone and finishing my charting instead.

When the major returned from her Tuesday morning

staff meeting, she pushed Xe's gurney in front of her. A rosy glow surrounded her. He looked gray around the gills.

"Joe says it will take a couple more procedures to get Xe's stumps in shape for prostheses," she said. "But he came through this like a champ. Get his vitals, will you, Kitty?"

As I bent over to listen to his blood pressure, the amulet fell out of my shirt. I pulled the necklace off over my head. "Here you go, papasan. Safe and sound," I told him, and looped the thong back over his shaved head. His color and my vision immediately improved. That is, the gray around him vanished and a little warmth touched his cheeks, not above them but right there in the skin, where it belonged. The glow disappeared from around my hands too. I knew something strange was happening, and remembered what Heron and Mai said about the old man, but I misunderstood even then and got it backward. "You must be a holy man, papasan," I said. "You seem to have cured whatever was wrong with me."

# 6

I suppose so far it sounds as if we never treated anyone but Vietnamese patients. Sometimes, the slower times, that was almost true. Joe kept the native patients as long as he could, until they were as completely well as we could make them, because life outside the hospital was more conducive to dying than to healing.

But we did treat GI casualties, of course, and when they came, it was in swarms that all but swamped us. The first big push came the day after Xe's surgery. It was what I had imagined it would be like while I was in training, while I was at Fitzsimons, while I was working neuro, where we seldom got mass casualty patients except as overflow. The pushes weren't as constant as I'd believed they would be, which was just as well, because despite all my imaginary scenarios of how I would handle that kind of situation, when the first one came I definitely was not ready.

Partly, that was because of the way I had spent the night before.

Tony had ambled onto the ward during evening report and hung out at the coffeepot until I finished. "Carry your books home for you, Lieutenant?" he asked, grinning.

He'd pushed his aviator specs back into his curls and looked like a movie star playing a helicopter pilot. "Hi, soldier, new in town?" I kidded back, slipping into the space under his arm as we walked out of the hospital.

"I had to see you. You glad?" he asked. Well, I was glad he wanted to see me, yeah, but I wished he'd waited till I'd taken a shower.

"Sure am. But who's going to fly all those helicopters while you're away?"

We just fit walking hip to hip, up the barracks stairs. "I

told Lightfoot, my crew chief, where to find me if he needs me," he said, slamming my screen door behind us, flipping on the fan, and attacking my top button in a single fluid motion. The room was smothering, as always, but Tony was a lot hotter. He finished my buttons and helped me with his during what was probably a fifteen-minute French kiss, if I'd been counting. And that was just the one on my mouth. "Come on, baby," he said, sliding with me onto my bed. "Tell me how you want it."

Well, what the hell. The dialogue wasn't exactly from *Gone With the Wind,* but the action was certainly impressive. He was innovative and skillful, all over me and that bed. The man had to have pored over the *Kama Sutra* as thoroughly as he'd studied his helicopter manuals, and he handled me with the same sort of competence. The trouble was, I wasn't a helicopter. Don't get me wrong. The sex was great, and I enjoyed it even more because I felt maybe I was finally going to have a real boyfriend, someone I could get away from work with and confide things in. So I snuggled next to him, waiting until he was comfortable to tell him about the crazy thing that had happened that morning, with the colors and so on, and about Ahn and the old man. We wedged ourselves spoonlike in the bed with the fan finally evaporating some of our mutual sweat. He tapped a pack of Marlboros against his chest until one popped up, lit it, and took a couple of long, satisfied puffs. "You'll get a kick out of this, Tony," I said. "Something really weird happened to me on the ward this morning . . . ." I leaned up on one elbow to watch his face. He was already asleep. I sighed, wondering why I felt it was so much ruder for me to wake him up to talk to him than it was for him to screw my brains out, then fall asleep. If he was going to sleep, I wanted out of the bed and into a cool shower. I ran my fingers through his hair to remind him that I was still stuck between his butt and the wall. He rolled over, smiled lazily, and everything started all over again.

I climbed over him while he was in the process of lighting up the next time. He was sleeping when I returned, and I pulled off my clean clothes and slid in beside him, getting slick again from his sweat. I flipped the sheet up over us and wondered fleetingly if this was what a real honest-to-God wartime romance was like before I, too, dropped off.

I don't know how much later it was that someone pounded on the door. I woke up a little disoriented, felt Tony next to me, and thought, Oh shit, it's the colonel. "Who is it?" I asked.

The door cracked and a round brown face with a hawkish nose poked in, looked mildly interested at what it saw, and backed out again. "Spec-5 Lightfoot, ma'am. I came for Mr. Devlin. We're on red alert now. Need to—"

"Tonto? That you?" Tony asked sharply, sitting up and pulling on his shorts and trousers as quickly as any fireman. "That's a roger, kemo sabe. Time to saddle up. We gotta didi."

He did lace his boots, but he was still buttoning his shirt as he ran out the door. He ran back and dropped a kiss on my nose. " 'Bye, babe. Call you later."

I nodded and listened until his boots hit the bottom stair.

Still, it was a good thing I'd spent a little time in bed that evening, because the rocket attack started a short time later and I spent the rest of the night under the bed, in a T-shirt, panties, flak jacket, and helmet, keeping the cockroaches company, hugging the plywood.

What I was actually supposed to do, what we were all supposed to do, was grab flak jackets and helmets and head for the sandbag-reinforced bunker hunching up between my barracks and the one facing it. Usually, nobody even bothered to vacate the officers' club. We hadn't received heavy fire in so long that the bunkers were not taken seriously. During my first rocket attack, I had dutifully reported to the cavelike little shelter to find the chief of internal medicine suavely sipping a martini and reading an Ian Fleming paperback by flashlight. By the next time, he had DEROSed (left the country) and the bunker was unoccupied. I took one look at the dismal, hot little hole and thought of coiled cobras and scorpions and snuck back up the stairs to hide under the bed.

Which was what everybody else who paid any attention to the shelling did. I had the procedure perfected by now. I took my pillow, flak jacket, helmet, usually a paper fan and a Coke, a book and a flashlight. It was a little like playing house under the dining room table when I was a kid. Usually I didn't mind it too much. The floor was hard, but you needed your mattress on top of the bed to shield you. That particular night I read the same sentence several times before giving up. I was plenty cool now, and I cursed Tony for being out there flying around making Vietnam safe for democracy when he should have been under the bed with me.

Then I thought about him flying around up there with all those rockets whistling through the air, and I wished I could be working, just to take my mind off it. Over on the wards, the staff would be moving the patients who could be moved under the beds. Those who couldn't would have mattresses piled on top of them. Several times already, I'd had to give meds on my hands and knees. The GIs with the facial injuries kept asking for their weapons, which were locked up, and I kept wishing I could slide under one of the beds, too, and huddle next to someone till morning. Even though I was supposed to be protecting those guys, I felt better knowing that they were there, under the beds.

You could joke your way through a shelling over on the wards, and act tough. It was less funny to lie alone listening to the shrieking rockets, the mortars crumping like God stomping around out there thoroughly pissed off.

Mentally, I composed a letter describing the rocket attack. Not to Mom and Dad, of course. I glossed over this kind of stuff when I wrote to them, knowing it would scare them a lot worse than it really scared me. But it sounded nice and dramatic when I wrote to Duncan and might make him worry about me a little, the shit. In my imaginary letter I told him about Tony, too—well, not everything, but enough to make him jealous. I'd have to get around to writing that sometime, I thought. Then, if I was ever found with shrapnel through my throat like that nurse who was killed while sitting on a patient's bed, Duncan and Tony would both be sorry.

I had some good moments there imagining Tony berating himself for leaving me alone, and Duncan in tears when they sent my pathetic medals home to him (of course, they wouldn't. They didn't send anything to people you wished were your boyfriend. They sent all your stuff to your parents). But I got tired of that eventually. I was pooped, and the noise was giving me a headache, and my own dumb game didn't make the one going on outside seem any less stupid.

It was fine for those guys to run around at night and shoot things at each other, but how was I supposed to work if I had to toss and turn all night on the damned plywood? Probably I'd catch my death of cold, too.

If something was going to hit me, I wished it would just hit me. Otherwise, the whole war should just shut the hell up so a person could get some sleep. All that noisy crap was just a nuisance anyhow. Nothing ever hit inside the compound. The VC couldn't afford to hit the 83rd. Who else would they be able to trick into taking care of their wounded? Once when George spent the night on guard duty and got pulled to work the E.R. the next day, he returned to the ward shaking his head and muttering, "They had a gunshot wound of the buttocks down there? Man, I swear that looked like the same ass on the same sapper I hit last night. Friendly as hell this morning, though. Loves baseball, apple pie, and Elvis like you wouldn't bee*leeve.*"

Finally, about 0300, choppers began thudding onto the pad, and their steady drone lulled me to sleep.

When I went to work that morning, the ward was transformed. The day before, we'd had only two beds on the GI side filled; now we had only two empty. Twelve bottles dangled from poles and Sarah sprinted from one to the other upending bottles long enough to squirt meds into the rubber caps or inject them straight into the new, special little chambers that came with some kinds of tubing.

The corpsmen and Sergeant Baker ferried wash water, razors, and cigarettes from the nurses' station to the patients.

"Hey, Sarge, can this dude have a drink of water?" Meyers called.

"Private Garcia here wants a cigarette, but he's got a chest tube and bottles. What d'ya think?" Voorhees called.

Sarah rehung a bottle, then consulted her clipboard. "No, he's going to surgery," she called to Meyers. "Absolutely not. Not till he's off $O_2$," she said to Voorhees. "But you can give *him* a drink of water if he wants. They operated on him last night."

Marge grabbed an armload of charts and threw a clipboard at me. We followed Sarah through the ward and she gave us a running account of each patient's wounds and what had been done for him.

The patients were mostly quiet, not saying much. They were fresh from the field, from the ambush or firefight or whatever it was that got them. Most of them had been waiting wounded for a chopper, then waiting on the chopper and in the E.R. to see if they were going to die or not, how much of themselves they were going to have to lose to get out of the war. Some were still groggy from surgery, others groggy from pre-ops before going to surgery. They all looked a little dazed, pale under tans or sunburns.

The ward buzzed with a kind of macabre carnival frenzy like the feeling I'd always had in Kansas after a long hot spell when the wind blew up and the radio blared cyclone warnings. My adrenaline rose to the occasion, jerking me from being half-awake to a clarity of mind that damn near amounted to X-ray vision. Sergeant Baker and the corpsmen, and even Marge, rushed from one end of the ward to the other, frowning with concentration but with a lively urgency to their voices and movements, making little jokes with one another and the patients.

I scribbled fast notes and started preparing the next I.V.s, slapping bottles onto the counter and decapitating them, injecting sterile water into dry powdered antibiotics and shaking ampoules until my hands were streaked with white grainy leakage of ampicillin, Keflex, and Chloromycetin. I picked up some of the manic feeling from the others. We looked like a recruiting poster, selfless healers doing our bit for the boys.

As the patients began to wake up, from sleep or shock or anesthetic, they mostly seemed fairly happy, and in spite of their wounds, there was some justification for it. They would be out of it now—out of the boonies, out of range, out of Vietnam. Clean sheets and a bath and a pain shot were more comfort than some of them had had in a year and clearly filled them with awe. Most of them remained somewhat subdued, but relief was at least as prevalent as dismay in their reactions to their situation. The magnitude of their losses, the full impact their wounds would make on their lives, didn't hit most of them right away. It was like jet lag. One minute they were in one piece in the middle of a firefight, the next they were safely tucked in at the hospital, not feeling sick but with some part of them they had come to take for granted broken, crushed, full of holes, or missing. But that was the bad news, and it would take time to sink in. The good news was that the show was over and they were going home. It was as if they thought that when they went home, everything would be made okay again. They'd be given their DEROS papers and their medals along with those pieces of themselves they would need to make it back in the States. I don't think it dawned on very many of them at first that those pieces had to stay behind, in the field, on the E.R. floor. Back in the States, they'd begin to realize they'd been gypped.

I'd already seen that side of it back at Fitzsimons, on the orthopedics (read "amputee") ward.

My civilian experience with amputees had been with elderly diabetics who lost limbs to wound infection. The guys I treated at Fitz were not elderly. They were all about nineteen, and before getting wounded every damn one of them thought he was immortal, that getting hit was what happened to the other guy. And their wounds were not gradual. Overnight they lost their mobility, their manual dexterity, their futures, their self-respect, and, in their own minds at least, their manhood. Sometimes they lost their families. Strong young men weren't supposed to be cripples.

And there I was, barely twenty-one years old, fresh out of a dorm full of other girls, knowing nothing about war, and damned little about men, maybe less about myself, or what kind of messages I was sending, or how to handle the responses I got.

The idea was I was going to be professional, tough but understanding. I wasn't going to mind a little old thing like a missing limb. I was a nurse, after all, I saw whole people, not just wounds or the space where parts that were missing were supposed to be.

It didn't quite work out how I'd planned it. My patients at Fitzsimons were experts on tough. I tried being seriously empathetic, but that was taken for pity and I was told angrily by a man who almost believed it, "Hey, I got nothing to feel sorry about. Sure I lost a leg, but you know how much they're gonna have to pay me for that sucker?

Man, thousands and thousands. I'm set up for life!" And I didn't know how to take it when somebody offered me a necklace of Vietnamese ears, showed me pictures of mutilated bodies, or told me about the torture of prisoners.

The one that bothered me most was the handsome young guy with football muscles who purred in my ear the whole time I was wrapping the stump of his right arm, telling me with considerable relish about the rape and execution of a Vietcong nurse. I made the mistake of meeting his eyes once while I bandaged him. His eyes shone like a little kid's on Christmas Morning and a drop of saliva dewed one corner of his mouth as he told me how they had shoved explosives up the woman's vagina and lit the fuse, and what the mess looked like afterward. I could see him getting off on it, telling that story and watching me, putting me in her place. I wanted to slug him with the nearest bedpan. I wanted to tell him how sorry I was that it was only his arm that had gotten blown off.

That was only the one guy, of course, and now that I think of it, that and all of the other gross-outs, the coarse randiness, must have been a kind of advance revenge on females for anticipated defeats. A wounded war hero can be a romantic figure, but he'd better have nothing worse than some colorful scars or some vague disease he picked up in the tropics. He'd better have all his parts in pretty good working order if he comes home from an unpopular war and wants to impress girls with his potential as a combination lover and meal ticket. Some of the patients had already been rejected, put down hard. The worst example of that I knew of was Tommy, who had a crazy tobacco-stained grin and an ironic sense of humor, and who wheeled around visiting the new guys, giving them shit to keep them going. "Hey, babe, c'mon to the beauty shop with me," I heard him say in his broad Brooklyn accent to a guy with a bilateral amp of the legs who was busy cussing out his physical therapist. "You need a pedicure to get in shape for swimsuit season." And the guy laughed a little and settled down to work. Tommy could get away with that because he had lost an arm, an ear, and an eye as well as both legs. And when his family came to visit him at the hospital for the first time, his wife and his parents took one look at him and left, and that was the end of it. Atrocities were by no means confined to Nam.

But even understanding all that, I had trouble dealing with the horror stories and with the angry, aggressive sexual advances. If you'd asked the colonel, she'd probably have told you that I invited them, that I teased the poor, helpless patients. And okay, when I say I was relatively inexperienced, I do not mean I was a virgin. I was, in fact, the black sheep of my nursing class, and all of the gently reared small-town girls in my class came to me as they got engaged and asked me where the heck to put their knees. The thing was, I didn't consider myself easy to offend and I tried to act as if anything that was said to me was cool, that I could handle it.

Usually I could. Usually passes were joking or wistful, frightened guys asking for reassurance that they were still men.

There were maybe only four or five out of over a hundred patients who really gave me a hard time, but nobody told me how I was supposed to deal with it, and nobody stopped them, so I went to work every morning with my gut in knots.

I wanted to do what I was taught in training and be accepting and nonjudgmental, see, or at least act as if I were. But these guys saw through me, or thought they did. What they saw was that I was rejecting them as maimed. And it was true that the stumps bothered me at first. It was true that what I found sexiest physically about Duncan was his beautiful strong hands and his long legs. But lots of guys had those and they didn't turn me on the way Duncan did. What I loved the most about him was his wit, his passion for history and poetry, and his ability to make stories come to life, his silliness. I would still love him if he lost a limb or two as long as he kept those qualities. But I guess that was the problem, really. With rare exceptions like Tommy, the loss of limbs seemed to mean the loss of those other qualities, too—temporarily, at least. That was what I really couldn't deal with. That and the fact I knew that if I were in their place, God forbid, I wouldn't take it any better than they did.

One day three of them surrounded me while I was changing a dressing and suggested that maybe since I was this helping person who cared about their problems and all, I could help them out with a little physical therapy at a local motel. In a normal setting, I'd have told them flatly that nurses don't date patients, period. But quoting rules at them provoked the same response as spitting at them. I *wanted* to tell them that even if I had been the whore they seemed to think me, I didn't do gang bangs. But then, part of me felt like, Why can't you guys be fair? You know how this game is played. If one of you had the decency to say thanks, we appreciate your trying to help, how about coming out to dinner and we'll get better acquainted, well, yeah, even if I wasn't completely bowled over by your charm you might guilt-trip me into something, which wouldn't be as good as if it was real maybe, but at least we'd both get laid, and feel moderately okay about it.

Instead I told them I was in love. Which I was, but Duncan determinedly had nothing to do with my sex life. I thought, these guys don't want to make love to me, they don't even like me. They want to hurt me, they want to make me feel worse than I already do. So I said I was sorry, I was not available, then added with hypocritical nursely courtesy that maybe somebody else would be interested. They said who. I was squirming by then. And it honestly crossed my mind that maybe I just was too prudish, that maybe if I were nonjudgmental, more secure sexually, this would not sound like an invitation to rape. Whatever. The bottom line was that I threw them a sacrificial name, another lieutenant who had confided in me that she was horny. Needless to say, she never spoke to me again, and when the story got back to our C.O., I was bawled out and accused of pimping and, what my instructor seemed to think was worse, not delivering what the men said I promised.

But promises were being broken all around. Most of us in Nam were the children of the last war that was ever supposed to be fought anywhere in the world. All of the baby boys were promised that they would grow up and become successful and all of the baby girls were promised that someday their princes would come. Then along came the goddamn government and bingo, it sent the princes off to battle communism and issued them the right to hate anyone not in their unit. Then it sent them home in body bags, or with their handsome faces melted or blown away, their bodies prematurely aged with disease or terrible wounds, and their idealistic souls turned into sewers. And *those* were the survivors. Where the hell did that leave me

and all the other women? Realistically, I knew that
Duncan was not going to change his mind and fall madly in
love with me. So what if the guy who was supposed to, my
real true love, my Mr. Right, was on one of these wards
somewhere, so fucked up I'd never recognize him? Worse,
what if he was lying in some rice paddy decomposing under a poncho? If he was among the merely wounded, I
could only hope that whoever was taking care of him was
better at salvage operations than I was.

Having to deal with all that again was part of what
scared me about facing GI casualties on ward four, but as
my grandmother would have said, I was borrowing trouble. Nobody offered me ears, nobody made any moves
toward me except to grab my hand for reassurance, or to
tell me I smelled good. Even the horror stories were somehow changed, though actually, many of them were the
same garbage I had heard at Fitz. Hearing them batted
back and forth across the ward among members of the
same unit, I realized that some of those stories were nothing more than folktales the guys told one another to keep
their courage up, make them feel like the meanest, the
baddest, the worst, so bad even hell wouldn't want to fuck
with them. So I tuned it out, and watched the major and
Joe and Sarge and did what they did and listened to what
they said.

One thing Marge did not do was put on the same kind
of phony act the nursing instructors tell you to. She
worked, she medicated, bandaged, and said normal, mundane things, asked trite questions that were easy to answer. "Your name is So-and-so? Where are you hit? Are you
allergic to anything?" and later, "Where are you from?
How did this happen?" No matter where they were from,
she always knew somebody from there or had visited the
place, made the guy feel like somebody who had once had
a background and people.

Her ward policy was to give pain meds a half hour
before dressing changes, and always to soak bandages in
peroxide or normal saline before trying to remove them.
We made a good team, and when she had a day off, I hardly
noticed, because she had shown me very clearly what to do
and how simple it was. Dressings and meds were all I was
responsible for. Sergeant Baker was in charge of the staff

and they mostly knew what they were doing better than I did. If they didn't, Sarge told them.

He was a 91-Charlie, the same as a licensed practical nurse, and he checked my pre-op meds with me since I was still nervous about them. But Joe Giangelo always wrote his orders and, if I had even the slightest question, dropped everything until we were both sure he had written what he intended and I knew why.

The only problem was, we were all spread much too thin. Joe was in surgery constantly after each new influx of casualties, Mai was often needed to translate in E.R. for the fresh Vietnamese casualties that frequently accompanied or arrived shortly after the GIs, and no matter how full or busy we were, some other ward always seemed to need to borrow one of our corpsmen.

And once we'd gotten the I.V. bottles hung, the next ones mixed, one round of pain meds given and dressings done on the GI side, there were always the Vietnamese patients. Dang Thi Thai's neomycin irrigations to her hip needed to be monitored. She was still our most critical Vietnamese patient, but her surgery had been postponed until after the crunch was over. Ahn's surgery, which was a relatively quick and simple debridement, had been left on the roster for Wednesday, which was two days after the casualties started arriving. If the kid didn't get in soon, he was going to rot away.

Marge had a day off that morning, so as soon as I'd done the rock-bottom morning necessities on the GI side, I left the ward to Sergeant Baker and Voorhees and crossed to the Vietnamese side to see how Mai was doing.

Ahn, who had been fairly quiet and tractable for a day or two, was once more in full voice. O.R. should be calling anytime to tell me to give his pre-op, and it didn't look as if one thing had been done to get him ready for surgery. If he wouldn't cooperate, the very least I expected was to find Mai trying to shush the kid or talk some sense into him. Instead, she appeared to be engaged in furious gossip with Xinh, both girls frowning and gesturing in the boy's direction.

I held my temper. Mai was highly regarded by Joe, Marge, Baker, and both corpsmen. It had to be more than her pretty face and wet coiffure. So in my best head-nurse voice I said, "Miss Mai, I'd like to speak to you for a mo-

ment, please." Mai ignored that, but both she and Xinh
began flapping their hands at me to join them.

"Tell her, Xinh. Tell her what he say," Mai said.

"You know Vietnamee soldier next to babysan, Kitty?"

"Private Dong?"

"I hear him say babysan, I hear him say, 'Babysan, you
go with them—' " She turned to Mai and broke into frustrated Vietnamese.

"Surgery," Mai supplied. "He tell babysan if he go to
surgery, they cut off all his arms and legs."

"He did, did he?" I asked, very calmly, under the
circumstances. The days of handling big-time crises really
had done wonders for my self-control. "Xinh, thank you
very much for telling us this. Mai, would you come with
me, please? I'd like you to set babysan straight for me and
then there are a few choice things I'd like you to convey to
Private Dong."

We stood before them. Ahn looked up at me, not with
the same fear and hatred he had before, but with disappointment and hopelessness. I wanted to wipe that away,
first. "Please tell babysan that when he goes to surgery,
Bac si Joe will only work on what is left of his left leg to try
to save as much as possible. Later, the doctor will give him
a new wooden leg so he can walk again. Tell babysan that
Private Dong was not telling him the truth." She shushed
Ahn and talked to him for some time, answering his inter-
ruptions until his expression changed to one of skepticism
and worry. He glanced down at his soiled dressing and up
at me and seemed about to cry again.

Then I turned to Dong, who was blowing smoke rings
and smirking. I pulled the cigarette from between his fingers and crushed it under my boot. "Mai, please tell Private Dong that I'm very sorry if he thinks we amputated
his legs without cause, but that is untrue. Please tell him
that if I ever again hear of him frightening this child or any
of my other patients with such stories, I'll personally take
care of his remaining limbs with a rusty butter knife."

Mai looked a little puzzled at some of the terms, but
got into the spirit of the thing and, I think, invented Vietnamese equivalents for the parts of my threat that didn't
translate.

Sometime during this discussion, the phone had
started ringing. It stopped of its own accord, but shortly

thereafter Joe stormed onto the ward, still in bloody green scrub clothes and paper scuffs. "What the hell is going on, Kitty? They've been trying to call to tell you to give Ahn his pre-op for fifteen minutes. I'm going to lose the room if—"

I told him what had been going on. Fortunately, he was the sort of person who, when he demanded an explanation, listened to it. While I was explaining I drew up the pre-op, checked it with him, and gave it to Ahn, who accepted it with surprising readiness. Joe chewed his fingernail while I talked, looked at the little boy, and looked at Dong, who had turned over on his stomach sometime during Mai's lecture. Then kindly Geppetto turned on his heel and jerked a thumb back at Dong. "Lose the bastard," he said. "Send him to the ARVN hospital or, if that's full, to Province. I don't want to see him again. I'll write the order when I'm through in O.R."

I caught Mai's eye. Her mouth was compressed, with a little quirk at one side, and she nodded once, sharply, with satisfaction. I almost expected her to dust her hands as if she had just finished taking out the garbage.

Rounds on the GI side were no quieter. A second push had come in around 0200 hours, so most of the men had been quiet earlier that morning, still sleeping or sedated. I knew them only by which antibiotics they were getting, and the name on their plastic wrist tags and at the foot of their beds, all of which I double-checked before handing them the pill cup under the little card carrying the same name.

I passed pills to two wan young men who accepted them with gratitude. The second one had some questions about his cast, followed by a brief chat about the medevac procedure and his telling me he was from Pennsylvania and had I ever been there?

"Hi," I said, all unsuspecting, to the third patient. "How you doing this morning? Need anything?"

"Out of this fu—out of here, that's all," he said.

"I think that can be arranged," I told him. "You'll be going to Japan pretty soon. I see the night nurse gave you a pain shot just before we came on. That holding you?"

He nodded, but didn't look much interested in talking, so I moved on.

"Hey, Lieutenant, I could sure use a pain shot," the

guy next to him said. He had his arm in a cast and the whole thing suspended in a sling from an I.V. pole.

I checked his chart. "Looks like you had a shot about two hours ago, too, corporal. It's ordered every four hours."

"But this arm still hurts like shit!"

"I'm sorry. I can give you something in about another hour, but it's dangerous to give you too much too close together."

I checked his cast. There was about a half inch of extra room around the wrist and another half inch above his elbow, so it didn't seem too tight. The color in his fingers was fine, tan, still grimy around the knuckles. His nail beds were pink. A bloody spot had already appeared at the cast's pristine elbow, but that wasn't unusual, unless it got larger. No, clinically everything checked out. Unfortunately, the first couple of days, fractures just plain hurt.

"Oh shit," he said and smacked his head back down on his pillow, jingling the dog tags, love beads, and roach clip around his neck. "I don't *e*-ven believe this shit. Come to a fuckin' hospital and they can't even give you somethin' for the fuckin' *pain,* man. Anybody got a fuckin' joint?"

Nobody offered him one, at least in front of me. I probably should have had Voorhees take him out to the Vietnamese tent to get high on the atmosphere. But it was no wonder his pain medication wasn't holding him. Even pot raised people's tolerance to pain meds, so that the same dosages were less effective. I'd had the same problem with civilian patients addicted to their prescription Valium or Librium. I decided to ask Joe about increasing the dosage, at least for the day, but didn't say anything to the patient, in case Joe didn't go for it. No sense in raising false hopes.

Farther down, a red-faced young man still wearing a splint on his left ankle suddenly sat bolt upright. He strained his neck toward the entrance to the ward, his Adam's apple bouncing up and down, and the veins in his arms stood out so clearly I started imagining how easy they would be to hit with an I.V. needle. "Hey, ma'am," he whispered hoarsely. "Ma'am, I don't want to alarm you or nothin', but I think I just saw a zip go past the doorway."

I almost said, "What? A zip in Vietnam? Surely not!" but remembered in time that the grunt sense of humor was usually dampened considerably by being wounded. So I just told him casually that he probably had, since we had lots of Vietnamese patients and staff members.

"But this is an American hospital!" he said indignantly. He was as young as they all were, his face deeply sunburned and peeling, with a white line near the hair where his hat or a bandanna might have been. He had frag wounds in both legs as well as the fractured left ankle. When he saw that I wasn't going to rush out and correct what he seemed to think was a terrible oversight, he continued. "Man, I don't want to just lie here with no weapon with damn zips runnin' around. You can't trust 'em. Not any of 'em. The kids will blow you up, the babies are booby-trapped— Hey, ma'am, no offense, but you know what they say about the way to win Vietnam. You take all the friendlies and put 'em in a boat in the middle of the South China Sea, nuke the country, then sink the boat."

Yes, indeed, I had heard that one. Many times. Way too many times. But I ignored it and said, "Well, most of the patients have been here for a while, and we don't let them have weapons either. They're mostly hurt as bad as you are, or worse. And the interpreters have been working here longer than I have, and haven't hurt anybody yet."

But he was still shaking his head as I moved on.

Two beds down, a man was moaning low heretical obscenities that rose in volume as I approached, to, "Oh, why me? Why did this happen to me? Awww, shit. Goddamn, this hurts like a motherfucker."

The two patients between him and me had rolled onto their stomachs with pillows covering their heads.

I checked the noisy one's chart. Crushing injuries to the soft tissue of both legs, it said. Nasty. The crisp smell of antiseptic gauze was overlaid by the tang of old blood and a touch of the sicky-sweet reek of rot. His bandages were soaked with the breakdown fluids from his crushed skin and muscle. Soft-tissue injuries were often more painful than broken bones—and healed more slowly.

"Sounds like you're really hurting," I said, checking his chart, which identified him as PFC Ronald G. Dickens. "You need something?" It had been only two and a half hours, but I was willing to stretch it and estimate a long fifteen minutes to prepare the injection. Fifteen minutes' leeway on the three-to-four-hour limit was usually permissible.

"I sure as hell do. I need you to get your ass over there to your little stash, sweetheart, and get me a fuckin' pain shot before I go through the fuckin' roof. Oh God, oh Gawwd."

Nursing is such a rewarding profession. All that gratitude. Restraining myself from strangling him, I drew up the Demerol, but when I swabbed the alcohol wipe on his thigh before administering the injection he started bellowing in my ear again. "Jesus fucking Christ, woman, you can't give it there. Not in my leg, oh shit—"

"Well, if you want to wait until I get help to roll you over—"

"And move these legs? Lady, are you out of your fuckin' mind? I'm *hurt*, you stupid—"

"Hey, man, cool it," the fellow across the aisle told him. "The lady's just trying to help you."

"Fuck you," Dickens said, and while he was flipping my would-be rescuer the bird I shoved in the needle, aspirated, and pushed in the plunger before he said something I really couldn't ignore.

"I'll let that take effect and be around to change your dressing pretty soon." I ducked around to the other side of the next bed to put maximum distance between us, and tried to calm myself down. I knew the guy hurt and hurt badly and was probably still shocky. But he still pissed me off. Maybe he wouldn't be so nasty once the Demerol took effect. He probably realized he might lose some or all of both legs with injuries like that and would undoubtedly lose some function—it was one thing to express those feelings, even loudly, and another thing to take it out on me.

My hands shook as I disposed of the needle and syringe at the nurses' station. Then I took a deep breath and concentrated firmly on the next patient, a Navy corpsman who was lying on his stomach because, in addition to having lost both legs, he had sustained multiple deep lacerations to his buttocks and back. I thought he was sleeping, but he turned his head toward me. "Hi, Lieutenant. Having a nice day?" he asked, grinning. "Don't answer that. Listen, I think it's about time for the heat lamp to my butt. Would you do the honors?"

I pulled back the light sheet that covered his lower

half—his upper half, like that of most of the men, was already bare except for dog tags and assorted GI jewelry. His stumps were bandaged, with drainage at the ends, and I made a note to bring more gauze to reinforce them when I changed the dressings of the charmer in the next bed. The lacerations on his hips were deep and infected, seeping green and smelling to high heaven of pseudomonas, a germ that got into everything. I pulled the silver gooseneck lamp over and cranked his bed down so that the lip of the lamp was high enough above him that it wouldn't burn him. "There you go," I told him.

"Thanks a lot, ma'am."

"Uh—you need anything for pain?"

"I think I'd better hold off. I'm going to need it a lot worse later," he said ruefully.

"How—uh—how did you get hurt?" I asked.

"Oh, I was helping out when the compound this bunch came from got hit. I saw this dude get hit out by the perimeter and was trying to drag him in out of range. I screwed up and dragged him across a live grenade. Threw him up in the air and blew the shit out of my legs. I don't remember any of that. I guess the Army medic saved my life, but he couldn't save my legs. They tell me I landed in a nest of concertina wire—that's how I got cut up."

"Yeah? How about the guy you dragged?"

He shrugged. "Nobody's said. I think he just took some frags, but hard tellin'. If you hear anything, I'd appreciate it if you'd let me know."

Tony called as I was finishing my charting on the Vietnamese side.

"Keeping busy?" he asked.

"Sure am, thanks to you."

"No problem. Happy to be of service. When can we get together again?"

The red-haired Special Forces type, Heron, flipped a mock salute as he passed the nurses' station on the way to visit Xe. The old man lay like a poor man's skinny Buddha, hands crossed on the concave spot where his belly should have been, eyes closed. They opened when he saw Heron and he actually smiled.

"Uh—I don't know," I told Tony. "Can you come over here after work tomorrow?"

"I doubt it. We're still on alert."

"Well, I'm off Monday next week. We could go to the beach or the club, maybe. . . ."

"Okay. Then, if not before. Gotta go. 'Bye, babe."

I said good-bye to a dial tone.

Both the ARVN and Ahn were gone, I noticed. I'd passed Joe's order on to Sergeant Baker, who'd said he'd take care of it. Apparently he had. Even as I was thinking Ahn was a long time returning from surgery, recovery room called and said they were sending him back to us.

Heron sat on the edge of Xe's bed, talking to him in a Southern-fried version of Vietnamese. The old man listened and nodded and said something once in a while. Heron's large hand covered the old man's frail one. Xe's other hand was, as usual, stroking his amulet.

Sergeant Baker called for Meyers to come and help him lift someone on the GI side, so I took Ahn's vital signs myself, and made sure he turned, coughed, and took deep breaths, all of which he did so cooperatively I wondered if they'd sent us another kid by mistake.

Dang Thi Thai's hip needed attention next. The woman gave me a watery smile as I swished the irrigating fluid around in her wound. The wound wasn't as red as it had been, and before long might be ready for skin grafts. I returned her smile and with forceps removed the light gauze covering the surface of the large wound and replaced it with fresh. Her breath sucked in with a sharp hiss, but as soon as I was done, she released it with a sigh and tried again to smile, although her eyes were brimming. Her face reminded me a little of that of an aunt of mine, a good woman who had a strong will, a hard life, and a lot of Indian blood. If this kind of thing had happened to Aunt Do, I could see her taking it the same way as Mrs. Dang.

While I was passing meds, Sergeant Baker, carrying his supply list, tromped onto the ward, followed by Meyers and Voorhees. Voorhees looked slightly sick.

"Pretty bad, huh?" Baker asked, chewing on his cigar while he scanned the shelves as if daring them to be short of anything we needed. When he found something, he marked it down, frowning as if he were giving it a demerit.

"No shit," Voorhees said. "I'm sorry, Sarge, but that Province Hospital is not my idea of a place to send sick people. Compared to it, the stock pens back home are the damn Hilton Hotel."

"Yeah, it ain't much of a place," Baker agreed. "But that's the way these people treat their own. Myself, I don't see it, but it's their damn country."

"What's so bad about it?" I asked.

"They didn't even have any beds, ma'am," Voorhees said, almost sputtering with indignation, "just some cruddy old mats."

"A lot of the Vietnamese don't sleep in beds at home, you know," the major told him.

"Yeah, well, not ones like these. They were all soaked with old blood and pus and stuck to the floor, and the whole place smelled like an outhouse that's been used once too often. People were lying two and three together on these damn mats, without any clothes on, or all dirty, with untreated amputations and wounds and big running sores on them. And Mrs. O'Malley—that's one of the missionaries who was there when I took the ARVN—said they don't even feed them. If somebody from the family doesn't bring in meals, the patients just go hungry. I tell you, it was gross, ma'am. Bugs crawling all over people. We might as well just have shot that guy and put him out of his misery."

I was beginning to wish I'd argued with Joe, but I'd been as mad as he was about the way Dong had treated Ahn. Still, we accepted that our own casualties would have lots of hostile feelings they worked through in pretty antisocial ways. For them, there was treatment and at least a certain amount of tolerance.

Mai, who had been charting her 1300 vital signs, chimed in. "I tell you, honest, what Gus say is true. No one get well Vietnamee hospital. Everybody go there die. That why everybody so happy come here."

"I guess I thought Province Hospital was just like ours, only the doctors and nurses were Vietnamese," I said. But I suddenly remembered when, right after I'd started working on ward six, I met a visiting Vietnamese doctor, an educated man with a French accent and French training, touring the ward with Dr. Riley in some kind of exchange program. While the other doctors were off consulting about something, he'd stood there looking embarrassed, and, trying to put him at ease, I'd attempted to strike up a conversation. I asked, "Are you a surgeon, sir?"

"No," he'd said. He was smiling a mild and self-effac-
ing smile that didn't prepare me for his elaboration. "No, I
am not a surgeon. I am not really a doctor, by your standards. I am a butcher. I work in a charnel house." Apparently he hadn't just been modest.

Baker shook his head and waved his cigar for Voorhees to follow him into the storeroom. I was opening my
mouth to ask Mai if she'd ever worked in Vietnamese hospitals before when Heron wandered over to the coffeepot.
"You know, Lieutenant, we're always needing nurses
for medcap missions. Could be you'd find that a real interesting way to spend one of your days off. . . ." He was
carefully polite this time, but I could hear him thinking:
Instead of going to the beach all the time.

But dammit, I needed breaks from the hospital to
keep me sane. A secondhand report of a place like Province Hospital was enough for me, thank you. My martyr
complex only extended just so far.

Heron seemed to read me as readily as I'd read him.
"Going on a medcap isn't anything like going to Province,
you know. We take you nurses and the doctors and supplies
to the villages and you treat people right there."

"Is that how you met Xe?" I asked. "On a medcap
mission?"

"It's how I heard of him," he said, stirring his coffee
with the butt end of a ballpoint pen. "Wherever Xe had
been, we weren't needed."

"Why? What do you mean?"

"He's kind of a one-man AMA," Heron said ruefully.
"Only not as political."

"Xe's a doctor?" I asked, feeling ridiculously dismayed
that we hadn't extended the old man more professional
courtesy.

"Kinda. He's sort of a combination of doctor and
priest, but I guess you'd have to say he was practicing
medicine without a license, by American standards. I've
been studying with him since I met him after he'd saved
one of my people from rabies."

"You were the one who called in the chopper when he
got hit, weren't you?"

"Umm hmm."

"You say you study with him. Is he like your guru or
something?"

He gulped the coffee and pitched the cup in the wastebasket with a basketball twist of the wrist. "Yeah, something like that. Think about what I said about the medcap, Lieutenant. Every Thursday morning."

I didn't much like Charlie Heron. He was a little holier-than-thou. He made me feel like some stupid debutante who never did anything but polish her nails and have her hair fixed all day. What did he think I was doing in the hospital anyway?

What Heron hinted about Xe was intriguing, though, especially since the old man seemed to have amazing recuperative powers. The day after Ahn's surgery, the old man spotted someone using a wheelchair and nothing would do until Mai and Voorhees lifted him into it. He wheeled himself around the ward as if he were indeed making rounds and afterward returned to bed exhausted.

Later, Ahn moaned in his sleep and I took him a pain shot. The kid rolled over without a peep and, after I'd given him the injection, rolled onto his back again. His sheets had worked loose, so I began to straighten them and hauled him up in bed, lifting him with an arm under his shoulder, another under his hips. As I pulled my arms out and started to straighten, his good arm tightened around my neck and he buried his face against my shoulder for a moment.

The next morning, Marge was still off. Voorhees got pulled to ICU and Sergeant Baker spent most of the morning in his ward masters' meeting. Joe was in surgery with Dang Thi Thai. There was a new technique for skin grafts using cadaver skin to cover wounds like hers, and Joe was anxious to try it out.

I went through my morning routine and checked the charts for the orders Joe had been writing while we were in report. On Dickens's chart was a new order: the dressings on his crushed legs were to be changed daily.

Remembering the man's behavior when he first arrived on the ward, I knew it wasn't going to be easy.

Most of the new casualties had pretty well stabilized by then, and were relaxed, shouting obscenities back and forth across the ward, sometimes throwing stuff at one another. When I took them their meds or changed their dressings, most of them seemed anxious to talk now, to tell me about their wives or girlfriends or mothers or dogs, even, to talk about what a mess it was back in the unit, to gossip about things they'd heard in the bush. Some of them talked so much you couldn't get away from them—they had what is called in psych a "pressure of speech," so much stuff was waiting to come out, a way of releasing adrenaline, of coming down. A few still stayed silent and I worried about them a little bit more. But there was nobody else like good old Private Dickens, thank goodness.

He hadn't mellowed a bit since he first came on the ward, and I approached him for the dressing change in much the same spirit he might have approached a squad of Vietcong. I'd given him a pain shot first thing that morning and he'd fallen asleep soon afterward, but the rattle of the dressing cart woke him to all his snarling glory.

"Dr. Giangelo wants your dressings changed this morning, Private Dickens," I announced with false cheerfulness, and before he could say anything began scooting Chux, the blue paper-diaper-like absorbent pads, under his legs, eliciting a howl and several unflattering references to my sexual and scatalogical practices.

When I poured the peroxide over his old bandages, he squirmed and hissed as if it were boiling oil. Of course, it was cold, and it bubbled, but most patients didn't seem to feel that even on very raw wounds it really hurt—not like iodine, for instance. But when I pulled the first layer of gauze away he woke anyone who might possibly be dozing with a bloodcurdling yell. The scream went straight from his mouth into my eardrum and almost deafened me. My hands shook with the longing to backhand him, but I gritted my teeth, having already decided that I was going to be gentle and compassionate with this obnoxious jerk if it killed me.

"What are you anyhow, some lousy VC, what the hell do you think you're doing to me, what did I ever do to you, why the fuck did this happen to me, oh *shit,* be careful, oh God, you're killing me . . ." and then, as I began removing the most encrusted layers of gauze, soaking them with peroxide as I went and being as careful as my shaking hands would allow, he began writhing and screaming piercingly in my ear.

With my eyes on the wound and my ears full of his screams, it's no wonder I didn't notice the wheelchair gliding up until it was almost too late.

Dickens bucked up on the bed like a frightened horse and tried to climb the wall backward, his screams intensifying.

At the foot of the bed, Xe sat in the wheelchair and regarded the patient with a mixture of calm and bewilderment. Then he lowered his eyes and mumbled to himself as he spread his hands over the spoiled meat of Dickens's legs.

"Get that gook away from me, oh God, he's going to kill me!" Dickens screamed.

A patient named Miller, with one arm in a sling, jerked the wheelchair sideways and sent it flying with a kick. The chair careened down the hall, the old man trying to get control of it by grabbing for the wheels. He succeeded only in making it veer into one of the beds, where it crashed, sending its fragile old occupant sprawling.

Two more of the patients leaped from bed and started after Xe. I didn't think they were going to help him up.

I saw Meyers running, as if in slow motion, across the hall from the Vietnamese side of the ward. God, he'll never make it, I thought.

Just then an ungodly clatter drew everyone's attention to the Navy corpsman, Ken Feyder. "Oops," Ken said. "Dropped my bedpan," as if nothing else had been happening. He turned his trunk lazily toward the hyperventilating Dickens. "Hey, doggie, whatsa matter? The old guy just heard you bawlin' about your legs and wanted to trade ya. Me too, anytime, pal."

Meyers reached Xe and used his own bulk to shoulder himself in between the angry patients and the old man.

Dickens's mouth opened, then he stared at Feyder's stumps. His eye strayed to where Meyers easily hefted Xe's legless body and deposited it back in the wheelchair. He swallowed hard and clamped his lower jaw shut like a snapping turtle. I quickly finished his dressing change while Meyers returned Xe to the ward. I didn't say another word and, blessedly, neither did anyone else. If they had, I'd have exploded.

I rammed the dressing cart against the wall, stripping off my gloves so fast I broke the rubber and made the powder fly. I had to make sure Xe was all right, call Joe and tell him about the incident so he could check the old man over, and fill out an incident report.

"Ma'am?" Feyder's soft voice stopped me in my tracks as I stalked past his bed. "Ma'am, would you hand me my bedpan? I can't reach it." I picked it up and held it out to him. It wobbled up and down in my shaking hand. His voice was low as he spoke to me. "Don't be too hard on them, Lieutenant. The unit I was with when this happened to me? Their interpreter took off just before we got hit."

I grunted, still too furious to talk. My second day alone on the ward and I have a fucking race riot. Jesus.

"How is he?" I asked Meyers, who was standing by Xe's bedside. "Did you get his vital signs? Is there any bleeding?"

"His vital signs are okay, dressings okay too, but maybe there's somethin' wrong with his head. He's just starin' into space. Pretty shook up, I guess. I'm sorry, Lieutenant, I was down washin' bedpans like Sarge told me. I didn't see him go over there."

"It's not your fault," I said, though I wished I could blame it on him. Xe lay there with his arms limply at his sides, staring into space. I checked his clipboard. His vital signs did look okay.

"Can you feel this?" I asked and touched his arm with the tip of my finger. He shook me off as if I were a fly, and kept staring. I wished Mai were there. I wished Heron were there. What was wrong with Xe was very clear to me. His feelings were hurt. Heron said Xe was considered a doctor among his own people, and he'd heard Dickens screaming and come to help, only to be attacked. "I know how you feel," I said. "Dickens is almost as bad to me too, but he's an asshole. Don't let him get you down. We're not all like that, honest. Feyder tried to help. And I kept this safe for you, didn't I?" I didn't even mean to touch the amulet, just to point at it. I knew how sensitive he was about it. But he moved and my finger made contact with the glass for an instant. Now I know it wasn't a physical sensation I felt, but then I thought it might have been something like static electricity. Because pain shot up my arm and into my chest, like angina in reverse. And that blade of pain cut a swath for the hot surge of shame and anger that swept over me, leaving the nauseatingly bitter aftertaste of failure in its wake.

Xe's eyes fastened on mine as I stepped back, his eyes brimming with a feeble old man's leaking tears.

My hand was on my chest, but as soon as I stepped away, the pain within me disappeared. It was as if I was feeling all over again what I'd felt that night by Tran's bed, only worse, much worse. And it was all there, in that old man's face.

I returned to my desk and filled out the incident report.

"What did you do when the incident occurred?"

"I attempted to calm and restrain Private Dickens while Spec-4 Meyers assisted Mr. Xe."

"What could you do to prevent such an incident from recurring?"

I chewed on my pencil for a long time over that. Maintain strict segregation of patients? Gag all over-wrought patients during dressing changes? Never start a dressing change until the riot squad is handy for backup? I gave it an appropriately vague answer in bureaucratese: "In the future ensure that all patients understand ahead of time that they are not to interfere when staff members are treating other patients."

That night I went straight to the club from work and systematically proceeded to get very, very drunk.

In spite of my hangover, the following day started out a little better. Marge and Joe took care of Dickens's dressing change during Joe's morning rounds, and I learned that most of this particular batch of casualties would be transferred to Japan the next day.

Sergeant Baker kept Meyers and Voorhees scurrying all morning cleaning up the ward. Blaylock informed Marge that VIPs would be touring the hospital later on. And sure enough, sometime around noon a handful of colonels and a general or two arrived with little jewelry boxes full of medals, Bronze Stars and Purple Hearts, and so on.

We all stood at attention and they handed Marge a list of patients to be decorated. I was supposed to help prepare everybody to be honored.

Ken Feyder was up for a Silver Star and a Purple Heart. He was basking his buns under the heat lamp when the VIPs started their rounds. "C'mon, Ken, time to turn over and get your just reward," I kidded him. I couldn't be

more pleased for him. After yesterday, I didn't need anybody to tell me he was a hero. And I always liked my
heroes to be nice people, too. But I was a lot more thrilled
by his official recognition than he was. For the first time
since he'd arrived on the ward, Feyder was less than coop-
erative.

"Just have 'em pin it on my butt, Lieutenant," he said,
and withdrew and refused to discuss it, pretending to be
asleep. They finally presented it to his pillowcase.

A surprise came when Heron appeared on the GI side
that afternoon and had a long visit with Ken Feyder.

"Okay if I take Feyder for a little wheelchair ride,
L.T.?" he asked me.

"I don't know. He's got those wounds on his hips and
Joe hasn't authorized—"

"Do me a favor, will you? Call Joe, ask him. Ken's
about to go nuts in here with the heat and the noise. He'd
sure like to go out for a spell."

He was giving me his most helpful good-ol'-country-
boy routine, his eyes trying hard to look round and sincere.

"Are you and Feyder old buddies or something?" I
asked. "I thought you were only interested in Xe."

"I heard what happened yesterday. You know, surely?
Meyers said you were standing right there." The way he
said "standing right there" made it clear he thought I
should have been doing more than that. And he was right,
of course. But I had been so taken by surprise I hadn't
known which way to move or how fast. "Meyers could
come too, for that matter," he continued, hurrying past
the reproachful jab at me, no doubt having been told by his
Southern mama that he could get more flies with molasses
than with vinegar.

"Oh, okay, just a minute," I said. Joe okayed it, providing the chair was amply padded with Chux and heavy
dressing pads. I asked Ken if he wanted a pain shot and saw
him look toward Heron, who shook his head, very slightly,
which I thought was a little odd. Meyers and Heron loaded
Ken in the chair and the three of them left by the back
door.

I passed them on the way to pick up my mail. I'd have
missed them except for the wheelchair. The three of them
were huddled behind some canvas and scaffolding between two of the wards. I saw only their feet, but I caught a

strong whiff of pot as I passed. I could have confronted them then, I suppose. As Meyers's superior officer, I should have. I didn't condone smoking pot on duty. But maybe he wasn't. Maybe it was just Heron, who wasn't on duty, and Ken Feyder. And I really didn't want to get Feyder in trouble after all he'd been through. I kept walking, and decided to send Sergeant Baker out to collect Feyder later on. Discipline was the ward master's province mostly, anyway. However, by the time I returned, Feyder was in bed sleeping and Meyers had resumed his duties, though he was wielding the mop in a very dreamy fashion. Heron had wisely made himself scarce.

When I made rounds with Joe that evening, the doctor tried to encourage Xe to try the wheelchair again, but the old man folded his arms stubbornly and refused to so much as look at the chair, which was about what I expected. But when we came to Ahn's bedside it was a different story. The boy said, "Mamasan, mamasan," and pointed at the chair, then, "Ahn, Ahn," patting himself on the chest. We got the point and Ahn got the chair.

As I passed my P.M. meds on the Vietnamese side that night, I felt something tug at my fatigue blouse. "Mamasan, la dai [come here]. Mamasan . . ." I turned and there was Ahn, enthroned in his chair, one hand tugging at my shirt, the other pointing at an I.V. about to go dry.

"Why, thanks, Ahn," I said, and hurried to replace the bottle.

Sergeant Baker looked up from the bedpan he was cleaning and shook his head. "My, my, looks to me like you done got yourself adopted, Lieutenant McCulley."

# 7

I chattered to Tony about Ahn, Xe, Xinh, and Heron in the Jeep on the way to the PX Monday.

"Yeah, those little gook kids are cute okay," he said when I told him about Ahn. "Just as long as you watch your wallet."

"Well, I think it's pretty amazing how fast a little hooligan like that can start acting like a normal kid once he's treated like one," I said smugly.

His arm was around my shoulders and he rubbed his hand back and forth, his long fingers curling and uncurling. It felt good, exciting and comforting at the same time.

"And did I tell you about Xinhdy?"

"Who?"

"Her real name is Xinh. She's a Vietnamese girl on the ward, really sharp. Mai's been teaching her English. She's always talking and laughing and polishing her nails and stuff—she reminds me of this girl I was in training with, Cindy Schroeder. So I called her Xinhdy the other day, just sort of teasing. She got real offended and said, 'No Xinhdy, Xinh.' I asked Mai to tell her she reminded me of my friend in America whose name was almost like hers, and that was why I called her that. Yesterday one of her friends came to visit her and called her Xinh, and she was so funny, Tony. She stuck her nose in the air and said, 'No Xinh. Xinhdy.' "

He turned his head toward me a little and I saw my face reflected in his sunglasses. "Yeah, well, babe, you want to watch getting too close to these people, y'know? Don't get me wrong, I know how you feel. Our hooch mouse is a great gal, and it's hard not to feel sorry for some of those poor bastards we pick up in the villes. But we're going to

96

be pullin' out of here one of these days, and these folks will be on their own. You better hope your friends are carrying rockets for the VC at night if you care about what happens to them later."

He wasn't telling me anything new, but I was trying to amuse him with human-interest stories and he was insisting on turning it into hard news. Nobody wanted to talk about that. I'd already asked him about his background and family and how it went in the field and he was vague about everything. What was left? Talking about helicopter chassis?

"Hey, cheer up," he said, giving my shoulder an extra-hard hug. "Have I got a surprise for you."

"What?"

"Wait till you see." He led me inside the PX, a hangar filled with counters and shelves holding junk food— nonmeltable candy like M&M's and Pay Days, potato chips and sticks, canned chocolate milk, sodas—paperback books, mostly either smutty or the action-adventure kind all about what fun war is, and magazines whose illustrations looked like a day in the gyn. clinic from the doctor's point of view. They also had cheaply priced expensive watches, which was good because the sand worked its way through watch cases, and I'd ruined two already, and perfume. The only other items for women were beaded sweaters from Hong Kong that looked like costumes for midget leading ladies in forties movies. In the back of the building was a walled-off section set up as a snack bar, where a Vietnamese entrepreneur offered anemic hamburgers certified by the PX to be beef instead of dog, and a plate of cold chips. That was where Tony steered me. But at the last moment he blocked the door with his body and said playfully, "What's your favorite Italian food?"

"Spaghetti?"

He shook his head.

"Pizza," I moaned.

"How long since you had some?"

"What's this all about?" I thought he was teasing me. It was a favorite game when the ward was quiet to dream of American junk food: "I'd give twenty dollars for a taco." "I'd give thirty dollars for a slice of pizza." Though we got spoiled rotten on steak and lobster regularly, we lusted for cuisine from McDonald's, Shakey's, and Taco Bell. One doctor, returning from R&R in Hawaii with his wife, had built a little shrine of a Big Mac Styrofoam container, foil wrapper from fries, and a fried-pie box.

He stepped aside and gestured. "*Voilà*. An authentic Vietnamese pizza parlor."

They'd tried. Under a nylon parachute awning, two skinny men and one bewildered-looking girl, wearing white aprons and chefs' hats, industriously made dough and popped things into ovens. The product was nothing for the Italians to worry about. It consisted of a crust, floury enough to make you pucker, topped with a little ketchup and pieces of hot dog. They'd completely missed the point about cheese. But we ate it and laughed and pretended it was the real thing.

We went to the beach for a couple of hours and swam and played in the water and lay on the sand. I enjoyed it more than I ever had before, because nobody interrupted us or tried to hustle me with Tony there. He acted as if he owned me, which was just fine under the circumstances. I was delighted to be with such a good-looking, sexy guy. I knew that back in the States I wouldn't have such a knock-out for a boyfriend. It was just that in Nam the competition was all among the men. I wondered if there was any way I'd be able to hang on to such a fellow when we returned home. Shared experience maybe? I was pretty sure my family would like him and Duncan would be absolutely mute with jealousy—if not on my account, then because Tony was everything Duncan just talked about being.

We drove back to the compound. My hooch maid bobbed at us as she emerged from my room. I turned on the fan. He put Joni Mitchell on the tape deck. And there was a lot more trying each other on for size in every conceivable erotic position. Instead of being all steaming flesh, as it said in the novels, it seemed to me that we were more all knees and elbows with no place on that narrow cot to go without being in the way. I started giggling and he growled, "What's so funny? Why don't you close your eyes?"

I thought he had to be kidding. I shrugged. "I don't know. Sometimes sex just strikes me as funny. Why?"

He didn't answer but finished soon after that and grabbed enough clothes to run over to the doctors' shower. I rinsed off too, but I returned to the room before he did.

Well, hell. Sex *was* sometimes funny to me, but mostly because I was having a good time and having a good time always meant laughing, as far as I was concerned. Jesus, I couldn't summon up all that dead-serious panting passion you saw in the movies. Tony was serious enough for both of us. At some points I'd felt like a patient getting a particularly thorough examination. I had the sneaking suspicion the whole afternoon would go on my chart with detailed graphs of my anatomical assets and failings. But I didn't want it to end. I just wanted him to think I was flawless for a little while before he started criticizing. I picked up my guitar and started playing a song I'd learned from a Tom Paxton songbook. Sarah poked her head in my door. "Do you know 'Blowin' in the Wind,' Kitty? There's one chord I can't get."

We sat on lawn chairs on the porch trying to figure it out, and by the time Tony joined us I was feeling better. The South China Sea was gleaming beyond the beach, the palms were waving on Monkey Mountain. Judy, who was also off for the day, and the corpsman she was illegally dating joined us, chiming in on the choruses as they sat on the porch swinging their legs off the side to the rhythm as we sang.

"I'm just learning this one," I said. "We could do the chorus together." I sang a couple of verses of "The Last Thing on My Mind" and Judy and Sarah tried it with me, but Tony hissed in my ear, "Why do you have to grandstand? You could sing something we all know."

I didn't much feel like singing after that. Or talking to Tony either. I retreated to my room while they sang outside. He was doing something nobody else knew either. Pretty soon Sarah and Judy and her friend drifted away. I sat against the wall in the corner, with my knees drawn up and a book I wasn't reading propped up on them. Tony lingered in the doorway. "I'd better get back over to the unit."

"Okay," I said, trying to sound indifferent instead of disappointed. " 'Bye." This time he didn't kiss me.

But he called later that night and said he had to go in the field for a while but would miss me and wanted to see me when he got back. His voice was warm and tender and I decided I got my feelings hurt too easily.

One side benefit of my new relationship was that I

could now fit right in when the other girls were bitching or bragging about not just men in general but a man, the man each of them was going with, in particular. Carol told me she thought her boyfriend might be a little bit more married than he'd told her to begin with. Judy was mad that she and her corpsman had to sneak around because the brass had ruled against nurses seeing enlisted men. Sarah's long face was wistful when she talked about her doctor boyfriend going home to his wife.

We confided in one another, and on the ward, during quiet times, I confided in Marge. She was older, had an upbeat but sensible attitude, and played the field. Or so I thought until she came back from mail call with her boots floating a couple of inches above the linoleum, a letter on Army stationery clasped to her bosom, and a silly grin on her face.

"Good news?" I asked.

She sighed. "It's from Hal. I knew him in Japan. What a guy! He's going to be reassigned here."

"Here? To the 83rd?"

"No, but in Vietnam. We can see each other sometimes. He's really a kick, Kitty. You'd like him."

"Is he a doctor or what?"

"An MSC officer. He'll probably be a hospital administrator somewhere. But between my contacts and his contacts, we're bound to be able to get choppers back and forth once in a while."

"When's he coming?"

"In a couple of months. God, I hope he gets assigned somewhere close. Too bad Colonel Martin just got here."

"Marge! You'd be the scandal of the post, making it with the boss—tsk tsk."

She grinned. "Yeah. I would, wouldn't I?"

Being rather young, I believed that if I was not the model-perfect specimen portrayed in the fashion magazines, no man would have me, so Marge's romance came as a revelation to me. She was probably in her late thirties to early forties and a long way from being a beauty, though her pleasant personality and warmth made you forget that. She was even tolerant of the Army, a difficult thing for a reasonable woman to be, I thought. She had the same attitude toward it that many nice women married to men who are jerks but good providers seem to have toward their husbands. It's a living, and he means well. She had lots of buddies and was friendly with both enlisted men and officers, married and single. But it was obvious that this was far from your casual kind of affair. You could almost see little hearts popping out of her head, the way they did in the cartoons.

And for a while there was ample time to daydream. We admitted casualties in twos and threes instead of bunches, and saw men with bad backs and twisted ankles. Most of them wanted rest or drugs or both.

Mai was teaching Xinhdy English in her spare time and Ahn hung out with them when he wasn't following me around. I decided to join them and see if I couldn't learn more Vietnamese in the process. I didn't, as it turned out, but provided everyone with a lot of amusement as I tried to pronounce Vietnamese words. Ahn and Xinhdy were both much better pupils. Sometimes we watched the Vietnamese TV station, which featured singers of wavery-tuned songs doing what seemed like a cross between the oriental version of grand opera and soap opera against backdrops that were strictly from Sunday school skits. It wasn't very interesting to me and sounded like fingernails on a blackboard after a while, but it was better than the bullshit you saw on Armed Forces TV. Mai, Marge, Sarah, and I sometimes had mock battles over who got the honor of changing Dang Thi Thai's dressing. Thai would watch us with her eyes dancing, and laugh through the painful procedure, encouraged by the healing she could see for herself if she twisted far enough. Soon she could be grafted, and once that took, we could start physical therapy in earnest and maybe get her back on her feet.

If Ahn had adopted me as his mother, he took to Xe as a grandfather. He'd sit by the old man's bedside and chatter at him, bring things to show him, try to involve him in conversations. Xe wasn't interested for a long time, but finally Ahn and Mai convinced him to join them at Xinhdy's bedside to chat.

This sort of thing went on intermittently for several weeks at a time, you understand. New patients were admitted and discharged, but our long-term patients were the core group and watched one another and us for entertainment the same way we watched them. But a lot of the time they slept or vegged out in front of the TV, and those times were pretty trying. Hectic as the pushes were, they were easier to deal with in some ways than the weeks and weeks of twelve-hour shifts that dragged by while you tried to find something to do.

When the patients were napping, the last roll of tape was neatly lined up with the next on the dressing cart, the bedpans were cleaned, and the empty beds gathered dust, the day shift sat around the nurses' station and talked to each other.

Sarah and I alternated on nights, so I rarely got to work with her, since the head nurse, Marge, had to be on days all the time. We were supposed to have another nurse, but she had yet to arrive. If she'd been there, she'd have been as bored as the rest of us.

So Marge and I sat around discussing such burning political issues as what we planned to order from the Pacex catalog before we went home. She also waxed lyrical recalling her tours in Japan and Okinawa, talking about the shopping in those places. If you wanted cameras or stereo equipment you went to Japan, everybody knew that. But Hong Kong was the best place for all-round shopping, tailor-made anything, fast and cheap, sequined evening clothes and sweaters, jewelry, pirate editions of the latest bestsellers.

I could almost see it in all its quarter-to-half-priced glory, and it cheered me in my hour of need, when the patients were surly, when Tony was gone or we'd had a fight. Nonmaterialism and spiritual values are all very laudable, but when you're in a situation where everything including your job involves questionable ethics, things are the safest possible topic for conversation and food for thought, except maybe for bargains, which are even better. Talking politics, work, or morality was confusing and depressing. Talking about home was even more depressing. Armed Forces TV showed news reports of what was allegedly happening in Vietnam, but to me they always looked wrong. Exaggerated numbers of Vietnamese dead and understated numbers of American dead and wounded may have been good propaganda, but seemed disrespectful of the sacrifice made by those dead and wounded who had not been counted. And anyway, only the naïve new recruits, the terminally gung ho, and lifers believed all that

crap about assisting the South Vietnamese in repulsing the
Red Peril.

The Vietnamese I saw seemed more worried about
getting enough to eat, keeping their families together, and
not getting killed than they were about political ideals.
Coming back late from China Beach, when the moonlight
glistened on the flattened Miller High Life and Schlitz cans
covering the Vietnamese huts with tin-into-silver al-
chemy, and the candlelight shone through the strands of
plastic beads (a phoenix, a peacock, a dragon) curtaining
the doorways, I imagined what the family gathered around
the candle talked about.

"How many watches did you nab today, Nguyen?"

"Thirty-four and four very fat wallet, honorable
mamasan. See here, thirty-four dollars and a J. C. Penney
credit card. Do you think you can get a catalog from one of
the Americans whose houses you clean?"

"I'll work on it. Daughter, how many tricks did you
turn today?"

"Fifteen, Mama. One soldier was mean and wouldn't
pay me, but then another gave me this ring. How much do
you think we can get for it?"

"We'll ask your papa when he gets home from carrying rockets for the VC. He's had a hard day of guard duty at
China Beach."

"I wish poor Papa didn't have to moonlight like that."

"War's hell, my son."

If I were in their shoes, I'd probably have done the
same thing. Tony had hit the nail on the head. The peace
marchers were eventually going to pressure the President
into getting American troops *out* of this mess, and when
they did, the people who'd been loyal to us were going to
be up shit creek. It probably didn't make much difference
to them if they were growing rice for South Vietnam or for
North Vietnam, as long as they were able to eat it themselves. Some of the senior officers I'd talked with said
America should have supported Ho Chi Minh to begin
with. And some of the guys with a couple of years of col-
lege claimed that the war was not about communism and
freedom but about boosting the economy and making
Southeast Asia safe for the oil companies and the in-
ternational military-industrial complex, whatever that
was. While that sounded pretty paranoid, it was less hokey

than saying that the whole war was strictly for the sake of political ideals. The only people who said anything about political ideals recited their lines in the same way church ladies said "blood of the Lamb" and "fallen from grace," or the Communists reputedly talked of "imperialist running dogs."

Shallow, materialistic bitch that I was, I preferred talk about something real like stereo equipment and clothes.

We were sitting there gabbing one afternoon when Sergeant Baker wandered in with the mail, eavesdropped a moment, and while Marge opened hers gave us the low-down on Hawaii and on Thailand, where he'd spent a tour and knew all the best bars and brothels. Meyers, returning from being pulled to ward eight, chimed in that *he* wanted to go to Australia because he'd heard the women were *real* friendly. Married men like Voorhees tried to go to Hawaii to meet their wives. I wanted to go to Australia as much as anything because nobody I knew had ever been there.

"Yeah, man, I really want to get out of here, go to that Australia, man," Meyers said. "But more'n that, I want to go home. Get outa this place forever and ever."

"Well, man, you ain't got it so bad," Baker said. "Think of them poor damn Vietnamese. They don't get to go no-where ever. They're home already and this is as good as it gets."

Tony hadn't called in a couple of weeks and I was about to start night duty, but I wasn't sure if I cared if I heard from him or not. Most of our dates had been spent in bed, with very little socializing or any other kind of activity.

"Look," I said, the last time he came over. "Could we do something else besides screw for a change?"

"What? You don't want to?"

"It's hot in here and it's been a long, boring week, okay? I'd like to get out and see something maybe, or at least go to the club and dance."

"Sure, we can go dance if you want to, but there's plenty of time before that—"

"Tony—"

"Baby, I'm risking my life up there," he said, slipping his hands up under my shirt and bra and nuzzling my neck. "Who knows? I might not come back next time."

Eventually we did go dancing, but it was one of those

nights when the band played line dances and the fast kind that I love. Tony danced one or two but then sat in the corner talking helicopters with one of the other men from his company. When I sat down, sweating and happy, he said, "Do you have to show off all the time? Why can't you just sit here with me and talk and have a drink?"

"Because I don't know anything about helicopters and, frankly, they're not that interesting to me," I said. "You're not the only one who needs to recharge when you're off duty, you know. I put in long days too."

"Don't I make you happy, baby?"

The argument was conducted in fierce whispers and nonetheless we were drawing a little attention. "Tony, you're a fantastic lover, but sometimes I think it's not me you love at all—I keep getting the feeling you wish I were somebody else entirely, someone who is quiet and demure and keeps her place. Probably somebody who doesn't work a twelve-hour day. Well, I'm not. I'm me. And"—I threw in a line from an old blues song, because it fit—"And if you don't like my peaches, don't shake my tree, okay?"

He slammed down his drink. "Okay. Excuse me, I think I'd better get back to the unit. I may be needed *there.*"

I didn't know whether I was madder at him for treating me like a whore who wasn't due any consideration or for spoiling my off-duty time. He was just jealous of the attention I got, I thought. He was used to being in the middle of things himself and couldn't take it that in this situation any woman would be more interesting to the vast majority of the population than any man. And that emotional blackmail crap about how he might not come back. The creep! After a week, I calmed down and realized that maybe some of it could have been my fault. I had to admit I recognized that he wanted me to be somebody else because I couldn't help wishing he were somebody else too.

Wednesday evening he called. "Hi, babe. How's it going?"

"Fine," I said. "How've you been?"

"I've missed you. You're off tomorrow, aren't you? How about if I come over?"

"It's my sleep day," I said. "If I don't sleep, I won't be any good at work tomorrow night."

"You can sleep some of the time," he said.

"I don't think so, Tony."

"We had a couple of close calls this week, baby. . . ."

"I'm sorry. Please be a little more careful. Maybe you could use the rest, too. Tony, we need to have a talk sometime soon, but I have to have tomorrow to think, okay?"

"Yeah. Sure. See ya," he said, and hung up.

Then, of course, I couldn't sleep that night, so I padded over to ICU to see how busy Carole was. She was bored stiff, sitting at the desk reading while her corpsmen played cards.

"Jesus, McCulley, what's wrong with you?"

I told her. "I don't want to break up with him, Carole, but dammit, if we're going to spend every free moment together I occasionally want to talk about something besides which position we should assume next and whether I came or not."

"I see where that would get old. Tom and I talk about everything. I dunno, Kitty, there are other fish in the sea, of course, but not many as sexy as Tony."

"I know. That's the whole problem."

"If he calls tomorrow are you going to let him come over?"

"No. It'll just be the same old thing. I don't think I'll be able to sleep, but I sure don't want to spend another goddamn day on post. Besides, if I'm here and he calls I'll give in. Want to go to the beach?"

"Can't. I'm having my own summit conference."

"If you hear of anyone going, let me know. I've got to get out of here. The last time I did anything interesting was the flying crane ride."

"Poor baby," Carole said, then chewed on her pencil awhile. "Hey, what's tomorrow? Thursday? Why not go on the medcap mission? I know it sounds like a drag to work on your day off, but if you don't mind losing the sleep—"

"So who can sleep? You're a genius, Swenson. I'll tell you all about it."

# 8

Well, well, look who's here," Charlie Heron said affably. "Bac si Joe, how's it going? Nice you could come, Lieutenant. Climb in, climb in. Lieutenant, you want to sit up front?"

He motioned to the ovenlike cab of a deuce-and-a-half.

"No thanks," I said. "I'll ride back here with the rest of the troops."

"Suit yourself," he said, and climbed in beside Joe.

The doctor and I hadn't exactly planned to come as a team, but the slow ward work had gotten to both of us. I met him as we were walking toward the gate that morning. Joe walked briskly and happily, a large camera and lens case around his neck. Photography was his other pet hobby, besides carpentry and orthopedic surgery.

"Hi, Geppetto," I said. "You don't mean to say that Marge is letting you go for the day, too?"

"Marge knows more about those folks than I do, by now. Things have been too slow. Got to go drum up business or I'll get rusty. Bob Blum can handle any emergencies that come in. I want to see a village," he said. "Do you think a wide angle and a telescopic will be enough lenses?"

"That'll feed two families after the kids steal them from you, and the camera will probably feed half the village, so—"

"You're as funny as a broken leg, Lieutenant McCulley, you know that? Speaking of broken legs, what's that limp about?" He cast an expert eye on my size nines.

"I don't know. Feels like I might have a rock in my boot."

By then we were at the truck and being hailed by

Heron. I wasn't that thrilled to see him. But even though his tone had been carefully indifferent, I could tell he was glad to see me there. Cathie Peterson, from ICU, came along too. She was already in the cab of the truck when Joe and I arrived.

A young Marine corporal helped me into the truck. "Glad you could make it, ma'am," he said. "The villagers are always glad to see you nurses. You don't know how much they appreciate it."

I looked around at all the Marine camouflage fatigues in the truck. "I didn't know the Medical Civic Action Team was a Marine-sponsored thing," I said. The truck bucked into action and rumbled through Dogpatch and out onto the highway.

A swarthy sergeant whose name tag said "Hernandez" and who had swung up into the truck behind me after making sure all personnel and gear were aboard, said, "Yes, ma'am. This one is. Though it started with Special Forces as a PSYOPS mission. Most of these men been out in the bush the best part of their tour. They're short—three or four months to go. They finish up the tour working in the villages."

"You mean they come off of combat duty and go right out on medical missions?" I asked, feeling a little uneasy about it. These men could as easily have been the numbed, miserable-looking wounded who cycled through the wards, enthusing about nothing but the joys of bayoneting gooks and how the difference between a VC and a friendly was how fast the individual in question could run. If the human target escaped, it was friendly. If it died, it had to be VC.

"Yes, ma'am. Sergeant Heron handpicked them."

I had to digest that. Although most of the men surrounding us were marines, and there were certainly a lot of decent guys among them, there'd been a couple of nasty incidents early in my tour at the 83rd that made me question the kind of training they had. Lindy Hopkins had come steaming off the ward one night, slammed into Carole's hooch, and sat there crying. "Those bastards. Those goddamn bastards."

"Take it easy, Lindy. What the hell's the matter?" Carole asked. She and I had been sitting around talking. Lindy worked on ICU with Carole.

"They brought her in—she was just a kid—eleven years old and they raped her—"

"Who?"

"The seven big strong marines who brought her in. They raped her till—till they broke her spine. She's going to be paralyzed, Carole. An eleven-year-old kid. And then the sons of bitches had the gall to ask when visiting hours were!"

Another time another marine tried to break into Judy's hooch at night to rape her. Fortunately, Judy's got great lungs.

So I was not crazy about marines. Maybe the only reason I associated marines with the vicious and cruel things that happened was because the Marine Corps dominated the area. Of course, I knew the enemy did horrible things to our people and to their own. But they were the enemy. They weren't supposed to be civilized. I'd grown up with men like these, and they were supposed to know better. I despised any kind of training that taught them to be less than human.

At least the men around me refrained from drooling or pawing the bed of the pickup truck. They looked perfectly normal—a little older and sadder than a lot of the GIs who passed through the hospital, but basically okay.

The man nearest me even offered me his truck tire to lean against and cushion my back. I accepted gratefully, reveling in the wind the truck made as it rolled down the highway to Freedom Hill. There it turned off onto a dirt road and bumped along through what could have been a rural area south of San Antonio, Texas. Golden fields were flanked by fences, and rows of fanning leafy trees shielded the houses from the hot, heavy sun. Water buffaloes with pajamaed people in tropical topees and coolie hats prowled the lone prairie instead of cowboys and longhorns, of course, but it was still cattle and cattle tenders of a sort, so what the hell. It was almost like home, lolling in the back of the truck, just enjoying the ride. The only signs of war were the uniforms and the weapons. The men acted as if they were going on holiday, although their eyes shifted toward the trees now and then.

A small boy wearing a blue shirt, shorts, and a baseball cap and carrying two metal jerricans over his right shoulder offered us a drink of water as the vehicles stopped beside the village pump. His shins were dusty, his face expectant. The men poured out of the truck, one of them knocking the kid's cap off and ruffling his hair, before replacing the cap, backward.

Joe started taking pictures the minute he hit the ground. The village was cool and shaded, made darker than the surrounding fields by a canopy of treetops lashed together overhead. Beyond the fields the mountains rose, and depending on where you were standing, you could see sparkles of a river glinting through the trees. This was not a newsreel-type village, bombed and half-burned. This was a collection of neat little unpainted homes, most of which bore trellises loaded with flowers and melons. The streets between the houses and trees were busy with bicycles loaded with baskets of pigs, Hondas with nets full of coconuts lashed to them. Grubby children with big brown eyes and bowl-cut black hair danced around them. Adults squatting on their heels in the shade looked up from their work or talk and waved.

Heron pointed out the school and the marketplace, and the hut that I later described to Mom as the "labor and delivery facility." It was windowless and dark and had the smell of old blood, rot, and other, pungent, vaginal odors very strong within this tropical bacteria breeding ground. My clinical description was a euphemism; the place was so ripe I had to suppress an itch to scratch my own crotch in sympathy. Little nests had been made inside, holes dug out of the dirt and lined with grass and old rags. One mother and her newborn, under the supervision of an unhurried-looking midwife, occupied the space on one side of the inevitable Vietnamese bedspread partioning the makeshift postpartum section from the L&D. "I'm afraid there's no delivery tables, Lieutenant," Heron said. "Vietnamese mothers deliver from a squatting position." Damned know-it-all. I'd assumed as much. So did my Indian ancestresses. So did a lot of women practicing the new natural childbirth methods.

He showed us to the clinic with another glance at me, as if he expected me to be horrified. I resolutely was not. The clinic area was a hut—a long, low one, also dirt-floored and dark. "You'll do fine," he told me. "I've done amputations in worse places than this, Lieutenant."

My "Goody for you" was drowned out in another introduction as Heron presented a boy of about eleven. "This is Li. He'll interpret for you. And this is Miss Xuan from Province Hospital"—he indicated a plain-faced girl in a white ao dai, the graceful tunic-dress of Vietnam, and conical hat—"and my ARVN counterpart, Sergeant Huong."

Li was as officious as any sergeant major as he lined up the patients for treatment. He strutted up and down the line while the examinations took place, as if supervising instead of interpreting. Li claimed that Miss Xuan, who was at least twice his age, was his niece. The niece didn't do much work but mostly flirted with Heron's ARVN counterpart, Sergeant Huong. Huong swaggered a bit, James Dean style, and flirted back.

I was nervous, not because of the conditions but because this was my first whack at public health nursing. Li's main usefulness was in telling the patients what I said. They were able to make themselves pretty clear with gestures and facial expressions. Besides the usual "owies" the children had, there were a lot of snotty noses and deep coughs and running rashes. Joe diagnosed a carpenter with sore knees as having tenosynovitis, an inflammation of the tendons caused mostly by being a carpenter.

"Oh boy, McCulley, come look at this," Cathie called me, peering at the side of a woman's head. The woman was youngish, with rather protruding teeth and a pained expression.

"She say she no hear too good," Li said.

"No wonder," Cathie said, and stood aside. The woman's right ear was completely blocked by a protruding tumor.

"Tell her she needs to come to the hospital with us to have this fixed," I told Li.

Li fired off twenty or thirty syllables that rose and fell like Vietnamese music. The woman shook her head and replied with fifty or sixty syllables of her own.

"She say no can do, co. Papasan work in field and she have these babysans." He indicated the two shorts-clad toddlers clinging to her pajama bottoms and the little girl, about seven, carrying a nude baby of about two on her hip.

"Well, tell her to talk it over with papasan, and if she wants us to help her, come to the hospital with the team next week."

My next patient was a sickly little girl whose round brown face, black bangs, and huge dark eyes made her look more like a doll than a real child. She was hot, her mother said, and cried all the time. I took her temperature, which was 103, and listened to her chest. For an FUO, fever of unknown origin, you also always checked lymph nodes routinely, so I raised the little girl's arms. Lumps the size and color of plums swelled in the child's armpits.

I took one look at them and said, "Whoopee shit," and called out to Joe.

"What is it, Kitty?"

"I'm not sure. I never studied tropical medicine or anything, but a couple of weeks ago I was reading this novel? And in it the heroine ends up treating a whole bunch of people in the Appalachians for bubonic plague. Joe, the book said the victims had big purple lymph nodes in their axilla and groin areas, just like this kid has. Come and see what you think." I tugged down the little girl's shorts and checked her groin while I talked. More plums. It was a wonder the poor baby could walk.

"Bubonic plague? No shit? In this day and age? Wait, let me get my camera. Damn, not enough light."

"Mamasan, if this is what I think it is, we'd better check you out too," I told the mother. Li didn't need to translate. The mother pulled her pajama top off and raised her left arm, pointing to the purple "owie" underneath.

Joe examined the nodules and whistled. "I dunno, Kitty. Your junk reading may have come in handy. Anyway, the kid's fever is enough to have her admitted and we may as well take the mother too."

While the patients gathered their belongings and arranged for their departures, Heron drove us to the marines' quarters, on the outskirts of the village. Wonderful cooking smells wafted toward us. The mamasan who looked after the marines had prepared a lunch of stewed chicken, rice noodles, and mushrooms in broth. The marines and Heron were already experts with chopsticks, but Cathie, Joe, and I all needed lessons. I began to wonder whether the Army chose olive drab for the uniforms of its Asian-based troops because the color went so well with chicken broth.

Heron sat next to me, which made me even clumsier

and more uncomfortable: exactly what he intended, I was sure. "I can see where Xe might be right about you," he said. "You don't go much by the book, do you?"

"Only bestselling novels," I admitted.

"I mean, you're more intuitive. I can see where he'd find you interesting."

He sounded so ridiculously, deliberately mysterious that I barely suppressed a desire to tell him that the rumors about me and Xe were completely false, that we were just good friends.

But my opinion of him had risen a little bit. After the incident with the marijuana, it would have been hard for it to get much lower. Still, the way the men behaved toward Heron and the villagers, and the obvious affection, even adoration, that the villagers greeted him with, made me realize that maybe the man could be more than a lot of talk.

"I can't get over how much different these people seem from the ones you see in Dogpatch and Da Nang," Cathie said.

"Uh huh," Joe agreed, simultaneously holding up his camera and slurping a noodle. "Look, we've been here half the day and nobody's tried to snitch my camera."

"Most of the folks you meet in town and around the hospital are refugees. They steal to get by. These people are farmers, but take away their land and their livelihood and they'd do the same thing, or worse, to put food in their family's mouths," Heron said. "Our mission is to make sure they don't have to steal to get by. Some of that livestock you saw, some of the clothes, cooking utensils, the men here bought for the villagers out of their own paychecks."

"Hey, that's really nice of you guys," I said.

"Naw, not really, ma'am," Sergeant Hernandez said. "It's like, see, well, last night a rocket landed out there and we went running out with our Band-Aids and Merthiolate. When one landed too near us a couple of weeks ago, the people were there to help us in a minute and a half. We figure what happens to them happens to us and vice versa, which is how this whole fuckin' war—excuse me, ladies— how this whole war should have been fought to begin with."

"If at all," said a thin-faced man with granny glasses.

"No shit, man," another marine said with feeling.

I seemed to have stumbled into a bunch of leather-neck Lancelots, no less—men who actually believed that there were good Vietnamese who were not dead Vietnamese. I can be flip about it now, but I had to look at my noodles to keep from "gettin' a little misty," as Maynard G. Krebs, the beatnik character from "Dobie Gillis," used to say. I also felt a little disoriented—why did some marines give their paychecks to better the lives of some South Vietnamese while others, and maybe even the same ones, earlier in their tour of duty, dedicated themselves to obliterating villagers who couldn't have been very different from these people?

"I guess you can mostly only do this because it's so close to Da Nang and protected and everything," I said. "I mean, out in the bush, people who need medical attention have to be medevaced, right?"

Heron abandoned his cool altogether. He waved his hands negatively and almost choked on his noodles, trying to gulp them down in his haste to set me straight. "No way. See, what you don't understand, L.T., is what a lot of people don't understand. This is my third tour. Last year, Da Nang was hotter than any little old village. Of course, some places we just don't have the supplies or men to do much—"

"That's where dudes like Sergeant Heron here come in," Hernandez said. "You know what this character's idea of a combat mission is, ma'am? He's the medic, right? *He* walks point into some hostile damn ville and starts patchin' people up before anybody can pop a shot off. Guy's got to have a charmed life."

"Hey. Sarge, I been wonderin' about that. Is it true you even sleep in the villages sometimes?"

"Mostly the Montagnard ones," he said, as if that was different.

"Holy shit."

"But you're not doing that anymore?" I asked. "You're involved with this now?"

"I do a lot of things," he said. "Helping the Marines matchmake these guys and this village is what I do lately."

"You beaucoup dinky dao, Doc," one of the men said.

"Yeah, I bet there's bets goin' down on the black market who's goin' to nail your ass first, Doc, the brass or Charlie," the guy with the granny glasses said approvingly.

"We've got a little something for Joe, haven't we?" Heron said, changing the subject. The mamasan was clearing the dishes, and as soon as she finished, Hernandez returned with a moldy bottle, which he handed to Joe.

"Homegrown penicillin?" Joe asked.

"It's one-hundred-day wine. They make it from sticky rice buried between banana leaves for a hundred days. Try it. I hear tell this is a very good year."

Joe did himself proud. His lips squirmed a little when he finished the wine, but he managed to pull them up into a smile and a thank you worthy of a ham actor taking a curtain call.

As we left the village, he photographed everything in sight. I shot a few pictures, too, of a young man in a straw hat who had infected sores on his legs but a beautiful face, a young girl holding her little brother, a water buffalo and its tender, a mamasan with her loads balanced at the ends of a pole.

But the good feeling I retained from that experience was eclipsed that night when I was pulled to help Carole in ICU. She had only a few patients, but one of them was an old woman, an ARVN general's wife, who had been sitting on her front porch when some sort of incendiary bomb was lobbed onto it, burning her over 100 percent of her body, mostly third-degree. Carole was devoting all of her time to that patient, while her corpsman covered the rest of the ward.

"What do you want me to do?" I asked.

"The POW is the other critical one. He's a burn case, too, not as bad, but he's got a collapsed right lung and a fresh trach."

He also had a guard, who had a green beret and a gun and who shifted as nervously as if he were surrounded by armed VC instead of standing over a relatively helpless one. He glowered at me as I approached. He was no more like Charlie Heron than Heron was like Barry Sadler.

He watched my every move as I extracted the prisoner's trach tube to clean it in a basin of hydrogen peroxide. Halfway through the cleaning process, the prisoner began gurgling, bubbles of accumulated phlegm collecting at the hole in his throat. I took off the gloves I'd already contaminated, put on a fresh glove, and reached for the suction tubing. The guard held his arm over the patient.

"Let him strangle," he said.

"What?"

"Let him strangle for a while. We're trying to get information out of him. We can't do it if you coddle him."

I glared at his arm and brushed past it. "I'm not coddling him, soldier. I'm suctioning his trach tube so he doesn't die. If you wanted to torture or kill him, you should have thrown him out of a helicopter when you had the chance. Once you bring him here, he's not just a prisoner. He's my patient and he is by God going to get the same care as any other patient in his condition, meaning the best I can give him."

The slurp of the suction machine drowned out the guard's protests for a moment. When I pulled the tip of the tubing out of the POW's throat, I glared at the guard. The muscles in his jaws bunched and relaxed, bunched and relaxed, as if he were chewing on a particularly tough nail. Finally he said, "Your kinda attitude is going to cost Americans their lives. This guy has information—"

"Bullshit," I said. "He can't tell you a damn thing if he's dead. You let us get him stable enough to talk, and then if you want to ask him questions, you do so under our supervision until the man is well enough for you to murder him. You bic?"

The only reason he didn't call me a stupid cunt was because I outranked him and could have had his stripe, and women were rare enough in Nam that fragging them was severely frowned upon even by gung-ho comrades. So the guard merely growled, but he got out of my way and didn't interfere again. The guard who relieved him was less zealous and sipped his coffee in peace.

The patient might not have been too with it, but he did seem to relax a little when the first guard left. Carole finished spreading a fresh coat of sulfonamide cream on her patient's burns. I thought I should warn her about the surly guard.

"Yeah," she said. "But you can understand how he feels. He may have seen buddies get blown away by that guy."

"I guess."

"God, I'm sick of burns," she said, tossing her dirty

gloves in the trash bag. "We had another guy last week worse off than this woman. He was a villager doing some painting for a civilian contractor, and this CIDG guard decided he wanted some of the paint. Apparently the guy told the guard that he'd have to ask the boss and the guard tossed a lit cigarette into the paint. Of course, the worker was already covered with paint and stuff and went up like a torch. His friends rolled him in the dirt and finally put him out, but he was third-degree over 90 percent of his body. He only lasted a few hours."

The night finally ended, and none too soon to suit me. A patient who needs constant suctioning requires you to be on your feet a lot, and mine hurt. I checked my boot again, but there was no rock, just a red place on my toe where I thought one might have rubbed. In spite of having been up for twenty-four hours, I had trouble sleeping the next day. The heat was a problem as usual, and I couldn't seem to get my foot into a comfortable position. Besides which, my mind was squirrel-caging with a turmoil of impressions and conflicting emotions from the events of the day and night. Also, I came fully awake every time the phone by the staircase rang. The few dreams I had were confusing, more troubled than restful.

I gave up finally and had time for a shower before work. My sore toe did not want to fit inside my boot, but I thought, all I have to do is make it through the night. I'll probably be able to sit at the nurses' station and put it up most of the time. It should be better in the morning.

# 9

It wasn't, of course. I got so sick that night that my memories of even the ordinary events are fairly surreal. Then Xe decided to intervene on my behalf and things got even weirder.

Though I secretly believed that wishing, willing, and praying would sometimes help some patients get well, I had been trained in a scientific tradition. Any energy I put forth could be nothing more than a random supplement to real help, such as antibiotics, surgery, and intravenous fluids. My feeling was just that any little extra effort I could throw in at a critical time couldn't hurt, so why not? Xe's perspective was the exact opposite.

I think that Xe must have already been considering using me—both from what Heron said and from what happened later. Some of Heron's antagonism toward me was because he had been passed over by the old man. We've talked about this, and he says he knows now that it wasn't a question of unworthiness. It was just that the old man could see clearly and graphically how much Heron's energy was depleted by the war. By the time I met him, the medic was on his third tour. He needed every scrap of energy to keep himself whole, and didn't have enough of himself left over for Xe's work. By the time I got sick, Xe was beginning to realize the full cost of his own wounds. He already had his eye on me, I think, because, of all the healthy people he was in contact with, I was the one who was already on his path, even though I'd never thought of it that way. Facts, figures, and procedures have always been more difficult for me than for most of the people I work with, so I'd always tried to compensate with some of the less tangible skills I'd tried with Tran. Unaugmented, of course, they didn't always help. But they were developed enough for Xe to pick up, even through the physically induced fog of a coma. He needed me well and strong and I think, if he had been a little stronger himself and time had been less limited, would have started trying to teach me. When I got sick . . .

But I'm ahead of myself.

The shift started at 1900 hours. The night started out to be even more hectic than the one on ICU. I was glad, in a way, because I was so sleepy that I wouldn't have kept awake otherwise. Sarah was on days alone and had received four fresh GI casualties at six, and had no time to settle them in before the shift change. I had their orders to carry out, two I.V.s to start, and a slew of paperwork. Besides that, Dang Thi Thai had had her skin graft surgery earlier in the day. The graft had to be "rolled," or smoothed down with a sterile Q-tip, every fifteen minutes to help it adhere. So I was constantly running back and forth between the wards and my sore foot got sorer every time.

I disregarded it. What was a sore toe compared to what the patients, especially Thai, were enduring? When I ran the Q-tip around Thai's wound she'd flinch, clench her eyes shut and her betel-blackened teeth together, and hiss. Her left hand, with the I.V. taped to its back, would clutch toward the wound, and stop just short of my hand. It must have felt to her as if I were sticking hot icepicks straight into her and twisting. But as soon as I stopped, her hand dropped back to her waist and she lifted her sweat-soaked face a little and blinked at me. Her mouth even tried to curve a little and she would duck her head in a sort of apologetic gesture and collapse against the pillow again. I noticed once that the case was wet where she laid her face, so I lifted her head and turned the pillow over for her, and from the look she gave me, you would have thought I'd healed her single-handedly and brought her husband back to life to boot.

Joe called around 2100 and said that, starting at midnight, Thai's graft could be rolled every half hour, which helped me a little.

Still, when I got up from charting my meds at one, I couldn't bear weight on my left foot and I hopped from bed to bed, and stood with my knee on a chair while I did Thai's treatment.

A new corpsman, Ron Ryan, was on the other side and there was no sound except the rush of the desktop fan, which didn't cool things off much but blew my charts apart unless I weighted the papers down with I.V. bottles and coffee mugs.

I felt funny hopping along, because with each little hop my head seemed to float right up to the ceiling and take a long time coming down. I felt as if I were looking out from a long way inside my brain, as if most of me were somewhere deep inside my body, smaller, shrunken inside myself, with the rest of me, this big ungainly shell, hopping around and sweating. Sometimes I didn't quite keep track of where I was and I'd think I was at bed three and I was already at five. I was well lubricated by continual runnels of sweat, but they almost felt cool by now. And I was oddly, dopily happy and unconcerned. Ryan appeared at one end of the ward with a mop and I stood staring at him for a moment and, hey presto, he disappeared without moving, just as I caught myself on someone's bed rail, falling backward.

Old Xe was still awake when I hopped to his bedside. He startled me by grabbing my wrist above the flashlight. He hissed as he touched me and his fingers felt so cool I thought for a moment his hiss was a sizzle, like cold bacon on a hot pan. "Numbah ten, co," he said, giving me a penetrating look from eyes that gleamed like pools of oil in the beam of my flashlight. I realized *he* realized my foot was killing me.

"Damn straight, papasan," I said from inside a tunnel somewhere. "Beaucoup dau," I agreed, but then felt a little ashamed to be telling him my troubles, telling this legless old man about my silly sore toe.

Ryan was on his break when the commotion broke out on the GI side. I limped over in time to see one of the new men standing in the middle of the aisle, swinging his pillow in a circle and shouting. Two of his buddies were wide awake, their eyes bright in my flashlight beam like the eyes of wild animals, watching him in the dark. I started toward him, and one of the others said, "Don't, ma'am. He's asleep, but he could still hurt you." But I did my best to sound motherly—"It's okay, sweetheart. You're just having a bad dream"—and talked him back to bed.

Walking back to the Vietnamese side, I felt as if I were on a single stable stilt. Suddenly Ryan popped up in front of me. He reminded me a little of an intelligent chicken: sharp nose, sharp but receding chin, shiny little eyes, and a bit of a forelock over his brow, like a coxcomb. He grabbed my arm as I tottered against him. "Steady, L.T."

"You keep popping in and out," I complained; "it's like, now I see you, now I don't."

"You better sit down, ma'am. You feel like you're running a fever. Anything wrong?"

"Got a sore toe. Isn't that silly?"

"You better go sit down."

"Gotta finish rounds."

"I'll finish them."

I was dubious. "Okay, but make sure everybody's breathing."

"Affirmative, L.T."

I limped back to my metal folding chair and landed heavily. I propped my sore foot on another chair, feeling like a comic figure of an old man with gout.

I wanted to take my boot off, but I was going to wait until the night supervisor made rounds, because I didn't want to be caught out of uniform and I knew that if I got the boot off, I wouldn't be able to get it back on. Actually, I didn't care all that much one way or the other, but to take the boot off would require bending over and I thought it very likely the top of my head would fall off and rattle down the aisle like a loose cookie jar lid when the jar is tipped too far. So I would just rest a minute and then I would start a letter to Mom.

My eyes just closed for a moment, but they wanted to stay closed. I fought them open again. I couldn't be caught sleeping on duty. I finally pried them open and started writing the letter. I found that I couldn't remember my last word and my pen kept slipping off the page, my words leveling out like an EKG gone flat when a patient dies.

My lids kept drooping and I wished I could use toothpicks to prop them open—the dim lighting, the muted noises, the intense heat, and the feeling I had of trying to move through molasses with my body while my mind was in free-fall made me feel drunk. I kept dropping off and startling myself awake a split second later, so that my surroundings took on the semblance of a clumsy animation with too few frames—jerky and discontinuous. I thought things would seem more real if only I could turn on more lights.

And then the ward lurched again and I saw that there *were* more lights, floating just ahead of me and a little above my chair. They were very pretty multicolored ones, patterned ones, a veritable Fourth of July's worth of lights, except that they weren't exploding and sparking but swirling out and dissipating like heat waves.

At first I thought there were seven, but they all sort of blurred and expanded into one big radiant pattern, flowing like smoke out of a central body, drifting, seeming to form ghosts, like the ectoplasm mediums were supposed to exhale, only in living color—rather faded color at first, but as I watched, growing more vivid. Clear blue and jade green and spiraling flames of amethyst flowed from what seemed a red-orange fountain with curls of blue smoke and rays of pure yellow, with a white spark near the center.

I thought: Far out, complimenting myself on my Technicolor imagination. I watched the colored thing's progress passively as if it were a weird movie. I could see perfectly well beyond the light and everyone was still sleeping.

Behind the light, at first dim but growing brighter all the time, was a man's figure. Initially it seemed legless, but as it grew brighter it lit him up like a Christmas tree. I could see that he had his legs tucked up under him, yoga style.

He was floating about five feet off the ground, just above the iron ends of the beds, and underneath his toes I saw the intake and output clipboard hanging from Xe's bed foot. Through the transparent white spark his hands clasped at his chest.

I don't know if I actually said it, but I thought: What a great trick, Xe. I didn't know you could do that. I also thought it was neat the way he'd grown his legs back, but I didn't want to say anything—it seemed crass to mention it.

As I watched, the light shifted with the same jerkiness as everything else, so when the pink tendrils started wafting toward me, it was again a case of presto chango, now I see them and now I don't know if I like this whole trip or not. I scooted back and my leg fell off the chair, which sent shafts of fire up it. The tendrils shriveled, and as they shrank back to the center, they deepened to bright red, then deep brick red, surrounding the whole pattern. Through the light I saw Xe's face, and that made me scramble even farther backward.

With another of those animated frame shifts, I blinked and saw only the little desk lamp. Xe was lying quietly, his eyes closed, looking maybe a little more tired and sadder than I remembered from before, but otherwise the same. I caught the glint of Ahn's eye as he rolled onto his stomach, looking around him as if he thought a cougar would pounce on him. I started up from my chair but blinked again and there was Ryan leaning across me over the desk. "L.T., you okay? You look real bad."

"I'm burning up," I told him and realized it was the truth. "And I gotta pee."

Inside the narrow toilet cubicle behind the nurses' station, I saw in the mirror that my face looked ghastly—if I had a patient who looked like that, I'd put them on the seriously ill list. My hair was matted with sweat that rolled off my pasty face and trickled down the back of my neck, though there were still goose bumps on my arms and ice water running through my spinal column. When I pulled down my trousers and tried to sit on the seat, my leg didn't want to bend from the hip. The rock in my groin was harder, and a ribbon of blush ran all the way down my leg.

I thought: Oh shit, and pried off my boot, which seemed embedded in my leg. I was glad I was already on the stool when I finally pulled my toe free because it hurt so badly I would have messed myself otherwise. Rolls of puffy calf and ankle flesh almost obscured my boot garter and I cut it off with my bandage scissors. The toe was red and twice as big as the other one, and the whole foot was bloated with edema. When I limped back outside, I shoved a thermometer in my mouth before doing Thai's treatment. I thought something was wrong with the thermometer. The mercury hit 105. I took three aspirin and left the rounds to Ryan.

When the shift was over, I reported to sick call and spent the next three days in my hooch soaking my foot in purple solution and popping antibiotics.

"Dear Mom," I wrote during that time, "I now know how it feels to be delirious. You wouldn't believe the dreams! And I think they may put me in for a Purple Heart on account of I got this service-incurred disability. . . ."

My toe was already turning toe-colored again, except for a slight residual purple stain, when Father O'Rourke made his sickbed visitation. The two of us sat in the lawn chairs on the porch outside my hooch and listened to my new Irish tapes, which had arrived from home a day or two before. The priest guzzled beer and I guzzled lemonade—alcohol interferes with antibiotics. I elevated my purple foot on the rail and tapped air in time with the music. It felt good to be alive and not in solitary and not baking with fever anymore.

And if there was any man I loved to hear talk almost as much as he loved to hear himself talk, it was Father O'Rourke. It was the brogue, mostly, of course, emerging deep and sonorous from that dark and burly man, who gave the impression of being large without physically taking up all that much space. He could have made supply memos sound like Shakespeare. Or Brendan Behan, more appropriately. But he was also a lover of music and books and knew more theology than what was in his breviary.

During the time I was recovering in my hooch, I'd had a couple of dreams about what I'd seen on the ward that night. While I could pass off Xe's light show as being due to my delirium, there had been too many other off-kilter occurrences between that old man and me for me to pass it off so lightly. The brilliant light had had a very spiritual feeling about it, and I thought it might be bound up with halos after all. Everyone kept telling me Xe was a holy man. Unlikely as it seemed, I wondered if maybe—*maybe,* because my illness had altered or expanded my consciousness as LSD was supposed to, I had been enabled to see his halo—maybe he wasn't just holy, but a saint or even an angel. Okay, so it sounded farfetched. But I hadn't expected to find bubonic plague in Vietnam either, and I had.

"Father, can I ask you a question?"

"After the song's over, my child," he said. The song was about an execution of an Irish patriot three hundred years before, and if I'd been paying proper attention I'd have noticed before I asked that Father had tears rolling down his cheeks.

When he'd mopped his face with a Kleenex, I tried again. "What I want to know is, who has halos and who can see them? Do saints have halos, or is it just angels? And can somebody be a saint without some sort of papal decision about it? I mean, could there be maybe Buddhist or Hindu saints that God knows about but hasn't let the Church in on yet? Could just anybody see their halos, if they let you?"

The chaplain glowered at me from under his bristling black brows. With such brows, he always seemed to be glowering, whether he intended to or not. "My dear child, what is it you're tryin' to do? Start another holy war? Is the one not enough for you, then?"

"No, it's not that, it's just that . . . well, when I first got sick, I was delirious, you know? And another time, I thought I saw—don't laugh at me, damn it, it isn't funny. I want you to regard this as being as confidential as if I were one of your patients."

"Flock."

"Okay, one of your flock. Even though I was delirious, I think this was sort of like a dream and it must mean something. I haven't experienced anything like it since I had the measles and heard this radio that wasn't really playing and smelled salted nuts when there weren't any in the house." I looked at him quickly but he had composed himself, his backwards baseball cap pulled down over his too assertive eyebrows, the words "God Power" machine-embroidered on the cap's hem. "The other night, when I first got sick, I thought I saw this giant halo that was all different colors and shapes around one of the patients, an old Vietnamese guy. And before, when the old man was in surgery, it looked like the major and our interpreter and Meyers and everybody had little halos too. Do you think, if the old man is a saint, well, could it be contagious some-how?"

O'Rourke tilted his cap back and stopped balancing his chair on the back legs, squarely setting it down. "Ah, life among the heathen isn't fittin' for ye of little faith, I see that now. Some of this Eastern stuff seems to be rubbin' off on you."

He was kidding me—the Irish always got a whole lot thicker when he was pulling your leg.

"What Eastern stuff? Halos?"

"Not halos, darlin' girl. The Holy Father holds the patent on halos and on saints and angels, since you ask. Auras, now. Anyone can have an aura. Buddhists and Hindus and the lot are lousy with them. They have quite a few over to Duke University back in the States as well."

"What did you call them?"

"Auras."

"Like the northern lights?"

"That's au*roras*, though I daresay it comes from the same root. Light, bands of light. Colored light, as a rule."

"Sounds like a halo to me."

"Only on your proper martyrs and such. Buddhists and them other Easterners are only authorized auras, martyrs or no. You mark my words, girl, and watch your step. They get you poor little lukewarm Methodists and all over here and pump you full of Asian germs and start showing you auras, next thing you know you'll be runnin' around shoutin' Harry Krishna and playin' with matches and gasoline."

The weather changed while I was on quarters. It started getting cooler in the evenings. At first I thought I just felt cooler because my fever had gone down, but long after I returned to work, the nights remained quite pleasant, balmy but no longer sweltering.

I'd walk home from the ward for midnight supper break and sit on the porch outside my hooch. At night everything was so much nicer. You couldn't see the barbed wire and the concrete and the raw plywood and sandbags and olive drab so clearly. The sky was black and velvety and star-studded, as glamorous as if there were no war on at all. Palms swayed on the horizon, and the South China Sea lapped gently at the beach. You could even forget the smell if there was a little breeze. I couldn't help thinking that if I were Vietnamese, I could hate the Americans on aesthetic grounds alone. Poor as the native houses and cities were, they blended with the countryside. Our compound reminded me of a strip mine I'd seen high in the Rockies. Everything else around it was breathtakingly beautiful and then there was this gutted mountain and a lake that looked like liquid cement.

On the way back to the ward, the compound was dark

and muffled, with only the red glow of a cigarette tip from the guard tower to remind you it was manned by a bored soldier with a rifle. Inevitably there was a little muted rock music from some corner of the compound, a radio turned down low.

The ward was quiet, too, those first few nights except for a whisper of pages turning in Ryan's book. I still took the flashlight and rolled Dang Thi Thai's graft, but now she sometimes slept through the procedure. I was more curious than ever about Xe, but he slept all night. Sometimes Ahn would wake up when I did rounds and climb into his wheelchair and come sit with me by the desk, watching with serious dark eyes as I charted or read or wrote letters. I showed him how to write his name in English and he drew the letters like an artist, his small grubby hands oddly graceful, the hooded light of the lamp at the nurses' desk gleaming on his bowl-cut black hair. He was very quick. The worst problem was keeping him quiet. Already his sessions with Xinhdy and Mai had him babbling away in fluent pidgin. Still, he would leave them to follow me if he thought I had a scrap of attention to spare him. I wrote my mother and asked her to comb the garage sales for children's clothes.

Evenings when I came on duty, Xe would be visiting with Dang Thi Thai or with Xinhdy. He nodded courteously to me if I happened to catch his eye, but otherwise paid me no observable attention, though sometimes I felt him watching me. I wondered about him more than ever. Thai always seemed to feel better after he left, but while her wound improved with each new procedure, the process was as long and gradual as Joe expected. I wonder now if Xe's power was really so diminished at that point, or if he simply felt that the hospital was the safest place for all of them to be.

Anyway, casualties came and went, including a pair of VC. I had no idea they were VC. They just looked like your average injured villagers to me, although, looking back, I remember them as a little more demanding and aggressive than most, but that could be my imagination. Anyway, one day they were admitted, seriously wounded, and when I came on shift again they were gone. I asked what had happened.

Mai chimed in. "Patients say they VC. Xinhdy say to

me if we not move VC patients, other patients kill them," and as she said the last she ran her finger across her throat.

"So where'd they go?" I asked.

"The POW ward," Marge said. "The MPs came and got them."

I tried not to wonder what became of them after that, and not to imagine what might have happened to us or our patients if Xinhdy and Mai weren't so close.

The last night I was on the ward was quiet and Xinhdy la daied me down to her bedside. She took my hand and looked at my ragged nails. "Numbah ten," she said and got out her file and polish and started giving me dragon-lady points. I let her. My work was caught up until midnight and I'd missed her cheerful, normal company. She more than anyone else let me imagine that at one time there must have been a happier kind of life in Vietnam, where people could be frivolous and worry about what was pretty.

"Kitty, when you fini Vietnam?" she asked.

"Oh, I still have months to go," I said.

"Good. I cry when you fini Vietnam."

"I'll miss you too," I said. "Do you think you might ever get to come to America?"

"I don't think so, but maybe. I like America. You know Hollywoo'? Vietnamee movie stars, they poor. Mai have more money than movie star. Not like Hollywoo'."

"I guess not. Why, do you want to be a movie star?"

"Hollywoo' movie star, yes. Vietnamee movie star not so good. My fam'ly say movie star not so good for Vietnamee lady."

When she gave me back my hands I resembled Madame Nhu from the wrists down, stiletto nails, blood-red polish, and all. But Xinhdy thought I looked glamorous.

When I got back to my quarters that morning, Julie Montgomery was waiting at my door. I didn't much like Julie, as I'd mentioned to Tony. She had two topics of conversation: how irresistible she was and how many men agreed with her. Most of the other girls disliked her, too, and openly snubbed her, but I'd tried to be at least polite. Being new in country wasn't easy. Still, I didn't welcome her visit. I had no desire to be bosom buddies with someone who was her own biggest fan.

"Kitty, I have to talk to you," she said, her voice carrying a tragic wobble to it.

"Sure. Come on in."

She stood in the doorway and lit a cigarette. Her gestures were short and jerky and she tried to make a tossing motion with her head, but hair as damaged by overtreating as hers doesn't move very well. In the sunlight streaming in the door, not one glint reflected off that pile of dead straw she had teased into a bouffant. "I couldn't bear the thought that you'd hear this from anyone else, so I decided, painful as it was, I had to come and tell you myself. You see, I don't want you to be *hurt.* You've always been nice to me. But he said—he said you wouldn't mind sharing. And since he's married, I figured it couldn't be really serious or anything and"—she giggled—"he's such a dish and he was so lonesome. . . ."

I had been getting her a Coke from the fridge, but I put it back and kicked the door shut. "Wait a minute. Are you talking about Tony?"

She nodded, giving me a soulful look through her cigarette smoke. "The way Carole Swenson acted, I thought maybe you might not know and I wanted you to hear it from me instead of her. Oh, Kitty, say you won't hate me forever. It was just a date and you *were* on quarters."

"Let me get this straight. Tony told you that he's married?"

"Well, yeah—"

"Thank you, Julie. I appreciate you telling me, but you'll have to excuse me now, I've got a murder to plan."

Well, at least I knew who the demure creature he wanted me to be like was. I supposed that was faithfulness, of a sort. I called Red Beach and told Tony what I thought of him and never to darken my doorway again. I surprised myself by not crying. Instead, I flopped onto my cot and read until I fell asleep, feeling strangely relieved for someone who'd been jilted, as if I'd just peeled out of a tight girdle.

At least now I wouldn't have anyone harping at me about being ladylike or nurselike or like anything else but myself, or as much of myself as I could still find after seven months in country. Tony's wife was probably having a ball at home. He ought to have sense enough to know that even his perfect wife would probably be a lot different if she were in my shoes. Being a dust-off pilot wasn't the only job that had to be done, after all.

I knew I'd miss him, but it was just physical, I told myself. Just because his legs were longer and prettier than mine, and his hair was so tritely perfect to run my fingers through, was no reason to fall apart. Just because his strong, beautiful fingers felt better than salt water and sun on my skin. In my mind's eye I saw him stride jauntily toward the pad. If only the jerk hadn't lied to me, damn him.

The monsoon drizzle started at around three that afternoon, in keeping with my mood. I didn't bother with a poncho but let the rain soak my red alligator-bedecked polo shirt. My flip-flops smacked against the wet cement walkway leading to the hospital and mail call. I didn't get mail, of course, but Marge Canon clutched another letter to her bosom, this one unstamped, which meant it came from in country.

"Kitty, you got time to come back to the ward for a cup of coffee? I want to ask you about something."

"Sure thing," I said, almost hoping she'd ask me to give up my afternoon off and work extra. I felt miserable and useless, and when I felt like that, the ward was the best place for me.

"Kitty, you ever been to Quang Ngai?"

"No," I said cautiously. Had I screwed up again or had it simply taken the powers that be this long to find somewhere to send me? "I never had any reason to. Why? Am I being transferred?"

"No, but I hope I am. Remember I told you about Hal? Well, he's in Quang Ngai now as hospital administrator at the 85th Evac. He wants me to try for a transfer."

Her eyes sparkled. I didn't know whether to be happy or bitter that at least somebody's love life was going well, but if anyone deserved to be happy it was Marge, so I said, "That's terrific, but when would you leave?"

"Oh, not till I'm processed. And after your promotion, of course. Which is tomorrow, by the way, in case you'd forgotten."

"Promotion?" I asked stupidly. Even though promotion to first lieutenant was supposed to be automatic, the brass could withhold or delay it, as Lieutenant Colonel Blaylock had pointed out to me on a couple of occasions.

"Don't look so shocked. You've grown tremendously since you came here. You're one of the best-organized charge nurses in the hospital and your rapport with the Vietnamese is outstanding. As a matter of fact, I shouldn't tell you this, but I'm putting you in for a Bronze Star and Joe is writing a commendation for your file before he leaves. And I'm recommending you for head nurse if my request for transfer goes through. So everything's going to work out great with you getting promoted right away. Lieutenant Colonel Blaylock wouldn't like leaving a second lieutenant as acting head nurse but plenty of first lieutenants are. So I won't have to wait until my replacement arrives in country."

When I arrived at work the next day, I walked about six inches taller and chirped my way around the ward with more energy than usual.

"*Good* morning, Melville," I greeted one of the GI patients, "How's the ankle doin'?" Melville had sprained it while stocking supply shelves. I suspected he had fallen off the ladder while stoned. He stayed stoned a lot, though nobody on the ward ever saw him smoke.

"Oh, sir," he said, "I think gangrene is setting in. Can I have a Darvon?"

Usually I would have snarled. Today the milk of human kindness filled my circulatory system.

"Of course you can, Melville. Just a sec." It was a wonder I didn't tell him to take two, they're small.

My promotion was held on the Vietnamese side, with Marge, Joe Giangelo, Sergeant Baker, Mai, and Voorhees in attendance. Meyers had been pulled to ICU.

I stood at attention while Marge read me the paper telling me in Armyese that I had met their requirements (though it sounded, in typically inflated bureaucrat language, as if I had won the Congressional Medal of Honor instead of merely an almost guaranteed promotion) and pinned a set of shiny silver bars over the embroidered ones on my fatigues that corresponded to a second lieutenant's butter bars. The shiny silver ones were for symbolism's sake. You didn't wear metal insignia on combat fatigues. I had learned this soon after coming in country, when the rationale of Army couture was explained to me by the supply sergeant. "No, ma'am. No shiny brass in the field. Sun catches on it and announces your arrival to the enemy, sure as shit."

But I looked at my new bars as if they were platinum and shook hands all around.

I felt a tug at my hip pocket and turned around to see Ahn wearing an officious expression. "Mamasan, mamasan, la dai. Chung Wi Long say you come."

Lieutenant Long, in the bed directly across from the nurses' station, was nodding a smiling endorsement of Ahn's summons. Long had been with us about two weeks. He was an educated man who spoke both French and Vietnamese and sometimes translated for us on nights. He'd lost a leg but seemed to have accepted his loss with equanimity. He was glad to be out of action, I think, but I wished we could medevac him too. After all, when the NVA took over, as seemed inevitable, Long would still be in Vietnam. I didn't think a disabled vet from the losing side would stand much of a chance.

I followed Ahn to Long's bed. In the next bed, Thai shifted painfully and gave me a tired smile. On the far side from us, Xe woke muttering from an afternoon nap.

Lieutenant Long cleared his throat. "Miss McCulley, you have promotion. You are now chung wi, same-same me, yes?"

"Yes. See my pretty new bars?" I flipped up my collar for him to admire them.

"Very nice." He reached under his pillow and held out a couple of small brass flower-shaped clusters, hooked together. "This is Vietnamese rank for chung wi. Please accept with my congratulations."

"Are these yours?" I asked.

"Yes. I have more. Please accept."

"Oh, I do. Thank you very much." And added formally, as I pinned them on my shirt pocket flap, where sometimes we wore extra little pins, unauthorized, of course, "I will wear this proudly. I feel very honored." And I did. Even though no extra pay came with it, I was almost more pleased at being promoted by Lieutenant Long than I was at being promoted by Uncle Sam.

Then, of course, Xinhdy and Thai and Ahn all had to admire my new rank, both American and Vietnamese. Thai bobbed her head respectfully. Ahn wanted to know if he could have my old ones. Even old Xe la daied me imperiously, gravely surveyed my new ornamentation, and nodded his approval. I patted his hand, despite his lordly air, and I thought his eyes brightened.

Xinhdy took out her lipstick and a Kleenex and polished the bars for me. It was the kind of totally off-the-wall thing she was always doing to try to please me, just because she was a generous and outgoing girl. I never got a chance to pay her back for her attempts to make me glamorous.

Sergeant Baker called me from the door. "Hey, Lieutenant, you got a visitor," he said.

I turned from Xe to see Ginger Phillips shuffle onto the ward, her hands on the shoulders of a gangly, crew-cut Vietnamese child in a faded pink dress.

They met me before I came around the bed and the child threw her arms around my neck. I returned her hug, though I was a little puzzled.

"Tran just wanted to say good-bye and thank you, Kitty," Ginger said. "She's going home today so she can spend Christmas with her folks."

"Cam ong, co," Tran said softly. "T'ank you." I had no idea what she was thanking me for, but I suspected Ginger had put her up to it. She had worked on ward six since a little before I had, and had continued to speak to me after my transfer.

"No sweat, Tran," I said, stroking her bristling head. The words had a hard time coming out. My throat had closed over and my eyes watered like an old woman's.

Ahn grabbed my hand as soon as I let go of Tran, and didn't release it until she left.

# 10

I was promoted on Wednesday, switched to days on Thursday. Sunday morning I worked alone on day shift. I walked onto the Vietnamese ward to find Sarah still running around trying to get morning meds and charting done. Her face was set and tight with emotion and she would not look at me. There was something else, too, something awful about the ward that made me stop at the door and hesitate to look around. My eyes went first to Dang Thi Thai and Xe, but they both seemed to be sleeping. I was noticing that the old man looked even more drawn and drained than usual when Ahn sat up, saw me, and catapulted into his wheelchair like a cowboy in a movie, barely stopping himself from knocking me over by throwing his arms around my waist and sobbing. I knelt down to pet him and that was when I noticed Xinhdy's empty bed.

"Sarah, where's Xinhdy?" I asked as casually as I could. She could have been in X-ray, or surgery. She was young and healthy and . . .

"Xinhdy died, Kitty."

"Died?" I asked stupidly. "What do you mean she died? C'mon, Sarah, get real. I'm talking about Xinh, in the last bed? She couldn't have died. All she had was a broken hip, for Christ's sake. She wasn't even on the seriously ill list. She wasn't *authorized* to die." I know that sounds like a bad joke to an outsider, but we had a seriously ill list and a very seriously ill list. If a patient was not on the very seriously ill list before he died, staff members were considered to be derelict in their duty.

Sarah didn't answer me, but Mai emerged from the bathroom. This time more than her hair was wet.

134

"Mai . . . ?" I began, still stroking Ahn's back and shoulders. Mai looked away, then covered her face with her hands, and I knew there was no mistake.

But there had to be. When I left the ward the night before, Xinhdy was perfectly okay. Well, she was restless and was sweating more than usual. She had a very slight temp, which I charted. I told Sarah in report I thought Xinh might be coming down with the flu. She'd been so cranky all evening Meyers had asked very carefully if she might be on her period. She kept thrashing around, shifting from one position to another, demanding that things be moved to accommodate each shift. This from the most self-sufficient bedfast patient on the ward. When the other Vietnamese visited, she complained to them in a loud voice until they left again, disgruntled. Still, I figured it was just a little upset. Hospitalized people can get colds and the flu too. My God, had I missed the beginnings of some horrible fast-killing Vietnamese strain of pneumonia? The empty bed stared blankly back at me. I expected a gurney to be wheeled in at any moment with Xinh in her hip spica cast leaning up on one elbow to smile and wave hello like a Rose Bowl princess as she passed the other beds on the ward.

"What was it, Sarah?" I asked. "Did she—was it some kind of flu? Were you able to get Joe?"

"Not till it was too late," she said. "He was over at that generals' mess at I Corps and didn't get back till later. Captain Schlakowski came over at eight and checked her but thought she was okay. Then we got three new patients on the GI side, and when I came back to do midnight meds Xinh was having trouble breathing. I was taking her pulse when she arrested. I started CPR while Ryan called a code and tossed me the ambu bag. The team got here right away but it was just too late."

"How could she arrest?" I asked. "She's twenty-two years old."

"I know, I know," she said, her voice getting softer and softer. "Joe came in to pronounce her. He said it was a fat embolism. Sometimes it happens with bad hip injuries who are bedridden for a long time. I never heard of that before, did you?"

"No—I—where's Joe?"

"In surgery with one of the GIs. I don't know how he

can do it, Kitty. He was more upset than anybody. Except maybe Xe. He woke up when the team brought the crash cart and I guess he was confused by all the commotion. He tried to get out of bed by himself and fell, then kept crawling toward us. It was awful," and now Sarah started to cry and I put my free arm around her. "I'm filling out an incident report now. . . ."

"Old guy's more trouble than he's worth, isn't he?" I said, but my voice cracked.

I didn't cry until toward the end of the day, though. You aren't supposed to cry in front of the patients, but that wasn't it. I just couldn't believe she was gone. Well, gone, yeah, but dead? I kept wandering back to her bed. The silence, without Vietnamese TV, was oppressive. Mai simply made herself scarce except when she had specifically assigned duties. The other patients slept, except for Thai, when I did her treatment, and Ahn, who clung to me and wanted me to carry him all day.

The day passed in a haze until mail call. I opened a care package from home when I got back to the ward. A nest of fat, bright yarn hair ties lay in the bottom and I pulled them out. My first thought was Xinhdy will love these; and then I looked at her stripped bed and gaping bedside table. My throat clamped down. I dumped Ahn in his wheelchair and bolted for the nurses' bathroom on the GI side. I don't know how long it took me to stop crying, but when I did, the fog had lifted and the pain had definitely set in. I wish I could say that I nobly comforted everybody else, but we all handled it as we handled most things in Vietnam, isolating ourselves from one another until we could convince ourselves that the anguish was nonsense, that war was a tough situation and you just had to do the best you could. The patients slept. Mai went home early. The corpsmen and Sergeant Baker furiously cleaned the ward as if the President were visiting the next day. Joe was a pain in the ass when he made rounds, ordering all kinds of useless things for patients he hadn't done more than cursory exams on for months.

On Monday, Sergeant Baker plopped a wad of R&R pamphlets on the desk in front of me. "Forms are right there, Lieutenant. Pick your spot, fill 'em out, and get the hell away from here while you still got the chance."

I leafed through them. The waters of the Great Barrier Reef looked abnormally blue, the mountains of Japan steep, and I already had a camera and a stereo coming from the Pacex catalog. As for the shopping of Singapore and Hong Kong, who needed sleazy silk clothes or outdated beaded sweaters? I couldn't work up any enthusiasm, yet I knew that Sarge was right, I needed to leave, and soon.

Heron was leaning against Xe's side rails when I returned from passing meds to the new GI casualties that day. He looked tired and ungainly, his body angling off in several directions to bring his face close to the still one of the shrunken old man. Xe's left hand fluttered like a moth until it lit in the medic's palm. As I approached them, the old man's eyes opened. His face was agonized as he looked up at Heron, like a dog asking to be put to sleep.

Without turning around, Heron asked, "How long has he been like this?"

"Since last night. He fell out of bed. He was trying to—um, he was—" I broke off and bit my lip, swallowed, and continued, "One of our long-term patients died last night. She was—a friend of Xe's. I think he was probably so scared for her he forgot he couldn't walk—"

"Who was it?"

"Xinhdy—Xinh. The girl in the last bed. It was—a sort of freaky thing. . . ." My voice died away as my throat closed off again. "I think—I think he's grieving—"

"That's putting it mildly," Heron said bitterly. Then he turned to face me. "Sorry, McCulley. But you have no idea how special this man is."

"I'm starting to. You've spoken of it before. And—some things have happened."

"Like the deal with the men on the other side of the ward?"

"Heron, I want you to know it wasn't that I didn't mean to help Xe. But I saw Meyers coming and I still had to dress Dickens's legs and I don't think the men would have really—"

He gave me a disgusted look. "Of course they would have. But I understand when you've got two patients who both need you, your inclination would be to stay with the white guy."

"That's a goddamn lie," I said.

"Okay, okay, cool it. Can you get someone to relieve you? Good. Then let's go for a nice walk. If you really want to know about Xe, I'll tell you. But I don't want to talk anymore in front of him and I don't much like spending time in rooms full of people. It makes me jumpy." He stopped, said something in soft Vietnamese to Xe, and bowed slightly. The old man wearily inclined his head and closed his eyes, his hands crossed on the amulet in the gesture I'd seen so often. Only this time it reminded me of the classic pose of a corpse holding a lily.

I let Sergeant Baker know I was going to be off duty for a few minutes and led Heron through the screen door at the back of the ward, through the curtain of rain draining off the roof of the building and onto the streaming sidewalk between the perimeter fence and the back row of Quonset hut wards. It wasn't raining hard then, but we were both wet in patches before either of us spoke again. A cool green smell wafted in from the perimeter, of ozone and fresh growth.

Outside I saw that Heron was in worse shape than I was, though not as bad as Xe. His eyes were infrared maps, and in the blue circles lining the sockets a large vein jumped. His mustache, waxed to ferocious points like the toes of Turkish slippers, twitched.

"Heron, I do care about Xe and I wouldn't have let anything more happen to him, you've got to believe that. I guess I just don't think on my feet that quickly and Meyers and Feyder were quicker. But I'm getting ready to go on R&R. Can Marge or someone on the ward contact you if anything happens to Xe?"

He shook his head dismally. "Nope. That's why I came over today. To say good-bye. I'm being reassigned to the field next week. I got in a little trouble I couldn't talk my way out of."

"Was it with drugs? Because I know you use pot—I saw you with Meyers and Feyder. . . ."

"Did you?" He looked mildly amused. "Is this a bust?"

"Come off it. What I mean is, you use drugs, well, pot anyway, you have access. I just need to know. The drugs aren't part of this power of Xe's you're talking about, are they? I mean, you don't have to be on something to see it? He doesn't, like, give people something . . ."

He stared me down. "What do you think?"

"I don't know what to think. You tell me Xe is some kind of native doctor and I've seen him get hurt twice trying to help other people, but the experiences I've had with him were like how I've heard LSD trips described. So when I saw you pushing pot to my corpsman and one of my patients, it made me wonder, you know?"

He looked down at his foot and nodded, his lips compressed. "Yeah, well. The smoking's got nothing to do with Xe, but I'll tell you how that is for me. I think we need a little light anesthetic sometimes to get through this war. A man who's good and stoned isn't so uptight he's going to go shooting up whole villages, you bic? But that's my thing. Xe doesn't need drugs for the kind of high he generates." He turned his back on me as if he had had the last word, and started walking back toward the ward.

I walked backward until I caught up with him, passed him, faced him. The sun came out behind him and I had to squint up. His lantern jaw shuttled back and forth beneath the pointy mustache. "Fine. I won't argue with you. Listen to me a minute, okay? Let me tell you why I even asked about drugs."

I told him about the ball of multicolored light around Xe and about the day I'd worn the amulet. "But was it really just that I was sick, or did I see something? Father O'Rourke said it could have been auras. Is that right? And if it is, why did I see them on everybody that one day when I wore the thingy he has around his neck, but then the other time I just saw his aura, but brighter, without wearing the necklace?"

"He allowed *you* to wear the amulet?"

"He insisted. He was going to surgery, and Xinh—I— he told her he wanted me to wear it if he was going to take it off."

"And you saw colors?"

I nodded.

"Shit. I wore it once, too, and I didn't see a damned thing. He's talked about you before, but he never let on that you'd worn the amulet. The way he explained it to me, the amulet is a sort of magnifying glass. It makes the auras of other people clearer to him, although he can see them, of course, without its help. But with it, he perceives physical and spiritual information about people that helps him heal them."

"I don't get it," I said. "It's usually pretty clear what's wrong with my patients, but I can't do anything about it just because I know what's wrong."

"Maybe not, but he can. The way I understand it, the amulet also amplifies his aura so he can use his energy to help someone else's. Before he got hurt he traveled all over the north part of the country—nobody ever gave him shit, not VC, not NVA, not ARVNs. Because he knew how to read them, how to heal the folks around, so that they always protected him from the hard-core badasses. Too fuckin' bad mortar shells don't have all that much of an aura." His voice was bitter again.

"How about the night I saw the ball of light, then?" I asked. "I wasn't wearing the amulet."

But he'd had enough of my questions and looked at me as if I were a sister who'd gotten more than her share of cake at his birthday party. He shrugged. "You said you were sick. You figure it out." And he returned to the ward to say a good-bye to Xe that I suppose both of them must have known was final.

When I dreamed that night it wasn't about R&R or about Xinhdy or Tony. I dreamed about Xe. I couldn't remember much except that he was floating around in a big balloon and seemed to be looking for something. I had the feeling he was looking for Heron, but I also knew, the way you do in dreams, that that wasn't quite right. And then I thought it might be me he was looking for and I wanted to tell him where I was, but Lieutenant Colonel Blaylock was hiding in the jungle somewhere with a rifle and if she found out I was watching that balloon instead of being back on the ward, she'd shoot me and make sure I wouldn't get my Bronze Star either.

I went to Taiwan for R&R. After Xinh's death and my cheerful chat with Heron, I couldn't bear to stay in Vietnam one extra minute. As soon as my papers were processed and Marge had rearranged the schedule, Sarge drove me out to the airport. Ahn rolled over on his stomach and wouldn't say good-bye to me, but Thai squeezed my hand and Mai handed me a folded paper fan. "Airplane too hot," she explained, fanning herself with her hand.

At the airport, the NCO in charge of the R&R flights said no way could he get me out. I started feeling panicky.

It was one day of my leave just sitting there. I told him to send me anyplace, anyplace at all, just get me out of country. He found one seat on a plane to Taipei. I didn't have the faintest idea what I'd do in Taiwan. The corpsmen told me proudly of their exploits and showed me photos of their bedroom-bound dates, but I was damned if I was going to spend my little taste of freedom from the 83rd in one lousy room.

Sick of the Army, tired of the military milieu in general, alone in a foreign country I had never explored before, I headed straight for the naval base. I don't remember why. Maybe I needed time to become acclimatized to a week playing tourist. But I found I'd been missing things I'd taken for granted, even despised, before. I met a Navy wife at the PX coffee shop and sat for hours drinking coffee and listening to gossip and routine marital problems that would have normally bored me stiff. It felt good to hear another woman, a non-nurse, nonmilitary woman, talk about ordinary, everyday housewifing business that had nothing to do with sickness or war or dying. I found her child-rearing traumas fascinating, her struggles with the base schools gripping. I cannot for the life of me remember if I even got her name.

After I left her I wandered around the commissary in a daze, and at one point stood between the rows of sugar pops and frosted flakes and remembered all my junk food breakfasts and Saturday morning cartoons and prizes and box tops and good old American come-on advertising, and I stood there and wept like a fool. I never thought I'd miss crass commercialism so much, and realized that I was capitalist to the core. I missed the damned radio and TV commercials. I wished Xinhdy could have seen, oh, a Maybelline ad, or a Clairol one. She'd have thought them very glamorous. On Armed Forces Radio, the only commercials were "Do preventive maintenance on your vehicle," and "Clean your weapon," and "Don't use captured enemy weapons and, if you happen to be an enemy listening, we wouldn't advise you to use your own weapons either."

Later I shopped and bought jewelry and presents for friends at the 83rd and the family and went to a Taiwan aboriginal dance where they dressed us visitors up in native costume and had us dance with them, something a lot like the squaw dances the Indians hold at powwows at home. I had dresses made and I smelled flowers and traveled inland to the gorgeous Taroko Gorge and saw a turquoise river flowing through the mountains and the marble factory. The funniest thing was getting on a FAT airlines plane and hearing only oriental voices and seeing only oriental faces all around me. I began to feel panicky when all the speeches by the stewardesses were in Chinese. To my relief, a man's voice with a heavy Australian accent announced that "this is your captain speaking." Of course, there are undoubtedly lots of marvelous oriental pilots, but I knew only of the mess the ARVNs made of our technical equipment, and the association was automatic.

I felt like a large barbarian, a feeling that was reinforced when I went shopping. I kept forgetting, surrounded by small oriental people, that I was no longer in Vietnam. I was looking at one ring in a jeweler's stall and said, "Oh, that one. I like. Numbah one." And the man in the stall said, "Yes, madame, that is an emerald of the finest quality. Would you care to try it on? Could I offer you tea, perhaps, while you are considering your choice?" I felt like a condescending fool.

And once my cab passed a construction site and somebody dropped a board or a hammer or something. I was on the floor of the cab before I knew what I was doing.

The driver was alarmed. "Miss, miss, you okay?" he asked.

"Oh, sure, thanks. Just—uh—dropped my contact lens. There you are, you little devil."

But the country was more beautiful than I had ever imagined, and I almost forgot about Vietnam in the fun of going shopping, dressing up and eating in nice restaurants. People were unexpectedly kind. I ran out of money before I could collect my developed snapshots and the man at the photo store told me not to worry, to send the money to him when I got back to Nam, no sweat, he had a brother who was a dentist in the States and so that made me okay too. And the girls in the hotel gift shop, where I had bought a couple of rings, called me over on my last day to give me a sack of dried pineapple as a going-away present.

I returned to the 83rd, if not eager to get back to work, at least eager to share my adventures with my friends and play Lady Bountiful with the presents: a book for Marge

and jade earrings for Voorhees's wife, a pirated rock tape
for Meyers and an ivory back scratcher for Sergeant Baker,
strings of beads for Carole and Judy, a woven Chinese
handcuff for Ahn, and a delicately carved wooden hair
ornament that struck me as something that would be beautiful in Mai's hair if she kept her locks dry long enough to
wear it. It cost maybe thirty-five cents in American money
and I intended to get her something nicer but ran out of
money. I felt guilty about being so chintzy when I had
been so little comfort to her over Xinh's death.

So I was surprised at her reaction when I intercepted
her and gave it to her.

"Very pretty," she said admiringly and handed it back
to me.

"No—it's for you," I told her. "I don't know if you
wear this kind of thing or not, but I thought it would look
nice in your pretty hair."

"For *me?* You buy present for *me?*" Her eyes started
filling as she handled it. "Thank you, thank you very much.
Is so beautifoo. Wait. I have present for you too. It not here
today. I bring it tomorrow—"

"Oh no, Mai, you already gave me a present. You were
right. The plane was very hot and I used your fan all the
time. I just wanted to bring you the comb because I think a
lot of you. It's so little really."

But the next day she was there with a bolt of purple
silk. She held it up against me, measuring. "It maybe too
long for Western dress."

"But that's good," I said. "I've really been wanting a
Vietnamese dress. I'll have mamasan at the gift shack
make me one. You always look so pretty in yours."

She took the cloth back. "No way you have her make
Vietnamese dress for you. *I* make you ao dai." The next day
she measured me for it and within a couple of days brought
it over to the ward, along with an invitation from her
family to come to the village and have dinner with them.
So far as I knew, none of the other girls had been invited to
a Vietnamese home. I had to get special permission, but
Mai was well known and liked at the 83rd and had doctors,
nurses, and corpsmen she had worked with in the past
writing to her from all over the world. Permission was
granted. The day we were to go, we both dressed in our ao
dais, my purple one so much larger than her little pink

flowered one, and Joe took our picture. We walked down the road unmolested though not exactly unnoticed through Dogpatch and to Mai's house. Her mother had fixed a chicken dinner and left the beak and the claws on top of the cooked meat so I would know that it wasn't dog or cat. Their house was large and spacious, with covered decks for eating and cooking and big fan-cooled rooms full of books. After dinner, Mai's brothers and I played guitars and I chatted with her mother while Mai translated. By then it was well after dark, and Sergeant Baker came for me in the Jeep.

I think Mai and I were trying to start a friendship that would expand to fill some of the gap left by Xinh's death, though we never spoke of her. But though the friendship was cut short, I remember that peaceful, relaxed evening with gratitude.

# 11

I had been looking forward to monsoon season as a break from the bleak simmer of the heat. The first weeks of rain were welcome, but soon everything stayed clammy with damp. The sheets were damp, the towels were damp, even my sweater didn't offer much warmth because it was damp, too. I worked an unexpected run of nights when Sarah caught amebiasis and had to lie on a stretcher and take I.V. fluids every morning before work because anything she ate or drank was lost to diarrhea and vomiting. The wards were cold in the daytime, and high winds brought storms in off the sea. Dressed in ponchos and wet jungle boots, we waded to work across half-submerged islands of sidewalk. About an inch of water covered the floor of the central corridor. The roof leaked and bedpans and urinals sat around everywhere to catch the drips while poncho-clad Vietnamese workmen crawled around on the roof, laboring slowly to plug the holes. Little lizards darted through the halls, and Ahn, now equipped with a crutch and a makeshift wooden leg Joe had fashioned from a crutch, limped after them with more agility than I would have thought possible.

Marge's transfer to Quang Ngai was reluctantly approved with the help of her boyfriend's connections. Joe's DEROS date was fast approaching, and between the two of them, you'd have thought the place was a photography studio instead of a hospital ward. We took turns snapping pictures of Marge and Joe, Marge with Mai, Joe with Mai, Marge and Joe together and separately with Ahn, me, Sergeant Baker, Voorhees, Meyers, Ryan, Thai, and any other patient or staff member who would stand still long enough to be snapped. Then we had to do more of the same because Marge's camera was a Polaroid and Ahn and Mai wanted duplicates of every picture with them in it.

Then Sarah suddenly got a drop because of her amebiasis, which meant they sent her home two months early to recuperate. I was pleased for her, but it made a lot more work for me, since her position and my old one were filled with two new nurses. I spent a lot of time being teacher. One of the new girls got amebiasis her second week in country and, like Sarah, had to report early for I.V.s every morning. She and Sarah left on the same plane.

Marge hugged me when it was time for her to leave. "You'll do fine, Kitty. Write and let me know how everybody is, okay?"

"Okay. Just take care of yourself and kick Hal in the shins for me for taking you away from us."

Soon to be ex-Major Joe Giangelo and another major made it to the door in time to block her exit. Joe grabbed Marge for a hug. "You be a good girl, Margie, and oh, I almost forgot, I have something for you here." His brown eyes twinkled as he handed her a couple of pieces of paper. "They're exercises to correct bowlegs—after you've been with old Hal for a while you're probably going to need them."

"Don't let me take the copies you were going to mail to your wife, Joe. How long have you got left now?"

"Six days four hours three minutes and"—he checked his watch—"twenty-one seconds. By the way, I'd like you all to meet my replacement. Major Krupman, Major Marge Canon, the best ortho nurse in Vietnam and possibly the entire military and an incredible fink who is splitting our fabled beaches. And this is Lieutenant McCulley, her second-in-command."

Marge said hi and then had to run for her ride. I said hi, but Krupman ignored it. "I'd like to make rounds now, Joe, if you don't mind," he said briskly.

"Sure thing. We'll start here."

"Here? But these aren't American servicemen, they're gooks."

Joe looked around him at all of the familiar faces and the few new arrivals. "No kidding? How about that? You mean you guys aren't from 1st Cav?"

Mai giggled. I decided it was a good time to get Thai up for her afternoon walk. Her grafts had taken and her hip was healed except for a single small area, from which a drain protruded. She had already walked twice. This time when I raised her, she only hissed between her teeth, but did not cry when I got her to her feet, slung her arm around my shoulders—which was a reach for her—and put my arm around her waist. She hissed again and groaned once.

"Sorry, Thai," I said. "Sin loi." I hated to hurt her.

She turned her face to me and on it was the biggest smile I had ever seen. She was walking. It hurt, but she was walking and she hadn't ever thought she'd do that again, the smile said. We made the route twice. In a couple of weeks the drain could come out and with a little help she could go home, wherever that was.

"Hey, Joe, look at Thai!" I said. Joe looked up and waved.

"Numbah one, mamasan!" he called to Thai from Xe's bed. "You gonna run footraces pretty soon."

Krupman straightened and glared.

Joe made rounds for three more days. Krupman usually made it just in time for the rounds on the GI side, but was unavoidably detained elsewhere when it came time to examine the Vietnamese. Even when Joe was not technically on duty, during the three out-processing days, Krupman didn't make rounds on the Vietnamese ward, despite our having a flock of new casualties, though he spent a lot of time patiently explaining back exercises to the incapacitated clerk-typist from Marine headquarters.

The day Joe got on the plane, however, I returned from lunch and saw that the new doctor had finally deigned to visit the Vietnamese ward long enough to stack a pile of charts where I could take off the orders.

The first chart was that of an old man with a fractured collarbone and possible pneumonia. He had had his arm in a sling and had had I.V. antibiotics for the last day or so. The new order said "Discharge," as did the orders on the charts of a girl with multiple shrapnel wounds to her lower body and a fractured humerus. The third discharge order was for Lieutenant Long, and already his bed was neatly made up and his bedside table cleared.

"Mai, did you see somebody take this order off already?" I asked, puzzled, since as the only nurse on the shift I was the only one who could pass along the orders to be carried out.

"No, Kitty. Chung Wi Long, he hear Dr. Krupman say, 'Send that man away, is no more we can do for him.' Chung Wi Long go."

"Go? Where can he go?"

Mai just looked unhappy.

"Does he have family here, Mai?"

Mai looked even more miserable and finally she mumbled that she supposed he must, and left.

"Sarge, Lieutenant Long just took off and Mai doesn't know where he's gone."

"Oh, yes, ma'am. Major Krupman said he could go. Only he didn't exactly put it like that."

"Go where? He's got one leg and no family around here anymore. He said they were all wiped out at Tet last year. Where could he have gone?"

Baker gave me a long look. It said I'd had a sheltered life and didn't understand much about people with no choices. It said what did I think happened to former Vietnamese officers with no family and wounds that left them helpless and dependent.

"Beats the hell out of me, ma'am," was all Baker said.

My hand went to my brass rosettes and my eyes swam as I opened the fourth chart, Dang Thi Thai's. "Transfer to Province Vietnamese Hospital," the order said.

I cleaned and dressed Thai's wound, helped her use her trapeze to swing herself free of the bed, and walked her, deliberately waiting until Krupman arrived the next day to talk to him about his preposterous orders.

He beat me to it. "What are these people still doing here, nurse? I have written orders that they were to be discharged."

"Xuan and Dinh are waiting for someone from their village to collect them, sir," I said. They might be waiting, but their village was near Tam Ky and their relatives had no idea how to locate them.

"How about the old woman?"

"I wanted to talk to you about her, sir. Thai's been making great progress—I'm sure Dr. Giangelo told you how hard we've worked with her, how hard she's worked, but she's not quite healed yet and—"

"Lieutenant, I am the physician here. I make that

determination," he said, despite the fact that he had yet to examine her. "She's on her feet. She's well enough to go to her own facility and give up her much needed space to a deserving GI."

"Sir, we haven't had to admit GIs to this side since I've been here and the census isn't especially high right now. We don't need the bed. There are four empty beds—"

"I've given you an order, Lieutenant. I expect it to be carried out. Do I make myself clear?"

"But, sir, when you've been in country awhile and seen what Province Hospital is like—"

"See here, young woman, I'm not listening to any more of these crappy war stories by you so-called old-timers. I want that woman out of here and I want her out of here now. Sergeant!"

He was talking to Baker. "Yes, sir," Baker said. "Voorhees!"

Voorhees dropped the thermometer he was about to put in Dinh's mouth. "Sergeant?"

"You heard the doctor. Get an ambulance and transfer the patient in bed four to Province Hospital ASAP."

"Yes, sir."

I glared at Sergeant Baker, but he didn't meet my gaze.

Voorhees moved slowly, rebelliously, but he was up for promotion, so he got the ambulance and he got the stretcher and he started loading Dang Thi Thai onto it. I went over to help, to try to reassure her. I don't remember where Mai was, but she wasn't there to translate or I would have tried to find someone else, a friend, a relative, to let them know about Thai's departure. I took her hand and said, "New doctor say you well, mamasan. Send you Province Hospital."

I hadn't gotten the words out of my mouth before she grasped my arm with both hands, digging in frantically with her fingernails. Her face, which had reflected slow and agonizing suffering for so long, was suddenly suffused with terror. "No, co! No!" She started climbing my arms, crying and begging. "Kitty, no—" Her eyes pleaded with me to change things, not to betray the hope and trust I had —we all had—encouraged her to have in us.

I held on to the stretcher, but Voorhees was pulling it away. Thai's nails grazed my arms as her hands lost their grip. Sergeant Baker tugged gently at my shoulders. "Come on, Lieutenant. No need to get hysterical over this," he said. "How many ladies like her you think are out there ain't had nobody to look after them?"

"No, Kitty! No!" Thai cried, but now Voorhees, who looked about to cry himself, was patting her and trying to calm her. He pulled the cart away from me and rolled her down the hall. I looked after them. Voorhees was still comforting, but Thai was silent now, her arms folded across her chest, her streaming eyes turned toward the ceiling.

I whirled around to glare at Krupman, but the bastard hadn't had the guts to stick around and hear her cry, so I glared at Baker instead.

"Thanks for the backup, Sarge," I said sarcastically.

"Don't go gettin' huffy on me, L.T. I just saved your butt. That doctor outranks both of us, and he said she goes, she goes. I didn't like it neither, but this is a war we got goin' on here. Lots of folks got less chance than Mrs. Dang out there on their own. At least he sent her to the hospital."

"You heard what Voorhees said about that place! She'll die there and she knows it." I was still shaking, so I concentrated on licking my finger and smudging the bloody tracks Thai's nails had left on my arms.

"You don't know no such thing, ma'am. It's the place these people would go to if we weren't here. They got their own ways, you know."

"I guess so," I said, and turned away because I didn't want him to see me crying. I was sitting at the desk watering the charts when I felt something warm close by. I turned slightly and Ahn leaned against me, nodding his head wisely, his eyes filled, not with fear, but with a mixture of cynicism and the sort of pity an adult gives a child the first time the child has a toy his father can't fix.

We got in a push of GIs later that week, and Krupman was too busy enjoying being a combat physician to banish any more of the native patients. I did my job and was barely polite, but as I worked with him that week and the next I couldn't help realizing that with the GIs he was a good doctor, caring, skillful, and thorough. I had to close my eyes and see Thai's face to remind myself what an ass he was. But I was beginning to be almost able to stand the man when Voorhees returned from the orphanage.

"We stopped by Province Hospital on the way back, Lieutenant," he said.

I was afraid to ask but I did anyway. "Did you see Thai? How is she?"

"She died a few days after she was admitted. Wound infection."

"Shit," I said, but that was all.

Mai returned from her daily shampoo in time to hear me. "What the mattah?" she asked, looking from me to Voorhees.

He told her.

I just sat there, and when I started to move, I felt as if I'd had a great big novocaine shot that affected my entire body.

Behind me, I heard the Vietnamese talking, but I didn't pay any attention. When it was time for dressings, I missed doing Thai's as I had every day since she'd left. Forty patients on the census, and I missed dressing one hollow hip.

When it was Xe's turn, I bent over to dress his stumps and felt his hands come up at the sides of my head. The numbness there began sliding away, and a deep ache replaced it.

"What are you *doing?*" I snapped, but then I looked at him to find in his face a perfect counterpart of my own pain and sense of failure. And I knew what had been slowly killing him. We were in the same boat, but his was sinking faster. We were both there to help, and he, who according to Heron had once been so much more powerful than I, was now even more powerless.

His hands, transparent as paper, hovered on either side of my head and he ignored my question but kept watching me. Something silken and balmlike touched the burning edges of the ache, then fell away. The sorrow in his eyes deepened even as he lowered his hands.

But the ache in my head receded and the numbness returned.

I walked away from the hospital, the cold afternoon drizzle soaking through my uniform. I didn't even bother with my poncho. I went straight to the club and knocked back three straight tequilas. The tequilas weren't so much to bolster my courage as to tranquilize me so I didn't attack

Krupman with my bare hands. Usually booze just makes me sleepy, but that night I had to quit drinking before I calmed down. The anger swelled up inside me till there was no longer room to swallow. I wanted Krupman to come into the club. I wanted to make a scene. I wanted to ream him out in front of everybody. But he didn't come, the bastard, so I staggered over to his hooch and stood there pounding on the screen while rivulets of water poured off my boonie hat and down my arms. The doctor was inside, headphones enveloping his ears while his reel-to-reel deck rolled shiny tape from one cylinder to another. He looked up, and no one could accuse him of undue sensitivity or second sight.

"What is it, Lieutenant?" he asked, almost amiably. "An emergency?"

"Not exactly," I said. "I just wanted to give you something to celebrate. I thought you'd like to know that poor woman you sent to Province Hospital accommodated you by dying. That seems to be what you wanted—"

He had lifted the headphones when I started to talk; now he tore them off his head and flung them on his bunk. "I didn't *want* anything one way or the other, Lieutenant. I just didn't give up my practice to treat slants." He picked up a photo of a group of people, and I admit I didn't register what they looked like because I thought he might be planning on using it as a weapon. "You see this boy in uniform here? That's my baby brother. He volunteered to be an American adviser and help these goddamn people and they let him walk into an ambush.

"I came over here to help boys like him and keep them from dying in this idiotic war. How people like that Giangelo guy and you can make pets out of the locals when you see what they do to your own people is a mystery to me, but as long as I'm in charge of orthopedics we are treating Americans, and the gooks can take care of their own. I'll tell you something else, Lieutenant"—his face was perfectly calm through all this and his voice was as even as a numbed-out marine's, though not as loud—"as soon as I have a little free time from the men who need me, I'm going to clean that place out, starting with those panhandlers who've been using up American medical supplies for the past few months. So you might as well start getting used to it."

He slammed the screen, then the inner door, in my face. As the door slammed, I saw him slip his headphones back on.

I could have pounded all night and been hauled off by the MPs, I suppose, but instead I sloshed back through the rain to the club to continue getting drunk. It wasn't my day. Tony was there. I hadn't seen him in weeks, except coming and going a couple of times from Julie's hooch. Carole had mentioned that they'd broken up and that Tony had cornered her and Tom to cry on their shoulders.

"Kitty, I have to talk to you—"

"Not now," I snapped. "Not ever. Let me alone, Tony. Take whatever you've got to say and put it in a letter to your wife."

"Don't be that way, babe. I didn't know it mattered to you. You were seeing Jake when I met you."

"I was not 'seeing' Jake," I began and then was just too tired to finish. "Look, I don't want to talk about it. I don't want to talk to you."

"Baby, I miss you. We're getting fired on all the time now. I almost got creamed last time." From his tone and the slight tremble of his perfect fingers around his drink, I thought he meant it this time. Usually, despite his fondness for military melodrama, Tony had as much faith in his own immortality as most of my patients had before they qualified as patients. But I, for one, did not give a shit what he believed.

"Tony, I'm sorry about that, but I have a few other things on my mind, all right? I'm cold and wet and I just finished talking to a so-called physician who cheerfully accepted that he murdered one of my patients and intends to go on murdering them, all perfectly legally and with the Army's blessings, because he blames *my* patients and maybe me for the death of his brother."

"He killed your patient?"

"Yes. It was Dang Thi Thai."

"The old lady with the hip?"

"I'm surprised you remembered. You never liked me to talk about my patients, if I recall. They weren't as interesting as your goddamn helicopters."

"Okay, okay, I deserve that, I guess. Carole tried to tell me a little how you felt, and believe me, I never thought you were cheap or anything. It's just, we were so good together I couldn't see why you couldn't just be happy with that. Why dwell on the war all the time?"

"I wasn't talking about the goddamn war. I was talking about my patients. The same way you talk about your fuckin' helicopters. It's my work and—and that bastard is destroying everything. . . ." I started bawling again, and could have shot myself for it.

But Tony had made up his mind to be charming, and I had forgotten how good at it he could be. He ran his hand up the back of my neck and kneaded, comfortingly, warmingly. "God, babe, I'm sorry. Tell me about it, come on. Let's go back to your place, or you won't be in any shape to do anyone any good."

I stopped crying before I told him because I didn't want to give him an excuse to hold me, much as I wanted to be held. He was unexpectedly concerned, however, and I remembered that a lot of my patients had been his patients first, in a way. He had delivered them. And Tony was a lot of things I didn't like, but for Vietnam, he wasn't much of a racist.

"Now he says he's going to do the same thing to the others—"

"Can't you head him off?"

"How?"

"I don't know. Where are they from?"

"Somewhere near Tam Ky."

"Okay, I'll check it out. If we can get some relatives up here, your patients will have someone to look after them at Province anyway."

He was talking about an awfully long shot and we both knew it. Uninjured Vietnamese were even lower priority than injured ones.

"Christ," I said. "It's like triage. It's bad enough for the new people, but old Xe and Ahn . . ." He reached over and stroked my cheek with that beautiful hand and gave me a melting look from those beautiful eyes and I almost fell into his arms. But I wasn't about to. Maybe he wasn't a complete rat, but Thai's death was the issue here, not my sex life or his.

"Don't they have anyone?"

"Nobody. Ahn's an orphan and Xe— Tony, do you know a Special Forces type named Heron?"

"Heron, Heron . . . no, babe. Sorry. I don't—sounds

familiar, but . . ." He let his arms raise and drop and the
pungency of his sweat rose up between us from the darkened green patches under the arms of his fatigue shirt.

"Will you ask around for me? Please? He's a friend of
the old man's. He got sent back to the field, but he might
be able to pull some strings and get Xe sent home. But I
don't know what to do about Ahn. If Marge were here
she'd know what to do."

"Where is she?"

"In Quang Ngai, with her buddy Hal, who runs the
hospital. If she hadn't left, that bastard Krupman would
never have gotten away with this."

"She knows the kid, Ahn, huh?"

"Sure. She knew all the long-term patients. Ahn's not
so sick, but his stump isn't all that healed over yet, even
though he has that prosthesis Joe cobbled out of an old
crutch. We've been waiting for a real prosthesis."

"He'd just sell it on the black market," Tony said.

I started to swing on him.

"Okay, okay."

"I'm sorry. You're right. But he doesn't have any place
to go or any chance."

"You could say that about half of Vietnam."

"Yeah, well, half of Vietnam doesn't call me mamasan.
Tony, I can't let him die like Thai, I just can't. Shit. If only
Marge were around."

"Well, hell, if she's the answer to everything, why not
take the kid down to her?"

"I can't. I—"

"I could. I go down there every once in a while. We
could go down and visit your friend and you could drop the
kid off."

"Is that—I mean, is it okay to carry a Vietnamese
civilian?"

"I do it all the time." He grinned. "Part of my job
description, babe, remember? And why do you care about
okay? You're the one who needs to get around regs now.
Just tell me when to pick you up."

"Well, I couldn't go—I mean, I'm on duty."

"You could go after, couldn't you? You're head nurse
now. Rewrite the schedule. Give yourself a day off. Nobody
will know. I'll have you back day after tomorrow night, and
if not, hell, what can they do, send you to Vietnam?"

"But couldn't you just find Marge once you get there and get her to admit Ahn?"

"Baby, I don't give a shit about Ahn, or Marge. I'm in this for ulterior motives, remember? I want my best girl back."

"Tony, you're married," I said wearily. "And you lied to me about it."

"Well, so what? She's not here and you are. Is it a deal or not?"

Thai's face flashed in front of me again and Ahn's sad, knowing eyes as Tony's scent smoked up my nostrils and his hand brushed my cheek again. "What you say, babe? Deal? Huh?"

"Okay."

"Seal it with a kiss?" His mouth came close to mine and his arms slid up mine.

"Tony, believe it or not, I'm just not in the mood right now."

He grinned. "I bic, baby. That's okay. I know a guy in Quang Ngai I can kick out of his hooch for the night. See you tomorrow."

"Tony?"

"Yeah?"

"You think this will work?"

"Sho 'nuff, baby. No sweat."

# 12

The atmosphere on the ward the next morning was as dismal as the weather. Navy-gray clouds rolled in from the South China Sea like tons of concrete, dropping rain in thick splats. The din of rain on a tin roof can be rather pleasant if you're inside. But combine the din with the discordant notes of those same drops plonking into basins and bedpans inside your shelter and the cursing of personnel tripping over the basins, and it's too noisy to think.

Sergeant Baker glowered at me when I came in and Voorhees declined to meet my eyes. I made old Xe's bed with him in it that morning. He was still asleep when I brought his medication, but his respirations were loud enough to be heard from several feet away over the rain. His chest sounded like a rattle. Ahn sat in bed and watched, his eyes as round as if he'd never seen anyone sick or hurt before. I thought again how quickly he had begun to act like a normal child. I wondered if I had done him any favors by convincing him that he could afford the luxury of a childhood, however brief.

The sheets I bunched under the old man were damp. Ahn slid out of bed, grabbed his crutches, and helped me. Watching Mai and the corpsmen, he'd learned to make hospital corners as sharp as any probationer's, and while he tucked, I rolled Xe toward me. When I rolled him onto his back again, his eyes were open—one of them, anyway. The other lid drooped heavily over the eye and the side of his mouth tugged at the corner. I grabbed a blood pressure cuff, but there was no particular change. At some point, while he slept, Xe had had a stroke. It could have happened to anybody his age, but combined with his amputations and the rattle in his lungs, it was ominous.

"Aw, shit," I muttered, half to myself, half to Ahn, who had moved to my side and was watching the old man as if he might explode. "Now I have to call Krupman in early." I couldn't help but take a hard look at Ahn.

"No, mamasan, no call bac si. He cat ca dao papasan, same-same Ba Thai. Mamasan, you make papasan numbah one."

"No can do, Ahn. Sin loi," I said, and started for the phone as Ahn continued his protests in ever-shriller Vietnamese. Xe's right hand curled over his chest like a claw, but his left one whipped out and grabbed my arm in a viselike grip.

He moved his mouth, but nothing save a dribble of spittle emerged.

"What did he say, Ahn?" I asked. "Does he need anything?"

"Papasan say he fini pretty quick."

"Give me a break, kid. You sound like Krupman now."

The right hand stayed hovering over the chest, but the left one steered my hand to the old man's neck and the thong, and my fingers found the amulet. Together we steered it back to its place over his sternum, and his good hand clamped mine over his bad one and the amulet. A violet-gray light oozed from him like a slowly spreading hematoma. I started to check his pupils, but suddenly life —real, knowing, painful life—leaped back into his good eye like a revived candle flame and focused on me. I felt as though we had clasped hands across a deep crevasse. I had seen, felt, such a thing from patients before, when they prepared to die, especially those who couldn't talk—this is who I am, remember me, it said. But never before with the bruising strength of will that flowed from Xe. In those eyes were my grandfather, great-grandmother, my favorite teachers at their wisest, my mother and father, Charlie Heron as I had last seen him, and another, stronger presence, a man who had been young and whom the war had made old, a man who had been even more than he was now—much more—and who was finally losing what was left. Those eyes held me fast, and then the power and the personality drained from them until only a stagnant pool was left in the good eye, which wearily closed for a moment.

I hugged Ahn close to me with my free hand. Papasan

breathed a deep sigh and opened his eye to fix it on us. He seemed puzzled for a moment, then the side of his mouth that was not drooping downward twitched up. His good hand nudged mine toward his chin.

"Xe want you take his joolry, mamasan. Same-same last time."

I rallied from the impact of that compelling stare, which had made me feel almost that I was Xe instead of me. I couldn't stop to think about it until after I'd taken his pulse, called the doctor, done what I could to preserve his life. I tried to untangle my hand from his so I could take his pulse. Refusing to release my hand, however, Xe carried it with him as he nudged at his amulet again. I had to take a set of vital signs before Krupman arrived, so I did as Xe insisted and removed the amulet. If Xe died, my logical side insisted I'd save it for Heron. I was just kidding myself—I knew there was more to it than that—but for Xe it was enough that I took it. He didn't insist I wear it this time, and as soon as I stuck it in my pocket, he relaxed.

Krupman had barely begun his examination when Xe expired.

"Well, Miss McCulley," Krupman said, "looks like your hangover from your little toot last night prevented you from giving decent care even to your pet gooks. He's dead. Perhaps if I'd been called sooner—"

"If you'd been called sooner you could have sent him to Province to die, right?" I demanded.

"That's it!" he said. "I've put up with you about long enough, young lady. You're earning yourself an Article 14."

I bit back what I would have said if I could have afforded to spend my afternoon at attention in Blaylock's office.

"I'm sorry, Doctor," I said more meekly than I would have thought possible. "But I called you as soon as I could. I didn't want to leave the patient alone." Yeah, Doctor. Unlike you, I care about my patients.

"I want those other people out of here by tomorrow morning. And I'm discharging the amputee kid."

I didn't say anything. I couldn't agree with him or he'd be alarmed, and since I already knew what I was going to do, I had no reason to disagree with him. So I shut up.

"Lieutenant?"

"Sir?"

"I mean it. I expect these patients to be gone when I return in the morning."

"Yes, sir," I said, and did busy work on the other side until he left the ward to go to surgery and heal the patients who *deserved* treatment.

Tricking Voorhees wasn't necessary. Fortunately, Sergeant Baker had a long ward masters' meeting and a farewell party for the command sergeant major of the hospital. So I refrained from telling the corpsmen about the transfer until the end of the shift. Then I gave the fastest report in nursing history and announced that I was going to ride along in the Jeep. But as Voorhees and I rolled Ahn's wheelchair out the door of the E.R. toward the motor pool, Tony landed. He cut it a little close to suit me, but he was there.

"Oh, wait a minute, Gus, will you?" I said. "Tony will want to say good-bye to Ahn."

I had to shout over the ripple of the blades. The spin and wind of them blew rainwater everywhere and lifted my poncho up over my face.

"What's going on, L.T.?" Voorhees shouted, trailing me to the pad. I helped Ahn out of the wheelchair and handed him his crutch. I didn't want to get Voorhees in trouble, but then, it wouldn't be so great if he reported me as AWOL the minute we left the pad.

I leaned over and cupped my hands to the corpsman's ear and shouted, "We're taking Ahn to Major Canon in Quang Ngai."

He shouted into my ear, "Krupman will have your ass."

I shouted back, "No way. He just wants the kid *gone*, bic?"

Voorhees seemed to think this over for a split second, then pulled back and gave me a wide grin and a thumbs-up sign. "All *right.*"

I climbed aboard the chopper, pulling Ahn in after me. Lightfoot, Tony's crew chief, handed me a pair of earphones, and the avalanche of noise around me dulled to a vibrating thunder. A splatter of CB-style radio talk passed between Tony and the ground and then we lifted off the pad like a pregnant hummingbird.

"Welcome aboard, babe." Tony's distorted voice crackled into the mike. "Want to sit up front? It's more comfortable."

"Nah, I'd better stay back here with the kid in case he gets scared."

"A gook kid? Scared of a little chopper ride? You gotta be shittin' me." But he didn't repeat the offer. Lightfoot knelt by the open door, watching the country go by. Gusts of rain swept in and I tugged my poncho tight around both Ahn and me for warmth.

Tony kept to the coastline at first, the sky drab pewter, the beach pale, the rain and sea shiny, and the jungle a brilliant ribbon of variegated green. Perfect squares of fishnets were suspended above the water all along the coast, isolated from the shoreline. I wondered how they caught fish in them. Ahn kept shouting curious questions at Lightfoot, who grinned and pointed at things.

I settled down amid the olive-drab-painted metal and webbing. Whew. So far so good. We were getting away with it. A little rush of excitement and anxiety zipped through my nervous system, only to be replaced by depression. Out of all those people I'd cared for all those months, I could save just one. Maybe. Xinh gone, Thai gone, and now Xe. When that guy said war was hell, he wasn't just whistling Dixie. I was racking up a body count a marine would envy. Ahn flipped water from a fold in my poncho and smoothed it across my lap, before laying his head in it and falling asleep.

Seeing little but sea, most of my hearing blunted by the roar in my earphones and the occasional staticky chatter, I soon grew sleepy, too.

Some time later, Tony's voice crackled in my ear. "Hey, babe?"

"Yeah?" I mumbled into the mouthpiece.

"You know that guy you told me to ask about—Heron?"

"Yes," I said, a little more alert. Heron would want to know about Xe. He'd be glad I saved the amulet. Even if he didn't want to use it himself, he'd know who should have it.

"I kinda found out and I kinda didn't. He's off in the field somewhere, but the mission is classified, no contact. Sorry 'bout that."

And after another minute, "Babe? You okay?"

"Yeah, sure, I'm fine, Tony. The old man died earlier today, did I tell you that? I just wish Heron could have been around." I fingered the cloth of my pants pocket where the amulet lay. The headphones went staticky-silent for a moment, and then Tony was humming "The 59th Street Bridge Song."

I was sleeping again when we got hit. I felt the chopper lurch and snapped awake, thinking for a moment we'd landed. It was too noisy to hear the round striking the bird. But when my eyes flew open, I saw Ahn's head raise up for a split second. His eyes glittered like a trapped animal's, then his skinny little arms covered his burr crew cut and he curled into a protective ball.

The round hadn't wakened Lightfoot and I thought it should have. Surely when Tony started dodging bullets the crew chief would have duties. And sure enough, Tony's voice called, "Tonto? Hey there, kemo sabe—Ben?" and he started to turn around. But I realized it was too dark for him to see anything and too dangerous for him to let go of the controls, so I unbuckled myself and crawled over to the crew chief, shaking his foot to wake him, as I had learned to do with the combat troops.

The foot flopped and I noticed that one of Lightfoot's arms was dangling out the door. I thought we ought to close that sucker anyway. I started to tug on him, and then I noticed the blood on his chest. I dragged him in and felt for a pulse, found none. I didn't expect to.

"Lightfoot's hit," I told Tony. "I think he's had it."

"Well, do CPR, for Chrissakes, while I try to find Quang Ngai. . . ."

I was way ahead of him, working on Lightfoot even as I tried to remember what I'd been drilled on with a plastic doll but had never had to do to a human being—clear the airway, tilt the head back, pinch his nose, take a deep breath, and cover his mouth with mine. His mouth smelled sour, and when my finger came away from feeling for the airway, it was smeared with blood. I breathed in anyway, and pumped on his chest, but all that did was force more blood out the mouth and the wound. God, Lightfoot, you could give a girl a little help here, I thought, but I knew I was working on a dead man.

"Get away from the goddamn door," Tony barked over the roar. I started to haul Lightfoot with me, but he was a big man, awfully heavy, and his foot caught on some webbing. Then the chopper lurched again and outside I saw a red tracer round streak past us. I couldn't help but remember what they'd said in basic about the red cross on medevac choppers making such a great target.

I was trying to dislodge Lightfoot's boot from a piece of webbed strap when another round hit, and Lightfoot's body jerked again. The chopper lurched and I fell backward as another round exploded through the metal floor of the chopper's belly, right behind me, and another. I abandoned Lightfoot and grabbed for Ahn, huddling against the metal pole that held the rotor.

The rounds kept coming and Tony was trying to fly us out of range, but something was wrong with the rhythm of the blades. Even I could tell that. Instead of a steady "thucka-thucka-thucka" there was a jarring grind every few beats. I lifted my earphones. I could feel the chopper's damaged heartbeat through the floor, through the walls, through my skin, and deep inside my guts—my hips and the backs of my thighs tightened every time that beat missed, every time a round hit. Ahn grabbed for my neck like a drowning boy just as the chopper wallowed onto its side, the open door yawning beneath my boots. Lightfoot's body was lodged between me and the opening or I would have fallen out then. Somehow we had left the ocean and were now heading over tall elephant grass toward an endless tangle of trees.

The taste of Lightfoot's blood in my mouth made me want to vomit, but Ahn had hold of me and I had grabbed on to one of those webbed straps and was pulling myself up as Tony righted the chopper.

"You okay, babe?" Tony's voice, crackly and almost unrecognizable, came through the earphones.

"Yeah—I think so," I said. Okay considering the circumstances. I fumbled as I talked. The wire to the headphones had wound around my neck and the mouthpiece, and I had to untangle it and pry Ahn loose before I could move freely.

"Kid too?"

"Him too. How about you? You okay?"

"That's affirmative."

I drew a deep breath. Good. Tony would get us out of this. He had been in plenty of scrapes before. This was only going to be a tragic delay. Everything was under control.

"Babe?"

"Yeah?"

"Listen, there's a field of elephant grass up ahead. I want you to push the kid out and jump, got it?"

"Jump?"

"Do it, dammit."

"Yeah, but . . ." What about him? He must have some idea how to maneuver the bird to safety but couldn't do it with us aboard. He wouldn't ask us to leave unless he had a plan. He'd get us out of this somehow. He wanted to get laid, didn't he?

The chopper jerked and shuddered over the elephant grass, and blades licked the sides of the open door. Ahn clutched me convulsively. I crawled over Lightfoot's body, trying not to step on him, wishing I didn't have a corpse to stumble over.

The broad grassy valley swept beneath us, the elephant grass rippling from the wind of our blades, spewing rainwater everywhere. The patients had shown me pictures of themselves in the elephant grass. The grass, which looked so soft, stood a good three feet above the heads of the tallest men.

The chopper convulsed and Ahn twisted away from me and dove through the door, the end of his crutch peg leg disappearing last. I grabbed for him—he couldn't jump with just one leg like that, surely—but the headphones tugged on my ears. I ripped them off and turned to set them behind me and saw Tony turn and rise in his seat, his mouth forming a scream: "Jump!"

From overhead came a horrible grinding and the floor fell out from under me as a blade sheered through the front windshield, metal, controls, and all, and through Tony, vertically, spraying me with his blood and burning me with its speed as it brushed past me and cut into the floor.

I didn't have to jump. The floor was somewhere to my right and down a foot or so and the chopper in a roll. I tumbled through the open door, scraping against the raw edges of the new holes in the red cross on the chopper's belly and dropping past the remaining prop, still swinging like some berserker's sword blade as it sliced the air and grass where my body had been just before.

The ground smacked up with a bone-jarring thud, and for a moment I was caught between the hard ground and a flattening wind as the chopper crashed past me, mowing a path through the elephant grass before exploding with a roar of flame and shrapnel that made the ground buck up under me again. The stench of hot grease, hot metal, and gasoline and the stomach-churning stink of burning flesh boiled into my eyes and nostrils, so I started choking and crying at the same time. One of the chopper blades poked out of the flames like the handle of a saucepan from a campfire.

I don't know how long I gasped and coughed and watched the billowing black smoke from watering eyes before the full impact of what was happening hit me in a shock wave harder than the blast of the crash.

All at once I took it in, along with the smoke, along with the heat of the flames, along with the rain: this was not me overdramatizing, this was not a movie, a joke, a stunt, or a nightmare. Tony was not going to come walking from the flames. What I had seen before I fell meant that he had died before the chopper caught fire. It's hard to scream when you're gasping for breath and gagging on the air, but a scream swelled up inside me and started to force its way out my open mouth. Maybe it was because that's what women always do in the movies, but I had to cry Tony's name, had to keen for him—

A bony arm slammed between my teeth. "Em di, co," Ahn pleaded, his voice a low hiss. His all too familiar tears were coursing down his cheeks again, and the sight of his frightened face jerked me back to my own responsibilities, which were to the living, Ahn and me. Tony would be really pissed if he knew I blew the chance he gave us by screeching our position to whoever had fired on us, or got roasted in the Vietnamese equivalent of a prairie fire while paying noisy homage to his memory.

Ahn already had his arms around my neck and I hoisted him up, piggyback, and ran for the trees. Every time my foot hit the ground I thought about land mines and unexploded bombs and trip wires. Every yard closer to the trees I wondered who was in them, if we were already in the cross hairs of a sniper's rifle or were running into a Vietcong ambush.

# PART TWO

# The Jungle

# 13

I tried to think what to do, where to go. In the States I would wait calmly by the wreck to be rescued. Here I might not want to meet the fire department, if it did come. Quang Ngai had to be around here somewhere—maybe a few miles, maybe more—but I didn't even know my directions here. And I couldn't remember what the hell it was the sun did, except that at noon it was in the middle of the sky and at night it disappeared, if it bothered to appear during the day at all, during monsoon season. VC would be all over the jungle, probably, but they'd see us even quicker in the high grass, if they hadn't already. I was glad Ahn had kept me from screaming. No need to announce that all of the occupants of our chopper hadn't perished.

Thinking about that put me in a funk again and I stopped, a little inside the forest, and stared off into space, my mind floating for a while. I wished I could float my body right after it and float away. When I looked down, Ahn was looking up at me anxiously, and also somewhat speculatively. I frowned down at him. He was probably calculating how much an Army nurse captive would bring him from the VC. The Army had warned all of us girls that we absolutely mustn't allow ourselves to be captured—in case any of us had been considering doing so for kicks, I guess. The propaganda value would be too great, they said. They would waste too many lives trying to get us back, they said. And, oh yes, the enemy would do terrible things to us. No doubt. I shivered and backed off a pace from Ahn, whose face suddenly broke into one of his monkeyish mugs as he began to cry in earnest.

I pulled him to me and smothered his sobs against my fatigue shirt, as much for both our safety as his comfort.

Poor kid. He'd already learned that his own parents weren't omnipotent enough to prevent their deaths and his injuries. Just when I'd made him feel safe and cared for, my grand plan to protect "my" patient had landed us both in this godawful mess, had cost Tony and Lightfoot their lives. I wanted to comfort Ahn but I started crying too.

We couldn't stumble through the jungle crying. We'd get blown up or caught for sure. Besides, I didn't want to get too far from the chopper wreck. Maybe it would draw some of our guys to see what happened. And I had the vague idea that maybe, after the smoke had cleared and things had cooled down, I'd find something in the wreckage that would help us. All I had with me besides Ahn was my poncho and my ditty bag, still tied around my belt loop, where I hung it when I didn't want to risk leaving it behind but wanted to keep my hands free.

I dug into it and pulled out a bag of M&M's, tilted Ahn's head back, and popped one in his mouth. "There, babysan, numbah one, eh?"

He wouldn't be comforted but chewed and cried at the same time.

"Look, honey, I couldn't agree with you more, but we have to do something."

The obvious answer was directly overhead, in the branches of the trees, which I figured, despite my conviction that everything in this jungle was out to kill me, would be the best possible cover. After all, hundreds of VC snipers couldn't be wrong, could they?

I pointed up to Ahn and gave him a boost. He shook his head and pointed to his makeshift prosthesis. I cut the bandage away with my scissors, and immediately realized I should have unwound the gauze and tape instead and saved what I could. God alone knew what we were going to need before we were—before whatever was going to happen to us happened. With the bandage gone, I gave him a boost and he grabbed on to the lower limb and swung up on it like the monkey he resembled when he cried. There was plenty of vegetation to use for foot and handholds and I was not many years removed from my tree-climbing days on the elm in my parents' yard, so I scrambled up after him and urged him to a higher branch.

We settled in like a pair of geese trying to roost where the hawks would least expect to see us. I fed Ahn another couple of M&M's and started to put them back without having any myself, since I was going to go on a diet. Then I remembered where I was and popped two, chewing them mechanically, looking out toward the red and black of the monsoon-drenched blaze. Though the area right around the chopper was still burning pretty hot, the elephant grass had charred out a fair distance from the wreck and died out, so at least we wouldn't be fried in our sleep.

Ahn had snuggled into a crook of a branch and fallen asleep. My bulk wasn't so easily accommodated. At least we were out of the rain, though we were both soaked from the grass. I thought of Tony, and of what we should have been doing right now—and I thought about all the things I would have done for him before, all those little things he liked so much, if only I had known. But who would have thought such a chickenshit would turn hero on me like that? My mind was racing too much to sleep, I was too scared, too relieved to be alive, too worried, too bewildered, too aggrieved. My nerves were jumping along the back of my neck, down my spine. Or was that bugs? There were certainly enough of those in the tree, though by and large the rain kept them from being too fierce as long as it lasted.

My ditty bag contained a change of dressing for Ahn; three bags of M&M's, one plain, two peanut; a can of shoe-string potatoes; six packets of fizzies; a comb; lipstick; change of underpants; and wallet. My fatigue pants held adhesive tape, scissors, scraps of notes I'd written to myself, a discarded medicine card, a small flashlight, pens, a pencil, several I.V. needles and a couple of syringes I'd neglected to discard, and Xe's amulet.

A spasm of bitterness swept over me as I fingered it. My mother hadn't warned me about days like this. She'd never dreamed there could *be* days this bad: starting with Xe's death, ending with Tony's and Lightfoot's, and me, an unathletic, very conspicuous uniformed woman, stranded with a one-legged child she could barely talk to in terrain she hadn't the foggiest idea how to handle. Where were all those goddamn marines when you really needed them?

I fell asleep wondering how I was going to explain Tony's death to his wife—I would have to do that, I figured, if I got out of this all right. I owed him that—or maybe that was exactly what I didn't owe him. No, no, I could lie and say I was medical escort for a critically injured child Tony was flying to emergency care and—oh, what the hell. How was the Army going to explain *my* death to *my* family? At least Ahn didn't have that kind of problem.

I'd been turning the amulet over in my hand like one of those jade egg-shaped worry stones I got in Taiwan. The worn old glass reminded me of Xe and the hospital and safety and of Charlie Heron, burned out and idealistic at the same time. I slipped it around my neck. It hadn't been such hot luck for either one of them, but Xe had died an old man at least. Anyway, it couldn't hurt. I fell asleep with it around my neck, my thumb tracing its smooth contours.

I slept very poorly. The foliage had shielded us from the worst of the rain initially, but soon the wind changed direction and we were taking the full force of it. The poncho kept blowing up over our heads. And I had fitful half-dreams full of fear that I would make noise and reveal our position, and self-reproach that I really didn't seem to feel all that much about Tony and Lightfoot dying. Why wasn't I grieving? Tony and I had been lovers for three months. He given his life to save ours—well, for the time being at least.

And instead of thinking nice thoughts to send him to heaven with, an ungrateful bitch inside me kept muttering, *Women and children first, huh? Thanks a lot, Tony. Now what do I do? You're the one with the survival training, the combat conditioning, all that good shit. What am I supposed to do when people try to kill me? Punch 'em with my bandage scissors? My recruiter told me this would never happen to me. The Army wouldn't let it—guess we outsmarted the Army, huh? They probably told you you'd never get knocked off those gorgeous pins of yours by a helicopter prop either.* And I would try to make myself cry, forcing up memories of those long legs storking about my hooch as he sipped a beer or smoked a joint, the smell of his skin, the feel of his curls, the way he felt inside me. Funnily, all I could remember of his eyes right then was those damned mirrored shades.

I knew it was healthy to cry, and this might be my only chance, but I just kept wondering hopelessly how we were going to get out of there. How I didn't even have the pioneer woman's traditional last round to use on myself if capture became inevitable. And even if we never saw a

VC, what would we eat? Where would we sleep? How would we keep from being blown to pieces by all of the things that were all the time blowing my patients to pieces? And we would get nowhere fast—Ahn's prosthesis, which worked well enough on the level concrete floors of the hospital, was going to be a problem in mud and rough terrain.

I opened my eyes in the middle of this rambling anxiety attack passing itself off as a dream and realized that I must have been sleeping in spite of everything. It was now fully night, with a steady hard pour. Across the elephant grass the chopper sat in a blackened circle, glowing with heat and little interior fires. And around it other things glowed, like huge fireflies. I could see the lights clearly through the rain, the elephant grass, and the darkness, but the funny thing was that many of the colors were not bright or light ones but dulled down—a brown glow, a taupe one, wine-colored, teal, brown with red spots, olive, rust, and even, I swear it, a black glowing deeper and hotter than the blackness around it. These mixed and wavered and changed often, but they danced around the chopper like so many Tinker Bells. And as my eyes adjusted, I saw within the glow people in military hats a little different from ours, with rifles in their hands. They were digging around the helicopter, looking for the bodies, I supposed, or usable debris.

I jumped as something touched me on the shoulder, and looked up to see Ahn, encased in a pale green glow sparked with grayed violet, putting his finger to his lips. I nodded.

The fireflies poked around for some time, then fanned out, looking up and down, side to side, rifles ready. I always knew where they were, however, thanks to old Xe's handy-dandy cosmic gizmo. Everybody was lit up like a Christmas tree.

A teal-blue glow stalked through the elephant grass, toward us, then below us, and at first I wanted to shut my eyes so the woman with the rifle couldn't see me. Because light was pouring from me, too, just as it was from Ahn, who was wrapped tightly around his tree limb, gray-violet rays of radiant fear leaking from him.

But the closer the woman got, and somehow I knew it was a woman, a girl really, even through the blinding rain and her personal light show, the more I felt I knew about her: *Poor kid, she's so heartbroken she doesn't even know how scared she is.* And the closer she got, the more the light grew distinct, into separate colors, brown overpowering the teal, gray-violet overpowering both, all three colors blending into one another before bleeding from her into the darkness, not in beams, the way you'd think light should, but in droplets, like tears. And the whole time her rifle was at the ready, waiting for us to make a false move.

We didn't, though. We lay there barely breathing for what seemed like hours, until, when I looked around cautiously, I could no longer see any of the nine glows I had counted—two mostly teal, three mostly brown, an amber, a rust, a black, and a dull red.

I patted Ahn on the arm and the little brat yawned at me. He'd gone to sleep, rain and all. "Come on, babysan, I think we better didi mau."

His purplish gray had been superseded by a brighter red and green which I knew, don't ask me how, were much healthier colors for a growing boy. The green was a shade that spoke of growing things, similar to the faint phosphorescence that was the aura of the tree that hid us, the plants all around us; the red, vital and strong, qualities in Ahn that were obvious watching that one-legged boy shinny back down the tree.

The sky lightened a little in one direction and the sun peeped out beyond the rain, splashing a rainbow across the sky. It seemed inappropriate, under the circumstances, but it had its uses. I didn't know if Vietnamese kids were ever boy scouts, but I thought they might have survival skills little girls who were bookworms in Kansas City might not have mastered. "Ahn, can you tell from the sun which way is the sea?"

"Sure. Sea that way," he said, and pointed toward the wrecked chopper.

I wondered how he knew, but even if he was wrong, it was someplace to start. I had about abandoned hope that another helicopter would arrive to find out what happened to the first one. If it did come, I hoped the will-o'-the-wisps from the previous night would be far away.

I found a stout stick and handed it to Ahn. "Babysan, you use this for crutch."

"No want stupid stick!" he said, his face screwing up

for a good cry as he poked through the underbrush below the tree until he found the piece of crutch that had been his prosthesis. "Want leg Bac si Joe make for me."

Kids. I humored him. Let him determine for himself what was going to work for him. I rewrapped his stump and bandaged it into the cup of the makeshift prosthesis.

The elephant grass gave off a faint greenish radiance, punctuated now and then by varicolored sparks as insects and lizards darted past us. I was glad for the cooler, damper weather and the wind. The bugs weren't so bad now as they had been earlier in the year. I took the lead, with Ahn just behind me. I watched the ground carefully for the sort of traps patients had told me about: punji sticks, trip wires, any trace of recently disturbed earth where mines could be buried. The VC might hope as I did for a second helicopter to investigate the loss of the first one. If I'd been them, I would have laid a trap for it.

I was not reassured when I didn't spot anything. After all, most of my patients had had far better training than I had before they became patients, and obviously they hadn't spotted anything either. I stopped short of the charred remains of the chopper. Fortunately, it didn't look as if anything remained that would have been of any earthly use to us, because I sure wasn't going to wade through that mess of smoldering wire and metal to find out if the wreck had been mined.

Ahn tried to take my hand, but it was shaking so hard he had trouble catching hold of it. His was small and hot in mine but reassuring nevertheless. My knees kept trying to fold and I had a queer, dizzy sensation. The color around me was mostly gray, though Ahn's aura by now showed a little less gray, a little more red, and he patted my hand with his free one and looked gravely into the wreckage, not because he cared, I thought, but because I did.

The red cross was not burned all the way off the bottom and I kept seeing it, feeling it against my shoulder as I scraped by, seeing the blade drop, seeing Tony fly apart, seeing the chopper scream by me and feeling the impact of the explosion, then all over again, from the time I first turned Lightfoot over to the lightning bug people last night, and again, and again.

A faint orange glow still shimmered near the bottom of the wreckage—the last embers of the fire? I scarcely noticed it at first, as my mind replayed the last few hours, but then I couldn't help but notice that the glow drifted against the wind, toward us. My own aura bristled around me, a fearful gray shadow, growing wider the longer I stood there, but the orange crept into it, warming it, interpenetrating it until my aura and a portion of Ahn's mingled with the brightness. My knees rebraced and my head settled down. My trembling fell several points on the Richter scale. And the instant replay stopped while inside my head a more sensible voice said: *Could be worse. You're alive, the kid's alive. Now try to stay that way. Ol' Tony didn't get greased helping some dumb broad who folds up when it gets a little tough. These woods are thick with VC, but they're thick with our troops too. Stay loose.*

And I suddenly realized what a great target I made and shook myself free of what was no doubt a major hallucination induced by fear and the weird psychogenic power of the amulet. I had no choice now but to accept what the amulet showed me, and be glad of it. Heron was right. Old Xe had known a thing or two and, bless his heart, had somehow in that last long look managed to pass some of it on, maybe knowing how much we would need it. If he could read me the way I read Ahn, read the VC woman last night, then he *could* have known. And however much his amulet confused me with the feelings and reactions it stirred in me, it had the quite practical ability to light up any human being in the vicinity as if that person were a shop window, and I couldn't think of a more useful tool to have when marooned in a jungle war, not even an M-16.

Ahn had wandered off. The rain was somehow colder and harder, but even though the orange light had bled away, that around me was no longer the pure gray it had been, but was flushed a somewhat healthier mauve.

I skirted the wreck to the forest beyond, watching silently for Ahn. A faint glint in the underbrush caught my eye and I stooped toward it. Tony's mirrored shades winked up at me, one earpiece broken. I picked them up and tucked them in my pocket.

I caught Ahn's glow in the brush ahead of me and quickened my step just a fraction to catch up with him, though I still moved as quietly as I could and kept my eyes moving.

Then the glow dipped and he fell with a rustle of brush and a sharp Vietnamese swearword.

He was no sooner down than another glow, one I hadn't noticed in my scrutiny of my surroundings, my pursual of Ahn, stepped into my line of vision and dove toward Ahn.

The hell with trip wires. I plowed through the brush toward them.

Ahn cried, "No, Joe! No. Me good boy. Me no VC."

"Hold still while I'm killin' you, you little muthahfucker," someone demanded unreasonably.

But he was demanding in black American English.

"Wait!" I called. I didn't mind being loud now. If one GI was here, his unit couldn't be far behind. No doubt they'd seen the crash and come to investigate and we were rescued already. "Wait! Don't hurt him. He's okay. He's with me."

A tall black man with his shirt tied around his waist unbent until he was standing, staring bug-eyed at me. Ahn scuttled out from under him and half crawled back to me. His prosthesis was dangling at an angle from his stump and he was crying again. I picked Ahn up, pulled the prosthesis off, and threw it in the brush.

"Shame on you for picking on a little sick boy," I said to the GI, wiping Ahn's tears away. "He's a patient of mine. I was medevacing him to Quang Ngai when the chopper went down." The man kept staring at me and I began to feel uneasy. "Wow, are we glad to see you," I said. "Where's the rest of your guys?"

He looked blank, and wary.

"The rest of your unit, where is it?"

He took a step toward me and I noticed his aura then. It was peat-brown and ash-gray—he was deathly afraid, even of me. I took a step forward to meet him. "I'm Lieutenant McCulley—Kitty McCulley—from the 83rd Evac at Da Nang," I said, trying to radiate all the warmth and gratitude I could. The mauve shadow around me deepened and was tinged with darker streaks of magenta. The first gray tendrils mixed with it, and the man stopped, and stared some more. "Two of the guys from Red Beach were taking me to Quang Ngai with little Ahn, my patient, here. But we got shot down. I'm so glad to see you."

He took one more step and the mixture continued. He

swallowed. I swallowed and slowly lifted a wrinkled brown package out of my ditty bag. "We wouldn't have had enough M&M's to last much longer, but now that we're rescued, we can use them to celebrate. Want one?"

He took it slowly, a red one, and popped it into his mouth, and looked mildly surprised when his tongue met the candy. Then he backed up a pace, still surrounded with gray, and started marching back into the forest.

"Hey, just a minute!" I said. "You can't leave us here. This little boy is crippled and I—I don't know where I am, and—" and I knew all of a sudden that something was badly wrong with this man—I wasn't sure we weren't safer without him, but he was an American. He must know where there were more. He must have come for us—

The soldier stopped, turned around, and picked Ahn up as easily as if he were a rifle and hoisted him onto one bare shoulder. "Lady, that just about make it unanimous," the man said.

We walked into the forest together and the GI remained silent, his aura still mostly gray, though it seemed the green of the plants showed through now and then.

We could hear the rain pouring harder, but under the forest canopy it took its time reaching us. Sometimes it was a fine mist, sometimes a steady drip, and now and then a downpour. The noise of the rain on the leaves was quiet compared to what it had been while Ahn and I were in the tree. The soldier's head rotated constantly, back and forth, side to side, up and down, and changing so he never got into a pattern, watching the ground, the trees, and air in front of him, the spaces on either side of him. I found myself doing the same thing.

He moved with thorough, automatic caution but very quickly. Too quickly for me. I lagged behind, panting to keep up. Ahn looked back over his shoulder, worried.

The man stopped abruptly and turned around. "Could I have another piece of candy, ma'am?"

"Sure," I said.

"They're all dead," he said when he had bitten into the M&M. He kicked a log and, when it didn't kick back, lowered Ahn to the ground and sat down himself. "My unit. I thought you was comin' to find me when I saw that bird."

"Dead?" I asked. "Who's dead? You mean the chopper crew?"

"No'm. I mean my unit," he said. Now that he'd started talking, his tone was conversational, ordinary. "We got overrun, I guess you'd call it. See, I was asleep in my bunk one night back at base and we was all in this, like Quonset hut, kinda, with a screen door? And somethin' wake me up. I always been like that, since I was a little boy. I sorta know when somethin' ain't right, like. Anyhow, I wake up and I see this shadow with a gook hat go by the screen door. And at first that don't mean nothin' 'cause the gooks, you know, they all over the place in the daytime. But then it come to me—they ain't s'posed to *be* no gooks there at night. And I'm just thinkin' that and I just start, half-asleep, you know, rollin' down under my bed when all of a sudden all hell breaks loose. Somebody starts afirin' in the screen door and killin' everybody. Everybody in there, all my buddies, all my friends, they get sprayed all over there, and when I crawl out, they all dead. Everyone dead and I ain't even had a chance to warn 'em. And outside the door I see fire and I hear guns and I see gooks runnin' this way and that and I crawl on my belly to the door and they're all over the place, all them gooks. Ain't s'posed to be there at night. Not at all. But they all over the place."

He was shaking his head like an old man with palsy. I patted his arm, the gray and mauve mingling again, spreading into each other. I felt his fear suddenly, as I had felt my own the day before, sharp and acid and helpless.

"How'd you get away?"

"Crawled. I crawled down off that hill, through the fence, and tried to find somebody. But I just got lost. Then I saw your chopper and I thought, William, they have come lookin' for you. Say, you *really* in the Army?"

"Army Nurse Corps," I said.

"I ain't never seen no Army nurse in Nam. They come for us with you here. We just got to keep out of Charlie's way. Army won't let you stay out here."

"They don't know I'm here," I said, realizing miserably that it was true. "I guess, officially, by now I'm AWOL."

"AWOL? And you a lieutenant? Whoo! That some kinda rich! Shake," and he held out his hand. I tried to take it, but he did that complicated black handshake instead and I couldn't follow.

"How long you been out here?" I asked him.

"I dunno. Two, three days maybe. You?"

"We spent the night in a tree."

"Yeah, me too, till a snake chased me out. I hate them things."

"Me too. But at least the VC didn't spot us."

"VC? Around here? Where?"

"All over the place last night. They're gone now."

"Fine with me." His aura flooded with beams of yellow, blue, and a hint of purple that went with the sudden wide, self-deprecating grin. "I hate them things too."

Seeing people as rainbows was a dizzying experience. Still, annoying as the side effects were, the edge the amulet gave me was too great to dismiss because it was a little disorienting. And the longer I wore the amulet and the more I listened to William and Ahn and had a chance to compare the feelings the colors gave me about them with their actions and words, the more eloquent the auras became. It was as if people had an extra feature to gesture with, one that expressed a whole side of them that mouths, eyes, and hands were unable to communicate. William's grin, by itself, was somewhat enigmatic, but while the basic gray-brown of his aura told me that he hated and feared the VC deeply and was in a state of shock explained by what he had just told me, the yellow, blue, and purple said, in the same way a grimace or a twinkle in an eye might, that his hate was not a customary thing for him, that he was a very bright guy, and more used to caring about the people around him than hating them.

That was part of the problem with acquiring an object of power without having studied its ramifications. I thought then that the amulet was giving me guarantees, that I could trust what it told me as absolute. From being a nonbeliever I was rapidly coming to rely on that one talisman as my salvation—rings of power and singing swords, as in Tolkien and King Arthur stories, aren't supposed to lie any more than just and wise rulers. The amulet abolished any reservations I would normally have had about William. But that was partly my fault, I guess. I desperately needed something to believe in right then.

In basic, the sergeant had given a little speech I

thought was amusing at the time. "Those of you who are going to Vietnam will need a god. We do not care which god you pick. Your god can be Buddha, Jesus, Allah, or Pele the volcano goddess. Your god can be sex or money if you so desire. But you *will* need a god. If you do not have a god, go to the quartermaster and he will issue you one." I began to see what that was all about.

"So," I said. "Have you got any idea where we are now?"

William scooped Ahn up with another smooth motion and started loping through the jungle again, which at that point was easy. The jungle floor was flat and the ground cover was mostly more elephant grass, though shorter than that in the field because the trees hogged the light. "Umm hmm."

"You do? Where?"

"In deep shit, woman. We in deep shit. Thass where."

# 14

John Wayne would have probably just shot me, but William stopped when I said I couldn't go any farther.

"Thass cool. Ol' babysan here ain't no lightweight. They feed you too much Da Nang hospital, babysan."

"No way, GI," Ahn protested. "Feed me tete. Ahn beaucoup hungry."

"Yeah, William beaucoup hungry too." William shrugged Ahn from his back and shrugged his shoulders together to take the stiffness from them. "You hungry too, mamasan?"

"I sure am. But I don't want to make my meal out of sweets. You haven't seen any rats around, have you?"

"Nah, why?"

"Didn't you guys get that speech in basic about what you do if you're starving and you only have a raw rat and a Hershey bar?"

"Oh yeah. You mean where you eat the rat and chase it with a piece of Hershey bar 'cause you ain't *even* gonna barf up the Hershey bar? It don't work, lady. I know a guy tried it. Says it just make you hate Hershey bars from then on."

"Well, maybe it's better with peanut M&M's," I suggested hopefully.

"Mmm," he said, lowering his voice a decibel or two. "Well, we ain't even gonna have to worry about it 'less we carefuler than this."

I took a quick look around and spotted no particular glows besides the amulet-enhanced phosphorescence of the greenery. "There's no one close," I said. "I think we're safe."

"Then you musta bumped your head in that chopper crash, woman. We not safe by a long shot."

"No, but there's no one close."

"You can't *see* 'em, lady. Thass the point."

"I think I could," I said, and then wondered how I would explain it to him without sounding like a superheroine refugee from *Teen Titans* comics.

"Yeah? An' how's that? Some special info only officers get?"

"Well, maybe you could say I have unusually good vision," I said. I decided I wasn't up to explaining about the amulet right then and William didn't look as if he was in the mood for listening to such explanations if I was willing to make them.

"Umm hmm. Well, find us some food, then, if you that good."

"*I* didn't have that much survival training," I said. "What have you been eating? If I were home right now I'd be having steak at the mess hall."

"Steak? Jesus, lady, you been on the gravy train for sure. What make you get your dainty steak-fed little ass into somethin' like this, taggin' along after some one-leggity child?"

"Someone has to look out for these people," I said.

William gave me a look that said it was too bad I was brain-damaged. "I been lookin' out for 'em okay. I lookin' real hard, and if any one of 'em come 'cross me, they ain't gonna need no more lookin' out for, and that, girl, is puttin' it polite 'cause you're a female and all."

Recalling what he'd just been through, I didn't argue with him but changed the subject. I didn't want to stop the conversation. As long as we talked, I felt less afraid.

"Where are you from, William?" I asked, only a little breathless from trying to keep up with him.

"Cleveland," he said, still mad at me, his aura bristling dull red.

"I'm from Kansas City. That's where my folks and my brother live. You have brothers or sisters?"

"Yeah. And a wife and two babies. An' I'd like to stay alive to see 'em again. Look, lady, it real nice talkin' to you and all, but I don't want no VC catchin' us shootin' the breeze."

I shut up, at first a little resentfully—after all, if we

were all stranded out there, it seemed pretty lousy not to be able even to talk to each other. Before long, we were climbing the side of a ridge, pushing through vines and shrubs that tore at my poncho and stands of elephant grass that made a ripping sound as we brushed through it, so it sounded as if our clothing were being shredded. Any VC in the area should be able to hear us for miles before we ever saw them. I remember Duncan, who was a hunter, telling a story in which he said something similar to klutzy hunting companions when they complained of not seeing deer. "Nope, you haven't seen them, but they've sure as hell heard you," Duncan would quote himself. Unlike the deer, the VC would not be scared away by hearing us. With that to think about and the work of climbing to occupy my energy, I was fresh out of conversation anyway.

Not that William was hurrying—he just sort of oozed up that slope like so much oil compared to me. He did let Ahn down, and the boy made good use of his foot, both hands, and, though I winced for him, his stump, as he climbed. He stopped and rubbed his stump occasionally, but didn't complain, and twice grinned at me as I stood panting for breath, trying to keep up. Nursing involves a lot of walking, stooping, bending, lifting, and running, but it's blessedly short on scrambling up steep muddy hills in dripping, steaming rain. The exertion more than made up for the slight drop of temperature caused by the wind and rain. Whereas in the clearing I'd been cold, within the heavy cover of jungle growth with big leaves overlaying bigger leaves, I felt like a pig at a luau. Sometime in late afternoon we broke through the thick cover into light rain sprinkling the top of the ridge. Here the trees were tall but the undergrowth was rocky and relatively free of tangly growth. I leaned against a rock and almost slid off it, I was that slippery from my own sweat. William looked like a ghost, wrapped in his own cloud of congealing moisture.

My head roared and my eyes weren't focusing all that well. The rain was warm but it was water, and I raised my head and let it trickle into my mouth. Ahn crawled over to me, dug into his shorts pocket, and offered me a Baggie of salt tablets. William was already on his stomach, lapping from a hollow rock. He gave me a turn, as he might at the drinking fountain in some park, and after a few laps I popped the salt tablets and lapped some more. It helped, but I couldn't knock it back and reach the most parched part of my throat. Still, I knew the systemic effects would save my life anyway.

When my eyes and mind had cleared a little, I looked at Ahn, who was pocketing his tablets again.

"Babysan, where'd you get those?" I asked him.

"I find them, mamasan. Numbah one, huh? I think maybe I sell when I fini hospital."

The Vietnamese version of free enterprise had for once proved useful. I had my own salt tablets, but having two supplies was better than having one. I had no idea what a salt lick looked like and doubted we would just run across one every time we got dehydrated. William had swallowed a couple of tablets too, but he had been in the bush long enough that his body had adapted somewhat. My sweat glands were spouting like Old Faithful and his just seemed to flow gently, like the Danube, adding a polishing gloss to his skin. Of course, he stank like a billy goat, but then, I was building up quite a pungent fragrance myself. The grunts were all warned against using scented American hygienic products like toothpaste and deodorant and after-shave. I wondered if it mattered. I'd heard that Americans smelled bad to Orientals, that eating red meat gives us a special odor they find objectionable. I wondered if the VC would kill you quicker for smelling good from toothpaste and after-shave or smelling bad from stinky pits, toe jam, dragon mouth, and crotch rot.

We walked along the ridge and over onto another one, with just a slight dip between hills. Once I stopped and removed the amulet for a moment, to see the country with normal eyes. I thought how much my mother with her love of nature trails and bird-watching would have loved this. Fields of elephant grass rippling like summer wheat were the only resemblance between this country and Kansas. The country was spined with ridges protecting low-lying areas of grass, paddies, and more jungle. Atop these ridges, spindly trees clawed their way out of rocky ground strewn with explosions of thin green tongues. The hillsides and valleys brimmed with forest green, emerald green, peridot green, bright, light, medium, dark, and drab olive green, lime green, chartreuse, and other shades of green I had no name for. Through the valley to the east of us, a stream glinted between the trees like fragments of Christmas tinsel.

"What you stoppin' for?" William asked.

"I bet you can see all of Vietnam from here," I said.

"I bet all Vietnam can see us too; think 'bout that and move your ass."

He didn't have to tell me twice. I slipped the amulet back over my head and followed. Although the footing was easier, and the wind and rain felt fresh against my face and arms, my feet burned as if I were walking on hot coals and my legs ached to my waist. William dumped Ahn onto the ground and rolled his shoulders back to relieve the tension. Ahn looked at me expectantly, but I shook my head, and without whining, he picked up a long stout stick and used it for a crutch.

The sky darkened from pale silver to the color of a new cast-iron skillet. The raindrops grew larger and the ground boggier. Below the ridgeline, the jungle covered us again. We slid down a slick embankment on our rears and dropped onto a spongy dead tree trunk that supported two more trees sprouting from its corpse. William stepped down from this and scuffed the ground cover up with his feet. Several lizards and spiders scuttled away, including two or three pretty large spiders. I wanted to ask if those were tarantulas but felt stupid for not knowing already, so I tried to look nonchalant as if, oh sure, I knew they *could* be tarantulas but I wasn't scared of anything like that.

"We better post sentry tonight," William said. "Which watch you want, first or second?"

"I'll take first," I said. "I'm beat but I don't think I'm going to be able to sleep—I hurt too much. What do we do if they do come? Spit at them till they drown?"

"No, but if we see them first, we're warned, we can hide. We don't see them and they see us, nicest thing they could do is slit our throats while we're asleep, but I don't think they'd let us off that easy, specially with you along."

"Thanks, William," I said, shuddering. "Any inclination I had to sleep is definitely gone now."

He nodded as if he thought I really was grateful and curled up between the tree and the lip of the ridge to sleep. Ahn was dead to the world as soon as the spiders were gone. I sat with my back to the cliff, my arms curled around my knees, and watched the auras of my companions dim with sleep, like private sunsets damping to dusky rose and slate blue.

Every once in a while I'd uncurl enough to peek up over the ridge, alert for the telltale glow of enemy auras. But I didn't think I'd see them in time if they overran us.

I rolled my head and shoulders and rotated my feet, feeling the deep pain in my shoulders and neck, my legs, arms, hips, my feet especially. I wanted to take off my boots. I knew I should or I'd get jungle rot, but who cared about that kind of thing when you could be shot—or worse —at any time? I understood how the grunts came in with some of the complaints they did. I didn't want to take off my boots. I wanted to be able to run if I needed to. I did not want to be captured.

Officers' basic at Fort Sam was pretty much a lark for my class of nurses—they needed us too badly to harass us. Unlike the men, many of us could have quit. Those of us who had contractual obligations could get pregnant and get out if need be. They did not want to bug us too badly. So when they took a group of us into a small classroom and closed the door behind the instructor and a Special Forces– type sergeant, I thought they were just being melodramatic.

"Ladies and gentlemen," the instructor said, "what we are going to tell you here is not to go outside this room. If you repeat it, we will deny it." Oh boy, I thought. "Mission: Impossible." The others showed varying degrees of concern—with most of the women it was polite. The male nurses responded a little differently. I saw Jamison, a fellow I'd chatted up at the O club, lean forward and look suddenly very intense. There were several male nurses in our group, but two or three, including Jamison, were already veterans before they got their R.N.s. As soon as they got their diplomas, they were eligible to be redrafted. Jamison told me he'd enjoyed Nam as a corpsman, had felt he'd really done some good on the medcap missions, but wanted the expertise he thought nurses' training would give him. He hadn't been redrafted, but from the expression on his face, I wondered if he wasn't having second thoughts.

The sergeant introduced himself first as a two-tour Vietnam veteran. We didn't really need to be told. And it was looking at his face, with its tired eyes, at his stance that was at the same time very casual and very tense, that made me realize that this part was not just more Army melodramatic bullshit. "Now I'm going to tell you something and I know you're going to think this is a cruel and inhuman thing to say and all that, but I got my reasons. You women, if it ever appears as if you are in a situation where capture appears inevitable, the best thing you can do is to kill yourself. You men, if you are in a situation with one of these women and it looks as if she may be captured, do her a favor and kill her. Because the tortures are atrocious." Then he showed us pictures.

I was a little shaken, but still thought to myself: Oh, what a load—there they go playing John Wayne again, the old saving the last round for the schoolmarm bit. The horribly hurt people in the pictures were shoved to the back of my mind with icky pictures out of medical books after a while.

At Fitzsimons, I met the nurse who told me her system for handling overseas romance. She had served in Nam during Tet too, which made her crazy enough to like me, I suppose, and try to help me out when the brass and all the other head nurses were so down on me. The day I got orders for Nam, she gave me the big-sister talk about men and we split first one, then two bottles of wine.

Toward the bottom of the second bottle, she started talking about the part of Nam she hadn't told me about: not the beach parties and the inconveniences, but her work. She had been triage nurse at Cu Chi during Tet and was talking about the way the Vietcong overran the place at one point and of some of the awful things that came through her E.R., the mutilations, the deaths. I asked, carefully, because we'd been warned not to mention it outside the room, "Did you get that talk about enemy torture before you went over there?"

She nodded. "Yep. I wish someone had told the civilians the same thing, because they were right on. We had a couple of American nuns come in; the VC had tortured those women till—well, one of them died, and I was praying to God the other one would too."

I thought about that while I huddled under the lip of that ridge. I could still see my friend's face. This wasn't something she had heard. She had seen it. American women like us. Only they were civilians. Surely it would be even worse, if there was worse, for military. And then there were all the officers trying to scare us, saying, "They know your names. They know who you are. The VC have you on a hit list." I thought about all the hideous things I had heard first- and secondhand, the Vietnam folk myths and the stories from other nurses, about torture victims, mutilations, Vietnamese and Vietcong women who had been sickeningly abused by either us or them, and I felt my own body, achy and sore because it was soft, easily pierced, of how I screeched if I stubbed my toe. Jesus Christ, what was I doing here?

The bugs were torture enough—my arms were sore from swatting at them, and big lumps itched and burned all over my face and arms and underneath my clothing. Even though I sat on my poncho, I was saturated to the bone with rain and plant sap and mud. How did the grunts take it out here in this shit? No wonder people got vicious —the discomfort alone was enough to drive you nuts.

There had to be better things to think about, but I'd never stood guard duty before. What would Duncan do if he were with me? Probably say that if he had his old .30-06 he would pick off the entire NVA, but since he didn't, he'd probably leave me alone "just for a minute, kitten, while I check something out," and go off with some Vietnamese floozy. Ahn whimpered in his sleep and crunched himself into a tight ball. I wanted to whimper too. I wanted my mother. I could just hear her saying, "Now, Kathleen Marie, it's not that I don't love you, honey, but you got yourself into this. Neither your daddy nor I, nor even the Army, forced you to go over there, so now you're just going to have to handle it the best you can." Thanks a lot, Mom.

She'd also tell me it was no use getting morbid. Good advice, but a little hard to follow. I tried to mentally construct a letter she would be able to relate to.

Dear Mom,
      A funny thing happened on my way to transfer Ahn to a different hospital. The darn chopper broke down and Ahn and I had to jump into the jungle. Tony, good captain that he was, went down with his ship, but we met this colorful character named William who's on his way back to civilization to get reassigned, since his last post

was terminated. Little Ahn has been learning lots
of new American expressions from him and wood-
craft tricks I'm sure will stand him in good stead if
he joins the Vietnamese Boy Scouts later on.

Anyhow, we've been spending the day on
this wonderful nature hike. Your African violets
would really take to this country. The place
looks like one big greenhouse, crammed with
angel-wing begonias, spider plants, ferns, mother-
in-law's-tongues, all kinds of vines and ivies and
flowers, most of which look as if they want to eat
you. Seriously, though, it's very beautiful, if in bad
need of a good pruning, and you'd enjoy the bird-
watching and identifying all the kinds of spiders
and lizards. We've heard monkeys too. Though
we haven't seen them, I know that's what they
are because they sound just like the sound track of
a Tarzan movie. There's supposed to be even bigger wildlife around, but so far none has crossed
our path. Fortunately, it's not too hot because this
is the rainy season now. A little wet, but don't
worry, I remembered my raincoat! Love to
Daddy and all . . ."

I wouldn't mention the amulet. She might not like me
accepting jewelry from strange men, especially patients.

I wondered if the amulet would give me aura-en-
hanced nightmares. At least the glow from the greenery
was fainter at night than during the day, probably because,
with the whole sun-chlorophyll reaction, plants put out
more energy during the daytime. That was good because
all of that unaccustomed visual stimulus had given me a
peculiar headache in the middle of my forehead.

Something rustled between the tree trunk and the
ridge, where William was lying. At least good fortune had
brought him to us, I thought, raising myself to my knees to
peer over at him as if he were one of my night-shift patients. Something hard caught me across the throat and
slammed my head back against the bank.

William's face loomed above me, his forearm pinning
me by the throat to the bank. He wore a strange expression
not of hatred or anger so much as concentration. Fortunately, the bank was crumbly and gave under my head, or

I think he would have killed me right away. I kicked out and felt my boot scrape Ahn.

"Cut it out," I said, though it didn't sound like that when it came out. "William, dammit, stop!"

Ahn flew into him, pounding him silently with bony little fists, dragging at his arm. William released me long enough to backhand the boy halfway down the rest of the ridge.

I couldn't wait to get my breath back, but gasped, "William, goddammit, what the fuck's the matter with you?"

He started to grab me again but I blocked him, rather feebly, with my own arms, and looked into his eyes again, trying to find out, before I died, what in the hell was going on. My arms were surrounded by a dingy mauve light that fused with his dull maroon glow and diluted it. He sat back on his haunches abruptly, overbalancing himself so that he tumbled backward a pace or two. He threw out his hands and grabbed a branch, sat up, shook himself like a wet dog, and blinked.

Ahn scrambled around him up the hill and hid behind me, rubbing his stump tenderly and sniffling. But he hadn't uttered a single cry throughout.

William crawled back up the hill. I scuttled back and nearly knocked Ahn over, but William just said, " 'Bout time you got some sleep, girl. I'll take watch."

"Oh, no thanks," I said, determined not to sleep a wink around him lest I inadvertently die before I wake.

"What you mean, 'no thanks'?" William asked. "Thass crazy. You gotta sleep." He said the last like a mother cajoling a youngster.

"*I'm* crazy?" I hissed. "You just tried to kill me."

He looked blank.

"Yeah," Ahn chimed in. "You numbah ten, GI. You get mamasan like this and . . ." He parodied choking himself and made a terrible face, then dropped his hands to his sides. "Hey, William, you some kinda VC?"

"Wait a minute, wait a minute. I did what? Is this child jiving me or what?"

"You tried to kill me, William," I said, and relaxed enough to try to figure it out, now that I was pretty sure he was himself again. "Maybe you were having a dream or something about being back at your unit again, do you think?"

"Yeah, yeah, could be. Hey, I'm real sorry—" He extended his fingers to my neck as if to stroke away the bruise I could feel rising. "I didn't mean—shit, I'm real sorry." His voice broke and I realized he was crying. He reached out a rather large paw and grasped Ahn's hand. "Sin loi, babysan."

Ahn gave him a measuring look that was older than he was, and nodded, dismissing the whole thing.

"It's okay, William," I said. "It's over."

But none of us slept, and as soon as it was light enough to move without falling over our own feet or tripping on one of the knots of roots and vines crisscrossing our path, we started walking again.

"Where are we going, William?" I asked.

"Hell if I know. I was just told, when you out in the bush, you keep movin'. So we movin'."

It was good enough for me. Only I wished I was sure we were moving toward a hot meal, a nice bunk, and lots of ugly wire and sandbags between us and other people's bullets.

Ahn clung to my hand all morning, but suddenly he slipped away, looking very excited, and peered intently along the side of the trail. I stopped and he took hold of the tail of my uniform shirt for balance and jabbed at something with his crutch stick. I thought it was a snake, but when Ahn shuddered backward I decided it might be even more dangerous.

"William?" I whispered. He was walking point. We were several yards behind him on the trail, though we were going as fast as we could and he as slow as he could.

"Yeah?"

"I think Ahn found a mine." I snatched Ahn back when he leaned forward to poke again, but he wriggled from my grasp and once more extended his crutch.

William rejoined us and caught the stick in mid-thrust, pulling it out of Ahn's grasp so that he fell back against me.

"You VC, kid? Try to blow us all up?"

"No VC," Ahn said. "Look," and he made eating motions, as if he were scooping rice out of a bowl into his mouth.

I took about four hasty giant steps backward as Wil-

liam prodded the mound of earth this time. I could vaguely
see little round shapes at the top. "What are they?" I whispered as William dug at the mound with a stick and flipped
something loose that rolled to his feet. "They look like
Sterno cans. Homemade bombs?"

"Don't seem like it, but almost as bad. Beans and
muthahfuckers."

"Huh?"

"Beans an' hotdogs. See here? Some dudes, when they
out in the field and they got C rats they hate, they just
buries 'em. How you get along with lima beans?"

William had the Army equivalent of a church key in
his pocket. A few hundred yards farther down the ridge
we found a stream, shallow-looking and only about fourteen feet wide. We choked down the cold food straight
from the can.

"Wisht I had my canteen cup and a little c-4," William
said. "I could heat this shit."

"What's c-4?" I asked.

"You know, plastic explosive."

We filled the cans with water over and over till our
arms ached from dipping and lifting. The morning had
been hot and muggy and the water felt wonderful when it
splashed me. William waded into the water. "You wanna
get wet, lady? Come on ahead, then. We gotta cross this
fucker anyway." He waded across without blowing anything up.

Ahn looked dubiously at the rushing waters of the
stream. I stepped into the bone-chilling water and could
see right away that he was going to have a problem. The
force of it was enough to knock you off your feet. "Come
on, Ahn. Hang on to me." I let Ahn hold on to my shoulder
while I dipped down to my knees to get wet and cold all
over. The night before, I'd thought I'd never be warm
again, but now I couldn't believe how great it felt. Then
we sloshed out. William, just ahead of us, began ripping off
his clothes.

I scarcely had time to wonder what in the hell he was
up to when I saw for myself. An inch-long leech was fatten-
ing itself on my forearm. I dumped Ahn unceremoniously
on the bank and started stripping too. So did he. I started
batting at the bloodsuckers, trying to pull them off.

"Don't do that," William said. "You'll break the head

off in there and it make you sick. Break up a salt tablet, put on its back. It'll pull out. Cigarette works better, but mine are long gone."

Ahn, bare as the day he was born, bent over his clothes and pulled a rather soggy pack of Kools out of his pants pocket. He also produced a Zippo, with which he expertly lit the cigarette he gave me. William was already at work on his crop of bloodsuckers with the salt. For his own, Ahn just plucked them out. You aren't supposed to be able to do that, but he did, pinching them up near their heads. It worked, anyway. When we were done, we had a total body count of about forty-eight leeches.

I turned my back on the men while I did a search-and-destroy mission on the leeches in my lingerie. I am really not all that shy, but guys who are not your lovers can be more modest than somebody's grandma, on your behalf as well as theirs. It is often ridiculously difficult to get a male patient to accept a urinal from a female nurse. I waited until I had my fatigue blouse on again to turn back around. Sure enough, William was buttoning up as rapidly as he could. Ahn was sitting in the grass, smoking a Kool with the savoir faire of James Bond.

In a debonair manner, he offered a smoke to me, to William.

"No thanks, kid. I tryin' to quit," William said.

The only thing I hadn't taken off was the amulet, and now it had fallen outside my uniform blouse, flashing back the sun like a mirror. William sat down beside Ahn to pull on his boots. "Uh, Lieutenant?"

"Huh?"

" 'Bout last night. I still don't recollect much of what happened, but what I reckon is I just sort of went dinky dao from all this duckin' and hidin' shit. You know I don't mean no disrespect to women, and it ain't got nothin' to do with black or white. I wouldn't want you to think I—to think—"

I knew what he meant, but then it was so soon after the time when blacks were beaten for using the wrong rest room or riding in the front of the bus, when civil rights workers were being murdered, that it was awfully hard to talk about racial stuff, especially between a man and a woman, especially an enlisted black man and a white woman officer, which is just sort of too parallel to the darky–plantation belle bullshit. "William, let's not get into that shit, okay?" I said. "I am not nearly as worried about the possibility of having you after my ass as I am about the possibility of getting it shot off. I'm real glad we found each other because I don't know a damn thing about the jungle. But I gotta know: is there some real sure way to snap you out of your sleep, something maybe your mom used to wake you up when you were a little kid? Because you almost killed both of us last night. I know you didn't mean to, but—"

He shook his head. "I never done nothin' like that in my life before. I never even had no nightmares before I come to this place. Used to sleep like a rock." He handed me the can opener. "Here. Maybe you can jab me with this if I go off again. Only be careful where you stick it, huh?" As he handed it to me, his aura wavered a little into the brown and his eyes suddenly got wet. "Goddamn, I am just fucking up all over the damn place. First I just roll under the bed and don't warn the men and they all get blown to shit, then I try to kill you—I don't know what the fuck is happening to me."

Ahn tapped him on the arm and offered him a cigarette again.

"Thanks, kid." He lit it this time and took a long drag, then offered it to me.

I don't smoke, but I took a drag too. "Look, man, you don't have the corner on fucking up." The chopper crash flashed across my mind.

I pulled on my trousers and tucked the amulet inside my shirt. William watched me with more relaxed interest now.

"What's that you wearin'? Where's your dog tags?"

"In my pocket. They got to irritating my neck."

"Yeah, well, if I'se you, I'd get shed of that rank sewed onto your collar too. Officers is the first individuals Charlie try to grease."

I cut off the ends of my collar with my bandage scissors. "William, how long do you think those C rat cans had been there? Do you think that unit is still nearby somewhere?"

"Sure. I do. Them and a whole bunch of others. And a whole bunch of VC too. Just depend on who we find first. You ain't talkin' to no trusty African guide, bwana. I didn't have much call to learn trackin' in Cleveland. Damned if I know how old them cans was. You the woman. You probably know more about canned goods than me."

"Not if I can help it," I said. I've never been the domestic type.

We walked just inside the edge of the jungle, down along the edge of a valley again that day. The valley was full of soft grass and little round fishponds and the rain blew gently across it, sweeping toward us, carrying a heady, fresh scent that reminded me of spring on Lake of the Ozarks. The jungle smelled more like a cross between the zoo, the alley in back of the A&P the day they tossed out the produce, and the aggressively green, earthy smell of a hothouse. "Can't we walk down there?" I asked William. "It'd be easier walking, especially for Ahn."

"Easier to get blowed away, you mean. See, some of them things hit but they don't explode. Plus the VC likes to set booby traps round that kind of thing. No way, mamasan. This soldier stickin' to high ground."

When he spoke to me, mostly William seemed perfectly okay. He was one of the nicest people who ever tried to strangle me, in fact. But when he was walking point, not looking back, not staying in touch with what was going on with us, his spine would twitch and his head circled and dipped like a snake's, sniffing the wind, looking for signs. We started climbing again, up and up into really thickly interwoven jungle with trees growing out of other trees and vines so thickly twined together that we had to stop and climb over them or separate them to climb through. Ahn and I had a tough time keeping up. The boy's adrenaline was finally wearing off and his little face looked pinched again. He started whining. He wanted to be carried, regressing, the way sick kids do, to an earlier age, where people were supposed to take care of them.

"No can do, babysan. You break my back," I told him.

He screwed up his face as if he was going to cry. "No way. You carry me before."

"Yeah, and I may have to again, but only in an emergency. I'm afraid I'm not strong like your own mama, babysan. No can carry water buffalo on each shoulder and a water jug on my head."

He smiled a little and patted my butt. "No sweat, mamasan. Ahn take care of you."

"Right. We're a great team."

William swung around on us with a look of such truculence that I feared for a moment he'd lost it again. "You people em di," he said, and whirled back around to take a step. Ahn was staring a little ahead of William with his eyes almost as round as mine.

"Dung lai, William," he yelped. "Stop!"

"What the fu—" William began, then abruptly stepped back and knelt down, feeling along a line in front of him.

"What is it?" I asked.

He didn't answer for a moment or two as he traced the thing back into the trees, made some sort of adjustment, and let out a deep sigh. "Thanks, kid. Mamasan, you better take a look at this."

"William, I wish you wouldn't call me mamasan," I complained as I clawed my way through the leaves and vines that kept smacking me in the face. "Or Lieutenant for that matter. What's the good of me cutting off my bars if you go announcing it all over the place? My name's Kitty."

"Yes, ma'am, Lieutenant Kitty, ma'am," he said snottily. "Now the private wishes to request, Lieutenant Kitty, ma'am, that you kindly take a look at this here trip wire so's you be able to spot a booby trap next time you be seein' one."

"Don't be a pain in the ass," I grumbled, but I took a look. It was a nasty apparatus—a dead log with a lot of pungi sticks set at angles that would make a porcupine out of anyone who tripped its mechanism. The whittled bamboo sticks with the excrement on the tips were more chillingly malicious than a grenade would have been. I had already seen the infections and damage they could cause— a man could lose his limb or life as surely to this sort of trap as to high explosives or gunfire.

"Right there is how these people be lookin' out for themselves," he told me. There was no anger in his voice. In fact, it was becoming increasingly remote and flat. The old wine color crept back into his aura, along with a grieving umber, and I knew he was seeing himself impaled on that device, feeling that maybe he should have been.

We climbed for two more days, through knots of gnarled root and twisted undergrowth that surely was usually handled with machetes. We were constantly climbing, tripping, trying to thread our way through it like darning needles through finely meshed silk. I feared I was going to grab hold sometime of a fat snake instead of a fat vine, and the thought of that slowed me down even more as I double-checked the aura of the growth in front of me to make sure the long things were uniformly plant-green. A little watery daylight filtered through from those towering top trees, splashing onto the broad flat leaves of the trees that grew to about half their height, and down through the undergrowth bristling above our heads, to sluice down the backs of our necks or splat into our faces. By that time the rain was no longer cool and refreshing but warm as sweat. As it evaporated, shivers ran down my spine without relieving the sensation of being slowly steamed.

Ahn started sneezing that afternoon, and his stump seeped pus and trickled smears of blood through the rough bandages I tried to keep over it. I was one big ache. My head throbbed from the constant glow of the jungle and my muscles burned. Every one of them, when asked to lift a body part over another clump of roots cannibalizing another giant log, felt as if heated lead slabs had been specially implanted in it. I had to think about how to position my fingers every time I grabbed another sticky, bug-infested vine, I was that exhausted.

In the dense forest we rarely saw the birds or monkeys. We heard them, like ghosts in old houses scuttling through the upper stories of the jungle, but they were almost always just out of sight, except for the flash of bright feathers or the suggestion of a tail. So much greenery lay above us that I saw animal auras only occasionally, like slightly bigger Christmas lights among the tiny glows of insects and reptiles. Much of the time all I could see of William was a glimmer of his aura, a flicker of wine or blue bobbing like a will-o'-the-wisp in the sea of green surrounding us. Except for the help of the amulet, there were several times when we might have become separated because Ahn and I slowed more as the day wore on.

Toward evening the watery green light diffused even more, until you got the feeling of being deep under the sea, surrounded by seaweed, a feeling enhanced by being continually soaked and with the smell of wet greenery always in our nostrils.

Ground fog swirled up from the forest floor, and soon

all I could see of Ahn was a grimy teal pool of light. William doubled back for us, his legs lost in the fog. He'd put on his fatigue shirt, but now and then he shook his shoulders like a dog having a bad dream and the goose bumps rose on my own arms. Ahn had a sneezing fit that wouldn't stop, and William glared at us and disappeared into the jungle again.

We couldn't even hear each other well because the sound of the rain blotted out everything but the shrillest cries from the creatures in the treetops. The beat of the rain thudded and splatted but was never regular, so that you couldn't get used to it or discount it. I was glad for it in some ways. It kept me from being hypnotized by the monotony of struggling through the shrubbery. Since I couldn't be sure I was following exactly in William's footsteps, I was constantly scanning the growth at shin level, looking for more booby traps. Once I nearly ran into trouble looking too low. I started to pass a tree vine, and a spade-shaped face surrounded by a tomato-red glow met me almost nose to nose. I fell backward so quickly I knocked Ahn into a fan-shaped fern. The snake slithered away until the last flick of red was obscured by the jungle's green glow. Mom always claimed snakes were more afraid of people than vice versa, and I was glad she was right.

After the snake, I slowed down even more, which was a good thing. We were barely moving when, a short distance ahead, a clay-colored triangular glow popped up from the ground and into the milky, roiling fog. It wavered for a moment and bent toward the ground, then with a scrabbling noise that sounded no louder than a mouse might make gradually elongated into an oval the size of a small person.

Ahn had to sneeze just then, and since he couldn't see what I saw, he made no effort to muffle the noise. The brown oval bobbed back and forth, searching for us, a metallic gray tingeing its edges, but the forest redirected sound. Although Ahn was standing right beside me, his sneeze could have come from anywhere. I bent low, clapping my hand over Ahn's mouth. He grew very still and we hunkered in silence, waiting.

The brownish aura floated a few paces away from us, and I heard bare feet on damp ground.

Then abruptly it doubled over and began coughing. I focused on the figure within the light and saw a small woman. She was pale, her skin wrinkled like a prune's, her hair caked with dirt, her pajamas black. She wore bandoliers draped across her chest and a rifle slung over one shoulder. Her left arm was raised, the wrist daintily covering her mouth, a foot-long dagger held negligently in that hand. She coughed, and melted silently into the green at the side of the trail. Moments later, where she had been, William's wine-colored aura bobbed slowly in on the fog, looming over a far vaster patch than hers had. It stopped a short distance away on the other side of where she had been, and as it hovered there, it gradually changed, the wine separating into rays of red and black, spurting from him like blood from an arterial wound.

Suddenly a second glow rose up from the ground between us, within it a man not so well equipped as the woman. I froze with my hand over Ahn's mouth. I had no idea how much I was able to see because of the aura, how visible I was to them, how much of them William could see. But a third, fourth, fifth, and sixth person issued from the hole without seeming to see us, their auras blending with the mist. As a seventh rose up to follow them and carefully turned to plug the hole behind him, William struck, and the small figure crumpled over the hole. Silently William stripped the body. Relieving the dead Vietcong of a long knife, he slit the throat with the efficiency of the neighborhood meatcutter. He took two more steps before he saw us.

The mist boiled up around him, curling in and out of a black and red radiance pumping from him. His face was hard and his eyes cold and resentful, but he raised one arm and motioned us forward. I hoisted Ahn onto my hip and stepped over the corpse. When we came even with William, he pointed into the mist beyond him, where he had already squashed some of the undergrowth.

I started, expecting that he was going to follow and keep the VC off our tail in case they were inclined to be there, but when I glanced back, the red and black stripes were overlaid with green as he cut into the forest in the direction the other Vietcong had taken.

Ahn clung tightly, silently, but I was making an incredible amount of noise trying to carry him and follow William's course through the foliage. I hoped if the VC heard us, they'd mistake my noise for their own. Or for

William's, if they discovered him. God, I hoped they wouldn't. What if they caught him? I prayed to God that wouldn't happen. I wouldn't know what to do. I didn't have a weapon. I couldn't save him. How could I live with myself if I just let him get caught, tortured maybe? Maybe I wouldn't have to worry about it. If they caught him, they'd probably get us too.

If we got away this time, maybe we could try to find a village someplace, somewhere where it looked as if there was enough food. Maybe I could pay them to take Ahn in at least until I could find help. If he'd had two legs, he probably would have left me by then, I thought. A lot of Vietnamese kids adopted Americans, but when it looked as if the bases were going to get hit, the kids suddenly became history, along with a lot of other friendlies.

We stopped dead in front of a huge snarl of roots, impassable as the Great Wall of China. Unable to go forward, I sat on the ground and waited. Ahn continued to cling to me, and I thought he might be crying. The wind shivered the grasses and smaller leafy plants, and the fern fronds swayed and danced, the bare trunks creaked, the leaves rattled like Halloween skeletons, while the rain beat its erratic patter and splash all around us, and on top of us. It had the advantage of keeping my own trembling limbs from shaking the shrubbery like a pair of Mexican maracas.

So we huddled there getting stiffer and stiffer, and I tried to distract myself by remembering what it was like to be dry. We were still perilously close to the VC tunnel entrance, which was what that hole had to be. I wondered if a second group would file out of the hole. Maybe I should have moved the dead VC. His body still emitted a faint mustard-colored glow, growing gradually darker, drifting on the wind, separating itself. The version of the Twenty-third Psalm that went "Yea, though I walk through the valley of the shadow of death, I shall fear no evil, for I am the evilest son of a bitch in the whole damn valley," went through my head and I felt a rather savage rush of pride in William; then, watching the VC's feeble aura fade like an ember, I felt ashamed and said a generic, universalist prayer, including in the scope of my entreaties the elderly gent with the flowing beard and kindly eyes and the cosmic forces of the universe and my own idea of Buddha, of whom I could conjure up only the image of a statue.

We had had to kill the guy—I felt I'd killed him as much as William. Or would have, if I'd had a means. Anyway, his death no doubt saved my ass, let's put it that way. But it had been nothing personal, and I wasn't especially glad he was dead.

As I watched, the dead terrorist's aura grew clearer, ruddier, within the milkiness of the mist, like fire deep in an opal. The discoloration from hatred, grief, and fear was dissipating with death . . . sort of like in the werewolf movies where the ravening wolf, after being shot by the hero's silver bullet, slowly turns back into the innocent human being infected with lycanthropy.

I was glad William had been so thorough, because if he had left the VC alive, I knew I'd feel honor-bound to try to patch the poor SOB up. As it was, I just wondered about the wisdom of leaving him draped across the tunnel entrance. Wouldn't that announce our presence? But if they didn't know how many of us there were, maybe that would make them abandon the tunnel.

Which shows you what an incurable optimist I am.

Ahn's face was next to my ear. "Mamasan, we didi now, huh? VC—"

"No can do," I mumbled back. "We wait for William."

"William dinky dao, mamasan, we didi."

Well, that was one vote in. Ahn, who had taken to William at first, was scared of him. And though I hated to admit it, I was, too. What kind of a nut would go unarmed after seven—well, six—VC? That was movie stuff, not what your practical, I-want-to-go-home-alive grunt would customarily do. The only reason I could imagine him doing such a damn-fool thing was to get supplies and weapons. Personally, when it came to getting supplies that way, my overwhelming hunger became a niggling little sense of peckishness, but nothing I couldn't handle till I found a particularly tasty-looking rat.

And William's behavior had been so erratic—the coolness that I at first admired I now saw as what was referred to in psych training as a bland affect, which meant simply that his face was usually expressionless and he didn't show much feeling. Of course, that figured, considering the trauma of watching his friends killed and being left to make it by himself in the jungle. But the blandness alternated with swings into irritation and I didn't know enough to be able to tell which was more dangerous: the agitation or the numbness.

The mist blew clear across the trail. I scooted back into the deeper shade of the root canopy, dragging Ahn with me. Normally I would have thought of snakes, but I really didn't care at that point, because I was convinced I was not going to live much longer anyway. It was just a question of when and how—a bite from one of those little bamboo vipers called two-step snakes because their venom could kill you before you'd taken two steps might be the easy way out under these circumstances.

A curse blew toward us on the breeze. The voice was so muffled the curse could even have been a Vietnamese one, though I didn't think so. What did it mean? Had they caught William and strangled off his last defiant words? I wished I could see what was happening—not as me, of course, but maybe as a bypassing lizard.

Ahn's small body shook silently and I thought how different he was from what he had been in the hospital, when he bawled so much the other patients were ready to throttle him. Maybe he'd been saving it up for then, when he thought it was safe, because now he knew without anyone telling him that weeping aloud could be fatal. I considered crying myself, but I was already losing too much water sweating.

The rain intensified, rattling the leaves, misting through the screen of interlocking growth, driving through the occasional opening where collective drops plopped like fat slugs from overburdened meaty green leaves. The jungle floor, steaming with recondensing moisture, reminded me of a cannibal's boiling kettle, with us in the stew.

An overhanging branch dropped one slow drop at a time on the crown of my head, reminding me of a story I'd read about the Chinese water torture, a procedure that involved letting water drip one drop at a time on the same spot on a victim's skull until it eroded skin, bone, and sanity. I decided not to think about that. The ground fog once more formed an opaque veil obscuring the faint path between us and the body. I could still see the outlines of the plants and the body, because of the auras. The fog hid Ahn and me from anyone else, however.

Ahn shivered again and emitted a small whimper.

When I looked down, his eyes were closed. He'd fallen asleep. His skin felt hot against mine. His rag of a bandage had come off completely and the wound was draining again. Damn. There was nothing I could do about that now.

The glow of the jungle shuddered and wilted to a shade ever so slightly brown moments before blood-red and pitch-black light strobed through like the lights on a police car, silently broadcasting death, hatred, fury, malice, and murder.

One of the VC, I thought. They'd caught William, he'd told them about us, and now they were circling back to get us. Before the malignant aura broke onto the trail, I pushed and prodded Ahn up over the root tangle and scrambled over after him. He whimpered once more, but as soon as I reached to cover his mouth he shut up, flipped over the top of the tangled root and decayed log, and cowered on the other side. I landed heavily beside him and lifted my face just far enough to reach a hole in the woven roots.

Like fire and char the aura burned in the clearing, then headed straight for where we had been. In the center of it, his face impassive except for eyes watchful as a jaguar's, and as impersonal, William stalked toward us, a machete in one hand, a .45 automatic in the other.

I was relieved to see him alive, but on the other hand he looked as if he was searching for us where he knew we ought to be, but did not look as if he was going to be happy to see us. He stepped across the corpse and began stalking up the trail, slashing at impediments. If we had been hiding in the jungle beside the trail we would have been spaghetti before we could say hello. I suppressed an urge to stand up and ask him what the hell he thought he was doing; didn't he know he could hurt somebody that way? I didn't because obviously he knew that very well. And it looked as though he no longer cared.

This was a bit of a dilemma. William was a swell guy when he was in his right mind. Even though he could get killed as easily as Ahn and me, he was a man, larger than me and with all that reassuring extra upper-body strength. I felt protected by him. He had training and know-how and had already showed me a couple of things that might help keep me alive. And now he had weapons with which he could protect us all, if he was so inclined. The trouble was, I was pretty sure, from the look of him and all that riot-squad energy shooting from him, that his inclination was to kill anything that moved, including us. Face it, William was nuts and I wasn't feeling so stable myself, which was why I sat back down, very slowly, and huddled with Ahn while William poked and prodded and eventually leaped over us, quite literally overlooking us. He stalked away, his aura blazing so intensely that he looked like a walking forest fire.

I watched until he was a mere flashlight beam in the greenery, then drew a deep breath. I tried to rise, but my knees wouldn't support me for a long time. When I put my hands out to brace myself on a log, they shook so hard it looked as if I were trying to play the bongos. Ahn pulled himself up beside me.

Ahn's aura was shallower than it had been, a washed-out sparrow brown with little veins of red. He looked as tired as I felt. "What we do now, mamasan?"

"We follow William," I told him. I didn't want to lose him entirely. Not only did we need him, he might need us. I didn't really think I'd be able to trail him for too long, but maybe I could until he was in his right mind and the three of us could band together again.

"William beaucoup dinky dao, mamasan."

"No shit," I said. But we didn't seem to have a lot of other options.

# 15

We lost him in less than an hour. Not that we didn't know where he'd gone. We only had to follow the machete slashes to figure that one out. But we couldn't keep up. Even with the support of his stick, Ahn fell often. Sometimes I carried him, but at others we both needed both hands to climb or brace ourselves for steep descents down muddy slides. We drank often from the rain pools on the leaves and stuck our tongues out at the rain, but it was a far cry from having a whole cool glass of water from mama's tap at home.

Soon the trail started heading mostly down, and when we finished sliding down muddy, root-riddled banks, the ground below was less overgrown, we stumbled less often, and none too soon we began treading on grass once more. The machete marks dwindled with the vines, and so did our ability to follow William.

Remembering what William had said about the other flatlands, I kept us in the trees. I kept thinking that soon the valley floor would turn into rice paddies.

The rain blew straight at us and I took my poncho from my ditty bag and tried to cover us both with it. I couldn't bear it in the heavy jungle. It was too hot. Now, however, as a wind and rain break, it was inadequate. Clouds like gray scouring pads blew across the top of the valley, squirting squalls every few minutes. The bomb craters, already full, flooded and ran into one another. I felt dizzy and headachy, as I did when I was catching cold. I wanted my mother again. I wanted her to bring me aspirins and antihistamines and a vaporizer with Vicks and comic books and fresh orange juice. The fact that she hadn't done that since I was about ten made no difference. Sick adults regress too.

"Dear Mom," I mentally wrote while carrying Ahn down the valley, "Ahn and I took a walk today—well, mostly I walked. He got tired. William had some business to take care of, and when he returned he wasn't in a very good mood, so Ahn and I decided we'd give him time to cool off. I bet we'll find a rice paddy today. William wants to avoid people, but I think the paddies are a good sign. They're so normal and agricultural, like wheat fields. William doesn't want to visit a Vietnamese village, but then, he's a city boy. I feel that, after all, these people are rice farmers just as the people where we're from are wheat farmers, so what really is the difference? I'm getting Ahn to teach me to say, 'Hot enough for you?' and 'Nice day if it don't rain,' in Vietnamese."

Thinking about home probably wasn't the best thing in the world, because my mind began drifting. Just because I didn't want to be in Nam, I started dreaming, with my eyes wide awake and my feet walking, that I wasn't. I imagined I was walking through the woods by my Aunt Janet's cornfield carrying my cousin Sandy, who was now about seventeen years old, though to my mind she was still as I had last seen her, younger than Ahn. It was like a mirage except that I didn't actually see anything that wasn't there, I just reinterpreted what I was seeing so that it seemed instead to be something I wanted to see. I have no idea how long or how far I walked thinking myself back in good old dull Kansas. It's a wonder I didn't mistake a booby trap for cow fence and kill us both.

Ahn pulled me back to Southeast Asia by suddenly rousing to point out what looked like a brilliant sunset. Indulging him, I stopped so we could admire the reds, oranges, and yellows of the sun, as I thought, reflected in the sky.

Around the next bend, I felt the heat, smelled the smoke, and watched tongues of fire lick at the sky as the field below us spouted flames. Acres of plants were already consumed and blackened, and the fire now fed on earth and roots. I wondered what burned so hot and remembered napalm. But why napalm somebody's field?

I hated the feel of it even more than I hated stumbling through jungle, so I started climbing again, up away from the fire. Just before nightfall we found another stream cutting a ridge in half. We bathed again and drank and I gave Ahn two of my Midol for his fever, and allotted us two salt tablets apiece after saving one for my new crop of leeches. I tore the sleeve off my fatigue shirt and bound it around his stump with a piece of his old bandage. The stump didn't look as bad as I feared, but there was a nickel-size sore where the stitches had once been, and it was draining.

We climbed back up and over another ridge before nightfall, and bedded down between two rocks under a very large tree that gave us some protection from the rain. I dreamed my grandpa was pointing at the field and laughing, telling me about strip-and-burn agriculture, but he was saying something about how they did it with crop dusters these days.

When I woke the next morning, I felt the warmth of a small fire, smelled meat cooking, and heard it sizzling. William squatted, Vietnamese style, beside the fire.

"If I be Charlie, lady, you be dead," he said.

"I almost was anyway," I said, prying Ahn loose so I could stretch a little. William's aura still had a faint edge of black and maroon but was mostly blue, a little yellow, clear green. "You remember coming after us with a machete and a .45 by any chance?"

"Me? Nah, I go after VC. Got some too. One got away, the girlsan with the heavy artillery."

"That who you thought we were?" I asked. But he just looked puzzled, and hurt, and his colors started swirling around in a confused sort of way.

"Never mind," I said. "How did you find us?"

"Easy. You not exactly Sheena, Queen of the Jungle, woman. You see any of 'em?"

"Any of who?"

"Our boys. They around. Who you think called in that napalm on the taro field?"

"Is that what it was? I wondered. What's taro?"

"Good food. But ten to one some asshole thought it was weed. Or maybe they just wanna make sure Charlie don't eat no taro. I dunno."

"Wait a minute," I said. "If that was one of our planes that dropped napalm, then there must be some of our guys around—"

"You catch on quick, Sheena. I spotted a patrol of about six dudes just as I got to that taro field, but they was 'way far down the valley, and about the time I started into that field after them the planes come up and it was weenie roast time. I had to didi mau. But that patrol is maybe a day ahead of us."

"Of you, maybe," I said. "I'm surprised you could backtrack far enough to find us. You sure are one tough act to follow."

"Yeah. Well, I think we should find them dudes."

"If they're a day ahead of us, we'll never make it. Ahn's leg is going bad again."

"We all gonna go bad we don't get out of this shit pretty soon. Want some of this primo monkeysan here?"

I nodded and looked back toward Ahn. He was sweating in his sleep. "You could carry Ahn again. That would speed us up."

"It'd slow me down, though," he said thoughtfully. "That patrol's already got a day's lead on us."

We chewed monkey and thought it over. I was tempted. I wished I hadn't brought Ahn out here. And William was undoubtedly right. We'd lose our chance at rescue altogether if we slowed down for Ahn. On the other hand, if he was an American kid, we wouldn't even be discussing it. I decided not to discuss it anyway.

"Well," I said, "maybe it would be better if you left us here and went after them yourself. I don't think Ahn's going to get very far. His stump's infected."

"Lady, you don't seem to understand. We ain't in the world no more. This be war, baby. I leave you here and when I come back, if you here, you probably be some kind of beaucoup messed-up fucked-over corpse."

"Okay, okay, I know, I know. Stop talking about it, okay? The whole idea makes me nervous. But frankly, buddy, I'm just about as nervous hanging out with you. That's twice you've nearly killed us."

"Will you stop sayin' that? I ain't harmed a fuckin' hair of your head—"

"It wasn't my hair I was worried about," I argued, ever as ready with witty repartee as I was when fighting with my kid brother.

"Nor nothin' else neither. Where you get this shit, girl? You ack like I crazy—truth is, you be the crazy one.

What you tryin' to do? Set me up to get lynched for rubbin' up against your lily-white round-eye tail?"

"Watch the names, buster," I told him. "I'll make a deal with you, you don't call me round-eye tail and I don't call you nigger, okay?"

The red and black was growing in his aura again and I realized that I was no longer dealing just with William, my fellow refugee, but with an armed and angry man who currently killed people for a living and was having a lot of trouble telling which people were the ones he was supposed to kill and which ones were on his side.

He half rose, then sat down again, his eyes full of resentment and hostility and something else that fueled both—the grief that cloaked all the other colors in his aura, and the self-reproach that was growing in prominence. The colors were altering so quickly, shifting from one emotion to the other, that I was having trouble naming them, although I knew what they meant.

"What you watchin'?" he asked belligerently. But he stayed seated and his hands were open on his knees. "You look like you about to shit yourself. What's the matter? I look like some nigger mothahfuckin' street gang rapist to you or what?"

"You got this all wrong, William," I said when I was able to detach myself from watching his aura. It had a hypnotizing effect that was soothing in a purely detached kind of way. But it was alarming how quickly his soft-spoken kindliness ran to anger. I was convinced it was misdirected when pointed at me, but I squirmed anyway. If I was not exactly a bigot, it was probably more from lack of opportunity than from actual ideals. There hadn't been any black kids in my classes until high school, though the neighborhoods near us had been integrating gradually—and with much paranoid grumbling and dire prediction from my relatives. I didn't mind talking to a black person, but the sexual stuff made me uncomfortable, all the more so because I knew that if I were the liberal person I thought I was, it shouldn't. But the real problem I was having was that even though William and I spoke the same language and were from the same country, I knew less about the problems and attitudes of the culture he came from than I did about the Vietnamese. Proximity to the soul brothers back at the enlisted barracks—hard-core groups who looked like the Army equivalent of street gangs and made nasty remarks as I passed—did not lead me to believe that I was going to be liked just because I was in favor of the civil rights marches on TV. But I was damned if I was going to be lost in the jungle with enemies all around and a sick kid and a crazy man and admit to being a bigot on top of it.

"Private Johnson to you," William Johnson snapped.

"You got this all wrong, Private Johnson," I began again. "You don't remind me of anything like a street gang."

"Nah?" he asked, sounding maybe a little disappointed.

"Nah," I said. "What you remind me of is this nice little old lady I took care of during my psych affiliation in training. She was just as pleasant and sweet as anything except that every once in a while she attacked clergymen and tried to castrate them. The rest of the time you couldn't meet a nicer person."

He didn't seem inclined to dignify my remarks with a response, so I speared a piece of monkey and turned around to give some to Ahn. He wasn't there.

"Babysan?"

"Leave him alone, will you, he's probably gone to take a piss in the brush over there," William said in the tone of an irritable father criticizing how I raised the kid.

"What if he runs into a booby trap or a snake or—"

"What would you do about it if he did? Scream?"

It was my turn to ignore him. I scanned the brush and the surrounding hills and valleys. No Ahn. But on the other side of our ridge was a valley with rice paddies. Across the valley was another ridge, and about a quarter of the way up this a few houses. No people that I could see, but curls of smoke rose from a couple of places in the village.

"Hey, look, civilization!" I said.

He didn't even look up from swabbing out his canteen cup with a wet leaf.

"Did you hear me?" I asked, forgetting to keep my dukes up. "There's a village over there. People."

"Yeah, but what kind of people do they be is the question."

"It's a village," I said.

He nodded. "Yeah, but it ain't San Francisco."

"But it's worth checking out. They might have some food we could buy, or medical supplies, or a radio—"

"Or VC. You act like it some kinda shopping mall. Well, it ain't, no more than I'm a platoon, even with you and babysan. You don't just go waltzing into those villages alone. Ho Chi Minh could be the mayor for all you know."

"Yeah, sure, but it could also be where those guys who burned the field are heading, couldn't it?"

"Unh huh, and it could be they're just going to call in an air strike and waste the place too, just like they did that field. I wouldn't say that was a real healthy place to be, especially not for just you and me."

"Yes, but with Ahn along—I mean, he's a Vietnamese."

"If he's not from that village or don't have relatives there, that ain't gonna cut no ice with them. Lotsa strays runnin' around the countryside. People look after they own folks. Can't take care of every draggly-ass kid who wanders in."

"Maybe not but—" In the trees below I saw movement, and Ahn broke into the clearing by the paddies. "Jesus, there he is. He must have spotted the village and gotten the same idea I did." I started off after him, but William was on his feet and pulling me back before I had time to take so much as a step.

"You can't go down there. They puts mines and booby traps all along the paddies. Babysan probably gonna get the rest of his ass blown off. No need to make it two of you."

"I won't abandon him," I said. "And I'm sorry, but you are crazy and you do scare me." He curled his lips and wouldn't look at me, intent on polishing the weapon he had captured. "William, I *know* when you're going to flip out if I'm awake, but when I'm asleep I can't—"

"That's *bullshit,*" he said in a low voice with so much force behind it I felt as if he'd slapped me. "You don't know no such thing."

"I do. Look." I pulled out the amulet and showed him. "This lets me see a light around a person that shows me what they're feeling—I can sort of read them. An old wise man—a magician, kind of—who was one of my Vietnamese patients gave it to me."

He smacked at it. "What you tryin' to tell me, girl? That I should leave you go wanderin' off by yourself through the jungle 'cause you got some gook *e*-quivalent of a mood ring? You think *I'm* dinky dao!"

"Look if you don't believe me!" I took it off over my head and handed it to him. "Put it on. Go ahead. And tell me what you see. Go on. I dare you. I double-dare you." Jesus, I was regressing to third-grade fights with my brother again. But he slid the amulet over his rifle barrel and very gingerly slipped it over his head.

"Now look at me!" I said. "What do you see?"

"I see one crazy white chick thinks she's Sheena, fucking Queen of the Jungle," he said, but his voice was a little more reasonable as he stared at me. He passed his hand over his face once in a weary gesture. "Look, sister, you better cool down now. You so mad you glowin' a little red around the edges."

"Aha!" I said. "See what I told you! See what I told you. Here, gimme it back." I felt blinded without it, like one of the mythological Graeae deprived of her eye. He handed it back, shaking his head, and when I put it on I saw that his aura was back to being predominantly blue and yellow again. He was beginning to understand, in spite of himself.

"William, I have to go now. I have to go get Ahn. I'll be able to tell if those people will hurt me and I'll be careful. But even if you weren't—pardon me—crazy sometimes, I'd be no safer with you than I am alone. Nobody's safe in this shit. You know it better than I do, for Chrissakes. But I can't let a handicapped kid go running around in the jungle by himself, and the longer I sit here beefing with you, the harder it will be for me to find him before he reaches the village."

"I could hit you over the head and carry you or drag you," he threatened.

"That wouldn't make for very speedy progress, would it?" I said.

"Sheeit," he said. "You go on, then, dammit. But don't go cussin' William Johnson when the VC are cuttin' your womb open while you still alive. You think *I* crazy and you scared. Let me tell you somethin', lady. I have been real scared travelin' with you and that gook kid. My ass ain't been worth nothin' since I took up with you. Get the hell out of here if you so het up to do it. I'm gonna contact that squad I saw. If I can get 'em to swing back by the village and there's enough left of you to put in a body bag, I'll see to it your mama gets it to bury." He turned around.

"William?"

"Unh huh."

"Did you maybe capture a smaller gun I could have just in case it does look like I'm going to be captured?"

He snorted and handed me the machete without a word and marched off. I looked after him for just a moment, feeling irrationally abandoned, but then I looked away and saw Ahn at the edge of the rice paddy, and a flurry of people in pajamas and conical hats running into the paddies toward him. I plunged down the hill and into the trees, expecting to feel the trip wire of a booby trap against my shin, or my foot step first into nothingness, then to be pierced by pungi sticks as I fell into a tiger pit. It must have been wishful thinking. I got to the paddy in one piece, in time to see that it was not Ahn who was causing the commotion among the villagers.

# 16

When I first saw the snake I thought, What's that fireman's hose doing here? I thought it might be something the villagers used for irrigation. Ahn sat at the edge of the paddy, very still, and I wondered if he was having second thoughts about being with his people again. I thought he was scared of something that insubstantial. Then I saw the fire hose more clearly, noticed that it had a distinct aura pulsing from it, the dark red of old blood, anger, malice, and hunger brewed together.

The villagers swarmed across the paddy and then stood watching uncertainly. The snake reared up like a self-motivated Indian rope trick to about two and a half yards above the ground. That made it taller than any of them.

They were very small people, short and lean from hard work and hunger and intestinal parasites, and there wasn't an able-bodied man among them. Ancient men, ancient women, pregnant girls who looked too young to have periods, and tiny children stood with their hoes and knives and watched the snake. It watched them too, swaying, and I thought its aura flickered with satisfaction as it eyed an infant on its sister's hip. The snake thought it was one badass motherfucker, and it swaggered toward the people as if they were so many mice.

For their part, they prudently backed up, considering, but looked at it mainly as if it was a curiosity. They chatted at one another, as if expecting one of their number to come up with an answer. The snake lay back as if it was about to strike, and the slimmest of the pregnant girls leaped out well beyond striking range and taunted it, flapping her arms and trying to draw attention away from the others.

Meanwhile, a few of the others circled back toward the snake's tail.

The snake was a no-nonsense-type creature. It decided that if the damn-fool girl wanted to get eaten so badly, it would accommodate her. It didn't so much strike as fling itself upon her. The others hacked at it as it flew past them, but it grabbed her in its coils and she cried out as it squeezed. Its jaws snapped onto her thigh and she abruptly stopped thrashing with her machete and collapsed within the coils. The other villagers tried to pull the coils loose, but the snake just squeezed more tightly. One of the babies, sensing the panic of its elders, bawled.

Ahn grabbed his stick and hobbled forward. I hadn't said anything as I came up behind him, and he still didn't know I was there. He grabbed the nearest old lady and held on with one hand and felt around the snake with the other until he found the tail, took it in his mouth, and bit. The snake stopped biting and the coils relaxed so that snake, girl, and Ahn all tumbled to the ground in a heap.

I couldn't just squat in the bushes and watch. There was already one corpse lying in the grass, near where the snake had risen. An old woman or an old man, I couldn't tell—just a mass of mottled skin and a hank of long gray hair in the midst of a bundle of rags. The snake was trying to free its head to reach Ahn. The others were pulling on various parts of the snake while an old man and a girl of about eight tried to whack at the reptile's head without whacking the victim or Ahn in the process. Ahn continued to chow down on the snake's tail.

I knew that however frail these folks looked, they were quite strong from years of work that would have killed me. I knew that they were much quicker than I was, and that I would likely get myself snake-bit or hacked if I tried to help. I also knew that I weighed almost double what any one of them did, and that maybe dragging with all my weight behind it might help. And I had a hell of a big machete. I also didn't think I would be able to live with myself, for however long I was going to be able to live anyhow, if I just sat there and watched that goddamn snake kill people who had survived bombs and bullets for so many years.

I waded into the paddy, my boots shedding pounds of

accumulated mud into the watery muck beneath the rice shoots.

Ahn sneezed, releasing his hold on the tail, and it whipped away from the girl, sending Ahn flying. The snake's head reared up about six inches from the girl's body to watch the kid and lunge for the nearest spectator. It had to uncoil a length of itself from the girl to make the lunge, and when it did, I hit it with my machete, not even sure I was using the right end.

The snake's body was bigger around than my neck, bigger around than my thighs even, so at first I wasn't sure I had done any good. But the blade had bitten deeply into the body just behind the snake's head and the snake hissed, shaking a head the shape and size of a spade, blood spattering into its eyes, and over me and several surrounding feet. I straddled it and bent over double so I could bear down on the blade, which was hard to do. The snake's writhing knocked first one of my boots and then the other sliding in the mud of the paddy, but I held on. I had to. The machete jerked in my hands, but I held it clenched in both fists. I heard a crack and knew one or more of the girl's bones were being crushed. She couldn't even scream with her breath cut off like that. The other villagers tried frantically to pull the coils from her. I leaned more heavily into my machete. There wasn't enough room between me and the girl for me to get good leverage on the snake's head. Any moment now it would crush her to death and round on me.

"Push her away from me. Ahn, tell them push her away."

Ahn started yammering in Vietnamese and the other people began rolling the girl's shoulders and legs away from my back as if they unrolled people from snakes all the time. I dropped to my knees and used them like a vise against the snake, and it bucked like a rodeo bronc beneath me. But from this vantage point I could put most of my weight onto the machete. If I let go and the snake's head snapped free, the war would be over for me.

I cringed inwardly every time the snake undulated, afraid the girl was being pulverized. I didn't dare look back to see, and that almost got me killed.

Ahn's tail biting, though I didn't know it at the time, had caused the snake to loosen its grip somewhat, and the people were able to roll the girl out of its grip. But as soon as she was free of the tail, the tail was also free of her, and the tip whipped up and around my shoulders, jerking me, machete, snake head, and all, backward.

As the coils started constricting around me, my grip on my machete started to loosen. I felt the people mass behind me, grabbing armfuls of slippery snake.

Then Ahn's head was beside mine, and his mouth grabbed an end section of tail and lightly chomped. The coils loosened and the villagers redoubled their efforts at straightening out the snake. That allowed me to keep hanging on to the machete and with it to bear the great head back to the ground.

"Got him," I gasped, and wanted to laugh in spite of everything, because anybody looking on would have seen that I was a little confused about who had whom. William was right. I did think I was Sheena, Queen of the Jungle, serpent slayer extraordinaire. But the truth was, I didn't exactly see a lot of other options. I was a big, strapping girl then and accustomed to wrestling three-hundred-pound ladies in body casts onto bedpans, having knockdown dragouts with grown men with the DTs, and subduing hysterical three-year-olds while giving them injections. The snake was bigger and more dangerous and more powerful than any of the situations I was used to, but not by all that much.

"Somebody chop off his fuckin' head, for Christssake!" I rasped. It was in English, no one should have been able to understand me, and Ahn's mouth was full of snake, but the old grandfather with the hoe hit the creature a blow on the noggin and the coils fell from me like a feather boa. I fell back against a pile of villagers and lay panting for a moment. The old man kept hacking, his aura as blood-red as the snake's had been, his face a calm, almost kindly mask.

I crawled over to the girl who had been bitten. Her aura was very dim, gray and muddy except for the part around where her leg had been bitten. That was deep black and spreading.

The bite was larger than any snakebite I had ever seen —the snake's mouth was bigger than mine, and almost bigger than my entire head. The standard treatment for rattlesnake bites was going to be useless, I knew it, but nevertheless I grabbed a knife out of the nearest hand and sliced at the wounds. The girl took her breath in sharply and her hand shot toward me, a knife in her fist. I dropped my knife and caught her hand, barely keeping her from stabbing both me and herself. She was looking at me with what I would normally have interpreted as hatred, aura and all, but considering what she'd been through, I just figured she was a little unhinged, probably confusing me with her former assailant.

"Come on, you guys, hang on to her or I'm not going to be able to help her," I said, and shoved her wrist into the bony hands of the nearest grandmother. I must have made my point clear enough, because three children and another pregnant woman rushed to help restrain her hands. Her eyes rolled in terror as she looked down at me and she moaned and squirmed under the blade. "Sssh, sssh, sssh," I told her, as I'd heard Vietnamese women shush their babies. I sat on her leg to keep it from wiggling, so I could do just a little incision instead of major surgery. "I know this hurts, but I have to try to get the poison out."

All around me the women were shushing her, hissing louder than the late snake. Hoping I didn't have any new cavities or canker sores I'd forgotten about, I bent over her leg and made like a vampire, sucking up mouthfuls of venom and blood and spitting it out again—sort of a reverse artificial respiration. It was a huge snake and there was a lot of venom. Even as I sucked I could see the blackness spreading through her pelvis, up her torso, toward her heart, down her knee.

I knew I was getting nowhere, and now the adrenaline was wearing off and I was feeling the effects of exhaustion, starvation, and exertion all at once. Helplessly I spread my hands along the perimeters of the spreading blackness of the venom, mumbling senselessly at it to stop, dammit. I was tired, muddy, and frustrated and about to lose this brave if somewhat screwy young girl in spite of everything. The venom on my tongue made it tingle, and I was starting to turn from her and try to wash my mouth out when I noticed that where the bright mauve of my aura touched the blackness, it gathered before my hands as if I were herding it. I stared at it stupidly, then ran my hands down her trunk, up her leg, and across her pelvis, as if I were sweeping the venom out of her system. Where I touched the black, it retreated before my palms, until it gathered at the wound and bubbled up out of it, like an artesian spring. When it was gone I kept staring at where it had been for a moment, then ran my hand across my tongue. A sheen of black appeared on my palm, and I wiped it off against the rice.

The girl lay still, panting, her eyes wide and her face still terrified.

"Ahn, tell her I think it's going to be all right," I said, my tongue so thick I had to repeat it. "Tell her I think the poison is gone."

I hoped I wasn't raising false hopes. I hoped I wasn't hallucinating. My head seemed too heavy to lift as I looked up at the faces around me: the girl herself, as pretty as Xinhdy had been, except for a gold tooth in the front of her mouth; the old man who had hacked the snake, most of his teeth gone; the children, wide-eyed and looking half-scared, half-excited. Finally the old man picked up the snake's head and the children followed, trying to lift portions of the body. When I got to my feet, the man shifted his grip farther back and tried to hand me the head. I declined, and emptied my breakfast of stewed monkey into the rice paddy. I hate snakes. I can't stand to look at them, much less touch them.

One of the girls helped the injured woman to her feet, while Ahn leaned on his stick and supervised. I felt the wounded girl flinch as I put my arm around her waist to support her on her injured side, but among us we got her back to the village. No mines, no booby traps. Just mud and rice and a concertina-wire barrier.

Later, four of the girls took a mat back out to the field and dragged home the snake's first victim. I watched mutely as they laid the body out. She was not as old as I thought, just very gray. Her face was purpled from suffocation and her body had been crushed, her features so ugly with her death that I had to look away. The injured girl cried out and argued at length with one of the women who was attending the body, but was finally persuaded to lie back. Her aura radiated grieving, a gray as cold and empty as a midwinter sky.

As they cleaned the body and arranged the features back to a semblance of normalcy before laying a banyan leaf across the face, it seemed to me that the dead woman

looked nearly like the live one. No wonder the girl had
been so ready to kill the snake.

Ahn wasn't allowed in while they dressed the corpse,
and the injured woman looked at me, still angrily, as if I
were committing a terrible breach of manners, but the
truth was I didn't have the strength to drag myself out of
there. I fell asleep while they were finishing the prepara-
tion of the corpse.

I awoke some time later to the groans of the girl beside
me. She was on the mat and I lay beside her on the dirt
floor. I was so stiff I could scarcely move, and it flashed
across my mind that perhaps the snake had done me more
damage than I realized.

But the girl's groan gave way to a sudden, panicky
scream. I sat up and automatically reached for her pulse
and stared at my watch, counting. Her stomach was rolling
beneath the light cotton of her pajama top, and she
clutched it with both hands.

This time she looked at me entreatingly, "Dau quadi,"
she breathed. "Dau quadi."

She was aborting, of course. It was actually inevitable.
Even if the venom had never crossed the placental membrane, being squeezed in the coils of a giant snake was
bound to be damaging to any growing fetus. I stretched
out to the door of the hut and yelled, to whom it might
concern, "La dai, la dai," and hoped the urgency in my
voice would make up for the lack of explanation.

It was almost over before anyone else could reach her.
Blood and water gushed from between her thighs, soaking
her pajamas and the mat before I could turn away from the
door again. As the first village woman ducked into the
house, the fetus, a very small fetus, delivered. It was not
well developed. It could almost have been any sort of a
baby creature, poor pathetic little thing. It hadn't had a
chance. The women brought cloths and we wiped her
clean and I wrapped the fetus in one. She grabbed my
wrist. She wanted to see it. I shook my head at first and she
persisted, so I showed it to her. It helps sometimes when
you know what you're mourning.

She began to cry, then to wail, and one of the other
women touched me on the shoulder and nodded that I
should leave the hut. I rose ponderously to my feet, feeling
like an out-of-shape water buffalo behind the small lithe

figure ahead of me. We hadn't far to go—just to a hut a few
yards away, which was blessedly empty except for Ahn,
who was tucking into a bowl of rice. He looked up long
enough to nod at me and went back to eating.

The woman showed me a mat with a roll of cloth at the
head for a pillow. I sat down gratefully and started to go to
sleep, but she sat on her heels and reached for my boot-
laces, as if she thought she was my maid or something.

"No, no," I said, and tried to wave her away. "Ahn,
please tell this woman I don't need a maid, just some sleep.
She should get some sleep herself or she could lose her
baby too."

"I tell her, co, but she be mad—lose face."

I compromised by sitting back up again and helping
her take my boots off. A little girl brought me a rice bowl
and a bottle of hot Pepsi, which I opened with the church
key William had given me. She took the bottle from me
and poured the Pepsi into a bowl.

The little girl put her hands together and backed off,
leaving the Pepsi beside me. I put my hands together and
bowed at her too. I was going to receive a crash course in
Vietnamese customs, I supposed. But tired as I was, I was
elated. William had been wrong and I was right. These
people seemed no more threatening than my patients. I
hadn't walked into the clutches of the enemy, I thought,
just into a strenuous one-woman medcap mission, with a
side dish of indigenous prehistoric wildlife.

Ahn stirred and coughed in his sleep. I felt his forehead. He was burning again. The rice and the Pepsi were
something I wouldn't have touched ordinarily, but I had to
have something in my stomach if I was going to renew my
strength. As the food took effect, my perception of his aura
deepened. Blackness spread from the stump up his leg. I
was sure that if I disturbed him to do so, I'd find a knot in
his groin. Well, now that I'd gotten the hang of the old faith
healer bit by trying it out on a perfect stranger, the amulet's power was bound to work on Ahn too. I spread my
fingers so that each touched the end of one of the threads
of infection and concentrated on thinking of the veins as
being clean and clear, with nothing but healthy blood flowing through them. The black threads knotted near the
stump and, with a little urging, drained out the end. While
I was working, the little girl was on the ball. She brought

me water in what looked suspiciously like the same sort of basin we used for patients at the 83rd. I supposed it was just another of the instances of the black market moving in mysterious ways.

I went through the bowing routine again and smiled at her. The poor kid had fought that snake just as hard as I had and she must be just as tired. I unwrapped Ahn's stump and he woke up, hissing. My old fatigue shirt sleeve was thoroughly be-nastied.

I turned back to the little girl, who was sitting on her heels watching with the expression of a nursing instructor checking to see if I was doing everything right. Disinfectant was too much to hope for, but I made motions of pouring some over Ahn's wound and bandaging it up again. My other fatigue shirt sleeve was grimy and slimy from the snake fight.

She dipped out of the house, and a few minutes later, an elderly man dipped back in and sat down on *his* heels. He was holding a bottle, from which he took a swig before handing it to me. It was Jim Beam. He passed it over, indicating that I should take a swig. I only pretended to, because the last thing I needed was a drink that would knock me on my can, and wiped off the bottle mouth before pouring a good inch of the stuff over Ahn's stump. He winced and hissed and started to cry.

The old man winced and hissed and started to cry when I poured his booze over Ahn's stump. I handed it back to him and made the steepled-hands bow again. I couldn't remember how to say thank you in Vietnamese.

He nodded wisely and looked me up and down in the manner of dirty old men everywhere. "Mamasan beaucoup," he said. He sounded a little awestricken.

"No," I said, grinning and shaking my head. "No, papasan tete." Which was perfectly true, of course. Walking along beside me on the way back to the village, he stood only as high as my bust line, which might have been what led to the personal remarks. He laughed and shook his head at my incomparable wit and he and the Jim Beam disappeared.

The little girl was gone a long time and I began to think that bandages were too much to hope for. People probably didn't have any spare clothing that was in better shape than mine, which was pretty sad. I used the rest of the basin of water to rinse the mud off myself and tossed the thick residue into the ditch surrounding the house. A regular moat. Well, I'd already met the monster.

The old man was out in front of the house, admiring the snake again. He had technically killed the thing, though he'd never have made it without the rest of the village, Ahn, and me. But he walked around it and nodded to himself. I thought he was preening until I paid attention to his aura. It was the gray I was coming to associate with grief. I left Ahn for a moment and stepped across the ditch.

"Some snake, eh, papasan?" I asked, nodding to our kill, which still made my vertebrae stand at attention.

"Yes, numbah one snake," he said sadly, pronouncing snake uncertainly, a new English word.

"I've never seen one that big," I said inanely. He continued staring down at the snake as if I hadn't spoken. "Beaucoup snake," I said and spread my arms and rolled my eyes for emphasis. "Are there more like that around?" I asked, and indicated our snake, plus another beside it and another.

The old man shook his head sadly. "Snake fini," he said and repeated my gesture to indicate that he meant all the snakes were gone, then threw his arms up like a child imitating a bomb, making the appropriate explosive noises. It should have been funny, but the grieving gray and sparks of red in the aura belied his smile, and the whole demonstration was as grotesque as if he had plucked out his eye and asked me to laugh at him.

I looked down and nodded. Bombs might make you nostalgic for the comparative harmlessness of enormous snakes at that. He picked up a stick and drew a few deft lines in the mud and a hungry crocodile slithered within them, mouth open and tail lashing. The old man threw his arms in the air, miming the bomb again, and tapped the picture of the crocodile. "Fini."

As the mud oozed back together and the crocodile sank into the mire, he flourished his stick again and eels, otters, huge fish, and a hungry tiger populated the mud. "Fini," the old man said each time, his voice grimmer with the vanishing of each species. The tiger had figured in our word games on the ward, however, and I thought I might use it to change the topic to a lighter one.

"Mao bey?" I asked, pointing at the picture.

He looked at me as if I'd done something astonishing and now his smile deepened and some of the gray sank back into him in the same way his pictures sank into the mud. He nodded enthusiastically. An educable American. How astonishing.

I drew a picture of a house cat. "Mao?"

He nodded. I was on safe ground. Maos had come up frequently in the word games Xinhdy, Mai, Ahn, and I had played.

I said, "In English, Mao same-same cat same-same Kitty same-same me," and pointed to myself.

He thought that was pretty funny and catcalled at me.

The little girl ran toward us, her black hair flying like a scarf behind her. In her hot little hand was a roll of gauze bandage, still in its white wrapper with the red cross in the blue circle.

"Co, co, see, see!" she cried. She was such a gorgeous child, like a doll with that Kewpie mouth and little pointed chin and that shining hair.

"Co Mao, Co Mao," the old man said.

It was no good trying to get him to go ahead and say my name untranslated. I ducked back inside the house to bandage Ahn's leg. He was sitting up now, and supervised while I wrapped his stump. The little girl again watched as if her life depended on it. I smiled at her when I was done.

"Ahn, we should introduce ourselves."

He looked dubious but said his name and a string of words after, looking as if he had just been elected to the dubiously honorable office of President of South Vietnam.

The little girl pointed to herself and said, "Hoa," and bowed to me and said, "Co Mao."

Ahn shook his head furiously. "Mamasan Kitty, chu—" I shook my head at him before he could say "chung wi." These people didn't need to know me by my rank any more than American civilians did.

"Ahn, I have Vietnamese name here. I like Mao."

"Okay, okay," he said, as if I were very upset about it, and looked at Hoa as if to say, Americans, who can tell what they're going to want next?

She nodded gravely, as if, because of his advanced age, his position and wisdom were unquestionable.

I wanted to rest a little longer, but thought I should first check on my other patient. She seemed to be asleep as

I poked my head in the doorway, but as soon as I set foot in the room she jerked awake and glowered at me. Ignoring the glower, I knelt beside her.

Her aura was mostly a muddy jumble of anger, grief, fear, and pain, but the basis of it was an appealing brilliant aqua and clear yellow, with tendrils of spring green and a bloom of pink. The brighter colors were smothered beneath the layer of muddy ones, like the rainbow in an old slick. She looked at me with a rebellious hatred that struck me as totally unfair, considering I'd helped save her life twice.

"Okay, be that way," I said aloud. She looked healthy enough now, her aura bright and strong despite all the muddiness surrounding it. This village had managed its ob. problems before I came along and I wasn't about to intrude on the privacy of a woman who obviously didn't want me there.

I was turning to leave when the woman who had brought me to the hut stepped into the doorway. Ahn squeezed in beside her. She seemed chagrined and bowed two or three times. I reciprocated. She started speaking rapidly to Ahn, gesturing toward the woman on the bed with lifts of her chin, watching me anxiously. Clearly, she had expected the girl to be rude and was apologizing for it.

"What did she say, Ahn?" I asked.

"This one name Tran Thi Truong, very please to meet you," Ahn said, inclining his head to the woman beside him. "Truong say that one Dinh Thi Hue."

Dinh Thi Hue interrupted suddenly, with a spate of imperious questions, her words sounding harsh and accusing.

"Well, what did she say?"

"She want to know where are other American soldiers."

I started to say there weren't any more and then thought maybe that wasn't such a good idea.

"What's it to her?" I asked Ahn.

Truong pulled us outdoors and started talking again, in low, emphatic tones, her eyes full of apology, but also some anger.

Ahn looked wise and said, "Last time Americans here they boom-boom Dinh Thi Hue." He made a graphic gesture with a circle of the forefinger and thumb and the forefinger of his other hand as casually as an American eight-year-old might wave hi. "Make babysan. She no like American soldiers."

No wonder. I turned back to her with more sympathy, which I had no idea how to express. I murmured, "Sin loi, Dinh Thi Hue."

Ahn was defensive on my behalf, however, and hobbled over to Hue's bedside and regaled the girl for several minutes, nodding at me, slapping the thigh above his stump with a gesture that said it was now sound as a dollar owing to my expert intervention, and clearly told her I was a GI of a different kind than she had known before. I hoped he wasn't telling her I was the only one of my kind.

She let out a long sigh and lay back against the pillow, her face sweaty and her hair still matted with mud and blood. Her face seemed familiar to me, but I thought that was because she reminded me of one of the patients. She had a banty toughness about her that reminded me of Cammy Dover, a four-foot-eleven biker I'd met at a folk club in Denver.

Ahn picked up her hand and la daied me over to her, and put our hands together. She didn't look into my eyes but inclined her head a bare half inch and muttered something in English.

"She say, 'Thank you, Mao,' for helping her when big snake have her. She say thank you to Ahn also, because Ahn *bite* big snake, make him let her go. She say Ahn and Mao numbah one team and she love us too much."

I laughed and patted his shoulder. "I say Ahn numbah one bullshitter and full of wishful thinking, but thanks for trying."

"Com bic? What means 'wishful thinking'?" he asked.

But about then Hoa came to the door and gestured urgently to Ahn to la dai. He turned away from the peace conference and hobbled toward the door, negotiating the ditch with more agility than I would have thought possible. I wished we'd been able to save his crutch during the crash.

The little girl appeared in the doorway again and this time la daied me. Truong frowned at her, but the child didn't notice.

Dinh Thi Hue watched all of this through slitted eyes, as if taking notes.

"It's been great having such a warm friendly chat with you," I said, "but I gotta go now. Kids. You know how it is. Probably want me to car-pool them to the Little League game or take them to the Dairy Queen."

She blinked, mildly puzzled. Her aura looked a little less muddied now. I thought I would be able to tell from it if she was losing blood. It would be dimmer surely. The way she felt about Americans, I didn't want to invade her privacy to check under the Army blanket someone had laid across her. Truong bent over her, murmuring something.

The rain started again, a thin gray drizzle. It made a pewter backdrop for the wet brilliance of the jungle.

As soon as I was outside, Hoa took off at a run, leaving me standing beside Ahn.

In a few minutes, Hoa returned, her pace slow and solemn this time, her arms cradling something that turned out to be a puppy.

"This Hoa's friend, very fierce tete guard dog, Bao Phu," Ahn told me. "Protecting Hoa, Bao Phu is hurt. Hoa want Mao to make better."

Wow. Snake charming, faith healing, and veterinary medicine all in one day. Ought to look great on my résumé.

# 17

The funeral procession for the old woman was a slow, thin line of people bareheaded and barefoot, people in conical hats and B. F. Goodrich sandals, people in what seemed like patched Sunday best, trudging, sometimes slipping, up the muddy incline, carrying smoking incense that refused to stay lit and stubs of guttering candle protected by open palms or a leaf shield. Children blew noisemakers and pounded on things—a shell casing, the basin I'd used to clean Ahn's wound. The noise, I've learned since, was meant to frighten away demons. I got the feeling from the auras of those around me that having a funeral so late in the day was irregular—that there might be more demons out than usual. Hue limped, with Truong anxiously offering support and mostly being spurned. Both women wore white with bits of gilt paper and red cloth attached to their hair and clothing. Hue, who should have been in bed after her miscarriage, walked with the help of two friends. She walked hunched over and I guessed that was because the snake must have broken some of her ribs. Ahn and I joined the procession, and he leaned on the old man, Huang, for support and knocked another stick against his makeshift crutch to make noise. I caught up with them and it was all I could do to keep pace with an old man and a crippled boy. I was that exhausted, and the path was very slippery.

Ahn looked up at me with the lugubrious expression of an amateur undertaker doing his best to look depressed about an improvement in business. He wasn't pleased about the old woman's death, I knew, but with the practicality of the poor and dependent, he knew she was dead and he was alive. The cause of her death was also a chance for him to fit in, get himself adopted and become one of the villagers. He didn't want to dissociate himself from me, exactly. My world had been his home for some time. Together we had done something that earned him a place in this world. But although he was a child, he could not afford to be an innocent. He was hedging his bets for his own survival. His faith in my omnipotence was not what it once had been. Which was in line with my assessment of the situation. I patted his shoulder and trudged beside him.

I didn't understand many things about that funeral, but the need for the incense was obvious, and not just for symbolic or religious reasons. The body already stank—the crushing from the snake would have ruptured the organs and hastened the decomposition. It was carried on a board and draped with a red cloth, jungle flowers scattered on top of it. Fortunately, the pallbearers walked very slowly and were as sure-footed as mountain goats. There had apparently been no time to build a coffin.

Everyone made lots of noise chanting and weeping, but since I was brought up to think that funerals were hushed affairs where it was almost bad taste for the bereaved to weep in public, I kept still. Mostly I attended out of curiosity, and, of course, to pay my respects to the family. My own family believed that even if you didn't know or hated the deceased, if you knew someone in the family you turned up at the funeral to show your concern for them. But it was awkward. I not only didn't know the deceased, I didn't know the family, really. And I didn't know anything about Vietnamese funeral rites except that they had them rather often.

This was apparent from the number of stone-covered graves on the breast of the hill. There were probably a hundred times as many graves—just the newer ones—as there were villagers. Many bore small shrines of red-painted wood, rain-sodden paper, and framed photographs, or other objects. We wound our way through them to what seemed to be the old lady's ancestral burial plot where the fresh hole, already filling with water, waited to receive her. The pallbearers were excruciatingly gentle as they lowered her, but the body still splashed a little when it hit, and the red cloth began darkening where the edges sucked in the water.

The people with incense wove tendrils of smoke in

graceful arcs around the body and laid things beside it: a rice bowl and chopsticks, a cracked cooking pot, and a book with a French title. Old men in black pajama bottoms, dirty white tops, and coolie hats chanted prayers. Children in shorts and shirts, some of the younger ones wearing shirts with no pants, kept beating on their pans and artillery shells, crying and wailing ceremoniously, and looking up at their elders to make sure they were performing their roles properly. Their auras were bright as tropical birds against the gray sky, the silver rain, and the collectively dull aura of the adults. Huang lit a stick of incense and after what sounded like a sentence or two would circle the incense over the body. A young pregnant woman tossed flowers, one at a time, on the cloth-covered corpse.

At the proper time, when the old lady had apparently been given the respect due her by her own rites, Hue came forth carrying a small bundle, the remains of her baby, wrapped in a scrap of silk. Her friends helped her kneel. Her breath came in quick gasps. Her face was ravaged with pain and anger, and wet with sweat, rain, and tears as she leaned far into the grave and laid the bundled infant beside its grandmother. Hue's friends helped her to her feet again.

I waited for the people to start shoveling the dirt back into the grave, but after what seemed a time of communal prayer, Huang, Truong, and a couple of the others I recognized from the snake killing started talking among themselves, then broke off and looked expectantly at me. Ahn said something to them that sounded questioning, received a short answer, and turned back to me. "Mamasan, people want to know: what Americans do when bury dead?"

I was so tired I felt momentarily annoyed by the question. What did they think we did? Obviously, we dug a hole and buried people, or cremated them, same-same Vietnamese. But Truong, Huang, Hoa, and the rest of the village obviously wanted an answer, so I said, "Well, it depends on your religion, or the uh—loved one's—religion, but generally we say prayers, bring flowers, and sing a hymn."

Ahn relayed this information. They held another discussion, then Huang said something to Ahn that sounded like an order.

"Papasan say, you sing for Ba Dinh," Ahn told me.

I started to protest but caught papasan's eye. He nodded once sharply, his aura rigidly contained in a red-violet binding of pride, the pride of face. He and the others were trying to do me an honor by including me in the service. If I declined, he would lose face. The only problem was, I never learned hymns. They were usually pitched too high for me. I stared into the grave. The barest glimmer of aqua leaked around the saturated scarlet cloth, and from the baby's a tinge of blue. I remembered reading on the back of an album cover once that in New Orleans, the slaves used to have parades and parties for the dead because they believed that it was a sad thing to be born into the world, a happy one to escape it. That was why "When the Saints Go Marching In" didn't sound like a funeral song. I sang the chorus and the only verse I could remember as well as I could by myself, resisting the urge to ask everyone to sing along. I doubted Ba Dinh had been a saint, but her next life, next world, whatever, could hardly be any tougher than the one she'd just left. And the snake had probably spared the baby a sad life as an unwanted Amerasian child of rape.

I sneezed twice during the song, but other people sneezed and coughed and blew their noses too. Hoa threw a last garland of jungle flowers on the grave and we all half walked, half slid down the muddy path, away from the all too populated cemetery, back down to the funeral feast.

I was given a pair of freshly carved bamboo chopsticks and a white bowl that must have been somebody's treasure. Everyone else ate out of earthenware rice bowls. The dinner was buffet style. We filed up to the cookpot, and the attendant on duty—everyone took turns—filled our bowls with snake stew and stirred while the rest of us huddled in doorways, under the nearest trees, and talked. Or rather, they talked. Nobody seemed to notice the rain soaking our clothing and running in rivulets off our faces to join the mud that caked sandals and bare feet. The fire looked more eerie than cheery and I kept thinking of the witches in *Macbeth*. The sky grew black very quickly, and the fire and an occasional oil lamp or candle were the only illumination in the village.

I choked down the snake stew. Protein wasn't to be scorned, no matter what it was, and cooked snake was better than raw rat. Besides, it was only fair that we ate the snake. It would have eaten us. Ahn scarfed down bowl after bowl. Finally there was plenty of something hot besides rice to fill our bellies with after all these days.

The heat of the food made my nose and eyes run and every once in a while I had to wipe them on my remaining sleeve. I was shivering then and sneezing as often as Ahn.

To the east, what looked like sheet lightning lit the sky, bright yellow for a few seconds, then died. Other light, streaks of it this time, followed. Slapping feet retreated from the funeral gathering, toward the jungle. Everyone's aura darkened with apprehension. The rolling thunder of mortars crumped, almost gently, in the distance. The sound gave me an odd sense of security. Then, almost as muted, the "ba-da-da-da-da-da-da," wait a beat, "ba da dada da" of automatic weapon fire repeated many times, solo and en ensemble.

Most of the villagers looked quite calm, very much as we did back at the 83rd, as though we were watching a fireworks display. But the sludge of fear oozed out around their individual auras until it lay like smog enveloping all of us. I found myself growing more afraid. Here were no bunkers, just a few flimsy houses, nowhere to go for decent cover. Suppose my countrymen didn't come through on a search-and-destroy mission but simply opened fire? Suppose the village was suddenly declared a free-fire zone? Suppose some pilot decided to empty his old spare bombs on us on his way back to base? And they didn't even know I was there, I whined to myself, it wasn't fair. They might kill me, and I was *American.*

Old Huang was carving on a stick, with the children around him. Truong and Hue weren't in sight. I thought maybe I should go see Hue; maybe if I paid my respects, told her I was sorry about her mother, we might be a little friendlier. Her hostility perplexed me. I hadn't done anything to her—just because her rapists had been American men didn't give her reason to hate an American woman.

Hue knelt amid a cloud of incense in front of a small shrine with photos of different people, a few flowers, what looked like a military decoration, a bit of embroidery, and a little piece of wood carved in the shape of an elephant.

I stood quietly in the doorway and waited for her to finish her devotions. The pictures were of men, two of them, and, recently added, one of her mother. A little covered bowl like a sugar bowl was there too. With the incense rose a gray-umber shade of mourning, and like the scent it filled the little hut, scumming the cooking pots, tainting the rice, staining the bedding and the mats.

The longer Hue knelt, the more the mourning color, and the smoke, rose, filled the room, and crept through the corners and cracks of the house to dissolve in the rain.

Her own aura, the bright colors, grew slowly stronger, clearer, until at last she rose. I was going to announce myself in a soft voice, but instead I sneezed.

Hue started and whirled around. A spasm of guilt passed through me for interrupting her, but her mouth twitched very slightly, more acceptance than annoyance. She was still dressed in her funeral clothing, white pajamas, with streaks of mud at the knees where she had fallen on the way up the hill. Her black hair was combed and shining now, the blood, mud, and sweat washed away by the rain.

I made the little hand-steepling bow. Looking troubled, she returned it, nodding over her own hands.

"I—I just came to see how your leg was." I nodded toward the damaged thigh. Her aura was still less strong there, with flecks of black reappearing. Tissue damage, I thought. The venom was gone, but its toxins would have caused some tissue necrosis, a source of infection, possibly gangrene.

She looked down at her leg, her eyes clouding with confusion. Her aura clouded and swirled again, fogging over with shock. Well, who wouldn't be in shock? She'd almost been killed, sustained a terrible injury, and lost her mother and her baby all in the same day.

I nodded toward her shrine and said as gently as I could, "Sin loi," and she steepled her hands and bowed her head again. I wasn't sure the "I'm sorry" I knew was the proper one to use, but she seemed to accept it in the spirit offered.

The light of the oil lamp glinted off her dark eyes.

I wanted to do something, to say something, that would let her know that I understood at least partially, that I sympathized. I dug into my pockets and found the crumpled package containing the last three peanut M&M's. It seemed as silly as the time I'd put my costume jewelry earrings in the collection plate at church because in a movie I'd seen a deposed duchess give the church her diamond ones since God had kept her husband alive. But I couldn't think of any other way to tell her.

"In my country, when someone dies, people bring food to the family. Please accept this candy as a symbol of my respect for your mother and for your grief," I said formally.

She looked down at the crumpled package and I expected her to open her hand and let it fall.

Instead, she slit the package as delicately as if it were an elaborately wrapped gift, extracted the three M&M's, an orange, a green, and a yellow, and set them in a triangle on her mother's shrine.

Then she dipped her head over her hands again and turned away from me, confusion whirling around her in a Joseph's coat of clashing emotions. I had to leave it at that, having done the best I could to make friends.

Outside, the wind had risen, carrying with it the acrid scent of smoke, drifting on the ozone freshness of the storm, overpowering the heavy blossom-from-decay fragrance of the jungle, the faint stench of the sewage trenches, and the mingling of incense and snake stew. It was hard to tell now what was war and what was storm. The rumbling and the flashing in the eastern sky could have been either. Rain splatted across the thatches on roofs, dinged on tiles, plopped into mud, and rattled the leaves, creating an ungodly din. The tops of the trees bobbed from side to side, bowing like an obsequious butler in some old movie. The palm-type trees bent easily, giving under the storm until they arched to the ground. The little ditches outside the houses were rapidly becoming substantial moats. Earthenware jars and plastic jerricans were set out to catch rain. People scuttled about like land crabs, spring-green anticipation mingling with the fear I'd seen earlier.

At home during such a storm the dogs would be barking, the cows stupidly heading for trees under which to get struck by lightning, and the cats curled up watching the windows, congratulating themselves on having the sense not to be outdoors. I wondered suddenly where the animals were here. With the notable exception of the snake and Hoa's puppy, I hadn't seen any animals, not so much as a chicken, much less a water buffalo. Where could they all be? I was never a genius in 4-H, but I knew enough about farming to know that not everything went to market all at once.

My GI patients told me that sometimes, to add to a body count or avoid shooting people, they shot animals, but that was mostly when they were on search-and-destroy-type operations. This village did not look as if it had been searched or destroyed. There were no burned marks on the earth, though I supposed the fast-growing greenery would have covered them up fairly quickly; it seemed that if the animals had been destroyed long enough ago for traces of other damage to be erased, the villagers would have managed to replace at least a few of the beasts.

My feet, legs, and hips ached from slogging around in the mud. Everything else was stiffening up too. Snake wrestling used muscles that I had somehow missed noticing in anatomy class.

I popped a couple of Midols without water, since I had no idea what was safe water and what wasn't, and didn't feel like going through the charades it would take to ask anybody, and lay back on the mat.

Sometime in the middle of the night a rocket whistled overhead and woke me. Ahn was not on the next mat, and our hostess, Truong, was missing too. White, orange, and red flashes popped up before my eyes as I glanced toward the door. The war was getting closer. Well, if it was going to kill me, I preferred that it land on top of me. I was too worn out to be curious about the whereabouts of anybody else. I rolled over on my stomach and pillowed my head on my arms, my eyes in the crook of my elbow so the lights wouldn't wake me, and slept again.

# 18

I woke up when they laid a bleeding man next to me. He screamed when they dropped him, and that's actually what woke me. I rolled over, looked at him, and looked up at Truong, who was heading back out the door. "What the . . . ?" I mumbled. She gave me an apologetic glance but continued on her way. In another moment an old woman with a rag tourniquet around her upper arm and a bleeding stump where her lower arm should be was dragged in beside him, followed by another young man with several bloody holes in him. That was all they seemed able to fit for the time being, so I got up on all fours to see what I could do, since I seemed to be in charge of triage and emergency room here.

Waking exhausted from nightmares to a strange room filling with mangled bodies, I had trouble focusing. What was I expected to do with these people? There was no soap, no clean water, not even an emesis basin; certainly no pain medication, no way to do surgery even if I knew what to do. Maybe this wasn't the emergency room after all. Maybe it was the morgue.

The glow of the corpses had been brighter than the auras of these people, but the man next to me began to moan and call out what sounded like a name. A pitiful little strip of rose beamed amid the rest of his aura, which looked less like a spirit's glow and more like a personal fog.

I pulled my bandage scissors from my ditty bag and cut off his shirt, though I already knew where his wound must be because the abdominal area was so bloody. He was partially eviscerated, his intestines perforated, mashed together, worms crawling in and out of them. Now I needed the emesis basin. Had there been a surgeon, he might have

been one of the mid-level patients for triage—the ones
who are salvageable but take a little longer. Without a
surgeon and proper equipment, he was a dead man. I
crawled over him to reach the old lady.

She sat rocking back and forth, holding her stump and
moaning, "Oi, oi, oi, oi," over and over. Her wound was not
as bad as the man's, though the blood loss and shock were a
bit of a problem. Here there was no poison to herd out, no
infection to rinse from her system. I was thinking that
before I could start experimenting with the amulet, I really needed to get some clean bandages. That was when
Hoa showed up with her shirttail full of gauze. Behind her
came the girl who had had her little sister on her hip
earlier that day. She was carrying the basin, the one that
had last seen duty as a funeral noisemaker, once more
filled with water. Not hot water, but water. Whoever was
playing hospital administrator was doing a pretty good job.
Hoa threw the bandages at me and ran away. I took the
water from the other child but followed her out the door.
Along the water-filled ditch, lying directly on the mud,
were a half-dozen other injured people. I didn't even look
at them. I saw Ahn with the old man and called to him.

He looked scared, and a little reluctant, but old Huang
saw me waving for the boy and scatted him toward me.
Ahn leaned on a new crutch made of a single long tree
branch, the stick I had seen Huang carving earlier. It reminded me of a wizard's staff.

"Babysan, I need help here. *Hot* water, rags."

He leaned close in toward me, his face looming large
for a moment. "Mamasan, these people are—"

"Babysan, I don't care. Just get me the stuff, okay? Ask
Huang. Ask Truong. I don't care. I'm too tired to argue. I
don't know where anything is and I don't have anything to
work with and I wish everybody would leave me the hell
alone and—" I realized my voice was rising shrilly and I
felt close to tears. "Oh shit, just tell them," I said, and
ducked back inside to try the amulet on the patients.

The amulet's power let me see right where the
wounds were, in case the shrapnel and the burns and the
bullets weren't graphic enough, but though I tried as hard
as I could to herd the blood back into the arteries, to mend
the flesh, not a damned thing happened.

I was feeling really rational. I took the amulet out of

my shirt and shook it, rubbed it off in case the accumulated grime was getting in the way of the power, like dirt on a car's headlight. I couldn't see anything wrong with it, so I put my hands close to the exposed bone and muscle of the old ba's stump and tried to think about healing. I closed my eyes and almost fell asleep then, imagining I was dreaming the carnage around me, the weird shadows of scurrying Vietnamese like flickering demons outside the hut.

Voices exclaimed from the doorway and a wet, chilled body squeezed in between the casualties, beside me. Ahn patted me on the shoulder as if I were the child and started chattering so fast that I knew I must look and sound like hell, he sounded so worried. "Mamasan, mamasan, no cry, mamasan. Mamasan, Truong say, so sorry put these miserable people next to numbah one bac si. She say, you touch Hue, Hue no die. You touch Ahn, Ahn no die. When hurt people come, she say, lay them next to Co Mao. They touch Co Mao, they get bettah pretty quick. No have to clean wounds, mamasan, no have to wrap. Just touch."

I held up my hand and it was then I noticed, without immediately realizing what it meant, that there were no broad bands of color radiating from it, just thin wisps of muddy gray with an infrequent scrap of winy-pink crawling away from me like an infection creeping up a vein. I sat and stared stupidly at the hand while my patients continued to bleed to death, to moan and shriek with pain.

Ahn grabbed my hand and forced it toward the woman's stump. "Look, mamasan, see, touch, like this," and he shoved with his own hand around my wrist till my fingers brushed the wound and the old woman screamed. I grabbed the amulet with my free hand and turned on him with all the ferocity of exhaustion. "It's not *me*, dammit. I'm not magic. I can't heal them. It's this damned thing and it's on the fucking blink."

Ahn reached up to touch it. Truong, whom I hadn't noticed in the doorway, leaned over us, watching, her hand on Ahn's shoulder. The old lady sighed. I looked down at her, thinking the sigh was her last breath.

But the first thing I saw was a soft gray-pink ring surrounding her. The next thing I saw was that it was coming from Ahn's hand and mine. Where he touched the amulet and my fingers, the green of his aura turned to mauve-pink as it blended with mine, and where my fingers touched her, the wound was closing, dirt and drainage pouring bloodlessly out as the skin crept across the bone and nerve endings. Her breathing steadied. I felt as if I'd just discovered penicillin.

Truong had been holding a lamp and now darkness flooded the room as she backed off with a hissing intake of breath. She didn't think I'd just discovered penicillin. She thought I'd just turned into a ghost.

But my exhaustion had turned to a sort of high and I grabbed her and pulled her back to us. "Ahn, it isn't just this," I said. "And it isn't just me. It's you and Truong too. And the patient. Come on, both of you, maybe we can save this man over here."

But Truong fled, her voice rising in a harsh singsong of superstitious fear.

Abruptly the doorway filled with light again and Hue and Huang stood there, with Truong behind them, pointing to the old woman and wailing. Well, it had been a long day for Truong as well, and she'd already adapted to a lot of strange things. I realized that at the time, too, with a detached patience in my mind that had nothing to do with the way I was able to act.

"Oh, shut the hell up and get lost if you can't make yourself useful," I growled. "Come on, babysan, just like before, only this time try it with one hand on mine and one on the amulet. . . ."

He tried, but the last effort had taken something out of him and his aura had shrunk and faded, the skin of his little face pulled tighter across his cheekbones. Hue stepped forward, protectively, and grabbed his shoulder to pull him away. Our mutual aura at once intensified. I held out my spare hand to her. Her aura was shot with gray-violet too, slightly weaker than either of ours, but underlying it was that clear strong yellow which spoke of high intelligence unintimidated by the appearance of magic, and a courageous, idealistic blue. She took my hand and the two of us touched the patient while my free hand held the amulet. My own aura brightened and bled into that of the man with the belly wound. When we started, the only bright aura around him was surrounding his intestinal worms. As we worked, his own aura throbbed into visibility, if not vitality, the blood stopped pumping out of him, the gut began knitting together, and the worms vacated the premises.

Ahn almost fell into the poor man before we moved on to the next patient. The job really was too draining for a young boy who had all but starved for three days.

"Babysan, you tell these people that if they want these hurt ones to get well, they had better come and help me. I cannot do this alone, and you and Truong and Hue can't be my only help. Everyone must help."

He nodded wearily and stumbled out the doorway.

Hue helped me with the man with the shrapnel wounds, who wasn't as bad as the others and under normal triage conditions would have been the first treated. By the time he was mending, no one had arrived even to watch, and I could still hear Ahn jabbering away to his countrymen to help.

Truong looked back in cautiously, and hissed again, but touched the amulet with a fleeting, reverent poke as if she was afraid its power would electrocute her. For a second I felt a flash of terror, followed by acceptance of the terror, resignation to it, feelings that I knew from her face belonged to Truong, not me. When her hand dropped, she gave me a hard, quizzical look as if she couldn't quite believe something she'd just been told, then drew close and took my hand.

We knelt in the mud beside the first patient, a deep scalp wound and left-sided enucleation (the eye had been poked out). Hue, Truong, and I made very slow progress alone, and no one stepped forward to help us until a couple of the children leaned forward and began to play with the amulet dangling from my neck as I bent over the patient, clasping hands in a ring-around-the-rosy with Hue and Truong. I felt a blast of the children's curiosity and energy, and the circle enclosed by our hands filled with rosy light. The eyeball could not be replaced, of course, but the bleeding stopped.

With the closing of the scalp wound, the rose light drained to a dirty pale pink. There were still four more patients to be treated.

I was aware of people standing around and watching, of Ahn doing his carnival-barker best to get help for me, but everyone else seemed afraid. The next patient had so many wounds it was a wonder she had any life left in her. I crawled through the mud to reach her. A girl of about fourteen, she was so covered with mud and blood that it was impossible to tell what she might have looked like if half her face hadn't been missing. I tried. Hue, Truong, and Ahn tried to help me. But we were all so drained. The girl's ragged breathing stopped. Maybe we managed to ease her pain a little before she died; I don't know. I had told Ahn that what we had to do when trying to heal these people was think about them as they might have been when well and wish hard that they be that way. The other two women, to whom he had passed on these instructions, stared at the girl in the mud. Hue's aura waned for a moment until it looked as if she was coated all over with two inches of mud that flowed out of her skin. Truong's flared, and she took the girl in her arms and began to rock her. I crawled to the next patient, looked into the face of an eight-year-old and the devastation of another gut wound, and turned away again. Ahn scooted on his butt to my side and patted me on the shoulder, but his hand didn't have much force behind it. He looked as if he was about to cry too. He kept patting me and I kept bawling. Truong was still silently rocking the dead girl, but Hue crawled over beside us. Her face was stricken, stunned with pain, but she plastered her tough look over it and started to harangue me in a slow, angry voice, trying to snap me out of it, I suppose.

"Babysan, tell her I'm sorry, but it's no good. We need more help. There's not enough magic in me to do it alone, not enough magic in all four of us."

Hue leaned over and touched the amulet as I said this and her tough face dissolved into remorse and more confusion that pierced me during the contact, so that I could hear her asking herself a jumble of angry, bewildered questions.

She raised her muddy hand to my cheek and touched it, then turned to her fellow villagers and spoke to them beseechingly, almost begging, but with an underlying steeliness that insisted on respect, insisted on attention, even while she was apparently imploring the compassion of the village.

Although I was far too wasted to consciously translate facial expression, tone, and aura in combination, something began clicking, and I became aware of what she was saying to the others. She told them that they were being shamed, that they were handing over the lives of their loved ones to a foreigner and then refusing to help her save them. The rain washed clear streaks in the mud on her face, and her plastered hair made her look as if she had drowned and returned as a banshee to haunt them.

Huang, who had been hauling bodies, was the first to react. He quieted her, patting her hand, but she placed the hand on my shoulder. Behind him came Hoa's mother, and the little girl who had carried her sister on her hip, and her brother. Ahn took Hoa's hand and put it on my shoulder. She pulled away from him for just a moment, but as the others crowded around her, her face took on a rapt look. The power flowed, flooding from the people all around me, touching me, Hoa, the patients, and one another. Then Hue spoke again and I knew without needing to know Vietnamese that she was telling them, "These are not bodies. These are not corpses. These are not merely wounds. These are your daughters, sons, fathers, mothers, sisters, brothers, aunts, uncles, cousins, neighbors, friends. Remember them working in the fields beside you, helping you build your home, doing business with you in the market, celebrating holidays with you. This child has played with your children. This child could be your child. Comfort her."

The people stood around me, or sat on their heels beside me, their hands on my shirt, my bare arms, fingers in my hair and touching my knees, my back and waist, one or two pressing too hard, most of the contact more tentative. Two of them, men I didn't recognize, touched the amulet, and from them I received an initial stab of suspicion and anger, rapidly followed by a rush of excited, strengthening energy, indecipherable amid the rest of it. I wedged my fingers between theirs and the amulet and their fingers closed over mine.

And then I remember the little girl I was touching, her gut wound healing, the skin coming together smooth and even clean, and her breathing slowing, the look of pain fading to one of fear and childish anger at being abandoned. When she started demanding her mother, I noticed the next patient. There wasn't enough room for all of the villagers to touch the girl or me, so some of them were jammed up against their neighbors but touching the other patients. All but the girl who died were already healing.

I wanted to go back to sleep, right there in the mud. But two young men helped me inside another hut. Just before I fell asleep I thought: These young men must have come from the other village, with the patients. There were no young men in this village yesterday.

Nothing should have been able to wake me, but the voices did. For one thing, they weren't the voices I'd become familiar with in the last twenty-four hours. For another thing, as tired as I was, my nerves were taut and I had a series of half-waking nightmares. A Russian in a tall fur hat was bending over my mom. I knew it was my mom, even though she didn't have a head. It was under her arm and she kept saying, "I hate to put you to all this trouble, sir. Really, my daughter can take me to the doctor in the morning." But the Russian had a secret invention, and I understood it had something to do with what Sputnik had found in space, and he was going to use this to put Mama's head back on except he didn't know which way around it was supposed to go.

Our neighborhood was up in flames and the Vietcong were marching into Bethel and pretty soon they'd cross the bridge over the gully down by Foster's house, but I knew they didn't know the land as well as I did, see. I seemed to be at home alone in our house. The family had gone someplace, or maybe had already been killed. I slunk through the backyard, past the crab apple tree, down the broken cement sidewalk, through the garden, and into the gully. I could hide in the gully and the Vietcong would never find me because they hadn't grown up on our street and only kids who had knew about the gully. Later, I snuck down to Foster's house in time to see them march across the bridge, and I crossed under it and ran way down the gully behind Foster's house. They'd never think to look for me there.

But then, even though Foster's house was two blocks away from ours, when the Vietcong got mad and set fire to our house because nobody was home, I could see everything clearly. The house went up like matchsticks and I thought: No, wait, let me get the quilt Grandma made, and the elephants Mama had been collecting, and my scrapbook of the Kingston Trio. And my kitty, Blackie, where was Blackie? And then I saw that Blackie was dead and knew they'd shot him for fun. They were burning the crab apple tree and our garden and had started on Sortors' garden when I remembered that Blackie had died when I was ten, so this had to be a dream.

I thought: But I'm good. I haven't done anything to anyone. I try to help the others, I translate, I am friendly and helpful, I assist those less fortunate. And I saw that I was pounding on a door shouting that I wanted to return to a safe place, while all around me people like zombies or lepers clawed at my clothes and tried to infect me. I was in hell, but that couldn't be right, because I had been good and done as I was supposed to.

I tried to wake myself up, but I was lying on the ground and something was wrong with my belly and I saw my intestines and knew there was a lot of blood, and I wondered why it didn't hurt. Patients always cried when they got their intestines torn out. And I said, "Hey, somebody help me stuff these things back in and sew myself up," and when I looked down again I looked like the scarecrow from *The Wizard of Oz*. And all the neighbors were standing around, not looking like factory workers and secretaries, but like farmers, wearing overalls and housedresses and carrying pitchforks. They all had that closed-off "I refuse to discuss it with you" look that Mom and Dad get sometimes—the one they get when I think they're mad at me but later I find out they're scared to death and don't want to think about it because it will scare them worse. And nobody would help me, until the guy who was guarding the POW on Carole's ward at the 83rd stepped out of the crowd, still wearing his uniform but carrying a pitchfork and wearing a nasty grin as he aimed his pitchfork at my guts.

This time I woke up. Ahn's cane tapped me on the side. "Mamasan, mamasan," he whispered.

"Huh?"

"Hurry, mamasan. Run to jungle. VC here. Hue say you go to jungle, hide."

"Okay, okay, keep your pants on," I mumbled, only half absorbing what he was saying but feeling the adrenaline zinging back into my veins like a strong jolt of caffeine.

I peeked out but saw nothing. "Where are they?"

"Hue's house. *Hurry.* Hue fool them. Have meeting. You go quick."

"Okay, but . . ." I pressed the amulet between our hands. A rush of inarticulate desperation, grief at losing yet another parent, and fear for himself and me swept to me from Ahn. I tried to project reassurance, but apparently the charm reflected only what was really in the wearer because Ahn just looked more afraid. "Didi mau, mamasan. Didi mau," he begged.

I had to slip around the front of the house, since if there was a back way I didn't know what it was. I must have slept several hours. The sky was relatively bright gray, with part of it yellower than the rest where the sun was trying to burn through. The jungle steamed with a sweet, earthy smell that made me want to lie down and bury my face in it. But I needed to find cover, and fast.

Just inside the trees I hesitated for a bare moment, undecided where to go, frightened again of mines and booby traps. Someone grabbed me from behind and I whirled around, ready to fight. Hoa tugged on my hand and pulled me behind her.

She was fogged in gray and muddied with olive-tinged brown, a color that would have made me uneasy if I wasn't already just plain terrified. She led me through some brush that had a track wide enough to have been made by a large dog or a small child. She lifted a bush and there was a hole dug beneath, not terribly big but big enough. The spot was within shouting distance of the village, without all that much cover, but it looked just like the rest of the jungle and the bush was high enough that nobody should step on me by accident. I crouched down and she pulled the bush back on top of my back. I could still see out a little, between the roots.

I waited for a long time, watching the village, watching particularly the space between Hue's house and Truong's. The voices continued shouting, but it was muffled and I kept nodding off, despite being scared to death.

How did Hoa know about this hiding place? Could that sweet little girl be a VC? Then I remembered the puppy. Of course, this must be the doghouse. I should have been able to tell by the smell . . . and the stuff that squooshed under my hands and knees.

While I was wondering where the dog was, the meeting let out. I had no idea Hue's house was so large. The whole village was there, many of the patients from the night before, and several young men and women whom I'd never seen before, plus one older man. It was to him Hue was appealing. Suddenly he backhanded her, knocking her to the ground, and one of the others, like the guard in my dream, leaned forward and jabbed her in the leg, where the snake had bitten her, with his bayonet.

The older man asked her another question, but she shook her head and kept talking. The younger man threatened her again, but his superior restrained him.

The auras of the people this morning were mostly dim and muddy. Even Hue's usually bright, fierce one was toned down with gray and the olive-brown Hoa's had shown. But the senior man's contained a burst of brilliant lemon yellow within a spotted aqua, a deep teal, and a lighter, less definite green. And though all of these were encased in a rim of brown weariness and umber depression, the yellow of the intellect, the blue of his devotion to his ideals made his aura outshine everyone else's except that of the sadistic younger man. His aura was all too familiar to me, though he wasn't. He strobed with black light that cast warped shadows on the red of his fury. Just like William on a crazy rampage.

Hue ignored him, appealing instead to the older man.

He shook his head and turned away from her. The younger man kicked her on the site of her injury and planted his foot on her abdomen, setting the bayonet blade against her face. Hoa ran shouting from among the villagers, toward my hiding place.

Staying alive around here appeared to be a popularity contest and I had just lost. I flipped the bush back, stood up, and started to run for it. I saw the trip wire just in time. It was stretched between the two trees, just beyond the dog hole.

If I had been thinking straight, I could have managed to run smack into it. But then it might not have killed me. It could have been a pungi stick trap, which would merely maim or poison me, not a grenade. My reaction time was way too slow, and by the time I made the decision and avoided it, someone was twisting my arms up behind my back so hard I heard the joints pop. The pain shot like a branding iron through the arms, into my heart, down my gut, and straight to my bladder and bowels. A knife blade twirled itself before my eyes.

Then all at once a strident voice began talking in rapid Vietnamese and one of the younger men, probably no more than a teenager, stepped in front of me while talking fast to my captor. The young man looked vaguely familiar, and though he spoke in Vietnamese I understood the gist of his speech, which would have translated to something like, "Colonel Dinh, perhaps I misunderstand the situation, but if I may venture a suggestion, I with my own eyes and all these people saw this woman—excuse me, sir, this foreign whore"—he spit at me, for effect—"perform magic that healed last night's casualties. Perhaps the Colonel would find it less embarrassing to interrogate her elsewhere."

Hearing him, understanding him, I knew him. He was one of the men who had helped me into the hut the night before, one of the strangers who had touched the amulet, and he was trying to save me. His aura was cyanotic with fear of being thought a traitor, but it also bore a blue brighter than that of his superior, blue that spoke of a part of his spirit that had been revived. When he touched the amulet, when he helped heal his comrade, he had healed a little, too. Furthermore, he was still a little linked to me, even though time had passed and contact was broken. He carefully avoided looking at me.

The colonel strode in front of me, glared at me, nodded abruptly, and I was manhandled back to the village. The little creep who held my arms had to bend me over double to keep my wrists between my shoulder blades, because he wasn't tall enough to reach my shoulder blades easily when I stood up straight. So I stumbled ahead of him to where Hue sat painfully erect, watching our progress with an aura cloaked in battleship-gray and her eyes desperately hard. Something gleamed in the mud: her gold tooth.

The others had disappeared—including Ahn. The villagers were still protecting him, which I took to mean that the young soldier who had spoken to the colonel was right. The village was too frightened of the VC to try to save me, but the colonel would be pushing his luck to mistreat me here. Damn. William knew I was here and there was a slim chance he might have found other men, that I might still

be rescued, although I wasn't sure that by the time that
happened I would be in any shape to know the difference.

While I was thinking this over, surrounded by small
people who were smirking at me, poking, groping, and
otherwise trying to make me jump so that my arms would
hurt even worse, the colonel stooped and extended a hand
to Hue. He said something gruff and disapproving to her.
She looked up at him and spoke again. And again I understood what she was saying without translation. The words
of my captors, except for the boy who had talked to the
colonel, were still a blessed mystery to me. Obviously, a
detached part of me decided, the amulet formed a link
between those who touched it, one that conferred understanding—I supposed it must simply get clearer and more
literal with practice, or length and intensity of contact. Or
perhaps I simply understood more because of the urgency
of my need to know what was being said.

Hue's face was swollen, bleeding, and covered with
filth, but she said in the calm, soft voice appropriate to a
well-bred Vietnamese girl, "I have done nothing incorrect,
Father. You are mistaken about the woman. She is not
really an American. She's a magician who has made herself
look like an American, to test us, if you ask me. She saved
my miserable life. Would you have me dishonor our ances-
tors by betraying her?"

The colonel stood, and just for a moment the brilliant
yellow of his aura flickered with indecision; then he
marched us out of the village.

I couldn't keep up. The VC trotted through places my
body wouldn't fit, and the branches tore at me. I kept
closing my eyes to try to protect them, because bent over
as I was, my face was even with the backlashing brush that
hit me when the others passed. Small hard bodies crowded
me on all sides, shoving so that I was afraid of being tram-
pled. Finally I fell.

I fell forward, face down into the mud, without being
able to use my hands to break my fall. My teeth bit into my
lips and cheeks and my nose started bleeding. The little
bastard who had been holding on to me fell onto my back
and I rolled over angrily and dumped him. "Let me alone,
dammit," I squalled. "I haven't done anything to you." My
feelings were hurt as badly as they had been in my dream
when I found out I was in hell. And even while I was

bellowing, I realized how stupid it all was. I was going to get killed in an undoubtedly nasty and painful fashion by people I had absolutely no quarrel with. How many of their relatives had been killed the same way? How many of my patients had survived the same sort of thing? It was all so dumb. I screamed something to that effect.

The young soldier who had tried to help me that morning knelt beside me, placatingly, but the colonel backhanded me the way he had done his daughter. I saw the blow coming and ducked away from it. That was a mistake. He knocked the young soldier out of the way and reached for me with both hands. His aura didn't change, except for a few sparks of red, and I knew that he didn't really care about me personally one way or the other, but was angry that Hue had taken my side against him. And though no one else could see, I knew from the foggy gray encompassing his aura that he was mourning his wife, the woman who was killed by the snake. His movements were precise and mechanical as he cut his way through a swamp of shock and loss.

He grabbed my hair first, but it was short and slick with mud and rain, so he switched his grip to the thong that held the amulet around my neck and jerked on it. The thong cut across my windpipe and I started to cough, then didn't have the breath to cough, gagged, and felt my face swell with unoxygenated blood. My lungs pumped like crazy, my whole chest burning, and water streamed from my eyes and nose. My ears rang and everything started to cloud over.

And that detached part of me thought: Oh boy, the press is going to love this one—Kitty McCulley, girl martyr. I wonder how many extra innocent people are going to get wasted as payback for me? The thought did not fill me with a savage thrill of vengeance. It just made me sadder and angrier and more frustrated with the whole miserable mess. I was going to die poorly and stupidly and senselessly. Shit.

Deadness tried to enter through the amulet, but my own fear and anger cut through it like a red-hot chain saw.

Oxygen flooded back into my lungs like water poured over a burn as the thong was released. My head kept swimming for several moments, but no blow, no questions followed. The little bastard with the hot-lava aura griped in a high-pitched voice and was very plainly saying something like "Let me at 'er, let me at 'er," but nobody was touching me anymore, and I was allowed to bury my face in my hands and gasp until my heartbeat and respirations resumed something like normal function.

When I finally looked up, the colonel was half a step from me, staring at me. He looked as shaken as I felt. When I looked at him, he looked away. Lava-aura made a disgusted noise in his throat and growled something at the colonel, which earned him a glower. The colonel did bear a family resemblance to Hue, especially in his truculent expression and the intelligence in his eyes. But he was balding on top, and his sharp cheekbones and chin triangulated to give him a closer resemblance to the snake that had killed his wife.

He seemed to come to a decision and, elbowing aside both lava-aura and my ally, squatted down before me and spoke clearly, distinctly, and loudly—in Vietnamese. My ally protested that I didn't know Vietnamese, so the colonel raised his voice and spoke louder. But it wasn't necessary. While his individual words didn't make sense to me, I still was able to catch his drift. He looked into my eyes, pointedly away from the amulet.

"They say you have healing hands, woman. I should cut those hands off to keep my people from falling under your spell. But my ignorant daughter says you mean no harm, that you use this power to help our people—that you are a compassionate person. If that is so, you have other power to help us. You come up North with us, you talk to your American press, you tell them that your men rape our women, murder them, but we treat you with respect. You tell them how wrong this war is. You say to them that your healing hands can make no difference when for every person you save, thousands die. You do this, woman, and earn your life. Do not think to trick us. Up North they have good speakers of English."

He kept looking directly into my eyes when he spoke, and I knew that he knew I understood what he was saying. I nodded. I wasn't lying. I was so relieved I felt faint with it. Right then I wanted to please him more than I wanted to please my own father, more than I wanted to please Duncan, more than I had ever wanted to please anyone. He could have me tortured to death or he could protect me, and he had chosen to protect me, for the time being. Once we got "up North," wherever that was, it might be another story, but for now I was going to live. I dipped my head and nodded, and snuck a glance at his face. He looked as relieved as I felt, and there was something else in his face too, something that he tried to conceal from everyone —something that embarrassed and intrigued him at the same time. Without knowing anything of my background, family, language, or customs, he now knew me as well as he knew Hue. Better, maybe. And if he killed me, he would know exactly who and what he was killing. Not that he hadn't killed many times before, women, old people, children. But he had steeled himself not to hear those people, to think of them as something besides people, as something he had no responsibility toward, no obligation to understand. He would not be able to bullshit himself about me. Holding on to that amulet, strangling me, he'd inadvertently become closer than my mother, closer than a lover, and he couldn't weasel out of it without damaging himself even more than he had already been damaged. While he held the charm, what I was had poured toward him and, taken by surprise, he had been unprepared to reject it. Only now, as he began to wrestle with his reaction to the amulet and to me, could I understand his share in the link.

Gruffly he ordered me to stand, but when my former guard tried to manhandle me again, he berated him, told him to tie my hands in front of me and lead me, what did he think he was doing, hobbling me that way so that I slowed us down? He could get his jollies feeling me up when they weren't in such a hurry.

# 19

I couldn't keep up. My captors breezed through the jungle as if it were a city park and they were the street gang in charge. They ate a handful of rice once a day and took a drink maybe twice. I was woozy with hunger and thirst before we'd been traveling an hour. Colonel Dinh thinned his lips irritably but had my other friend give me a drink of yellowed water and a salt tablet and off we went again.

The first night we slept in a tunnel. I've heard there were great complexes of them, but the one we were in was more like an underground bunker. The passage was narrow, obviously not made for an American girl's hips. The other men preceded us, with my village ally going just before me, and the colonel just after.

Oddly, now that I knew I was in no immediate danger from the colonel, I felt less frightened than I had at any time since I'd come to the jungle. I didn't have to worry about booby traps or mines. These were the guys who set them. I didn't have to worry about enemy capture. That had already happened. I had nothing to worry about except what might happen when we got where we were going, which was still a long way off, and whether or not an air strike might accidentally hit us. So with my friend from the village on one side of me and the colonel on the other, and the passage too small for any moving around, I slept better than I had since I'd left the 83rd. My captors could sleep soundly too. The colonel was watching the entrance. If any Americans stumbled across the tunnel, the colonel could shove me forward as a shield.

My eyes opened on darkness, and I squeezed them shut again. I remembered that something terrible had happened, something irrevocable, but for a moment I couldn't remember what it was and I didn't want to. I smelled the earth, rich and musky, and something dead. I stretched out my hand and touched flesh and hair, withdrew the hand quickly. My heart pounded with panic. Was I dead? Buried? Was this another corpse in some mass grave? Slowly I forced myself to calm down, felt the area around me. Someone groaned. Someone else's sandals were in my back. I opened my eyes. Along the tunnel passage lay the sleeping bodies of my captors, cloaked in their various-colored auras, looking for all the world like the ghosts of Easter eggs lining some subterranean nest. I tried to sit up and bumped my head on something hard. A restraining hand pushed me back down. The sandals dug into my back as the colonel sat up. A pencil-thin shaft of light fell across my eyes, then a volleyball-sized shaft, as the colonel lifted the cover away from the tunnel entrance. He climbed out and extended his hand. I climbed out after him.

He sat on a log and lit a cigarette, offered me one. I took it. He sat staring into space for a long time. He was wearing a pistol. I could have taken it during the night, I supposed, but I'm not sure what I would have done after that. "Babe in the woods" didn't even begin to describe my degree of total helplessness and ineptitude.

He caught me looking at the gun.

"Do not force me to kill you, co."

"I wouldn't dream of it," I murmured in English. He looked surprised, then wary, at my response. I don't think he understood precisely what I said. I think his comprehension was general, in the same way that mine initially had been. I saw him wondering if perhaps I wasn't a magician after all, because, of course, he didn't understand the power of the amulet. He was puzzled by the sensation that he understood me, when he knew logically that he couldn't have.

The drizzle wet my cigarette through almost at once, and I chewed on the end of it, bringing saliva to my mouth to relieve the dryness. The jungle was thick here, the undergrowth tall and twining.

The colonel stubbed out his cigarette, field-stripped it,

put it in his pocket, and poked the man nearest the tunnel entrance with a twig.

Before we left the tunnel site, one of the soldiers, a boy of about fourteen, rigged a mine to the entrance.

We spent the morning climbing. My guard and I were the very last in the column, with machetes hacking up ahead of us. The trail was so steep that my thighs started throbbing with exertion after only a few steps. Gradually the ground yielded to more rocks than brush.

At the top of the ridge we rested, or rather, the colonel ordered a halt so that I could rest. As I caught my breath, I found I was inhaling stale smoke. It was coming from the valley below us. What I had mistaken for jungle steam was still drifting up from the charred ruins of the village hit the previous night. Among the few buildings still standing or partially intact, a few people wandered dazedly. The colonel gave me a smug look. This was the village from which my patients came. We had skirted it carefully, avoiding the survivors, lest anybody be grateful enough to help me, I supposed. I shrugged at him. He'd been overly cautious. Those people below us looked to me to be too out of it to care.

I was trying to be casual for the colonel's benefit, but the sight of those people, homeless, grieving for who knows what losses, and alone in the jungle, shook me. Their fields were bombed and blackened. How would they eat? They were hurt. How would they work? Right now they apparently were sympathetic to the VC and taking fire from us, but it could as easily turn the other way, I knew. Would Hue's village be bombed soon? I wondered. Or would it be invaded again—what if William found those GIs and told them about me and they returned to the village to find me gone? What would they do to the villagers? Jesus, out of the frying pan into the fire for those people. It must be like living in a Stephen King novel you can never finish—a new fate more horrible than the last on every page. Well, I'd gotten too close and now I was in it as well and I didn't even want to think about what would happen to me—unless William stayed sane long enough to bring help.

Ahn would try to tell a rescue party what had become of me, I was sure, but how could he do that without condemning the people who had taken him in? I wondered if he would be alive by the time help came. His wound could break open again or, worse, someone might decide he was dangerous to them and kill him. Sometimes, I heard, children who had lost limbs were poisoned. The reasoning supposedly was that they would not be able to lead useful lives and would be more abused as they grew older. I hoped Ahn's stubborn streak and the self-interest that had caused him to flee William would stand him in good stead. Some mamasan he'd picked. I'd wanted to protect him so that I would not have to watch him die or hear of it, but how soon after I took him to Quang Ngai would he have been in a situation as bad as his present one, if not worse? They couldn't keep him in the hospital forever. If I really cared, if I'd fought hard enough, couldn't I have adopted him? I doubted it. Even GI fathers married to the mothers of their Amerasian children had trouble moving their Vietnamese families to the States. It was a good thing I hadn't promised to adopt Ahn. I would never be going back to the States myself now. I stopped thinking then. It was much less painful to agonize about what would happen to Ahn and the villagers than it was to think about what would happen to me.

We ate dry handfuls of uncooked rice, a little harder to chew than unmilked Grape-Nuts, and I had another swig of water. I still needed to rest. My wind wasn't up to this. The colonel took three men aside and started pointing things out, a few yards away from me. I was staring at my boots, feeling the mud run off me with the rain, wondering idly if part of my shortness of breath wasn't encroaching pneumonia, when something sharp jabbed my left breast. I looked up and there was lava-aura, pointing his bayonet at my chest, grinning as if he'd done something clever.

When I looked up he jabbed me again, on the other side. Trying to deflate me, the adolescent asshole. He jabbed again and, swinging my bound hands, I shoved the damned thing aside. It laid open the side of my arm, which bled freely since I couldn't even put pressure on it to stop it. He smiled unpleasantly. "Let me alone, you jerk," I said, half-sobbing. He smiled even more unpleasantly and twitched the bayonet back and forth at eye level, my blood mixing with rain and dripping off the tip.

We had creeps like that on our side too, congenital sadists, probably, little boys whose favorite sport was tearing wings off butterflies or torturing kittens, boys who finally had a little authority and used it to abuse anyone who came under their control. And he had me good. If I screamed, he might not kill me but he could very well put out my eye, just for the fun of it. He wanted to scare me and was doing a damned good job of it, but I was getting so angry at his bullying I was beginning not to care. The balance between being afraid of mutilation and being determined to shove that damned thing up his ass was rapidly tilting toward the more suicidal choice. I didn't have much to gain either way, except satisfaction.

I was steeling myself to lunge at the damned thing when someone picked up my tether and jerked it sideways, slamming me down into the mud. In almost the same instant an explosion lifted my tormentor off his feet and knocked him halfway down the hill.

I brushed the mud from my eyes as my ally helped me back onto my rock and started fussing over my cut. I lifted my hands to my neck and took the amulet in my fingers, brushing it against my guard while he examined my cut. The blue of his aura had been darkening a little, but now it brightened and grew a fragile shoot of mauve. I could not see what was happening, but I felt the bleeding stop. I dropped the amulet casually back into my shirt as the guard looked back at me, awe and guarded hope in his face. He had been with the liberation movement since the Diem government executed his family. He had thought the movement would be a way to avenge his family, help his country. He was not so sure now. Sometimes the scene he had watched from hiding—his parents, grandparents, sisters, and brothers being deliberately murdered—came back to him in the things he and his comrades did. He had wanted to be a Buddhist monk and then for a while he yearned to be admitted to the Party. He had wanted to drive out foreign aggressors and their puppet governments. Instead, as a child, he had carried bombs to blow up boys not much older than he who were sometimes trying to be kind, and "punished" villagers the way his parents had been punished. He had begun to doubt the good in anything until the night in the village. He was Hien. He would do for me what he could, but what was his unworthy protection compared to that of Colonel Dinh himself?

The colonel frowned down the hill, his .45 already

replaced in its holster. With Hien's help, I rose to my feet. The body of lava-aura sprawled halfway down the hillside. His death aura did not change or clarify. It remained black and red, almost indistinguishable from his physical appearance—half of his chest covered in blood, a black cloud of insects already gathering around him. Was I right about his being vicious since boyhood? Was he simply a naturally talented sadistic psychotic killer? I wondered. Perhaps his aura had started out like William's, just occasional flashes of killer craziness, and had eventually taken over his whole personality. From my standpoint, it didn't matter much.

"Thank you," I said, bowing to the colonel, but he turned on his heel and walked away from me, making a small gesture that mustered the group back into action.

Lava-aura's body was left where it fell. I examined the auras and faces of the men around me. I was afraid some friend of his would blame me and try to kill me out of revenge.

But the men around me didn't even look at the body. Hien hummed softly to himself. He wasn't the only one to seem relieved. Some of these men were hard-core dedicated troops, true, but several were virtual draftees from the villages, men who had joined the Vietcong because to do otherwise would cost their lives or those of their families. Most of the auras never changed, just remained the same muddy brown, indifferent, numbed, and hard as nails, but without the vitality their late comrade had derived from hurting people. No one seemed to blame me. I would have been flattering myself to think the colonel had killed one of his own men on my account. The man had been executed for disobeying orders. Even a guard dog that doesn't mind its master and bites unpredictably has to be put down.

Just before dark we headed down the ridge, toward another village. Everyone grew marginally more tense, the colonel's aura sparking with anxiety. A few yards from the perimeter, we saw a man with a rifle. He yelled, "Dung lai," but as we got closer, he saw that this was no time to play *High Noon* and scuttled off into the village, his aura leaving a light trail of gray-violet fear.

The colonel exchanged a few words with his men and nodded into the jungle, the paddy, up the hill. One of the men with flat, muddy auras took the point position walking into the village. I tried not to allow myself to feel excited. If the colonel was being so wary here, that must mean this was not a VC village. Or at least not entirely. Maybe they were even hiding American troops, right now. Maybe . . .

I was looking the other way, squinting into the hills, trying to see what the colonel had been nodding at, when the point man stepped on the mine. I heard the explosion —no big thing, really, for Nam—and the howl of pain almost at once. Some of the others started to run forward, but the colonel stopped them with a gesture and strode over to the man with a confidence only I could see was tinged with fear.

He hollered to Hien, who suddenly looked as if he might faint. His aura was whirling with teal, pale grayed olive, and violet, underlain with mustard. He believed I was special, a saint perhaps, and should be protected and helped, but he was a simple man, not a brilliant one like the colonel, and he was afraid. His very thoughts were traitorous. If there was help here for me—but the colonel was beckoning us across the minefield and Hien removed the rope from my wrists and took my hand to lead me forward, showing me by example that we must step only in the colonel's footsteps.

The colonel nodded to the injured man, telling me to do my thing, whatever it was. Then he signalled everyone except Hien to follow him into the village. Now the yellow in his aura swirled with a sad brown the color of an old bloodstain, and red kindled in the blue. The auras of the men blended in similar combinations with his—the influence, I suppose, of a leader more charismatic than he wanted to be or realized.

I cut away what was left of the point man's trousers. His left leg was severed above the knee, the femoral artery spurting. I started applying pressure, as I normally would, and imagined the artery sealed, the wound mending, a smooth clean stump, but the wound continued to spurt until I took Hien's hand in one of mine and held it, trembling, against his comrade's wound. Blood covered both of us now, but gradually it receded, like a film of a flowing river shown in reverse. Hien looked from the patient to me with eyes as large as bomb craters. The injured man had groin wounds, too. He would father no more children, but with Hien holding him with one hand and holding my hand with the other, the wounds magically began forming granular tissue from the inside, one of the initial stages of the healing process. This time the process looked like a film run on fast forward. But it wouldn't be fast enough to save him from sepsis. For that we would need more hands. My strength was gone and Hien's had been drained with the healing we'd done together.

I looked up from the patient to see if the colonel was anywhere close, to ask him to send us someone else to help.

He was not close, but he was close enough for me to see what happened.

They had gathered the village together, with the frightened perimeter guard, now unarmed and scared halfway to death already, in the center. His aura shot sickly pus-purple. He looked like a teenager—a good-looking boy with his black hair parted on one side. He was probably not old enough to have been drafted by the ARVN. His eyes looked like a frightened horse's, the twilight bouncing off them, and he kept babbling at the colonel in a tone at once apologetic and argumentative.

The colonel gave an order and one of the VC, a man whose skin was mottled as if he had been burned at some time, stepped forward. Another man pushed the boy to his knees and forced his arms up so that his head bent low. I thought they would shoot the boy, but the man with mottled skin drew a machete from his belt and started hacking the boy's neck.

I buried my head in my hands and screamed, my screams lost in those of the others, the moans and wailing and "oi oi-ing" of the frightened villagers. I didn't want to look back up, but I couldn't help it. One by one an old man and an equally ancient woman, a middle-aged woman, a girl and the baby on her hip, and three older children, the boy's family perhaps, or village elders, or both, were kicked into the center, bent over double, and butchered as the boy had been. I was on my feet now, screaming and screaming for them to stop.

The colonel had been as coolly intent on the executions as if he were supervising a ditch digging or a concrete pouring. Almost casually, he glanced our way and his eyes met mine, cutting through the twilight. His face looked just the same, but his aura was a bare wisp of drabness around him.

Hien grabbed the amulet and jerked me back down beside him. His hand flew up and first stung my cheek, then burned it, and I thought my head, too, would fly off as I fell across our patient, Hien still holding the amulet. The pain in my face was nothing compared to the fear pouring from Hien. Fear more overwhelming than anything I had ever felt flooded through me, and I knew what it meant to be literally spineless as my backbone and knees turned to jelly. We'd be killed, we'd both be killed, the worst possible deaths would be needed to set an example, deaths that would make the simple beheading of those villagers look humane. I must be quiet, I must pretend not to be there, or I would force the colonel to kill me and then kill Hien for not shutting me up.

Hien released the amulet and pinned my arms as the colonel left the troops, now firing on some of the huts, and marched toward us. I was at the same time angry with Hien for slugging me and furious with myself for my own idiocy. Hien's recriminations echoed through every capillary and nerve ending in my body. How could I have been so stupid, so spoiled, as to think the pragmatic mercy that had been shown me so far meant that I had any influence on the normal course of duty? This village had caved in to the enemy. This village had set mines that were responsible for the death of a soldier of the liberation. This village had been punished, and now my foolish actions would force the colonel to make an example of me, to show these people how worthless their American allies were.

Footsteps slapped through the mud and the colonel stood over us, the light from a torch carried by one of the men behind him reflecting off his head. He scowled down at us and examined the patient, who was now conscious, briefly. Then he nodded to my guard and put his pistol to the head of the wounded soldier. Blinding pain shot through my own head, breaking the auras into millions of light motes that spun like galaxies through the darkness.

# 20

I was dead. I knew I was dead. They'd shot me in the head and that's why I saw all those stars. I was nothing but an aura looking for a place to land. When I opened my eyes to darkness again, I knew I was definitely dead. I had felt the shot. They shot me because of my wounds. A soldier with one leg and no genitals would slow them down and the nearest hospital was many kilometers away. . . .

No, that was wrong. I was alive. It was the point man who had lost his genitals and leg. He was the one who was shot. But I was the one lying in darkness with a terrible pain in my head, scared almost literally to death. I tried to sit up, and if there had been anything in my environment that could have spun, it would have. I fell back again and lost the day's rice ration, having to twist suddenly to keep from vomiting while I was landing on my back, and choking myself. It was difficult because my hands were bound again, and my feet too.

I did the old deep-breathing routine and sat up much more slowly. My head hit pay dirt before I'd done a complete sit-up, and I raised my hands. A wedge of cold black, a little lighter than the blackness in my hole, poured in as something slipped back from my palms, and hot shadows danced across my face. I was in another tunnel, perhaps a rice storage bin.

I was not dead, I had not been injured, I was not even imprisoned. I was hidden. My patient had been murdered and I was alive and hidden. A whole family had been murdered, and in the village beyond my hiding place I saw that the thatch of two of the whitewashed mud houses had been set afire. Had the colonel casually burned the houses to make enough light to finish his punishment of the village?

I could not have been unconscious very long. The people had not changed position. The colonel had returned to the village, though the body of my poor patient still lay in the mud, among the mines.

Pigs squealed and chickens squawked madly as some of the VC troops tried to round them up. Children shrieked and cried while their mothers tried frantically to hush them. One old woman tried to crawl to one of the bodies and was kicked away.

The colonel made a circle with his arm, and his men stopped chasing chickens and started grabbing children from their mothers or herding them toward the gate. The shadows of flames burned across Dinh's face and hands, making an aura of their own for him.

The children were lined up at the village gate, facing the mined path as if they were to run a footrace. Dinh took two of the oldest by the shoulders and pointed across the minefield to my dead patient. His arm dropped as the roof of one of the houses collapsed in a fountain of sparks and flying, flaming thatch straw, and the boys half ran, half stumbled through the gate.

I closed my eyes to focus. When I looked up again, Hien's agonized face covered the opening of the hole. His lip was swollen so that his back teeth were bared. Firelight caught the gold in one of them. His eye was cut and swollen, too. He had given up on trying to be gentle. He put his hand on top of my head and tried to shove me back in the hole. He must have been sitting behind it, or to one side, so intent on watching the village it had taken him some time to notice that I'd opened the hole.

The force of the next explosion startled both of us. He jumped away from the mouth of the hole. Earth and rice tumbled to the floor of the hole as the vibrations shook the ground and the smell of gunpowder joined the acrid stench of burning thatch. A woman screamed short, staccato screams. I poked my head back out the hole again.

The colonel stood in the midst of the executed villagers, who lay at his feet like so many disassembled store dummies. Four of his men held automatic weapons on the adults of the village. Four more held automatic weapons on the children who had been walking cautiously down the mined pathway. For a split second, the children froze as if they were playing a grotesque game of statues. Then one of the smaller ones, a little naked boy of about three, began crying and tried to run back to his mother. He and his screeches were lost in the flash from another explosion.

I knelt back down in the hole and vomited bile down my legs and onto my feet. I didn't want to look back, but I did. The guards stood menacing the two older boys, who had reached the dead VC and were now trying to drag him between them back to the gate. Only one of them made it.

I didn't watch the rest. I retched and retched into the hole while the crackling of a fire, the sobs of the bereaved, were punctuated eight more times, I counted, with fresh explosions and shrieks.

After a very long time Hien pulled me, dizzy and shaken, from the hole. The colonel and all but one of his men stood nearby, with several new recruits from the village. Some of the new people were the mothers of the children; one I recognized as one of the boys who had been hauling the body. He was reeling from shock but trying to smoke a cigarette and look as if he'd been plucked from the unemployment line for some routine job. No one would ever be able to tell the difference between him and a regular Vietcong, and in time he wouldn't be able to tell, either.

The fires from the houses were burned out and I did not look for the auras of either the dead or the living. I did not look in the direction of the village at all. I allowed myself to be led away from it, through a lesser nightmare of biting insects and vines and tree roots that tripped me and made me fall. Toward morning, Hien dragged me after him into another tunnel bunker. I felt him shaking beside me, as if he were palsied. Even after he grew quiet, I couldn't sleep. I was afraid to. I could not believe, when Dinh had done such terrible things to his own people, that he would let me live much longer. My God, what if he had found Ahn? What would he have done to him? He'd never find out from me. And neither would Hien. Poor Hien. He was too damned scared of Dinh to really be of any use to me. But maybe he would send some last words to my mom, if I could think of any.

On my other side, the colonel flopped restlessly. I pulled as far from him, as close to Hien, as I could get. I could still smell the blood, the gunpowder, the smoke, on Dinh's clothing. He rolled toward me once and I flinched away. He sat halfway up in the tunnel, and tugged my rope.

He pulled me after him into the open, where he lit a cigarette and put it to his mouth as if it were an Aqua-lung and he were underwater.

He handed it to me after a puff, but I waved it away. I was already coughing so hard my sides hurt. "Hien saved your worthless life last night, woman," he said.

I nodded listlessly. I had dragged myself through most of the trip away from the village. Of all the terrible things that happened, the deaths of the family and the children, I think what did the worst harm to me was when Dinh shot my patient out from under me so soon after I had poured all of my energy into his cure. Part of me was still gone, out there in the twilight zone somewhere with the augmented aura of my former patient. I don't know if it was the same for Hien. Maybe. I never found out.

I looked down at my filthy feet and ran my tongue around my blood-and-bile-fouled mouth. It tasted as if it had been stuffed with filthy dressings. I couldn't stand to look at Dinh. Never in my life had I hated anyone so much. The way he had butchered that whole family. Those poor babies in the minefield. That helpless man who thought we were going to help him. It made me thoroughly sick to think I had ever regarded such a monster as a human being, much less a protector.

I was chilling so badly it felt as if a winter wind were blowing straight into my marrowless bones. When he touched me I felt I'd been thrown into a pit full of rattlesnakes. I couldn't seem to stop shuddering.

I thought he winced ever so slightly as he withdrew the cigarette, as he had not winced at killing children in front of their mothers and one of his own—no, two of his own men. His aura was little more than a thread of light around him now, the colors so smudged and muddied it was hard to tell what they had been.

But he only smiled and blew a smoke ring that was immediately dispersed by the drizzle. And he spoke quietly, almost offhandedly, in Vietnamese, as you might speak to a dog or a cat, or perhaps to a total stranger when you have something so terrible to say that you don't want anyone you know or care about to hear. "You were displeased by what happened in the village, co. I could not allow you to undermine my authority there—it would have proved fatal for you if you had even attempted to intervene. But now you can tell me what you would have told me then."

I licked my lips, and flicked the rain into my dry mouth. One of my teeth was loose. I started to speak and he casually leaned over and touched the amulet. I pulled away, resenting the gesture as fiercely as if he had stuck his hand in my crotch. I didn't want this man to know me any more. I didn't want to know him. He grimaced, trying to make me think he was amused at my repulsion, but he wasn't. I relaxed just a little with a sense of revenge. He had already known I hated him. Touching the amulet wasn't a sadistic act toward me—it was a masochistic one for him.

"I was just going to say stop," I said. "I was going to say, don't do it. They're your own people. How could you?"

"But I had to do it. By sparing you, by sparing the village that harbored you, by sparing my backsliding daughter, I was already in grave error. Believe me, I would not have done so if it was not that I think certain influential men will be pleased to have you among us."

I wondered then if he intended to lie for Hue and the village, to say that they captured me and had the foresight to keep me alive and hand me over. I hoped he was that human, anyway.

"You could have let me help the injured children, the ones who survived," I said.

"I did not wish them to survive. I did not wish to make a folk heroine of you, to have legends of you spread over the countryside. I wish no one to know of you until we reach the North. I will tell you something between the two of us, co. I am still attached to that worthless daughter of mine. I am grateful to you for saving her and for what you did for those people. Did you know that the entire village risked my wrath, risked having happen to them what happened to this other village today, to plead for your life? They have not cared about the lives of anyone outside their own families for decades, and now that you are gone they will forget you as if you were a disturbing dream and revert to their apathy. Though I try not to be a superstitious man, I believe that my daughter is correct about you. I believe that you are a holy woman in a rather unusual guise, and I respect that. If it were up to me as a man, I would take you back to your people. If it were up to you as a simple woman, I believe that you would continue to use your gift as you have been doing, for the benefit of anyone who needs you. But it is not up to me, or to you.

"If I release you, your gift will be discovered in time and your government will use your gift to lead my people to the false conclusion that the Will of Heaven is with the Americans and resistance useless. Do you understand? Wandering among us in normal times, you would be a mendicant holy woman. Among your people, what you mean as good is a weapon against us. Even if you do not mean to cooperate, they can force it. You and your gift will be scrutinized, analyzed, and your talent ultimately perverted to military purposes, which I know, and you know, are the thing furthest from your heart. Unfortunately, I can promise you that if you cooperate, my side will do much the same, but it is *my* side. I cannot betray it by allowing you to fall back into the hands of the enemy. I can protect you only so far."

"As far as you protected that man who stepped on the mine? Or those children?" I asked.

"It was necessary that the village pay in its most valuable currency for its treachery. The soldier would have been no good to us alive. Dead, he made it at least seem a fair trade. I have done many things to your own countrymen you would like even less well," he said with deliberate menace that failed to frighten me nearly so much as his gentle tone of regret. "You are overly sentimental."

"I am overly human," I said bitterly. "What's your problem?"

He sighed and extended his limbs in a gesture that was more writhing than stretching, then returned to his relaxed pose, the cigarette dangling from his fingers, which dangled between his knees. "I knew I should have killed you back at the village. I hope you don't think I'm a good example of a dedicated Communist. I'm not even a Party member yet, though perhaps you will help me become one. I'm not really worthy. I haven't yet purged all of the reactionary Confucian notions from my heart." He grimaced when he said the last, too. Neither communism nor Confucianism really meant anything to him, his voice and face said. They were constructs that were useful because of how other people used them to define him. Then he looked back up at me, and though his aura had been too slim for me to read it, I could read his eyes. They were like those of a patient who's had a stroke and has just awakened to find himself paralyzed, his face crooked and his mouth unable to make intelligible sounds. "Damn you, woman," he said finally. "Do you want to know why I really saved your life?"

I blinked assent.

"At first it was because it would have shamed me to kill you, shamed my daughter, shamed my wife's memory, shamed the movement in front of my home village. And, of course, I would have had to kill my daughter, to whom I am incorrectly sentimentally attached, before I could have killed you. But later, in the jungle, when I intended to kill you, I did not because when I looked at you, started to question you, for the first time in years I saw another person—a living person. Everyone has been walking corpses to me for years, even my daughter. But I think now I should have killed you at once after all. Life is not meant to return to a dead limb, and now that it does, it burns with the fires of hell."

Hien crawled out of the hole then, followed by some of the others, and we resumed our march. We were doing most of our traveling in the evening, at night, just as the American troops were making camp and starting to assign patrols.

I think Hien must have heard some of what the colonel said. He stuck very close to me, the blue of his aura all but buried in an avalanche of depressed brown. The night before must have been more horrible for him than it was for me, must have made him relive again the massacre of his own family. Knowing how frightened he was, and how he had acted to save my life, painful as it was, I felt protective of him that last day. And something strange happened. We had to walk close to each other, as the brush was very thick and the machetes slow to cut it clear. Hien held on to my tether and pretended to push me around while actually inspecting the damage he had done to my face and trying to slow the pace so that I could keep up. It was a great effort for him, because he was, as I say, very low. But I noticed that my aura, though very weak and faded to the dirty pink of a tenement baby's sixth-hand Goodwill Easter dress, gradually engulfed his. It was like what I had seen happen with the colonel and his men, and it confused me.

I did not know what to do, or what to say, about the way he, the village, and the colonel were reacting to me. It was like when the wrong guy falls in love with you for the wrong reasons that have nothing to do with you. These people were assuming that I did the things I did because I was who I was, that I was making the amulet do what it did, instead of simply discovering what it would do as I went along. Even when I totally lost all my ability to use it, back at Hue's village, and the villagers and Hien had to help me, they thought I was sharing my power, not borrowing theirs.

And yet I couldn't just take the amulet off. The big reason, of course, was that without it I was just another American invader worthy of no special attention except the kind I could do without. But also, in some strange way, I had become what I can only describe as addicted to the amulet, dependent on it. I drained myself through it into patients, but as long as it was with me, I felt as if I had a way of renewing myself. I realized why old Xe had waited until he was dying to give it up. It was as invested with my life as I was with its power. And of course, so long as I had it, I might be subjected to some unrealistic worship but I was not tortured or summarily executed as I would have been without it.

I think that if I had had Xe's years of experience and wisdom, I could have done much more with the power while I had it. I wish I had at least been able to do more for Hien.

When the ambush came, he was the one who knocked me down and threw himself on top of me, taking my share of the bullets and frags. Dying, his body twitched on top of me, and I hesitate to say it, but it was as if he were making love to me. And I guess he was, at that.

# 21

Jesus fucking Christ, you ain't even going to believe what I found."

A rifle barrel prodded me, plowed a path through the matted tangles of my hair, rolled my dead guard off me. A man with a blackened face, too much stringy dishwater-blond hair for regulations, and a gap-toothed grin reached down to wipe the grime and blood off my arm as if I were a pile of animal shit he was examining for tracking purposes.

"Yeah?" another voice challenged. "Whass that? Don't tell me that slant had on an earring you can use for the centerpiece in your necklace."

"Better. Lookit."

"Sheeit. Hey, lady. Lady, where the fuck you come from?" This from a pockmarked swarthy-type kid with some kind of a New York accent mixed with the redneck patois most of the grunts used. The auras of both men were flashing, red, brown, black, olive, mustard, orange, a confusion of high emotion that blurred together for me. I sat up, feeling as if I'd been in an elevator that had suddenly dropped two floors. We had been wending through the jungle as we had for the last four days when all of a sudden all hell broke loose and there I was, on the ground, with my guard bleeding on top of me and automatic bursts and hand grenades exploding around me and my bound hands pinned down by the body on top of me. A deep groan issued from someone nearby.

"We got a live one here."

"Well, pull him out. Where the fuck is Bao?" This was from other disembodied voices. I was still trying to focus on the two faces in front of me.

"Jesus, lookit her hands. Lookit her *arm*. Baby, did

270

they hurt you bad? Hey, Didi, you save that little bastard. They had themselves an American woman, the little fuckers."

"A *whut*. Maryjane, what the fuck you smokin' now—"

"No, man, I found her. Let her alone. Can you get up, baby? Show papa where it hurts," and he tried to scoop me up and I wanted to collapse in his arms and sob but he was flashing so heavy with all that red and orange and black it seemed he was on fire. I looked around me. Dinh was half-sitting, his arms being wrenched behind him. One leg was covered with blood, the calf lying at a funny angle from the thigh. Maryjane, the dishwater-blond, saw the direction of my stare. "That the fucker who did you, baby? I'll fix his ass." He rose and strode over to Dinh.

"No, you don't, man. We gotta squeeze him first. He's some high-rankin' motherfucker," said the man who was tying him, the one called Didi.

"Yeah? Okay. I won't kill him, then," and he reared back and kicked Dinh's injured knee. The colonel let out a sound like brakes being applied at high speed and fainted. The smell of fresh urine added itself to the stench of death and evacuated bowels from the corpses of my former captors.

"Cut it out," I said, I thought loudly, but it came out a bare whisper.

"Hey, you asshole. You're upsettin' the lady. She been through enough." The guy with the New York accent helped me to my feet, but I didn't stay up very long. I took one look around me and doubled up again, losing the little rice I had kept down that day and retching long after the last of the bile had poured from me.

After a while I was able to tell them who I was. Someone got on a radio, back to base, and told them about me, about Dinh. There was a long pause, then: "Hold it right there, son. This is General Hennessey, on inspection tour. You say this is an American nurse you found? And she was in the company of these Vietcong guerrillas?"

"That's affirmative, sir."

"Give me your coordinates again."

He did, and the general set up a rendezvous. I thought at the time, I didn't think generals probably remembered how to do that anymore. I guessed I should feel honored.

Maybe he'd want me to attend at party at his mess. I was dressed right for a mess then. My fatigues were in tatters, and I was covered with bites and scratches and that one long bayonet wound.

Someone picked up Dinh like a sack of potatoes and carried him, shattered leg dangling. I don't think they had a medic. Maybe he'd gotten killed. Maryjane and Zits, the guy from New York, supported me. I don't know how long it took, how far it was. I wasn't entirely with it. I kept getting confused, thinking we were still back at the village with the point man walking into the minefield, and that was Dinh. When I looked down at my own hand I couldn't see any color at all around it. I heard myself giggle. Maryjane grinned at me and wiggled his eyebrows encouragingly. "I'm outa juice," I explained. It made perfect sense to me, but he drew a spiral by his ear with his finger and Zits nodded. That was pretty funny and I giggled again.

They tied Dinh to a tree. He couldn't stand, even on his one good leg. He was out of it. They tried to question him, but he didn't say anything. I thought he was conscious most of the time, but no matter what they asked, how they hit him, what they threatened, he didn't say anything, except to groan and scream a lot.

Some of the questions were about me. The sergeant who was running the show would ask in broken Vietnamese, then the interpreter would ask, then they'd hit Dinh and he'd scream again.

"Not a fuckin' thing. What we gonna tell the general?"

"Maybe he don't know nothin'."

"He knows what they did to her. Where she's from."

"Hell, man, she knows that."

"Yeah, but she's dinky dao as shit."

"Fuck it, man, he ain't gonna tell you anything. I'm tired of this shit. Let's play a little 'guts,' Sarge, whattaya say? That's first-class round-eye tail he was fuckin' with, man. We don't even get none of that. He's got some payback comin'."

"Damn straight."

"Nah, man, the general's gonna want to question this dude."

"You ain't been listenin', asshole. He ain't talkin'. We'll just loosen him up a little."

"Lookit him. You'll kill him before the general gets here, man. He's gonna be soooo disappointed."

"Ain't that a fuckin' shame. So we'll save him a piece. A tiny little piece."

I looked inquiringly at Zits. I was still having trouble talking. It had been only a few days, but it felt like forever since I'd heard English spoken by other Americans. It seemed to be going too fast for me. I still didn't get what they were up to. I wasn't tracking very clearly.

"You'll see, baby. Maybe you wanna play too."

Oh goody. Vietnam was so wonderful. In school nobody had ever wanted me on their team, and here the boys were, choosing me first.

"Me first, man, I found her," Maryjane said. He cut off Dinh's clothes.

"Hey, man, leave him a jock. There's ladies present."

"How can I cut off his balls if I leave him a jock? Besides, she's a nurse. She's seen it all."

"Don't cut him there yet, man. That's too much. He'll die too soon."

"I don't give a fuck," he said. But he stood in front of Dinh, and when he stood away, he was holding a bloody piece of something and there was a long bleeding strip where the colonel's right nipple had been. Dinh made that braking sound.

"See, baby, that's how it works. Wanna play?" Zits said. Then, "Hey, she's next, man."

"Umm, yeah, I'd like to play guts with her," someone said lasciviously. I think he was kidding and meant something else, but my whole back convulsed. I stood up slowly and walked over to Dinh. I started to look at the knee. Touched the amulet slowly. But my eyes were drawn back to his face. His eyelids peeled back about a quarter inch from his eyes and he saw me and groaned. I stood up.

"She's takin' a long time to decide what she wants. Somebody ought to tell her it's spontaneous, like. Hey, baby, give somebody else a turn."

"Shut up. You don't know what that slant bastard did to her."

"No, but it's fun to imagine, huh?"

"You make me sick." Zits came up beside me. "Hey, baby, you need somethin' to work with, huh? A field knife maybe?"

I was looking at Dinh. His eyes struggled open a little bit more. Hue's father, who had blown up all the children in one village, murdered a family, shot one of my patients. I saw with a shock that while his screams might not have been faked, his degree of being out of it was. He was more alert than I was. And his aura, a bare thread, was the gray of a concrete overcoat. He stared at me steadily, challenging at first, and then, in response to whatever he saw in me, imploring, pleading, demanding, calling in a debt. Without even speaking to Zits, I lifted his sidearm from its holster. He didn't seem to notice, he was watching me so hard. So was everyone. I don't know what they thought I was going to do. I pulled the gun out and, still watching the colonel's eyes, which lit with approval, his head nodding imperceptibly, stuck it in his mouth and pulled the trigger.

"Damn!" Maryjane threw his helmet angrily to the ground. "Ya see? Ya see? Women! Jesus! You let them in on something and they spoil everything!"

"Not everything, sweetheart!"

"Aw, come off it, M.J. It's just 'cause they don't get taught how to play football and like that."

I handed Zits' gun back to him, returned to my rock, and sat there, staring at Dinh's body and the tree as if the whole thing were part of some abstract work of modern art I was trying to understand. Actually, I wasn't seeing anything. I was resting my eyes. Resting my mind. Everybody stayed the hell away from me. The yelling died down to angry muttering. That was okay. I didn't feel like talking to anyone.

Sometime later the chunking of chopper blades drew my attention. A Huey descended to hover in the clearing, blowing the hell out of everything. I just sat there and ate its wind, the rain, watching a fit-looking tanned guy with white hair jump out. Some other guy was there too, but I was watching the general as if I'd never seen one before. He wore a shiny gold buckle at his waist. I thought what a great target it would make. He was clean, pressed, authoritative, and handsome in a steely sort of way. Like the successful older man every secretary yearns to marry. I didn't much care for the mossy-green aura camouflaging his intentions, but at least it went nicely with his uniform.

In a couple of minutes the chopper lifted up again and swung away from us.

Maryjane and his sergeant, who looked perpetually stone-bored, walked up to the general. The general stalked up to the corpse still hanging from his bonds against the tree, and examined him, his expression growing angrier and tighter with every second, so that I thought pretty soon his skin would split open from the tension. Maryjane pointed at me.

The general strode over and stood above me like a wrathful God.

"You don't rise when a general officer addresses you, Lieutenant?" he asked.

I just stared at him. I thought about trying to straighten out my knees, stand up again. Nope. Too much effort.

"From what the men here tell me, I have to conclude that you're a VC sympathizer," he said as if accusing me of something shocking. I thought it over. It was at least partially correct. I had certainly sympathized with Colonel Dinh in his last moments. But generals weren't much for such nice distinctions.

"I was performing according to my MOS, sir. One of my primary goals is to relieve suffering."

"As a member of the United States Army, Lieutenant, your primary goal is to help win this war. Do I make myself clear?" I didn't ask what war, when did we declare war. I didn't want to cause the man to have a stroke. "I understand you just executed a valuable enemy prisoner, of your own volition, costing us the opportunity to extract vital information. Do you realize the loss of that information will result in the deaths of thousands of Americans?"

I shrugged.

The moss green in his aura erupted into a study in angry, arrogant reds and oranges, mingled prettily with the mustard of a low order of intelligence, and a swamp of deep blue and teal for fanatical devotion to selfish causes. Like his own career. His face was rapidly growing purple. He grabbed my arm and yanked and I found that I did have a squeak left in me after all. It was my bayoneted arm. It was growing increasingly edematous and inflamed. Might have to amputate that sucker, I thought idly.

He released me and wiped his hand off on his fatigues, swearing.

"Where the hell did you say you found her?" he asked Maryjane.

"I got her off a dead VC, sir," Maryjane said.

"How do you know she's one of ours? I don't see any dog tags."

"Want us to search her, sir?" someone asked eagerly.

"Later. Young woman, I want to see your military ID."

"Okay," I said. Then I remembered that I'd taken it out of my pocket and put it in my ditty bad and my ditty bag was long gone—back at Hue's village. "Oops," I said. "It got lost."

"Very convenient. Men, I want you to hear this. Our enemies are very clever. There is a report that a Lieutenant Kathleen McCulley went AWOL about two weeks ago. She went down in a Huey headed for Quang Ngai. She, the pilot, and crew chief and all presumed dead. It's an open secret, been talked about over the phone, over the radio. Now here is this girl, claiming to be McCulley. How could a lone girl have made it this far? And didn't you say, private, that when you found this woman she was being shielded by one of her comrades? Doesn't that tell you something? You know, all Communists are not Vietnamese. There are even American women in the employ of the enemy. Now, I would hate to think that an American Army nurse might have been so foolish as to have succumbed to Communist propaganda, but these women aren't real troops, after all. They can be scared and intimidated. The giveaway with this one is that she killed her leader over there before he could tell you anything about his operation, himself—or her. Gentlemen, I think we're dealing with a traitor here. I have my doubts if this woman ever was Kathleen McCulley, but if she was, five will get you ten she lured that chopper into an ambush and then rejoined her VC buddies."

"Wait a minute, sir," Zits said. "Sounds like you're going to court-martial her."

"Well, that would be one option, private."

"Sir?"

"If this gets into the press, it will cast a shadow over all of our loyal girls in the service, all of our brave nurses and other female personnel. You men wouldn't want to see that happen, would you?"

There was a lot of random mumbling basically to the effect that they didn't really give a shit.

"Well, there's an alternative. Nobody knows about this but you men and me. Supposing this woman was killed with the rest of her comrades? Supposing for the classified files, Kathleen McCulley was killed by the enemy. For the official files, she died in a chopper crash. To spare her family, of course."

I stared at him, hearing the words but not believing them. He had to be kidding, didn't he? No, of course not. Generals didn't kid. But he was coming to take me home. That's why he was here. I was going to go back to the 83rd and have a last swim at China Beach and get my stuff together and go home and see my mom and Duncan. I had been drifting along with the shock and fatigue, thinking that I was so close to being out of all this, if not the beach, just a warm bed and a bath . . .

"I want to go home," I said, but everybody else was talking and nobody heard me. That was just as well. Whining about home wouldn't do me any good. Everybody— well, almost everybody—wanted to go home. I was being a privileged character again. The people I'd been among for the last week or so were home already and a fat lot of good it did them. I felt a little strength start to course through me, a few tendrils of anger start to warm my cold-clotted blood.

Behind the crisply uniformed general, Dinh's body hung lifeless from the tree, like a modern version of the crucifix, his rain-diluted blood still flowing in pink rivulets down his chest, his mouth. What's wrong with this picture? I wondered, and when I looked down at my own legs I realized: the aura was missing. It wasn't clinging to the body as I had seen the auras do so often right after death. It was clinging to me, overlaying my wisp of muddied pink with that clear blue and yellow, and sparks of red.

No wonder the general thought I was a VC spy. I was wrapped in the late colonel's aura, and it was a little like being wrapped in one of those cloaks of invisibility from the fairy tales, only not quite as useful. Still, I was beginning to feel a little stronger. It could be worse. What if I were Vietnamese, with no right and no desire to leave this

beautiful, blighted land? If this were my home, and I had
nothing to do but stay and try to fend off wave after wave
of invaders while my family, the culture I knew, the very
landscape rotted around me like an old silk curtain in
monsoon season? Nothing to look forward to but struggle
and more struggle. The last few days had been horrible,
but I still had options, another home, one of my own—but I
needed to snap out of it if I wanted to live long enough to
see stupid TV commercials and eat Sugar Pops for breakfast again. What Colonel Dinh had said echoed back to me
from what seemed like years before, but was only that
morning: "Life is not meant to return to a dead limb, and
now that it does, it burns. . . ."

"Well, young woman, if you have any explanation I'd
like to hear it. What were you doing in the company of the
enemy?"

"I was a prisoner, sir," I said. "That's why my hands
were tied." Obviously. Jerk.

"Yeah, but what about that guy on top of you, sweetheart?" Maryjane asked nastily. "Looked to me like he was
takin' your share of the heat. Some enemy." Maryjane's
tone had raised in pitch to the shrill and malicious end of
the scale.

"And that guy." Zits jerked his thumb at the colonel's
corpse. "Why'd you off him? Like the general says, we
coulda got valuable information out of him."

"You didn't want valuable information," I spat back.
"You'd already tried questioning him and you knew he
wasn't going to say anything. You just wanted to hurt him."

"So? What was it to you? Hadn't he hurt you? Or
maybe you liked it, huh, baby?"

"No, I just don't like to see people mistreated."

Somebody laughed harshly. "Well, lady, you are in the
wrong war, then."

From being protective and solicitous, the men had
become hostile, aggressive. Looking up at the general,
who wore an expression of smug satisfaction that must
have been much the same as that worn by an early witch-
hunter, I saw what was happening with graphic clarity.
The blackness in the general's aura cannibalized the other
colors that had been present in it, and grew, webbing out
to touch the blackness that was the primary component of
Maryjane's aura, to sprout more blackness in Zits, to web

with the hatred and anger that had become part of every man's aura, and where the blackness met blackness, it was amplified, until the clearing was filled with it. General Hennessey sure was a leader of men, okay. He just didn't have much use for women.

One of them looked at the other while the general thumbed his side arm. Maryjane gave me a lopsided grin and pulled out his machete. "You know, General, if the Cong had done her, they'd have made it hurt." He grinned and winked at me. Big joke. Very funny.

"Oh, great, soldier," I said. "What did you do when you were a kid? Rip the legs off of frogs? Did I take away your toy and—" I was stopped in mid-sentence by a commotion on the perimeter. The sentry was yelling something and somebody else was yelling back. Several of the men ran over to see what was going on. The general merely turned around, annoyed at the distraction.

"Goddamn, sir, will you look at that? They must be havin' a fuckin' sale on 'em today," Maryjane said as two men wrestled a third between them into the clearing. The third man wore crossed bandoliers slung over his bony shoulders and prominent rib cage.

He was still fighting, and one after another flung the men who held him away from him and jumped Zits, trying to wrest his weapon from him. Three more men pulled him off and held him down. Zits covered him.

The general came out from behind a tree he had just happened to step behind. "What seems to be the problem here, men?"

"We found this dude pokin' around the dead gooks, sir. We started, you know, rappin' with him, and he fuckin' attacked us."

"I was gonna off him, but Darby said since he was American we should, like, try to bring him in," the other man said.

"Okay, soldier, what have you got to say for yourself?" the general demanded.

What was left of William spit and a glob landed right in the middle of the shiny gold buckle. The red and black aura was strobing like crazy and so was the aura surrounding Zits.

"Goddamn it, cut it out," I said. "He's dinky dao. He thinks you're VC. Leave him the hell alone." I pushed past

Maryjane's machete and knelt beside William. He spat at me, too, but I'd seen lots worse lately.

I didn't have much aura left to share and there was nobody I much wanted to touch, but the general solved that problem for me. He came and stood so that his leg brushed my back.

"Do you know this man, young woman?" He was trying to intimidate me, but his well-fed, rested energy was what I needed. Only nothing happened. No change took place and William spat at me again.

So I slapped him, and glared at him.

He rolled his head back and forth, back and forth, trying to shake that aura. After what seemed like forever to me, it receded and he opened his eyes.

"Lieutenant Kitty, baby. Hey, girl, what's happenin'? I thought you was takin' babysan down to the ville."

I sighed, sat back on my heels, and buried my head in my hands.

"You know this woman, soldier?" the general asked. "What are you doing in this sector? Where's your unit?"

William blinked several times, as if trying to focus on me. His entire aura extended only about a quarter of an inch from him and was as wavery and uneven as the EKG of a patient with a myocardial infarction. "What the fuck is goin' down here? Man, I was trackin' you dudes, only I wasn't always certain if it be you or if it be VC, dig? So I sort of follow along. Then, I dunno when, I see some other dudes humpin' through the bush and I'd have thought it was you only they was draggin' the lieutenant like she be the doggie in the window, if you can dig *that?* And then, man, I don't know. I was layin' down fire at someone and then somebody else opened up, but I'll be damned if I know who the fuck I was shootin'. I got like hit, see?" He touched the back of his head, and when he held up his fingers, they were bloody. "When I come out of it, I go to look at the bodies and then these other dudes come at me and—oh shit, man, was that you? Lieutenant Kitty, you right on, girl. I must be dinky dao as shit to take these dudes for gooks. Ain't no gooks that ugly. That's a joke, man."

The black radioman guffawed and two other black guys snorted.

"He may be dinky dao but he ain't blind," one of them said.

But William was taking stock of his surroundings now, and the same instinct that had told him when to roll under the bed sent blue-gray needles of alarm prickling from his aura. "Oh hey, man, hey, now, look, I didn't—I mean, no way did I off one of our guys, did I? I—"

The general cleared his throat and Zits and Maryjane glared at him, but the black soldier leaning against the tree said, "No, man, nothin' like that. Just seem like the jungle full of lots of folks 'sides Charlie out for a walk today."

"I told you we were both lost—" I began wearily, but William cut me off with a nervous spate of chatter. It was a side of him I hadn't seen before, another defense, I suppose, besides an automatic weapon or a stranglehold.

"Man, I dig. This is really wild. 'Cause I can tell you for dead sure I never expected to see this woman alive again. How's babysan, Lieutenant?"

I shrugged and mumbled, "He's at the village."

William plunged right on over my words. He was sitting up now, while the medic, who was one of the other black men, cleaned and bandaged his wound. His arms flew around as he talked so that the man had trouble bandaging him as he told the story of his unit being overrun.

"Yeah, I heard about that. Numbah ten, man. We didn't know nobody got out."

"Why didn't you report to headquarters, soldier?" the general demanded.

"General, man, that's what I be tryin' to tell you. I be tryin' to report back for weeks, man. But you know, I got me no radio and you the first bunch of dudes I see and I'm not sure most times whether you ours or theirs."

"But you managed to contact Lieutenant McCulley."

"Wasn't like she was in no headquarters, though. She was lost, just like me." He frustrated the medic by scooting away from him to put his arm around me. "But hey, girl, we made it, didn't we? Here we be, safe and sound in the bosom of whatever the fuck this unit be." He gave me a squeeze. "Now, I want you dudes to take notice of this woman here. She be one amazing chick. I see this chopper crash, see, and here comes mamasan, deely-boppin' through the jungle with a one-legged kid, tellin' me her boyfriend got greased in the crash and do I know the way to the nearest Howard Johnson's. Then she decides my company is too rough for her and goes down to this village to park the boy and ask to use a phone. I thought she'd be dogmeat for sure by now, but here she is and she sure is somethin', ain't you, mamasan?"

"Soldier, I want your name, rank, and serial number and your unit," Hennessey said.

"Whoa, there, sir, lighten up," said the radioman, whose aura was veined with mauve that had been deepening as he listened to William.

"I want to know your connection with this woman, soldier," Hennessey persisted.

"Connection? Got no connection. Don't you listen, man? I done told you my connection. Her an' me is friends, ain't we, Kitty? My unit got overrun and her boyfriend's bird crash and here we be in the jungle together. Only she had this kid to look out for, see, so we decide to split up— she goes to the ville to dump the kid and I come lookin' for you dudes. Only she beats me here."

"She was found in the company of a party of Vietcong," the general said.

"No shit? Baby, you all right?"

"Fuckit, man, I'm callin' in medevac," the radioman said. "My brother here, he's hurt."

"You'll do no such thing," Hennessey barked. "I'm conducting an inquiry here."

"Man, look at him," the medic said. "He's manic as hell, runnin' on a scared-stiff high. He gonna burn himself out from that all by itself, you don't get him back home. It's not just this head, sir. This man got a bad case of exposure."

"Me too, Washington. Send me back too," Maryjane said, and shut up when the medic glared at him.

The radioman spoke up. "With respect and all that shit, sir, you do the rest of your inquirin' back at HQ. You gonna hang around here long enough, somebody's gonna come lookin' for us."

Maryjane stubbed out his smoke. "That's a-fuckin'-firmative."

Although the general tried to throw his weight around, the men were drifting away, marking notches on their helmets or openly toking on joints.

The radioman called for the medevac chopper to take

us to the hospital at Quang Ngai. He gave a thumbs-up sign as we lifted off.

The general pulled his hat down over his eyes and affected sleep for the journey.

William and I leaned together on the bench seat of the chopper, but neither of us tried to speak above its noise. William had gone from wildly talkative to dead quiet. He was so weak he stayed seated only because he was strapped in. His aura was almost nonexistent. I laid my head on his arm and tried to share strength, but Dinh's aura had deserted me and I didn't have anything left to share. We were both carried into the hospital on stretchers, but William was taken to a different section. He gave me a tired wink as they took him inside. I know they asked him more questions about me, and that he was reassigned to another unit, but beyond that I've never been able to find out what happened to him.

# 22

Vietnamese vermin and parasites saved me more than once in the ensuing weeks. General Hennessey did not give up easily, and many times while I was in the hospital, people came in and asked me a lot of questions about what had happened in the jungle. Most of them seemed more intelligent than General Hennessey, and one or two of them even had the grace to look embarrassed. If it wasn't obvious to the general that I had not been having a grand adventure running and playing with the Vietcong, it was obvious to almost everybody else. My skin was a mess of infected bites, my scalp lousy, and my hair falling out. The wound on my arm had to be debrided to three times its width and depth; the superficial puncture wounds on my breasts gave me a bad case of mastitis that made breathing painful and coughing, from the pneumonia, excruciating. My feet were so covered with sores and crud I had to wonder how I'd been able to walk at all. I developed malaria from not taking my pills, and intestinal parasites. The interrogators knew that when I said they'd better clear a path, they'd better clear a path.

I had been transferred out of Quang Ngai, which was set up for emergency surgical care only, as soon as my arm was debrided, and sent to the larger facility at Long Binh. I don't remember the switch. I was delirious with fever during that time, and stayed that way for a week. I'm not sure why it took me so long to begin to get really sick. Perhaps the anesthetic lowered what little resistance I had. Perhaps the amulet had afforded me some protection while I was using it for healing so intensely, but when I was knocked out, with no generative power for it to feed on, it conked out. Or maybe it was just the usual pattern, that my body knew while the stress was the greatest that I would not survive if it caved in, so it kept me going until the pace slowed a little.

At any rate, I was too sick to answer questions, too sick to do anything but sweat, have dreams that I knew were hideous but I couldn't remember, and mumble.

The staff was as kind as they could be initially, as busy as they were. My doctor was one of those bloodless men who sees medicine as a science and patients as specimens. His aura was almost pure yellow, with only bits of mauve and blue, like colored thumbtacks, binding him to his career. The nurses wore white uniform dresses, which I noted with pity. Nylons in 110-degree heat will try to fuse with your legs. But my bed was dry and had clean sheets and I had been bathed. The first day I was able to shower, I tottered back toward my bed feeling dizzy and light-headed, but I stopped at the desk and told the corpsman, "That felt so good. Maybe I could rest a little while, then help you with your next set of TPRs or something?" He was another of those kids who looked as if they were fresh out of junior high, with a blond butch and a sunburned face. The face got redder when I talked to him. He wet his lips and said, "No thanks, ma'am," then, "You have a visitor who's been waiting for you."

"Oh? Who?"

"Just one of them people that's been here every day since you got here. Head nurse ran 'em off but said we had to call them as soon as you were strong enough."

I wasn't strong enough. Nobody is strong enough to put up with the kind of shit I took from those intelligence people day in and day out for weeks after that. They made Hennessey's accusations sound like "Tsk tsk." One guy in particular started getting really hostile. They were trying to break me down, and that was easy. I've never been able to bear mental battering. But it didn't do a lot of good. I was confused and whiny, and weepy, and even to me my story never sounded exactly the same each time I told it.

But Marge came to visit me once. I told her as much as I could about where Ahn was and said if she could find Heron, I was sure he could find Ahn. I just wanted to know he was okay. She listened to me carefully and nodded noncommittally. On her way out, she stopped and chatted with the head nurse, and after that when the interrogators came, one of the ward nurses made it her business to be nearby.

Otherwise, most of the staff steered clear of me, except for treatments. I was at the end of the ward, and a curtain was drawn between me and the other patients, so I could hear them but I couldn't see them. I even had a guard, usually a woman, so she could go right into the bathroom with me, if necessary. I was surprised they spared the handcuffs, but at least having a guard meant there was *someone* I could talk to. I suppose that's what they counted on, but since I didn't have anything incriminating to reveal, it didn't do much good. Some of my guards ignored me pretty much to flirt with the corpsmen or the patients, but one WAC in particular was someone I thought I'd have liked for a friend under other circumstances. She reminded me a little of Hue, short, tough, and very quick, deceptively young-looking, with an aura of bright yellow intellect, creative lavender, and idealistic blue slightly overlaid with deceptive gray-green. I almost told her about the amulet, once, but then I remembered what the inside of a mental hospital is like and knew that that was not where I wanted to spend my first few years back in the world. Also, in the back of my mind, I kept hearing what Colonel Dinh had said about the way the government would use the power to prolong the war. I thought, if Charlie Heron turned up before I left, maybe I would give it to him. But he never did.

Sergeant Janice Mitchell, the one who reminded me of Hue, never grilled me. She just sat inside the curtain and chatted with me, leaving only long enough to light up a smoke away from the oxygen I had flowing through a cannula into my nose, as therapy for the pneumonia. She listened to what I said sympathetically, not as if she was about to indict me for every word. Every time I had another session and she was there, I'd blow off what little steam I had left or whimper in her direction, so we went over the same story almost as often as I did with the interrogators. Maybe more. Besides, we got to talking about home. She was a Midwesterner too, from Nebraska, and had joined to get out of Nebraska and to be near her brother, who had been up at Phu Bai until he was injured. She was dating several guys, but she didn't elaborate, except in general terms. I gathered maybe she wasn't supposed to talk about that. I told her about Duncan, repeating some of his stories, and about my family. But somehow the conversation would always drift back to what had happened after my fight with Krupman.

I wasn't trying to lie, but I didn't want to talk about the amulet, nor did I want to be obviously withholding anything. So I told her about the villagers, okay, but I downplayed the injuries and upgraded the available equipment slightly. We had been talking for two weeks before we ever got past the ambush. I started telling her about what happened afterward, what Hennessey had said.

"Wait a minute, wait a minute," she said. "You trying to tell me that the general tried to talk these men into killing you? You have witnesses?" She looked a little like a pointer who found a scent just then.

"Well, yeah, like I told you, William Johnson was there, but he got there after the general said most of that stuff. And Zits and Maryjane but—no real names." I shrugged helplessly and stared down at my sheet. "Wait a minute. There was the radioman. A black guy. His name tag said Brown. He'd tell you."

"I'll check on it," she said ruefully. "There's probably only a couple thousand men named Brown in the area."

She stood up abruptly, flipped back the curtain, and stood at the foot of my bed. I heard the click of her lighter, saw her shadow take three short steps one way, three short steps the other, back and forth.

She and Sergeant Llewellyn, the ward master, struck up quite a friendship while I was there. He had mentioned once when he was handing me an emesis basin that Janice had been with me most of the week I was out with my fever. They'd gotten well acquainted at that time, I supposed. I heard him ask her if she wanted a cup of coffee and she ducked her head in and said, "Kitty, I'm going to the nurses' station for coffee. Want a cup?"

I shook my head. Later I heard whispers from the station and then voices raised in argument. I caught the words "your career" in a male voice and then "about as subversive as you are" in Janice's clarion tones, followed by "my career" and mumbles of grudging agreement.

Before day shift ended that day, Llewellyn, a lanky, rawboned 91-Charlie who had Cherokee cheekbones and a Tennessee accent, lingered by my bed after picking up my supper tray. His aura was a rather muddied mauve, the healing rose overlaid with anxious gray violet just at the moment, belying his casual tone.

"Well, how are you this evening, ma'am?"

I sighed and tried to smile, but the smile drained away before it got to my mouth. "I'll do."

"Yeah, well, it sure is exciting having you around here, y'know that? All these visitors and such. Why, it's the most excitement we've had in this place since the My Lai thing and all those newsmen and investigators all over the place. Sergeant Mitchell was on that one, too, but I didn't know her then. Noticed her, though. I don't know how you folks felt up there, but we thought ol' Calley sort of took a fall for somebody higher up. Gotta hand it to General Hennessey, though, he was right in there cryin' atrocity with everybody else, even though I met this fellow used to work in the general's mess?" His voice rose in the Southern interrogatory that means "you know?" but puts in the question mark and leaves out the words. "He said Hennessey was in favor of wipin' out the entire population. Not that that's an unusual idea. But it's commonly held that if it takes wipin' out all of us to wipe out all of them, he's gonna be right in there wavin' the flag and talkin' about the domino theory. Between you and me, the man ain't fishin' with a baited hook. He's been around a couple of times to pass out medals and he's downright rude to the female personnel. Why, I remember last spring one lieutenant got raped by a troop under Hennessey's command and she had to go to the I.G. and have her mama write her congressman for bein' a loose woman. Useful thing, the I.G. I believe General Torelli, same officer that was in charge when Lieutenant LaVeau had her trouble, is still OIC. Between you and me, I think he might like to get somethin' on that bastard."

My brain was not working at rapid speed, but the man had practically drawn me a picture. I had been too harassed and too out of it to wonder, but suddenly I realized I had had no letters, no calls, no solicitousness of any kind from home since my return. Nothing forwarded. I wondered what my family had been told.

"Well, I'd write home," I said wearily, "but I suppose it would be intercepted."

"It might be—unless you found a way around it. I think you better try, ma'am."

I did, because I knew he was taking a risk, and Janice was taking a risk, to try to help me. I didn't care all that much by then. It didn't seem to matter what I told anyone, they put their own connotations on it. I had always been a "gook lover," back on the ward. All my co-workers said so, the interrogators told me. I had no feelings for the GIs. And when had I learned good enough Vietnamese to see me through my alleged ordeal? I was sick of it, but no sicker than I was of everything else, and I was getting used to being sick of things. Having an easy time of it, having people in power be reasonable, being allowed to get well and go back to my job began to seem like a naïve dream of Disneyland proportions.

But from what Llewellyn said, Hennessey was even more of a crazy man than I thought, and could do a great deal more damage to a great many more people. So I wrote some more letters and filled out more papers and eventually answered more questions. An official inquiry was conducted, one that included other high-ranking people than General Hennessey. Janice told me they located Brown in Quang Ngai, just before he was medevaced to Japan for removal of half his radio from his back. Words were bandied, more papers filled out. William had been reassigned to III Corps, she said. They were still looking for him. The possibility of a court-martial hearing for me was discussed.

In the meantime I received a letter from home. My mother was so glad to hear from me. She'd sent an inquiry through the Red Cross when I stopped writing, but hadn't had an answer as yet.

Then gradually the interrogators, even Janice, stopped coming by, except to ask the odd, enigmatic question here and there. The silence made me more anxious than their presence had. I thought this was never going to end. I was never going to be allowed to go home.

One morning the head nurse, Major Hanson, personally took my vital signs and tenderly took me in a wheelchair to the shower, straightened my bed, and helped me into a clean patient gown. I had been walking to the shower and changing my own bed for about a week, so I knew something official was going on. I wondered if my last meal was going to show up on the breakfast cart, and I about knocked myself out in the shower trying to pick up the soap, which kept slipping out of my unreliable hands.

General Hennessey, a bird colonel, and a major proceeded down the aisle of the ward and stopped at my bed. The major ruffled a document and handed the general a box. The general opened the box and extracted something.

"Lieutenant McCulley, in honor of your . . ."

I didn't hear the rest of what he said. I was too busy flinching backward when I saw the pin he was aiming at my infected breast. Meanwhile, he was less saying the words than sputtering them, and started waving the pin around. The bird colonel, who wore insignia from the inspector general's office, took the object away from him and laid it on my pillow. My Purple Heart, I thought, without looking at it. Big fucking deal. Instead of court-martialing me, they were giving me a medal. An hour and a half later I boarded an orange Braniff freedom bird, back to the world.

# PART THREE

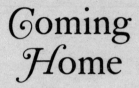

Coming
Home

# 23

The airplane ride back was like a big, long, raucous party, but I curled up in my seat and pretended to sleep. I didn't have any money on me when I got to Fort Lewis, and I was wandering around trying to think what to do when a warrant officer tapped me on the shoulder. A woman who looked about to explode was standing nearby, watching, trying to restrain two boys about eight and five.

"You lost, Lieutenant? The real world's that way." He pointed to the doors. I looked at him and saw Tony, who should be meeting his wife. It took me a moment to refocus.

"I forgot to get paid," I explained finally. "I need to get home and I forgot to get paid."

"Where's home?"

"Kansas City."

He looked as if he was going to say the hell with it and leave me standing for a moment, then he said, "There's a Western Union office at SeaTac airport. If we give you a lift that far, have you got somebody you can call to wire you the money?"

I nodded. They dropped me off and loaned me a quarter. I called my folks collect and talked to the woman in the Western Union office. She had teased hair and her uniform skirt was a mini.

I thought, it's good to be back in the world. A woman with Mary Travers hair and wire-rim glasses and a boyfriend toting a guitar passed me in the broad hall, and I smiled at them experimentally. The woman twitched the skirt of her granny dress carefully aside and looked pointedly at the fatigues and combat boots one of the nurses had loaned me for the trip home.

I wandered into one of the clothing shops in the airport. All kinds of batiks and cotton-gauze ethnic things were on sale there. And gorgeous long dangly earrings, the kind you could never wear on duty. I wished I had my back pay.

"Is there something I can show you?" the young woman behind the counter asked. She had on a nice silky dress of some sort.

"No, I'm sorry. I wish I could afford something, but I just got back from Vietnam and they didn't give me my pay before I left."

"You were over there? It must have been terrible." I felt like snapping that no, it had been a lot of fun, really, but restrained myself. She was just being pleasant. "What were you doing there?" she asked.

"I was a nurse," I said, and added, "I took care of GIs and also a lot of Vietnamese civilians." I didn't want her to think I was a baby burner.

"How interesting." The loudspeaker came on, announcing a flight, and she leaned forward over the counter. I leaned toward her to hear what she had to say. "You must have learned a lot about the people, then. Did you get your necklace there?" and she reached out and touched the amulet before I quite knew what she was doing.

She let go of it fast, the bright mustard and green of her aura darkening like snow after a slop bucket has been emptied on it. She backed off. "Well, if you don't want anything, excuse me. I have to finish this inventory."

I yearned to see Mom and Dad throughout the five-hour trip, but when they hugged me, I had to fake returning their hugs. I wasn't quite up to their smiles, so very soon those smiles faded. Kansas City looked as if nothing else were going on in the whole world. Trees grew unmolested, people dressed in suits and hats with veils and high-heeled shoes that would have made running impossible. It didn't look real to me.

When we reached our old driveway, I felt like a teenager again. The wind chimes sang cheerily in the breeze. The pine tree in the front yard looked a little taller. All of the pets were long dead. My brother was there, and my grandma and grandpa. I didn't know what to say to anybody. I went upstairs to my room, sat down on the bed, and stared at the pink Chinese print paper I'd picked out when I was fourteen. The last of my cat collection, a couple of Avon bottles, sat on the blond dresser Mom and Dad had bought secondhand for me. I walked over to the dresser and picked up one of the glass cats, to stroke it for comfort. Its surface was cool and smooth, but it felt warmer than I did. I felt as if my insides had been hollowed out with an ice cream scoop, cold, numb, and empty. I couldn't see my aura anymore. I thought the muddiness I saw in the mirror probably was real dirt. It had been a long trip.

I took off the amulet and tucked it inside my old jewelry box. I wouldn't need it here in the world. I put on a pair of jeans that had been too small for me when I left and were now miles too big, and one of Daddy's shirts, a pair of Mama's shower shoes. At least I'd lost weight. Maybe I could make money introducing the Exotic South China Sea Dieting Miracle—amebiasis and tapeworms. Most of them had been flushed out of my system by various antibiotics, fungicides, and other medications, but some of them were not easily gotten rid of.

Mom made my favorite foods: steak and homemade French fries, corn on the cob, and fresh green beans and tomatoes. My aunt made my favorite cake, buttermilk chocolate, and put on it the peppermint boiled white icing that only she seemed to know how to do. I couldn't eat much of it. I didn't say, "Pass the fucking salt," as I've heard some of the guys say they did, but I didn't say much of anything else either.

So when Mom found the medal, she thought it was a topic of conversation. "Honey, this is a Silver Star, isn't it? You didn't tell me you'd won a medal. Can I call Mr. Mingel at the *Kansan* and tell him? He's been wanting to interview you when you came home."

I should have unpacked it myself, before she got around to it. The fatigues I had been in when I was admitted were still in there, and that's not the kind of thing you want your mother to see. But my attitude was "burn the whole damned thing." My stuff from Da Nang was being sent later.

Mama's eyes were troubled when she opened the box someone had packed the medal in. I hadn't brought it along. I guess whoever threw my stuff in my bag had done it. I wished Janice had come back to say good-bye. Or Llewellyn.

"Silver Star, huh?" I asked, and glanced at it. Sure enough. I guess the general felt I needed a little higher bribe than a simple Purple Heart to keep my mouth shut. Those things take months to review and award normally. It made me a little sick to think that they were trying to buy me off with something most people earned with the loss of one or more limbs, or maybe their lives. "Don't mean nothin', Mama. Please don't call the newspaper man. I don't have anything I want to tell him."

"Well, if you're sure," she said uncertainly, then patted me on the cheek. "You know your daddy and I love you and we're very proud of you, honey."

I felt as if she'd hit me. Tears stung the backs of my eyes. Proud of what?

I'd killed a man, had been the cause of death for two others, and had abandoned the little boy I'd been trying to save in a Vietcong village. Nothing had turned out right. The medal was a mockery. A Hollywood happy ending. Fuck. I'd give it to Duncan. He liked that kind of shit. I'd make up a funny story about it, and give it to him. And then later, maybe he'd hold me and I could tell him how it really was. If I could just tell everything to him, I could really start to feel at home again. That was a good idea. If I could talk to him, he'd make me feel better and then I could be a little more normal around the folks. He was living in Independence, Missouri, now, according to the third and final letter I'd received from him. I sat down on my folks' bed and tried to call, but nobody answered.

I drove out to Independence the next day. Mom and Dad disapproved. They thought I should sit around and regale the relatives with more war stories. But I needed to see Duncan badly. If he was gone, maybe I could wait. I stopped and called again from a 7-Eleven store.

"Kitten! You're home!" He said. "God, that's about the most wonderful thing I've heard. Hell, yes, come on out. I've got so much to tell you."

Maybe it would be all right. Maybe he cared more than I thought. Maybe he had realized how much he missed me. I drove into the parking lot at his apartment complex and felt my stomach knot as I came to the front stoop of his apartment, rang the doorbell. The door opened.

A mane of wild red hair held back by a blue bandanna overwhelmed a girl who wore rubber gloves, cutoffs, and an overtaxed halter top and who had legs up to her armpits. Maybe I'd gotten the wrong apartment after all. Maybe he'd moved and had kept the same phone and had forgotten to tell me.

"I'm looking for Duncan—" I began.

She grabbed my hand in her rubber gloves and chirped, "You must be Kitty McCulley! Oh, that rat didn't tell me you'd be here so soon. I've been cleaning this place all morning trying to make it look nice for when you got here. Duncan has told me so much about you I've just been dying to meet you." She dragged me into the hall and peeled off her rubber gloves. "I'm Swoozie," she concluded, as if that was supposed to mean something. Duncan had definitely not told me all about her.

"Uh—hi," I said, looking beyond her to see if he was there. Across the living room was a stairway. Upstairs, a faucet shut off, there were a couple of footsteps, and then Duncan came bouncing down the steps, attired in fresh jeans and a starched, button-down shirt. I'd forgotten men could look that clean.

He grabbed me in a bear hug and, to my surprise, I didn't feel any more like hugging him than I had Mom and Dad. I just looked at him. If he really meant that hug, who the hell was she?

"I see you met Swoozie. Great, isn't she?"

"Umm," I said noncommittally.

"She's made us chicken for lunch. You like chicken, don't you, Kitten?"

He didn't wait for an answer. The chicken amply showed off her domestic skills, and the way she hung on Duncan showed off others.

When she had detached herself for a second I said, "Duncan, I've got so much I need to tell you."

"Oh, yeah, and I really want to talk to you too, hon. But it's going to have to be later. Swoozie and I have to run out to her folks' farm for an hour or so. You can entertain yourself, right? The TV's in the bedroom."

I didn't say anything and he didn't ask anything. The two of them piled into his Camaro and drove away. I wandered around the house, thinking I should just leave. He was behaving as if I came over every Sunday for dinner. As if I'd never been away. And to me, his apartment didn't even look real. I drifted upstairs. I'd have to look at the TV. I think I was still hoping he'd get halfway to whatsername's farm, slap himself on the head, say, "Oh, what a fool I've been! I need to get back and talk to Kitty. We can take care of these trivial errands later." But though I strained my ears listening, I heard nothing. I opened the closet door and the smell of his cologne and fresh-pressed clothes drifted out. I lifted a shirt sleeve and sniffed. Before I left, I'd asked him to keep my letters, and I wondered if he had. I didn't expect to find them so easily. But there they were, in a pile, with a rubber band. I picked up the pile, all written on stationery with helicopters and Big Chief tablet-style lines. When I removed the rubber band, I understood why his letters never made reference to mine. He hadn't opened them. Incredulously, I pawed through the pile. Not one was opened.

I picked them up, tucked them into my purse, and got back into Mom's car. I drove into the countryside, hoping by some coincidence I'd run into them and he could explain. It had been a rainy day, and as I drove down a small dirt road with trees on either side, it rapidly grew darker. I didn't care. I took the curves very fast and ended up plowing through the woods. I was still focused on the letters, and on Duncan, and it took me a while to realize that I wasn't on the road and was heading down a steep embankment. I forgot about braking until the shock of impact hit me, and the fender was crumpled against a tree, the radiator spewing water.

I got out of the car and walked until I found a farmhouse. I called Duncan, and he and Swoozie came to get me, and called a garage.

I didn't ask him about the letters then. But the next day I called a VA hospital in Fort Collins, Colorado, and was accepted as a staff nurse almost at once.

I thought what I needed was to get back to work, to get back into the swing of things, to stop dwelling on my problems and help other people. I was assigned to a drug/ alcoholism rehabilitation ward. The alcoholics were mostly suffering from DTs, the drug addicts had hepatitis. The alcoholics told the staff where the druggies were getting their fixes, the druggies told us where the alcoholics were hiding their bottles. I was not popular with my co-workers. I was used to getting myself organized and getting everything done at the start of the shift and waiting for casualties. I found myself getting irritable and brusque with the staff, and I resented it when they asked me to help them with their work. It was boring. I felt no empathy for the patients, and even wearing the amulet didn't help. Their auras were uniformly depressingly gray-green, deep with self-deception and shit-brown with self-loathing. My own was thin and brown. Once I worked on ortho, and was caring for a very nice man with terrible pain in his back. I tried to help him, tried to focus, using the amulet. Nothing happened. I gave him a pain shot, which did nothing either.

The day I got the letter from Charlie Heron, I walked on air. He left a phone number and I called him. He was living on the Coast, he said, in a great place in San Francisco, and he wanted me to come and see him. He sounded different than he had in country, aimless and unemphatic, but I figured he probably couldn't talk to anyone either. Maybe we could talk to each other. I could give him the amulet. He'd trained with old Xe. He'd know what to do with it.

One of his friends met me at the airport and took me to the house he shared with Charlie. Charlie was wadded up in front of the television with a joint in his hand. The house reeked so badly of pot you could get stoned just breathing normally. I smoked with the two of them, but didn't get two coherent words out of Charlie all weekend. I didn't even consider giving him the amulet then. His aura was only a slight variation on the ones worn by my patients in Colorado.

I worked at the hospital for another month, but finally quit. I couldn't stand it. As the patients sobered up, the yellow in their auras, a tendril of blue, sometimes some other healthier color, would bud along with sprigs of personality, only to be smothered again as soon as they were released. I found myself going home at night and drinking to relax from the misery of it. I crashed my car another time, and was nervous about driving for a long time after that.

I drifted from job to job, trying to work as a night float

whenever possible, working first on one ward, then another. I liked the variety and the adrenaline rush of occasionally having dire emergencies to deal with. That made me feel at home, as if I were back in Nam. But what I liked the best was that I didn't really have to get to know anybody. I wouldn't risk contaminating anyone else.

When Nixon ended the war, I was fiercely glad. Our men could come home and the Vietnamese could begin adjusting to having one boss instead of many. I expected the news of the Communist takeover, but the day it came out, I didn't go to work. I stayed in bed and tried to remember what Mai looked like, wondered if having been a patient in an American hospital would affect Ahn's status, and hoped Hue was reinstated in the good graces of the winners. I sat in bed and stared at the TV and ate junk food and held my knees in my arms and watched, and rocked, and wondered. Pretty soon I started to cry, just a trickle at first, and then great gulping sobs, such as I hadn't cried since before Tony crashed us in the jungle. Thinking about Tony and Lightfoot made me cry all over again, until I couldn't get my breath. I didn't go to work the next day either. I didn't have the energy to go anywhere, or to do anything. I couldn't bear to brush my teeth and it was a struggle to drag myself to the bathroom.

When I realized I was out of anything to blow my nose on, I pulled myself together enough to return to work. Everybody was talking about this new restaurant or that new movie. If you hadn't been there, you had nothing to talk about. I was home, but I wasn't. Everything here seemed trivial, superficial. Life was not sweet. It wasn't even bearable.

One night I was working the emergency room, in Gallup, New Mexico. There was a long lull between the night's stab wound victim and the drunk who'd been hit and run from. The receptionist and the nurses' aide were chatting about inconsequentialities. A new boyfriend, a new soap opera, the grandparents taking the receptionist's kids to Disneyland, a new crochet pattern. I wanted to scream. I had consoled myself by trying to jump back into everything, into jobs, into love affairs that were little more than one-night stands (I was still trying to find someone to touch me), into the whole pop-culture commercial scene. I spent most of my days in shopping malls charging stuff I didn't need on my charge cards and worrying over paying them off, eating out so I wouldn't have to eat alone. I lived in a singles complex with no old people, children, or pets but lots of predators of both sexes circling the pool like so many sharks, looking to score with the best body with the best tan. And I didn't give a shit about any of it.

I walked out to my car that morning after work and found I'd left the lights on and the battery was dead. I spent a sleepy morning learning about jump starting, and hitched a ride home with the service station attendant. I walked into my cute little studio apartment, around the breakfast bar, and gave the steak knives a serious once-over. I selected a sharp one and took it into the bathroom.

Why not? Duncan didn't love me, my parents would be better off without me, I was no good at my job anymore. Nobody wanted or needed me anymore. From being someone with special power, I had become someone who was another body, in the way, who had spent a year of her life doing something that was not to be mentioned in polite conversation. I would kill myself and then they wouldn't have to worry about me. Nobody had ever taken *me* to Disneyland. And I had always wanted to go, too. Tears ran down my cheeks and over my hands and onto the knife blade as I thought how unfair it was that here I'd fought for my country and nobody had even offered me a lousy trip to Disneyland.

Well, goddamit, I would kill myself, no mistake about that, but I'd do it after I took myself to Disneyland. Duncan hadn't kept his promise to be the man of my dreams, my parents hadn't kept their promise to always make everything all right, no matter what, and the Army sure as hell had never kept *any* of its promises, but *I* could keep my own promise to myself. I didn't expect the place to be wonderful. I didn't expect it to thrill me. I knew it would be silly and childish and commercial, but it was something the little girl I'd been before I went to Nam wanted to do, so whatever I thought now, I'd go for her. Like going to the funeral of Hue's mother. To honor her memory. Nobody else was going to.

I called in sick, and packed a bag. I drove to the airport in Albuquerque, and handed over my plastic for a ticket to L.A.

Flying over it made me think of Nam: the mountains,

the palms, the ocean. It also made me think of the line in the Joni Mitchell song about paving paradise and putting up parking lots. I had heard the city put down pretty often, but it looked okay to me. I'd heard one of the patients joke about returning there from Vietnam. "When you've spent time in hell, L.A. ain't so bad," he said.

Baggage claim seemed miles from where we deboarded. People were in a terrific hurry and the auras surrounding them looked like a psychedelic nightmare. I decided that before I went to Disneyland I would remove the amulet and stick it in my jeans pocket. I wasn't ready for Mickey Mouse with a black and red aura.

I've become pretty familiar with the baggage claim area by now, but that day I had only an impression of a large room with several entrances, one of which had an almost tunnel-like hall, like the endless corridors in VA hospitals.

I turned to scan the baggage racks, looking for my new tweed case, when I heard a noise as if the streets of downtown Da Nang had been crowded into the room. What was this, a flashback? I wondered, as I turned toward the stomach-wrenchingly familiar singsong cacophony of Vietnamese language being spoken in frightened, angry, defensive, awed voices, and saw what looked like half of Vietnam come pouring out of the tunnel

The familiar gray-violet fearful aura wrapped these people in a fog, but there were sparks of yellow around many, and clear, hopeful turquoise. Their bodies, normally small and slim, were emaciated now, some bearing sores. Children looked up at their parents with frightened eyes and the parents looked dazed, shell-shocked. Some carried small bundles, others had nothing. No one went to the baggage claim. I had long ago stopped listening to the news or reading the paper, and I couldn't imagine what they were doing there. I thought I was hallucinating. Then I noticed several American people and a couple of fairly well-dressed Vietnamese infiltrating the main crowd, detaching clumps of people who must surely be family groups. Waiting behind the barrier separating the luggage area from the rest of the room stood people with signs. "Welcome," they said, in English and in Vietnamese, with names below them. I wanted to cry again. Nobody had been there with signs for us. But at least most of us were familiar with airports, and heavy auto traffic, and how to catch a cab, and had someplace to go, eventually when we got here. Surely these people couldn't all be visiting relatives in Pasadena?

I watched until the throng disappeared. I found myself searching every child's face for Ahn's or even Hoa's, every young girl's for Mai's or Hue's, every old man's for Huang's, or even Xe's, though I knew he was dead. I knew now I wasn't hallucinating, that these people were not ghosts that had collectively come to haunt us, but I grew fascinated by them. When they stopped pouring in and had been picked up by the welcoming committees, I wandered off to a newsstand to see if there was anything about it. On the third page of the Los Angeles *Times,* I found a story I almost ignored: "Hundreds of Boat People Arrive Daily." But there was a picture with Vietnamese people in it. I scanned those faces too, but didn't see anybody familiar. I didn't understand how the people I had seen could be boat people if they arrived on an airplane, but I took the paper with me back to the baggage claim and watched several more planeloads of people file through the tunnel, people from many countries, but among them some Vietnamese.

I didn't go to Disneyland. Though I knew it was a long shot, I kept thinking, Maybe Ahn will be on the next plane and I'll take him with me. Wouldn't Disneyland knock babysan's eyes out of their sockets? Finally I got too tired to watch anymore and I checked into a hotel near the airport. But the next day I was back. And I went back every day for the week I had planned to stay, watching the planes, watching people being collected, searching the faces.

At last, among one of those big crowds, I thought I saw him, a one-legged boy with a crew cut and a thin, frightened face screwed up like a monkey's, ready to irritate everybody by crying. I'd been leaning on the railing near the luggage carousel, and I snapped to my feet and walked forward as if someone were pulling me on a string, toward that boy. Penetrating the crowd wasn't easy, but I did reach him, only to have a woman snatch him into her arms and glare at me.

"Excuse me, what are you doing?" an American voice said behind me.

"That boy . . ." I said and then braved his mother's glare and looked at him again. It wasn't Ahn. Too young. He looked like Ahn when he had first come to the hospital, but Ahn would be almost fifteen now. "I'm sorry," I said to the American woman and made a steeple with my hands and bowed to the mother. "Sin loi, ba." And to the American woman I said, "I thought he was a boy I knew in Nam. A friend of mine, a patient actually. I—"

I felt as dazed as they looked as the people poured around me like a stream around a rock. "I'm sorry," I said finally.

"No need to be sorry. Wait a sec," the woman said and signaled to one of her friends with the signs, then took me by the arm, out of the traffic. "You were in Vietnam?" I nodded. "What as, a missionary?"

"Army Nurse Corps," I said.

"No kidding. And you're waiting for your adopted son, is that it?"

I shook my head. "I just thought I recognized him. He —I don't know where he is. I left him in a village."

"Probably not here, then. We don't get that many peasants with this bunch. Mostly history professors and government people, intellectuals who'd be killed by the new regime if they hadn't escaped. But you never know. They keep sneaking in all kinds of shirttail cousins and old family retainers and what have you that they feel an obligation to. He might make it in with some family."

"Oh," I said, disappointed not to find something I didn't even know I was looking for. But I waited with the woman, who told me her name was Shirley Nussbaum, for the next planeload, and she told me about some of the problems the people were having resettling: no apartments, no job skills, worst of all no English. The government gave some help, but church groups and clubs did most of the sponsoring. And of course there was a lot of resistance to the presence of the refugees in some places.

I nodded, only half listening, and took Shirley's address as she shepherded her last group away. I lingered for a while as the crowd drifted away, then headed for the women's room. It looked empty, but then I heard a toilet flush and somebody shrieked. My adrenaline leaped up. A mugging? Heart attack? Somebody just freaking out? I searched every stall, flapping open the doors, until I came to the latched one. Sobbing issued from within.

"You okay in there?" I asked, knocking on the door. More sobbing. "Look, can I help you? Are you ill? I'm a nurse. Please, just answer me." But the sobbing grew louder.

Oh hell, I wouldn't catch anything on the floor of the L.A. airport I hadn't already caught in Nam. I lay down and peered up under the door. A skinny Vietnamese girl squatted with her feet on the toilet seat. As I watched she leaned back against the flush button and shrieked again. To go through a war, and refugee camps, and a brave new world, only to be freaked out by plumbing. I wriggled under the door, unlatched it, and helped her down from the seat. She couldn't have been more than seven. She tugged at my hand and I squatted down beside her so I wouldn't look so tall, and scooped her up, then showed her how the toilet flushed.

"Where's mamasan, huh, kiddo?" I asked her, and carried her to the sink and showed her how to wash her hands, then carried her out into the lobby. I had Shirley's number, but I didn't need it. Shirley, carrying a toddler, came barreling back through the door, followed by a frightened-looking young woman with a child on each hip and another toddler clinging to her skirts. When Shirley saw us she stopped and put her free hand over her heart, panting exaggeratedly. "You found her."

"Yeah," I said, looking for someone with a free hand to hold her. There wasn't anyone and it would have needed a crowbar to dislodge her fingers.

"Mrs. Huong has too many kids to keep track of, I think. Would you mind walking with us out to the van?"

"Sure," I said. It didn't look as if I had much choice. When everyone else was seated, Mrs. Huong reached for the little girl. The child clung to the thong around my neck until she was sure her mother had her, and as I released her, her fingers touched the amulet. A warm rush went through me as we formed a triangle, and the energy formed a circuit; a tentative mauve-pink light, a little grayed down, but definitely growing brighter, sprang up among us. Mrs. Huong did not smile, but her expression lightened with relief at another hurdle overcome. Life after war. It happened. I had seen hundreds of people in the last few days who had lived through it, who were still trying to live. And there was nothing I had seen that most of them hadn't seen, nothing I had had to do that many of them hadn't had to do, and maybe worse. I couldn't contaminate them, I couldn't shock them, and yet a kid who had been born and raised amid all that ugly, numbing horror had more awe and wonder at push-button flush toilets than I had at the idea of Disneyland. I watched the van depart and then headed back to the hotel. Shirley would pick me up tomorrow morning, to see some of the temporary facilities her group had arranged for the refugees, and to take me to the airport to meet more. They needed a lot of help, she said. Meanwhile, I had things to do, preparations to make. I wondered if Charlie Heron was still stoned all the time, if he was alive, if he was interested in making a trip to L.A., and if I still had his number.

# Why I Don't Tell It Like It Is, Exactly

When I visit the Vietnam War Memorial in April this year for the first time, unlike a lot of veterans I don't expect to recognize any of the names. My GI patients were in and out of our MUST unit hospital in Danang so fast that I never really got to know them. Besides, when they left, they were going back to "The World"—to Okinawa or Japan to stabilize and then back to the United States. The names I remember are not likely to appear on any memorials, although the people they belong to may by now be dead. The names I remember are almost all Vietnamese, the names of civilians I worked with sometimes for months because there was no place other than our hospital that was safe enough to give them the time to heal. I doubt any of my patients made it to the United States as refugees, even if they had wanted to come, because they were not officials or people with jobs important to us; they were mostly farmers and shopkeepers and people caught in the middle.

*The Healer's War* is as much about these people as it is about American nurses and helicopter pilots and ground troops. I told the story through the perspective of a girl very much like the girl I used to be because I felt that even in fiction it would be difficult for me to understand exactly the depths of pain, fear, and conflict my patients and other Vietnamese people experienced. Especially because there are so many Vietnamese refugees living in the United States now, I wanted to share what I knew of their stories. I hope it will give their new neighbors some insight into the world the refugees left. The only parts of *The Healer's War* that are not heavily fictionalized are the stories of my Vietnamese patients.

I chose to write the book as fiction because, as somebody is frequently misquoted as saying, fiction is supposed to make sense out of real life. And if there was ever an episode in my life that needed sense made out of it, it was Vietnam. In a nonfiction account, I could talk only about myself, what I saw and felt. I wasn't very clear about that when I started writing. At the University of Alaska in Fairbanks I studied Asian history, but the first time the professor pointed to Vietnam on the map I became nauseated. Like many veterans, I had deliberately shoved the experience away, and if friends had not started asking me questions and saying, "You never told me you were a nurse in Vietnam," I wouldn't have realized what a black hole in my spirit the war had become. I looked at it sideways, with shame and dread, and shared only the funny stories. I remembered well how uncomfortable and sometimes hostile even people very close to me had been when I tried to talk about my life in Nam when I first returned to the United States. As I researched the book in order to give it a broader perspective, as fiction, I began to realize how many other people in all capacities shared my feelings. Foot soldiers, helicopter pilots, and nurses alike spoke of tragedies they still carried with them, twenty years later. Vietnamese people spoke of homes lost, families divided, friends betrayed. Journalists, medical people, entertainers, Vietnamese refugees, former Viet Cong, and protesters for peace, as well as foot soldiers, were as full of conflicts about the war as I was. And the children and relatives of veterans and the ones who chose not to go just didn't understand. So I tried in this fictional work to blend my own story with the stories I had heard in Nam and later in the States from veterans and to be fair—to show the good and the bad, the help and the damage, the kindness and the cruelty, and the equally inexplicable bonds formed with an enemy and hostility from friends, which made it so impossible to deck everybody out in black hats and white hats or to know what was the right thing to do and when to do it, always supposing you wanted to do "the right thing."

Writing the book as fantasy helped me take it even further—I realized that many of my feelings about Vietnam, much of my emotional experience, were not the result of what I personally saw, but the result of what I heard, what I learned about, the undertow of despair at not being able to make any discernible difference. I wanted Kitty to go into the jungle, not to show what a heroine she was or I wanted to be, but to provide a more vivid picture of the terror felt by the villagers, who had to try to please both Viet Cong and U.S./ARVN troops if they wanted to stay alive, and the fear and bewilderment of American soldiers who wanted to be like their World War II vet fathers and give candy and nylons to the nice Vietnamese and kill the enemy Vietnamese, but who had no way of knowing which were which. In a true story, or a straight realistic novel, honest writing would have required that an unarmed American woman in hostile territory with only a Vietnamese child amputee as a companion be killed within the first couple of pages after the helicopter crash, which would have made *The Healer's War* a damn short book.

Writing a fantasy about Vietnam, however, allowed me to keep my protagonists alive by having a wise old Vietnamese healer give Kitty a variation on the standard magical enabling device. The device, unfortunately, cannot help Kitty destroy Evil, as most magical enabling devices are able to do. It can, however, help her recognize danger and try to avoid it, and it helps her recognize sickness and damage and try to change it.

In the course of researching *The Healer's War*, one day I watched a movie about American prisoners of war. That night I dreamed that I was taken prisoner in a place I knew was Tibet and put into a largish room with a whole lot of other prisoners, all of whom I knew to be heroes of some sort—astronauts, medal of honor winners, etc. It was a rather sexist dream—everyone else in the room was male and a hero except me. But the story that unraveled in the dream was so powerful for me that I woke up remembering it vividly. I won't say too much more about it here since that might spoil the story (it does have a bit of one of those O. Henry twists that I've always enjoyed so much but are so often deplored these days). But, ever the mercenary free-lancer, I decided before the goose bumps the dream had evoked had faded to write it up as a short story with the idea of selling it to the late, lamented *Twilight Zone* magazine.

Some time later, I mentioned to Janna Silverstein at Bantam/Spectra that I had this idea I couldn't get out of my mind and it was making current projects difficult to work on. I told her about the dream, and it gave her goose bumps too. She suggested that I might want to submit the story to the *Full Spectrum* anthology Lou Aronica and Shawna McCarthy were compiling. I spoke to Lou about it in terms of deadlines, since I was just finishing *The Healer's War* and trying to start another book. Lou expressed interest, if I could finish by the deadline. Meanwhile, still drained of words and emotion by *The Healer's War,* I attempted to get to work on a new novel, for which I had a six-month deadline. I got out a few pages, but as the deadline for *Full Spectrum* approached, I felt a compulsion to set aside the novel and work on the short story.

I am not a particularly fast writer—at least not of fiction. Usually I feed my conscious mind lots of information and then my subconscious takes a long time to process it and spits out a dollop for me every once in a while, while I sort of string words together in between times. So I had forty pages of short story that wasn't quite working and not much novel to show for two months' work when I met Lou Aronica at Norwescon, a science fiction convention in Tacoma, last year. I asked again when the *Full Spectrum* deadline was and over dinner told Lou the dream I'd had.

About a month later, when I was due to take a trip to England and the *Full Spectrum* deadline had passed, I had to confess that neither short story nor novel had come together yet. In trying to write the short story, I was finding I had neither enough external information from the dream to make a believable setting nor enough internal information about the characters. The story I had in my head was more about abstract symbols in a surreal place, and to translate that to readers, I needed to understand the people and place and what they symbolized. When I explained this to Lou, he said he had been thinking about it and wondered if my dream wasn't the skeleton of a novel rather than a short story. I had been arriving at a similar conclusion, and the story was still so strong for me that it continued to make work on the new novel hard. Eventually, we agreed that I would shelve what I had been working on and start working on the book about the dream.

Research had to be concentrated on two areas—the

setting, Tibet, and the characters, who were prisoners of war and heroes. This was all foreign territory to me, and other than the POW movie, I couldn't imagine why I had dreamed about Tibet of all places. Fortunately, I had recently moved from Fairbanks, Alaska, to a town full of adventurers, artists, and causes (our sister city is Jalapa, Nicaragua, to give you some idea). Unfortunately, our old library has been allowed to deteriorate, so I needed to buy the books I wanted to use for my research. To this end, I wandered into Phoenix Rising, the local New Age store, figuring it would have books about Tibetan Buddhism. It did, as well as books on adventures in Tibet, the people and history of Tibet, and an array of other esoteric information. The owner later took pity on my newcomer's blues and invited me to her Thanksgiving party. Several of her guests had traveled to Tibet, were involved with Tibetan Buddhist groups, and had read extensively about Tibet. From these folks I got many leads on good books to read for my research.

Among these were the classics, *Seven Years in Tibet,* by Heinrich Harrer, Austrian mountaineer and former tutor to the present Dalai Lama, *Warriors of Tibet,* by Jamyang Norbu, a Khampa tribesman tricked into collaborating with the Chinese during the 1959 invasion, *Wind Between the Worlds,* by Robert Ford, a British radio operator taken prisoner by the Chinese during their invasion and imprisoned for five years in a Chinese prison camp, and *Magic and Mystery in Tibet,* by the intrepid Alexandra David-Neel, a French adventuress (and Buddhist) who defied the conventions of the early part of the century to travel in Tibet and learn about the Tibetan religion and philosophy and the most secret ritual magic.

I also read *Neon Lotus,* by Marc Laidlaw, another Spectra author, who used the background of Tibetan magic and the Chinese invasion as material for a wonderful science fiction/fantasy novel. And of course, I reread *Lost Horizon,* by James Hilton.

Delving into the stories of prisoners of war has been another aspect of my research. I'd read lots about the holocaust as a girl, but the prison camp in my setting is very different from that. Nevertheless, I read Terence Des Pres's book on survivors of the death camps and learned about what sort of mentality allowed some to live, while others, perhaps initially healthier, died. Fellow writer Bill Ransom also suggested two books, one by an ancestor of his, John Ransom, who survived Andersonville Prison in the Civil War to write the *Andersonville Diary.* The other book he suggested was by the famous e.e. cummings, before he changed to lowercase, called *The Enormous Room,* about cummings's experiences being imprisoned by French allies during World War I. The conditions of the camps, the injustices perpetrated, and the prisoners' reactions are somewhat different, but gave me a more complete picture of the mentality of both prisoners and guards and just how much humanity it might be possible for each to keep.

And of course, to make the story real, I have to know not only the prison world but the world from which my characters come, an earth somewhat in the future, which makes this new book not only a fantasy but a bit of social science fiction. It seems to me that technology may be less of a factor for change than how people choose to solve certain economic, military, environmental, and social problems that exist right now. I want my characters to reflect their own backgrounds, which are, because of the nature of the story, from different periods in the development of the North American continent. The central viewpoint character is a woman who has been a perpetual student but can find little wisdom and even less application for it in her world, and who eventually, unable to find employment or to continue her education, submits to government imperatives that she leave the nicely ordered civilian world to go into the military and perform a meaningless and trivial job. Other characters are a medic who as a boy was an itinerant bird-cleaner, a test-tube baby raised by the army to accept his role as a killing machine, and a peace activist who is, as part of his job, a demolitions expert.

One sad aspect of my dream was that in its time period everything had been spoiled or exploited in one way or another. The best thing about writing the book about the dream is all of the new territory it has enabled me to explore.

ELIZABETH ANN SCARBOROUGH

## ABOUT THE AUTHOR

ELIZABETH ANN SCARBOROUGH, a former nurse and a Vietnam veteran, is the author of seven other Bantam novels—*The Christening Quest, The Harem of Aman Akbar, The Unicorn Creed, Song of Sorcery, The Drastic Dragon of Draco, Texas, The Goldcamp Vampire,* and *Bronwyn's Bane*—all humorous fantasy. She has recently moved from Fairbanks, Alaska, to the Washington coast, where she is working on a new novel about prisoners of war.

# Spectra Special Editions

# The Unbalanced Earth Trilogy
## by Jonathan Wylie

Fourteen years after the Destruction violently tore the very fabric of reality and drained the world of magic, the scarlet-haired princess Gemma, who unwittingly caused the cataclysm years before, is driven by a compulsion she doesn't understand to sail to the Southern Continent. Once there, she and her newfound love Arden begin to uncover the mystery of that voiceless call, as well as the greater mysteries of a constantly shifting reality, the nature of magic and finally the mystery of the very fate of their world.

☐ Dreams of Stone (27974-2 • $3.95)
☐ The Lightless Kingdom (28147-X • $3.95)

And coming in April 1990
the stunning conclusion to
**The Unbalanced Earth Trilogy**
**The Age of Chaos**

Buy **The Unbalanced Earth Trilogy** on sale now wherever Bantam Spectra books are sold, or use this page for ordering:

**BANTAM**
SHOP·AT·HOME
C·A·T·A·L·O·G

# Special Offer
# Buy a Bantam Book
# *for only 50¢.*

*Now you can have Bantam's catalog filled with hundreds of titles plus take advantage of our unique and exciting bonus book offer. A special offer which gives you the opportunity to purchase a Bantam book for only 50¢. Here's how!*

*By ordering any five books at the regular price per order, you can also choose any other single book listed (up to a $5.95 value) for just 50¢. Some restrictions do apply, but for further details why not send for Bantam's catalog of titles today!*

*Just send us your name and address and we will send you a catalog!*